ORDER OF SUCCESSION

By Maxwell Anderson

September 01, 2019

To:
George,
Thank you for your friendship, persistence, and all your suggestions – as well as your Trailblazing in getting your book published. I appreciate your leadership. I hope you are not disappointed when you read this one.

Eric Schittl (A.K.A Maxwell Anderson)

This book, *Order of Succession,* is a work of fiction. Any similarity between the names characters in this book and people in real life is coincidental. Most of the locations, local stores and restaurants, and the like are real; however, their names were changed with the exception of national chain stores and restaurants. The highways and roads are real and accurate at the time the book was written; they were included for those readers who want to follow the story with real places on real maps.

Copyright © 2018 by EDS Publishing

Front- and Rear-Cover photos and map sketches are courtesy of the author.

Library of Congress Control Number: 2019907926

ISBN 978-1-07-748802-1

All rights reserved. No part of this book may be used or reproduced in any manner whatsoever without written permission of the author or publisher, except in the case of brief quotations embodied in critical articles and reviews. For information, please contact: maxwell.anderson72@yahoo.com.

90609-OoS-KDP-V2R0 // 547P;161,818W

DEDICATION

This book is dedicated to my wife, who has provided motivation to 'write something'.

And also to the men and women of the Secret Service and the United States Armed Forces, who protect the Constitution of the United States and the office of the President of the United States.

ACKNOWLEDGMENTS

I want to extend my appreciation to:

The Writers Group of The Desert Rose Café, Williamsport, Maryland, for the encouragement to do something with the ideas rumbling around in my head.

JoAnn, my wife, who is an inspiration to me and who read the first proof version of this book.

And to Eoin MacErk, who critiqued the story-line and, more importantly, its presentation, structure, clarity, and syntax.

Also to Vincent H., who worked the magic of Photoshop® [1].

Judy W., who proofread the final proof version of this book

Dan S., who proofread the final version of this book and who suggested allowing friends of his (in the Secret Service) to also read it and make comments.

Additional appreciation is extended to Steve, Mandi, Michael T., Maria, and Gary for reading the book and for having patience with me.

And, of course, to Scott Schoppert and the team at Printing Impressions for formatting this book for publication.

---

[1] Photoshop is a registered trademark of Adobe Systems Incorporated

TABLE OF CONTENTS

DEDICATION iii

ACKNOWLEDGMENTS v

PROLOGUE 1

Part 1 – WTF Just Happened Here 9
  1 – Next Batter Up! 10
  2 – Securing the Site 25
  3 – Somebody Doesn't Want Us Here 35
  4 – Digging for the Truth 44
  5 – The Post Mortem 62
  6 – A Quorum of Minds 75
  7 – News from the Outside World 90

Part 2 – Untangling the Gordian Knot 97
  8 – Early Background 98
  9 – Ridin' His High Horse 109
  10 – 2 Recons of the Primary Target 113
  11 – Meet at the Gun Platform 122
  12 – 3rd Recon of The Primary Target 128
  13 – Where are Those Missing Cars 135
  14 – 3rd Recon (Cont'd) 138
  15 – The Plot Begins to Gel 141
  16 – 3rd Recon (Conclusion) 144
  17 – Still Unanswered Questions 152
  18 – The POTUS Phone Rings 158
  19 – Forming A Brain Trust 166
  20 – More for the Brain Trust 175
  21 – The 2nd Trailer 181
  22 – Relief from the Heat and an Old Buddy 186
  23 – Sleight of Flight 190
  24 – Cleaning-up the Rest Area 200

Part 3 – Recon, Planning, Searching, and Training 207

25 – Getting Back Into the Game 208
26 – Finally, the FBI Arrives 214
27 – New Accommodations 221
28 – Resolutions and Clearing the Plate 235
29 – Hunting for the Red Barn 243
30 – The President's News Conference 246
31 – Searching for the Bunker 255
32 – It's Gotta be Here – Somewhere 266
33 – Aha and More 275
34 – Hang-Gliders 280
35 – Prepping for the East Coast 288
36 – Modified Choppers at Quantico 292
37 – Parking Spots for the Helos 297
38 – Recon the Bunker and Camp David 305
39 – Recaps 312
40 – Learning New Skills 317
41 – Moving to New TDY Quarters 327
42 – Getting' the Skinny in D.C. 331
43 – Night Maneuvers 338
44 – A Helluva Party Boat 341

Part 4 – The Game Begins; Place Your Bets 343

45 – Act I – The Show Begins 344
46 – Act II – Smoke and Poor Doug 351
47 – Act III, Scene I – Forget Coming-In On Monday! 360
48 – Act III, Scene II – Missiles Away 370
49 – Act IV, Scene I – Securing Sites 386
50 – Act IV, Scene II – Raiding The Pentagon 394
51 – Perp Walks, Not Quite 406
52 – Pack Your Overnight Bags 418

Appendix 1 – The Order of Succession 439

Appendix 2 – Additional Quotes From Thomas Jefferson 441

Appendix 3 – Abbreviations and Acronyms 446

Figures

Figure 1: Map of Interstate 8 (I-8) Across Border in Southern California 5
Figure 2: Highways and Roads around Buckman Springs Rest Area (In Middle of I-8) 6
Figure 3: Buckman Springs Rest Area – Buildings, Parking, and Trees & Plantings 7

ORDER OF SUCCESSION
PROLOGUE

For whatever reason, someone in the White House's travel-planning department thought it was a great idea to arrange an international meeting about transporting goods across the border between the United States and Mexico.

And, furthermore, that meeting should also take place at the truck port-of-entry (POE) along the United State's side of that border just a few miles east of Calexico, California entirely for symbolic reasons about international trade between the two countries. The opportunity for this 'photo-op' could not be denied. The Secret Service agents, who were assigned to this 'meet and greet' wondered, "But, out in the Mojave Desert in July? Really? Who planned this fiasco? And why?"

Although Calexico claims to have an 'international' airport, the White House planners consulted the air crews at Andrews Air Force Base to determine if that airport could be used for this conference/meeting. It took only about 45 seconds to decide it was not possible to guarantee adequate support for Air Force-1 and the rest of the entourage at that airport. Consequently, the planners created a somewhat convoluted and tortured itinerary. They were told to have Air Force 1 fly into Yuma, Arizona, so the President could also meet with the governors of Arizona and California. And then drive over to Calexico together in "the Beast' (the President's limo) so they could discuss 'southwestern issues' prior to the meeting at the truck POE where the President of Mexico would join them.

Following the photo-op at the POE in Calexico, U.S. President Avery Jacobson would then be driven to overnight accommodations in El Cajon, California, to meet-and-greet local politicians. On the next day, a Saturday, additional meets-and-greets were already scheduled before re-boarding Air Force 1 to return to Andrews.

All this meant that Air Force 1 would fly into Yuma, drop President Jacobson off, and then fly empty westward to the airstrip at San Diego Naval Air Station and wait for the President to re-board Saturday evening for the return run back to Andrews Air Force Base.

Order of Succession

What a great plan; what could possibly go wrong with it!

How it actually worked out

Yuma is only about 60 miles east of Calexico, so this would reduce the miles the presidential motorcade had to be on the ground – instead of driving round-trip between San Diego and Calexico. This plan also reduced the total clock-hours of disrupting traffic in San Diego and all along Interstate 8 from an estimated 10 to 12 hours down to maybe only four – if they were fortunate.

Following the Calexico meeting, the planners were also told to route President Jacobson to visit a few small border towns in California prior to arriving in El Cajon, east of San Diego. So on Thursday, 12-July, President Jacobson flew aboard Air Force-1 into Yuma, Arizona, arriving at 03:34 hours (12:34 AM PDT, Friday). Air Force-1 was then scheduled to fly into San Diego later on Friday afternoon and wait for President Jacobson to arrive Saturday, sometime in the late evening after spending some time glad-handing with local politicians and visiting with local military commanders, followed by a red-eye flight back to Washington, D.C.

Jacobson was scheduled to meet with Arizona Governor Miranda Nicholson and California Governor Archibald (Archie) Calderon at 7:45 A.M. in Yuma to discuss international trade relations with Mexico. Trade Representatives from both governments had already agreed to all the pertinent points in this newest trade agreement – except for deciding who stands where during the photo-op. Jacobson and the governors were planning to use the drive-time in the limo (from Yuma to Calexico) to go over their notes for the conference and iron-out any last minute hiccups. The President and the governors arrived as scheduled at 9:30 A.M. at the 'truck POE' just east of Calexico, California (on the U.S. side of the border) and across from Mexicali (on the Mexican side of the border). The three of them would meet the President of Mexico, César Rodriguez at 10:15 A.M. at this seemingly insignificant spot. It was really just a wide spot along the All-American Canal, which separates The United States and Mexico along part of the border in this area of California. All of the news-media outlets were welcomed to have reporters there, in the middle of July, out in the Mojave Desert, to report about the 'truck-stop conference' covering transporting goods both ways across the border. At least, the three hoped, in both directions.

Order of Succession

President Rodriguez had no problem crossing the border from Mexicali. While he would not have to show a passport for this occasion, he had one handy just in case someone asked about it. Or, if he observed an opportune moment during the meeting into which he could add a little humor – and stick it just a little bit to the Americans (on International television) that he was, indeed, a 'documented crosser'.

Everyone shook each others' hands. Pictures were taken and news scripts written. After all of the pictures taken, each of the governors had pre-arranged their own transportation to depart from the Calexico Airport, where they boarded their own planes and left President Jacobson to enjoy the heat, alone and unaccompanied, as he headed further west toward the much cooler Pacific breezes. California Governor Calderon had been invited to attend the dinner planned later that evening in the El Cajon area. He, however, declined because he had to be in Sacramento for conferences beginning immediately after their lunch break.

Agent Michael Walters, an agent in the Secret Service Presidential detail, took orders for fast-food 'to-go'. He departed the POE area about 45 minutes before the motorcade was scheduled to form-up. He headed to a pre-selected fast-food restaurant along the pre-planned route, where he had all the orders tagged, bagged, and ready-to-hand-out when the motorcade slowed down and pulled-in along the highway's shoulder. Two managers assisted him distributing the bags – just so they could gawk at the occupants and maybe even shake the hand of 'the man'. Since Agent Walters was assigned to the last Chase Car, there would be little lost time waiting for him to rejoin the motorcade. Between gasping for breathable air and other security concerns, Walters muttered almost aloud, "Just who the hell planned this effing trip anyway? Who wants to travel across the southern-most part of the Mojave in the middle of July? Gotta speak to those planners and invite them to join us out here in this heat. Hope they like it better than we do. Talk about rotten planning." Walters dutifully handed–out meals and drinks to everybody in the motorcade as they slowed-down to a crawl, but did not fully stop. Then he hopped into his Chase Car, Number 8, and automatically took the rear-most position in the motorcade.

The motorcade followed the pre-planned (and vetted) route to Interstate 8 (I-8) and headed west toward El Cajon. There was no other traffic on I-8 in either direction because I-8 had already been closed-down all the way to El Cajon. Tomorrow would be San Diego's turn to

Order of Succession

deal with the traffic headaches. This portion of the trip was supposed to be a straight-shot over I-8 to the cooler side of the mountains – and most importantly, greatly above the posted speed limits. Additional local deputies were supposed to be stationed at various pre-planned points along the way, with a 'service crew' pre-staged at the Buckman Springs Rest Area if they were needed. That's about two-thirds of the way there.

Walters was running over the planning in his head when he noticed two local police patrol cars following his car about a quarter mile behind. He assumed that they were just part of local law-enforcement – sort of a 'sweep' team along the route.

In southern California, the route for I-8 places it very close to the international border between the United States and Mexico.

In the United States, almost all Interstate Highways that are routed across great distances have rest-areas for motorists; I-8 is no exception. The majority of rest-areas in the Interstate Highway System are located on the right-hand sides of each of the highway's respective directions, serving only the motorists on that side of the highway. However, in many other instances, rest-areas are located in the center (the median strip) and serve motorists from both directions.

The Buckman Springs Rest Area on I-8 is located at California Exit 51. This rest-area, though not unique, is built in the median area between the eastbound and westbound travel lanes. This rest-area was also built utilizing a pre-existing intersection of two county roads at the same location, Buckman Springs Road and Sheephead Mountain Road. Additionally, there is another county highway currently designated as 'S1', which is also is situated parallel to I-8 on the south side of I-8. Some maps also designate this highway as 'Old Highway 80'. Basically, all these roads existed before I-8 was even built. The Interstate designers added the rest-area, using the existing roads to access it from both I-8 directions – east- and west-bound.

This story begins at the Buckman Springs Rest Area. Diagrams of the Buckman Springs Rest Area and the section of I-8 described in this book are found on the following pages.

(Diagrams can be found on the following three (3) pages.)

ORDER OF SUCCESSION

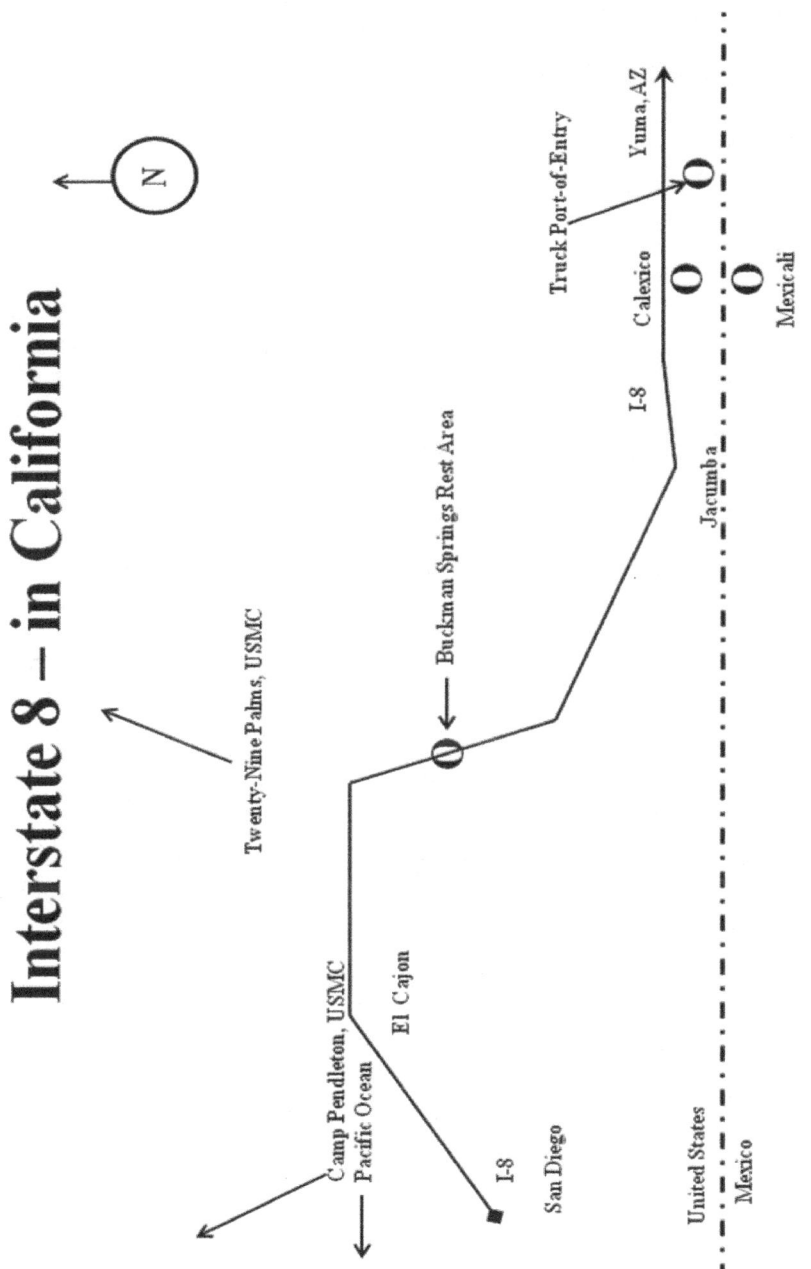

Figure 1: Map of Interstate 8 (I-8) Across Border in Southern California

ORDER OF SUCCESSION

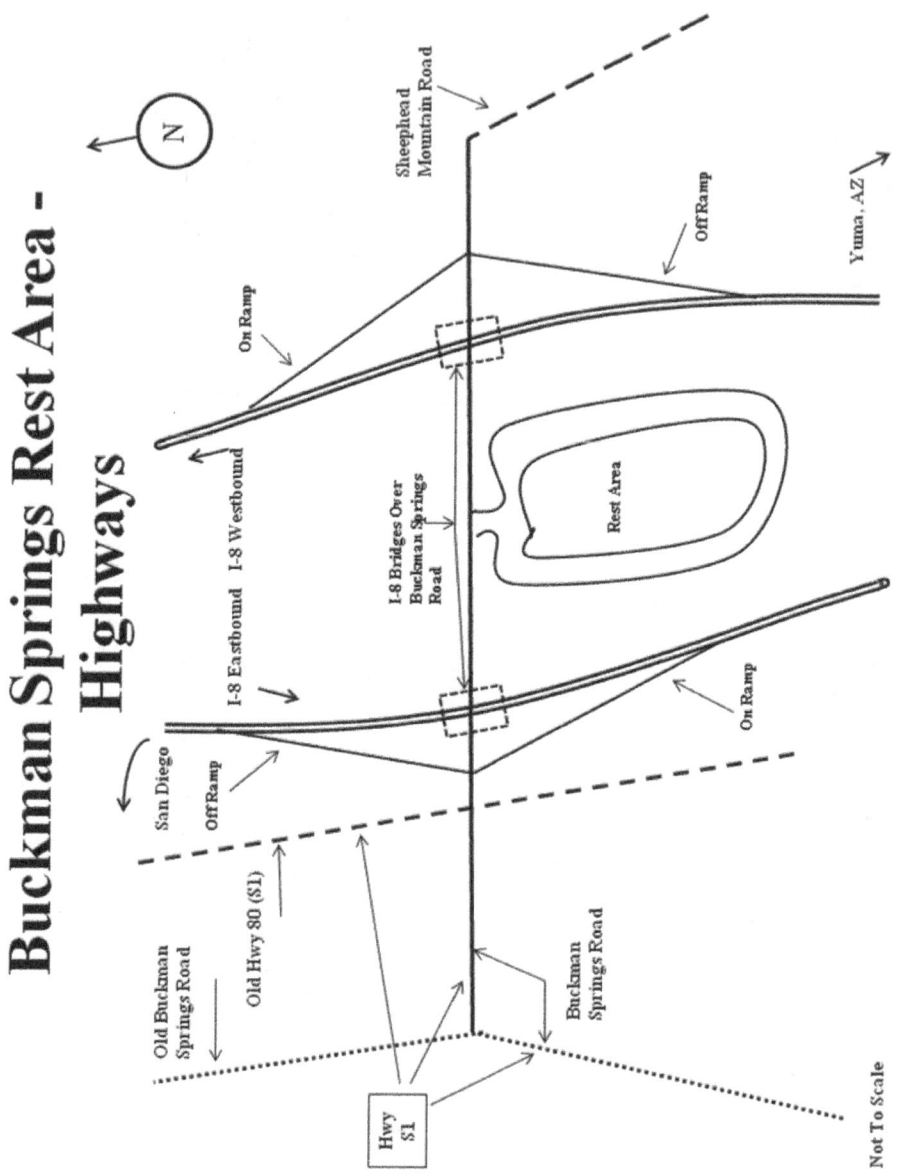

Figure 2: Highways and Roads around Buckman Springs Rest Area (In Middle of I-8)

ORDER OF SUCCESSION

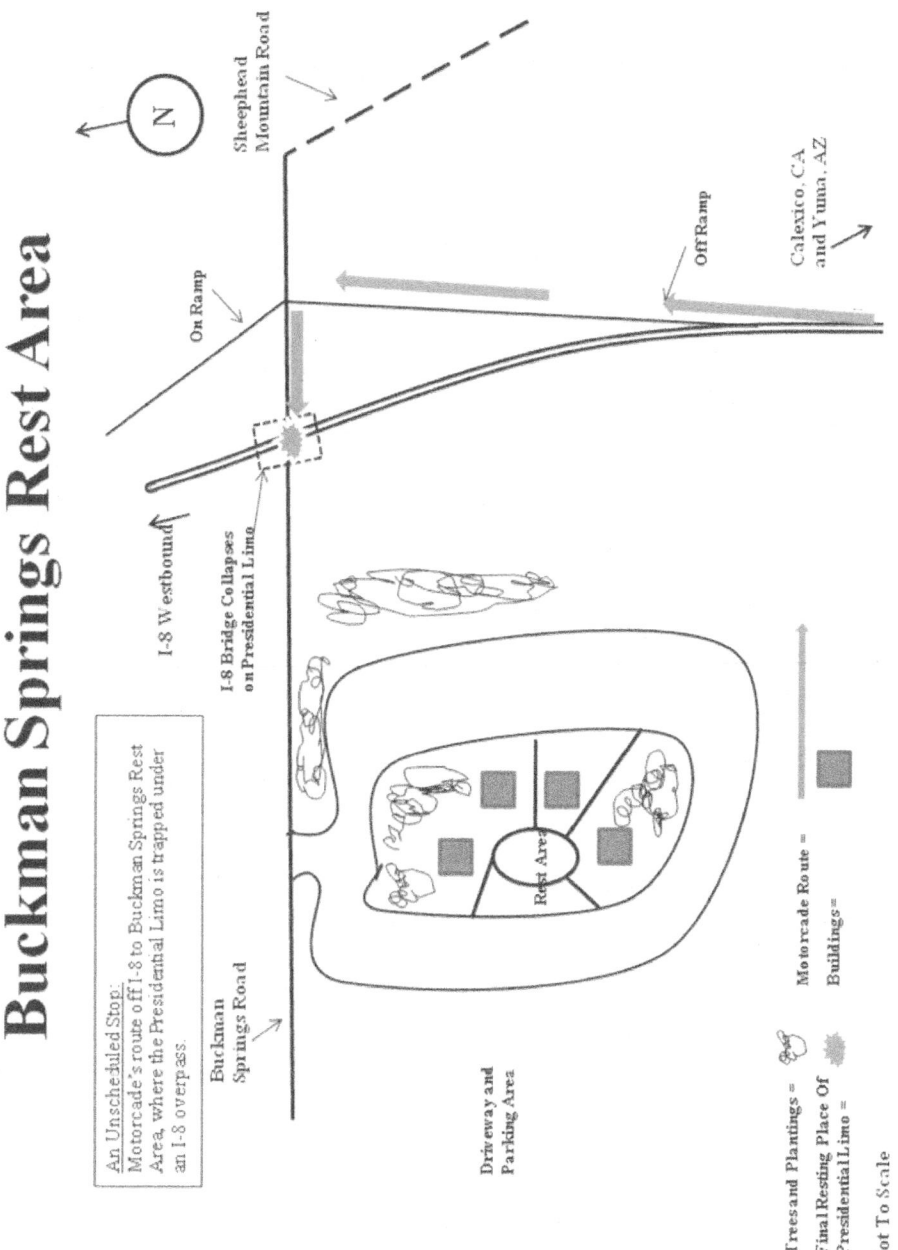

Figure 3: Buckman Springs Rest Area – Buildings, Parking, and Trees & Plantings

Order of Succession

ORDER OF SUCCESSION

Part 1 –
WTF Just Happened Here

Order of Succession

1 – Next Batter Up!

Mid-afternoon, Friday, 13-July: Westbound I-8, Exit 51, at Buckman Springs Rest Area (Intersection of I-8, Sheephead Mountain Road, Buckman Springs Road, and County Road S1), Mojave Desert, California

TIME: Friday, 13–July at 14:24 PDT

"Mr. President! Mr. President! Please answer me!!

"Answer me. . . . Answer me. For God's sake, please answer me! Dammit, please say something, moan, groan, something, anything. It's me, Agent Smitty from Chase Car-3. God damn it, say anything. Dammit, President Jacobson, say something, anything. Please."

Mumbling to himself now as he surveyed the crushed limo, "What the hell just happened here? What the hell happened? Where is he; is he okay?"

Using his car's radio, Smitty yelled at the mic: "Hey, Jonesy, tell CC [2] to get a lot of heavy-duty wreckers out here right now. And some cranes to lift the overpass. No, make that at least four cranes – mobile cranes and a flat-bed truck for the limo. And hurry, Jonesy, you got that?" The response to Smitty's request, no, make that his command, was just continuous radio static, just that damned continuous crackling. "Jonesy, you got that? Just say you got that. PLEASE say something, damn-it!" The damned crackling static persisted. "Jonesy, say something." Then it hit him; Jonesy was not in his usual Chase-car. He was assigned to the limo just this morning. Jonesy was inside the limo, or whatever remained of the limo.

Smitty's mind raced. Trying to make sense of this scene was a hopeless cause. No sounds came from inside the limo; all was deathly quiet. Even the flames from the fires seemed unsympathetically silent; however, their eerie dancing seemed almost like it was truly living. The

---

2 CC = Central Command

Order of Succession

two Lead- and the first two Chase-cars were still ablaze. Even the limo, that tank of a car, was wrecked, crushed beyond recognition as having ever been any type of car.

{Smitty (thinking to himself: "Maybe all their radios were out, too. Sure as hell mine is all effed up. What the hell happened?"}

Smitty couldn't remember how long ago it was since he got out of his Chase-3 car, directly behind the C-2 car. Now, maybe a quarter-hour later, he remembered that something looked weird on the Interstate's left shoulder as they passed it about 250 yards back. Whatever it was, it really looked out-of-place, but now he couldn't recall why it looked that way. But before he could even consider radioing his thoughts, the limo turned off I-8 onto the off-ramp marked for the Buckman Springs Rest Area – a VERY unscheduled stop – so fast, there wasn't even any radio traffic announcing the sudden change of route.

"Where are the others, the friggin' back-ups?" Maybe his adrenaline level was stabilizing; his thoughts seemed to be a bit more organized and methodical now. Smitty tried to lean and rest against the I-8 overpass walls, but his mind would not let him take a moment of rest.

{Smitty's mind: "Where the hell are the overpass walls? They're reinforced concrete; where the hell are they? They were here just seconds ago; they were holding-up the damned overpass bridge. Now there's nothing but blue sky up there – although, hazy through the smoke and acrid air. Where the hell is everybody? There's nothing down here but burning and wrecked cars. The limo is crushed. Wait a second, it's friggin' CRUSHED? I didn't even notice that! Am I the only one still alive? Where are the others? Am I the only damn one still friggin' alive? Is that a good thing or not? Somebody please just tell me what the eff just happened here?"}

Smitty's mind continued racing even faster trying to grasp the full extent of this destruction, and all of a sudden, it completely derailed and went way off subject.

{Mind: "Oh, Rita, I know I promised not to swear or curse. Please forgive me, but this is something very, very different. I don't know why I said those things; I'm sorry."}

The radio's continuous s static intruded once again. He tried to reach-out to other members of the President's Protection Detail: "Jonesy, can you hear me? Jonesy? Jonesy? Anybody on this frequency, please answer."

Order of Succession

Nobody answered his calls; not a friggin' sound – nothing.

{"Sorry, Rita. Okay, Brain, get back on the track, and make it damn fast; I got other things to do PDQ. Leave me the hell alone, and do it NOW!}

Habits, old habits. Smitty checked his watch. "14:22:32" "Oh, my God, it's been over 5 minutes."

{Realizations began sinking in: "Okay, Brain, think what this could be and how we got into it. Damn it, think. Follow the money. No, Brain, not money right now; follow the friggin' time-line. DAMN IT – THE TIME-LINE! THE DAMN TIME-LINE; NOTHING ELSE RIGHT NOW' JUST THE DAMN TIME-LINE! GOT THAT, BRAIN? THE EFFING TIME-LINE."}

Smitty's mind raced as he tried to follow the time-line. His mind kept replaying driving Chase Car-3 in the Presidential motorcade.

{Smitty's mind: "Hey why are all the cars ahead of me taking this off-ramp? That's Lead Cars-1 and -2, the limo, and Chase-1 and -2- they're all taking this effing off-ramp? This was not covered in the briefing. What's going on here? And where the hell is this – the off-ramp sign says 'Buckman Springs Rest Area'? Where the hell is this friggin' Buckman Springs anyway? Are we still in California? Mexico is just somewhere over there to the south. Isn't it? Are we still in the friggin' U.S.?"}

Then he saw the dust and debris of an explosion somewhere in front of Lead-1. A split second later, something in the rear view mirror caught his eye. Another explosion behind the procession lit-up the rear-view mirror. Seconds later, the dust spread rapidly, engulfing the entire scene in both the inside and both outside mirrors. Smitty made a quick mental calculation that the distance was a bit less than an eighth of a mile to the last car. Every car behind him was still on the off-ramp, and his was stuck in the middle of a left turn from the off-ramp onto this friggin' road. That meant the bomb, or whatever it was, was pretty damn big – or there are lots of friggin' IEDs under this road.

{Smitty's analytic mind: "Must be a pretty deep hole; wonder if the road is still there. WRONG! Wrong questions, you dummy! One IED ahead, and one behind. Front smaller than one behind us. How many devices are there? Whoever set-up this trap is driving us to get off the off-ramp and into a bigger trap. What's the damn reason?"}

Order of Succession

Old habit: "Passing Off-Ramp Exit Sign At 14:15."

{Smitty's brain, still analyzing: "Okay, Brain, I need some help here real fast. Keep replaying the off-ramp time-line. Wait, not so fast, slow down. What is that thing over THERE on the left shoulder. Replay that in slow motion. Still can't make sense of it. Just passed a second one of those strange 'somethings' farther along the right shoulder of the off-ramp. Haven't seen one of those since sniper training out in . . . . . Oh. OH NO! This effing trap is gonna get friggin' deadly damn fast.}

Back to the present: And then the limo stopped dead-center under the westbound overpass like it was trying to hide from some unseen aerial predator – hidden from all vantage points above it. Of course, any bad-guy aiming from either end of the local road under both overpasses, would be able to see parts of the limo – and probably reach out and thump it real good with an accurately-placed bullet – assuming he was a halfway decent sniper. The passengers would definitely know they could be within range of something powerful enough to damage their mini-tank. However, any good sniper with a scoped weapon would still have to have a lot of skill and a damn heavy-caliber weapon to acquire and hit the limo effectively, what with the Lead and Chase-cars blocking the line of sight. But, that could have been the last all of the limo's occupants ever felt – momentary security."

Time: Friday, 13-July, 14:15 PDT

This off-ramp was not a cloverleaf with gracefully curving arcs for the ramps. This exit was pretty much a straight line, dropping gradually down the side of the Interstate, just angled outward enough to move traffic away from the highway – maybe 400 feet long or so, with red octagonal stop signs at the end. At the bottom of the off-ramp, it met the on-ramp straight across from it. Only the local road passed between them, continuing past the rest-area that was built between the two Interstate roadways – east-bound and west-bound. It passed under the eastbound overpass and on to wherever it was supposed to go anyway [3]. Smitty rolled C-3 to a stop inside the intersection of both on and off ramps, blocking all traffic on the local road. From his car's position about 100 or so feet behind the limo, Smitty witnessed all hell break loose in front of him.

---

3   (INFO: This is Sheephead Mountain Road and Buckman Springs Road, all in one.)

ORDER OF SUCCESSION

{Immediate thoughts: "Man, if this is what hell is like, Rita, we don't want any part of it. It's worse than we were led to believe. If the world's religions only knew! Damn it, Brain, leave Rita out of this right now will ya? I love her and all that and would really like to be with her right now, but leave her out of it for right now, okay? We got stuff to do."}

Through the overpass, he could see the two Lead-cars rise above the overpass bridgework – each riding on a pillar of flame, violently belching smoke, and debris. Smitty did not see them fall back down to the ground because Chase Cars -1 and -2, immediately in front of his, suddenly rose the same way – blown sky-high and maybe only 60 feet in front of his own C-3 car. That detonation shoved C-3 backward about 10 yards off the local county road all the while pelting it with debris and pavement from C-1, C-2, and the roadway. C-1 rose directly into the underside of the overpass, flattening and distorting the car into a lumpy pancake before it landed. C-2 had been stopped partially under the westbound overpass. However, when the explosion blew it upward, the front of C-2 caught the edge of the overpass, causing the car to tumble and whirligig through the air; it landed in a smoking heap in the dirt between the Interstate and the westbound on-ramp.

{Smitty's thoughts: "Holy shit! Those poor bastards are all still inside all those cars! Sorry, Rita, that one doesn't count. Okay?"}

Suddenly, he was viewing the scene from somewhere off the road. Smitty looked ahead under the bridge and also back up the off-ramp he had just driven down, now on his left. It wasn't pretty; considering the situation, his C-3 car was still 'relatively' unharmed – at least, it was still on its wheels, but with most of its windows smashed to smithereens. Thank goodness the shatter-resistant windshield had been updated a couple of months ago.

{Smitty's thoughts: "Hey, Rita, what the hell are smithereens anyway? Ask Roger or Georgia; maybe they know. Brain, stop this. You know they're both gone. Now stop this right now. We've got a lot of much bigger things to worry about."}

Time: Friday, 13-July, 14:16 PDT

The driver in the C-4 car behind him (maybe Hank, or whoever) inched C-4 forward down the off-ramp to roughly where C-3 had just been just

Order of Succession

seconds ago. Smitty didn't give a damn right now who the driver is. More important things were happening right in front of him.

The burning Lead-1 and -2 cars and C-1 cars trapped the limo – damn effectively, he thought.

Before Smitty bailed-out of his car, he checked to make sure his Sig-229 was still in its holster along with a couple of spare magazines. Satisfied, he also grabbed the 9-mm HK-MP5 along with three magazines. The 12-gauge Remington 870 pump-action shotgun was the last weapon Smitty grabbed. In his haste, he almost forgot his ditty-bag, which he always stuffed full of extra ammo, but, now grabbing it with two fingers of the hand holding the 870.

Smitty wore a more comfortable vest when driving longer distances because he felt it was more flexible, and out here in the heat, well … his thoughts trailed-off. "Damn-it, the better vest is in the back! I'll get it later."

Glancing outside through the now windowless driver's door, he would have given anything to have an auto-loading shotgun about now with rifled slugs. But this Remington loaded with #4 buck shells would have to do for now. The rest of his standard emergency gear was in the trunk along with his better vest; besides he was running out of hands and fingers to carry all of it anyway. He scrambled out of C-3 as fast as he could, focusing all his attention on reaching the limo. Most of the glass fragments and shards fell off his clothes and lap as he gained his footing on the now rubble-strewn pavement that had been the off-ramp turn just seconds earlier.

The agents in C-4 and C-5 started scrambling out of their cars, when their cars also left the ground, followed by shots fired from behind him from some scrubby growth on the right side of the off-ramp. No agents returned fire.

{Smitty's realizations: "Oh, God, I was just sitting there 15 seconds ago. Hank, or whoever you were, hope you were on the right side of the Lord. Ask Him to help me, no, make that us, because we're gonna need all He can spare. I'll check-in with you later, but I gotta try to get to the limo. I hope you copy this. Whoever's behind this doesn't plan to leave any live witnesses. Just what the hell is this all about anyway?"}

ORDER OF SUCCESSION

Time: Friday, 13-July, 14:19 PDT

The C-2 car had already been blown off the road's pavement onto the shoulder of the west on-ramp. He quickly decided to check on C-2 later. Next, Smitty had to find a way around the still burning C-1. No signs of life in either one. The heat was unbelievably intense even from where he crouched about 100 feet away.

Smitty tried to skirt to the left side of where C-1 had been. He knew he had to try to get to the limo; he had to protect the President at all costs. But he was too late on all fronts. He was certainly too late for the agents in both Chase-cars – C-1 and C-2 in front of his C-3 and now C-4 and C-5 behind it. Had he just plain lucked-out to have his car still on its wheels? Some damn luck! What else could he think? He didn't want to exchange places after all he had seen. Some friggin' luck!!

Smitty heard his own voice for the first time since this mess began, "Gotta skirt around C-1 to get to the limo." Too late to even plan anything. If the first three explosions were all hell breaking loose, this next one was a much-worse Baghdad-size 'shock-and-awe' detonation, up-close, very intense, and turning-out to be very damned personal. Underneath the overpass bridge, the limo disappeared in explosive tongues of flame, debris, and rubble. Smitty, blown off his feet, found himself lying behind his C-3 car, sucking the ground. As he pushed himself off the ground, he saw the limo still sitting bizarrely under the overpass bridge – but with large piles of dirt and debris to its rear, left side, and front. It was going to be one helluva of a job to get the limo out of there.

{Brain: "Damn-it, pick-up some ear-protection next time, will ya? Screw it, can't think of everything." "Hey, Mr. Brain, will you just shut-the-hell-up for now; I can't listen to you yammerin' in my mind right now. Damn that was God-awful loud. I wonder what thunder sounds like to God. Hey, Brain, take a 15-second break will ya?"}

No one was stirring; it would not have done them much good anyway.

Time: Friday, 13-July, 14:20 PDT

The designer of this ambush still had the coup de grâce up his sleeve.

Order of Succession

{Smitty's conversation with Brain: "Your shoes look like crap; dontcha ever polish them?" "Hey, watch that, huh? I just polished them this morning before picking-up C-3. I thought I told you to take a break. Leave me the hell alone for now!!"}

Smitty began to advance toward the limo once again. Everywhere, the air was heavy with only the smell of explosives and dirt – just impenetrable everywhere. Smitty was mumbling aloud to himself, "Okay, this time let's get past C-1. Hey, that last explosion threw enough dirt and debris across the front of C-1, extinguishing some of the flames."

He advanced through the debris still mumbling as if expecting answers to his questions. "Hot damn, some good luck! The limo is right there. Strange – it looks like a big, black river-barge run aground and no water to re-float it. Or maybe sitting atop one of those western mesas with its wheels hangin' over the edges."

{Smitty's responses to Brain: "I told you to shut-up, Brain. Now, do it!" "Those run-flat tires ain't goin' anywhere. Hell, they ain't even touching the ground anymore; a lot of good that does the President. Frame looks like its sittin' right on the ground. Oh, man, it's gonna have to go to the repair shop as well as the paint shop for damn sure. A couple of the windows are cracked; let's see those suckers are what, six-inches thick – that means – that means the limo took a massive wallop."}

Now, Smitty even heard himself screaming, "Hey, anybody in the limo, can you hear me? Speak-up, yell if you have to. Tap on the windows. Anything. Can you hear me, Mr. President? President Jacobson, can you hear me? Dammit all, say something, anything, will you?"

{Smitty's mind: "Let's see if there are survivors in L-1 or L-2 who can help with the limo. Just climb over the dirt berm in front of the limo, and over to L-2 and then L-1."}

When something gnaws at you, sometimes it gets a good hold on you – right down to the bone. Smitty suddenly felt an immediate and deep chill – a very big chill – the kind that raises goosebumps at 2 P.M. in the mid-July afternoon sun. He tried to give a good once-over to everything as he clambered up the berm. The unexpected "thunk" of an impact near his feet, followed by the crack of a rifle shifted his attention damn fast. He may be the only survivor of this ambush, but, apparently,

ORDER OF SUCCESSION

that was not by design, but by BAL. Smitty hit the far side of the berm, diving behind the wreck of L-2, and hoping by all that's holy there's not another sniper on this side who is a better shot. And trying to stay away from L-2's hot metal body – still burning in some spots.

{Smitty's responses to Brain: "My God, a good sniper could be a quarter mile away and hit a knothole in the back wall of a dark barn through a crack in the front-door. Those other agents in C-4 and 5 were a lot closer and less smoke; crap, they gotta be friggin' dead. Two more thunks followed by two more cracks; maybe just to keep me pinned-down? Or giving a sniper out in front of me more time to circle around me for a better shot?" "A fine pickle you got us into. Why did you choose this damn job with the Secret Service anyway? Listen, Brain, LATER, WILL YA?"}

{Smitty's mind: "Good thinkin' dummy; the better vest and helmet are in the trunk of C-3. Boy, was I right, you can't think of everything. Hey, Brain, where the hell were you when I screwed-up that decision, huh? But you made sure I got the guns. Big deal; nothing I got is accurate past 30 yards or so. Well, to even hit them, I'm gonna have to lure them in here pretty darn close, that's all. Good going, Mr. Brain."}

{Mind: "Okay, there's a berm to the rear of the limo and L-2 and L-1. It might provide partial cover to the front – great. They're keeping me busy, aren't they? Oh CRAP, they ain't finished here yet, are they? There's no traffic on any of these roads, so help ain't here yet. There's an awful lot of damage right here in what, say, a 200-yard stretch of road – probably an historic amount of damage caused by how many bad-guys against so few of us. Why so few of us? That means ME; that's what that means, you dumb-ass. Where are the reinforcements supposed to come from anyway? Hey, Camp Pendleton is just about 100 miles or so; where are the Marines when we really need them? Choppers, a Harrier, CV-22 Osprey, or even an F-35 JSF, a strafing run, anything to help. God, help us please! They aren't friggin' finished here, are they? If they were done, why shoot at me? 'NO SURVIVORS', that's why, you dumb-ass. Dontcha get it yet? I got it, Brain; I got it – almost really got it – for real."}

{Realizations again: "Where's my radio? In the ditty-bag? Yes, here's the radio. Damn static! What did the briefing notes say about this leg of the trip."}

Smitty mentally checked-off the items he could remember. Brain finally got down to radio, and – OH CRAP – this short stretch of I-8 is

ORDER OF SUCCESSION

radio- and cell-phone dead, meaning the radio and cell services ARE WAITING FOR US ON THE WESTERN END OF THIS STRETCH.

{Smitty to self: "God, I hope the good-guys are wondering where we are. Maybe there's a working phone line down at the rest-area. Do they still have pay phones? Maybe my cell will work down there. Okay, how do I get there? Can't just pick-up my ditty-bag and stroll down there right now, can I? L-1 and L-2's fires are dying down. They're sitting catawampus over there in the left lane of this local road, Maybe I can hug the left side and get near the trees and shrubs between it and the rest-area buildings. The rest-area was supposed to be cleared of all travelers and personnel except necessary law enforcement to keep it closed until after the motorcade had passed. Where are those locals? It looks to be only about 80 to 125 yards away; why haven't they responded up here yet? Maybe they are dead or members of this gang? Is it worth trying to get down there? The answer wasn't long in coming. Well, here goes nothin'."}

Smitty low-crawled on his belly to the left front corner of L-1, the one closest to the buildings. Smitty raised-up to a crouch and took off running, zig-zagging as jaggedly as he could. He thought he was now out of the sight of the sniper to the rear – unless he, too, had changed his nest. Then it struck him like a dope-slap on his forehead!

{Smitty's brain: "Those things that caught your eye on the shoulders of I-8 and the off-ramp – they're improvised rifle rests – a stick in the ground topped with a "U"-shaped cradle. A sniper could quickly change his position and throw the rifle in the cradle with a known distance to the target. RIGHT ON THE FRIGGIN' OFF-RAMP. That's what I would do. Clever bastards. Now what?"}

If there was a sniper on this side of the rest-area, he didn't fire. Maybe Lady Luck was still favoring him – just maybe.

Smitty reached the shrubs for cover and tried to catch his breath. He was making sure all his guns and ammo were still with him when another humongous explosion shook the entire rest-area. The ground beneath his feet shook like one of those infamous California earthquakes – and kept shaking. Hell just got worse – a lot worse.

From his partially-hidden position, Smitty saw nothing but dust rising from the overpass area under the bridge. But this time, it all looked

ORDER OF SUCCESSION

different; gotta wait for the dust to settle to make sure. OH SHIT! Smitty saw nothing but dusty air where the bridge had been – EMPTY FRIGGIN' AIR. Those bastards had dropped the overpass on top of the limo.

{Smitty to self: "I don't think it was supposed to withstand that much weight. I can't check the limo out now – or should I even try? How can anyone still be alive?" Move from crouch to kneeling so you can absorb what had just happened. Okay, now, go to the rest-area buildings or to the limo?"}

He decided to check-out the limo as quickly as possible before he made for the rest-area buildings to get some back-up support. If there were any survivors, maybe he could do something for them. But the enormity of the assault left him with little hope. These bastards were brutally efficient.

Time: Friday, 13-July, 14:23 PDT

He approached the limo as stealthily as possible, taking advantage of as much cover as possible. The limo was now almost flat – like a car-crusher had practiced his trade. It was safe to say that this limo would never be rebuilt. The limo was just too well built using thicker and armor-plate materials – even the Jaws-Of-Life® will be useless. If there's anybody still in it, they are going to have to cut him out with a torch or bury all of them as a single unit – limo and all.

There were no sniper shots fired at him this time. Smitty eventually decided they were probably finished with their job and didn't care any longer that he had survived. He took off toward the buildings at a fast trot – still zig-zagging though.

Smitty turned and retreated cautiously through the trees, low-crawling across some of the more open areas so as not to tempt any snipers if they were still out there. He didn't even want to think the rear sniper might have moved across I-8 to get a better shot at him from above. Maybe they stuck one of those aiming-cradle sticks along the highway to also cover the rest-area. Too much to worry about at this point now. He approached the buildings from the rear, hoping not to attract attention by a more obvious – and shorter – frontal approach. At the side of the near building, he broke-out a frosted-glass window, hoping to find an office with a working phone. No such luck, but at least

Order of Succession

now he was on the inside with a little more cover. He looked over at the parking lot. There were three local sheriff's cars in the parking area and five uniformed bodies on the ground in front of them (probably corpses by now). No movements anywhere.

{Smitty to self: "This is getting really gory. Okay, now, where's a damned phone, a WORKING phone? There's a phone booth outside, but I can't see if there's a phone in it – and there's not much cover, anyway. Maybe there's a utility room where the phone lines come into the building? How do I even know what to look for or how to make a call without an actual phone? Keep looking, Smitty. Do they have phones at a visitors' information desk? There's the desk across the lobby; that's worth a try."}

{Smitty's brain scolding: "Crap, the Sat-Phone is in the trunk. Nice going dumb-ass. Try the radio again; where did I pack it – if I did, oh, yeah, the ditty-bag! Just more crackling static; no responses to radio calls. Look in the ditty-bag. Anything in there that's useful? Try the cell-phone. Hey, no damn bars. Okay, it's over to the information desk then. Hug the wall and as low as possible – GO! Okay, I'm here, and there is a phone. DIAL-TONE – HOT DAMN! Got the number to call right here. WTH? What do ya mean a recording that says I can only dial local numbers from this friggin' phone? I don't want to talk to a friggin' coyote. DAMN IT; I NEED SOMEBODY BACK EAST RIGHT FRIGGIN' NOW!" Okay, alternatives; what now? What's local here? Think; think; damn-it THINK!"}

Time: Friday, 13-July, 14:28 PDT

"9-1-1. What's your emergency and what is your location?"

{Smitty's brain back-talk: "Are they kidding me? Am I the only one who knows what's happened? Okay, Brain, shut-up."}

As calmly as he could, Smitty said, "I am with the Secret Service. Please connect me to the highest-ranking police official at your facility." It must have been the sense of urgency in his voice.

{Smitty's mocking brain: "Urgency, my ass; you're really just this close to sheer PANIC. You really oughta hear yourself."}

The call was transferred to a Captain Marcus Torgelson. Smitty continued, "Please record this conversation or write it down. I am Smit . . , just call me Smitty, an agent with the Secret Service possibly still

ORDER OF SUCCESSION

pinned down by snipers at the Buckman Springs Rest Area on I-8. The emergency is that the motorcade of cars with the President of the United States has been ambushed and all are probably dead, including five of your local deputies, except me. Do you understand? Yes? Good. Any questions so far? No. Good.

"First, I am going to give you a phone number you MUST CALL. When the call is answered just tell them 'AVALANCHE'. Yeah, that's right, like snow in the mountains. Also tell them 'Agent Smitty at Buckman Springs Rest Area'. Do you understand? Yes? Good. Then destroy and forget that number. Do you understand? Good.

{Smitty's brain, scolding: "You're breaking all the security rules, and you know it, you naughty boy." "Shut-up. I don't have a choice; I've got to do something. What the hell do I care at this point, huh? Just shut-up, will ya? Besides, the phone number and trigger word will be automatically changed when they hang-up. That number I gave him will be useless right after they answer the call. Now shut-up, okay?"}

"I need a couple of ambulances and a lot of morgue wagons.

"I also require a detachment of police or military to secure the scene. Better yet, instead of the local police, contact the U.S. Marines at Camp Pendleton, and ask for the Emergency Response Officer. Give him my name and the same code. Tell him to air-lift at least two platoons of Marines to this location ASAP, like yesterday. Oh, yeah, a couple of combat medics, and their best snipers, too. Everyone ARMED; THIS IS NOT A DRILL. Arms, live ammunition, automatic weapons, all that kinda stuff. He will also have to air-lift about one full week of field supplies for those Marines. I also want all available recon fly-overs they can provide to ascertain likely evidence sites and if there are any bad-guys still around this area. Basically, this section of I-8 was officially closed for the President's trip and has not been re-opened yet. Therefore, all vehicles on this section of I-8 in either direction must be stopped, drivers thoroughly questioned and identified, and they and their cars and occupants must be held for questioning by the Secret Service. Do you understand? Good. Shall I repeat any orders? No. Good.

"Tell the ERO that I-8 is closed, and I don't want any remaining evidence screwed-up. Airlift the troops and supplies onto eastbound lanes of I-8 east of rest-area off-ramps. Do not march down the off-ramps

Order of Succession

– they might be mined. Parking lot is crime scene; westbound lanes east of this rest-area also crime scene. Tell them to be prepared for a possible firefight; the LZ may be hot. The Supply Officer to include body-bags as well, maybe 15. Got that, Captain Torgelson? Yes, good.

"You will also have to set up detours for all traffic on I-8 in both directions. The westbound roadway is out of commission; the overpass has been blown-up and is now on top of the President's limo that was sitting under it. Do you understand what I have told you? Do you understand what you have to do? Do you understand? Although dispatched vehicles may be off-road capable, they are not to drive anywhere not paved. Again, got that? Any questions? Good and Good.

"Oh, hell, get the California highway department to figure-out how heavy that damn bridge is and how to lift it straight up.

"Contact your state's Highway Department – this is California, so that's CalTrans the last time I knew – tell them to pull out their maps and drawings for the west-bound overpass at this location. The bridgework and its abutments are destroyed; it will all have to be completely replaced. They will not, I repeat NOT, be allowed on site until our investigation is complete. CalTrans can make arrangements with the Secret Service and the Marines for a fly-over to estimate the size of the cranes and how much work they are facing. The rest-area is also closed. Eastbound I-8 will be closed in both directions for a few more days; they will be allowed on that roadbed for detour construction whenever it is opened. Do you understand?" Torgelson responded that he did. "Good."

"Thank-you for your cooperation, Captain Torgelson. Do you have any questions? Please call me back immediately on this number from an unrecorded line if you have one so I can give you the number to call. Thank-you again." And, Smitty hung-up his phone.

The phone at the information desk rang almost immediately after he had hung-up. "Captain Torgelson, here's that number. Now let's get this recovery underway ASAP."

{Smitty's brain, scolding: "You just said 'recovery', ya know that, dontcha? You know – RECOVERY. So, ya givin' up, are ya?" "Brain, reality really sucks. We're staring it in its damn face, and the reality is that the limo is gone, and I can't move enough debris to get anyone out. I know it's not my failure, but he's gone to. That's reality to me right now,

Order of Succession

so shut the hell up. I can't do anything about it by myself. I'm doing the best I can. I'm the only one; there's nobody else here right now. Now, leave me the hell alone, will ya. I got more things to worry about, and I'm plenty worried. Hangin' up now; bye. Over and Out!!"}

Smitty also knew, but didn't tell Torgelson, that 'Avalanche' would also trigger NRO to reposition two of their nearest satellites to scan the area with both photographic cameras and with a variety of scanners for heat, radiation, electromagnetic emissions, and all that stuff. Fortunately, in this instance, the satellites were already approaching this area in their normal orbits. The NRO just had to tweak their orbits a little so that this area was almost under constant surveillance. The local civilian officials had no specific need-to-know about this; he didn't tell them.

Time: Friday, 13-July, 14:32 PDT

Smitty, mumbling to himself: "Where the hell are the back-ups? It's already been over 15 minutes!" He felt his legs begin to tremble. He finally tried to sit on the floor behind the information desk and discovered his left leg had been wounded. So, instead, he braced his back against the desk and sort of slid down into a sitting position. And then cried a few tears, "Rita, I'm sorry about my language; please forgive me."

My left leg hurts, and my pants feels wet down by the knee. Man, just what I need right now! WHY did all of this happen? Let me sit here just for a minute and rest a bit, will ya? Maybe get some water, too."

His surroundings began fading and growing fainter until they completely disappeared. Deep slumber soon followed. Smitty was soon visiting with Morpheus, the Greek God of dreams.

ORDER OF SUCCESSION

2 – Securing the Site

Early evening, Friday, 13-July: Westbound I-8, Exit 51, at Buckman Springs Rest Area, Mojave Desert, California

TIME: 15:43 PDT

"Yo, Special Agent Smitty, you in here somewheres? Speak up. Where you hidin' at? You still alive or wounded? U.S. Marine Corps Gunnery Sergeant Cornell here. My Captain Rhodes wants to see you ASAP! Special Agent Smitty, please answer-up."

The nebulous voice echoed from the other side of the visitor information desk behind which he had taken refuge after calling 9-1-1. He hoped to stay awake to at least guard the front of the buildings. Apparently, he even failed basic 'guard duty' today.

{Smitty's alarmed, fog-enveloped mind: "Damn! You better bet this voice is not one of the snipers. Falling asleep on guard duty will get your dumb ass killed. What the hell is wrong with you? You're dead meat, you dumb ass." "Shut-up. Help is here – I hope. Now shut-up!"}

Smitty struggled to reorient himself to this sudden intrusion into his deeply-needed rest period. "Stand where you are, okay? For God's sake, knock-off all the noise, will ya? It's all fuzzy where I am. Who did you say you are? Why are you here? Wait a minute, first, what time does your watch say?"

The voice: "My watch says 15:46. Why?"

"It's been an hour and a half since all this started. You guys are fast; you got all this stuff standin' by or sumpthin'?"

"Okay. I'm standing still, but I got you pin-pointed, too. I'm not planning anything hostile, but I came prepared. Now, listen-up: your 10 seconds of waking-up time just ran-out. I am Gunny Cornell – Gunnery Sergeant Cornell, if you're not in the Corps. We're out of Pendleton like a certain Special Agent Smitty requested a civilian Captain Torgelson to

Order of Succession

call. Well, we're here. We have an advance party out there looking this mess over. Not touching anything but the ground on eastbound I-8 and gathering in the parking lot – stayin' away from the cars and county sheriff deputies' bodies. Isn't that whatcha wanted? By the way, the wounds on those bodies look close-up and very personal – if that matters to you. The Captain wants to see you right now, like half an hour ago. I am supposed to bring you to him. You better be Smitty, or we got us a mighty big problem, and you don't want him to have any problems. Understood?"

Smitty: "Roger that. Hang tight; I'm having some trouble moving my left leg. Didn't notice anything much before I called; must have picked-up a piece of shrapnel and didn't really notice it until now. Did Torgelson give the Pendleton officer some sort of password?"

Gunny responded, "You mean 'Avalanche'? Don't know what it means, but I've never seen so much structured panic in my whole friggin' Marine life; this must be damn important. Marines at my level ain't told crap about that, but we do know how to jump, and this one was damn high, too. Hey, Smitty – that's you right – I gotta get you to the Cap'n. You ready to go?"

Smitty: "Well, 'fraid not, Gunny. I'm gonna need some help getting' up. As you face the desk, go around the right-hand side and bring something I can use as a crutch. Oh, I am armed and prepared if you ain't in official Marine camo – the ones with 'USMC' woven into the camo pattern. Do you understand what I am trying to say? You had all the right answers so far, but with all those bodies outside – well, I'm just sayin', ya know."

Cornell: "Gotcha. Not a problem. I understand your caution. But, we gotta get movin'. I will walk slowly around the right side. Two corporals with a stretcher will follow me if you need it. By the way, that Captain Torgelson torqued-off the Pendleton folks pretty effing good; seems he also called the Army over at Fort Irwin 'cause he's got a buddy over there. Guess he thought they could beat us Marines here from the eastern side of this ambush. You better be prepared to make nice with Cap'n Rhodes 'bout that. Now, 'nuff of this jawin'. We are gonna get you up-and-out so we can secure this area." With that, Cornell eased around the right-side, also with his side-arm drawn, cocked, and ready, but pointed at the floor, with his finger outside the trigger guard. As a courtesy, Cornell offered to show Smitty his Marine ID Card.

Order of Succession

Smitty: "Oorah! Not necessary on the ID, Gunny. You look like every other Marine I trained with. Just help me get up and let's go." One of the corporals, who had been standing against the far wall, offered him a choice of a litter or a crutch. "Crutch, it is. I've holstered the SIG, but could someone please police-up the MP5 and the shotgun? I'd really appreciate that. Is there a hook or something on this crutch to hang my ditty-bag? It's got a lot of stuff I don't want to lose track of."

Cornell: "I'll be damned! You a Marine?"

Smitty: "Well, not exactly; I trained for months at a time with lots of Marines – Gunnies, like you up at Pendleton, Palms, and some other places I can't name. So, don't be insulted if I say 'Oorah'; sometimes, it just slips out. Okay?"

Cornell: "Damn straight. After looking around this area, I knew somebody had his friggin' act together! Well, hot-damn, guys, we got us a Gyrene, here, and a damn good one, too! Just look at that crap outside. Help us getting' him down to the Cap'n."

One of the corporals, "Don't worry about your weapons, sir. We'll police-up the area and bring all of it out to the parking lot for you. We're right behind ya. Say, sir, pardon me for asking, but you lugged all this crap around this site dressed like that? Slick-soled shoes, white shirt, which, by the way looks like crap right now, and civilian slacks? Boy, you'd never pass inspection for combat. But, just looking around out-there, there must have been a lot of shit goin' on. Glad you made it through that, sir, with just that scratch on your leg."

Smitty: "Believe me, me, too."

The four formed their own small squad hobbling at Smitty's speed across the grass toward the tables and benches in the plaza area of the Buckman Springs Rest Area. Following the concrete walks to the plaza would have been easier, but cross-grass was shorter. Six of one; half a dozen of another. Gunny led the squad over toward what looked like a makeshift command table. Smitty guessed that's where Captain Rhodes must be. Gunny yelled at the cluster of Marines around the table, "Cap'n Rhodes, Cornell here with Special Agent Smitty."

"About time!" a voice from the near side of the table. All eyes turned toward Cornell and Smitty. Smitty looked first for the railroad tracks insignia and then a name tag. Only one of them had the 'tracks' and 'Rhodes' on his uniform.

"Are you Smitty?" Rhodes asked; and then he saw the crutch. "I didn't realize you were injured. Anything you need for that?" Rhodes may not have looked like every other Marine Captain – shorter stature, average-looking build, and freckles, yet – but he had the intensity to bolster his authority.

Smitty: "If you got a medic, can he look it over later? About this mess, what do'ya need from me? I apologize for asking you all to land on I-8. I don't want to disturb anything useful down here. Hope you copy."

Rhodes: "You ready to walk and talk right now? We need to get a handle on this situation right away. Just what the hell happened out here? Can you walk over that way to describe what you did, saw, and how all that stuff lying all around everywhere got destroyed?" He motioned toward the area with the demolished overpass, the cars – L-1, L-2, the limo (which he couldn't really see yet), and the 'C-cars'. If Captain Rhodes hadn't been over to that side of the area yet, he hadn't seen C-2 lying in the dirt, C-3, and all of the bodies on the off-ramp yet.

Smitty: "Yeah, but first, sumpthin' musta happened to my radio and cell. It's been a while since all this assault started. You heard anything from the Secret Service yet?"

Rhodes: "Say what? They ain't in my chain of command, catch my drift? The first, last, and only contact since forever was a little over an hour ago – and it was with YOU. However, to answer your specific question: We ain't heard didly. Is that a problem? Maybe they figured you to be a Texas Ranger – you know, 'only one ranger to a riot'. Are you sayin' you ain't from Texas?"

Smitty: "Yeah, that is a problem, a BIG problem. They're supposed to be Johnny-on-the-spot whenever the President sneezes, and all this time has elapsed and nobody even asked how the weather is out here. What the hell is goin' on?" Smitty didn't go into how everybody thinks the agents are supposed to be willing to take a bullet for 'The Man'. But, he started to think long and hard about that and why nobody had shown up yet. Maybe we all were supposed to take a bullet or two about an hour and a half ago. He started to mull over lotsa other possibilities. Smitty decided to try to keep the Captain from jumping on the same conclusion train he already boarded.

ORDER OF SUCCESSION

With another nod toward the wreckage, he brought the Captain's attention back to the task at hand. "Say, Captain, I feel strange always calling you Captain; is there something else I could use?" "Yeah, first name's George, but in personal conversation, you can call me Rocky, a play on Rhodes and, besides, I like the ice cream a lot. But not in front of the troops, okay?"

"I like that, but we'll keep that to a minimum." Smitty nodded back toward the smoking wreckage. "Let's go give it a try. I'll even point out the limo to you – or where it used to be."

"What limo?" Rhodes sounded surprised.

Smitty: "The limo with the President in it. That's why we're out here – some scheduled political trip to Calexico and then over to El Cajon for another political dinner and a hotel stay. The next morning supposed to leave for San Diego by motorcade to catch the 'Big Bird' back to D.C." Smitty considered telling this Captain about some political criteria and how stupid the Captain was for not realizing how it all worked. Fortunately, he stifled any more-aggressive wording before he could really screw-up this meeting before it even got started.

Back to the problem at hand. Smitty (pointing toward where the westbound overpass used to be): "You see the overpass bridgework over there between what remains of the concrete abutments? What in the hell does the trade call it, 'bridgework'? 'Deck' I think; it really doesn't matter that much at this point, now, does it? The limo is still under the deck regardless of what its technical name is, isn't it?"

Rhodes: "Are you telling us the President of the United States was still in the 'limo', which is squashed under that bridge – or deck or whatever it's called? DAMN! That never got down to us! Don't know how it happened, but we got the impression that it was some sort of 'terrorist activity'. Must be like that parlor game; you know, the one where somebody tells someone else a short story, which is supposed to be relayed by everyone else in a row – and whatever comes out at the far end doesn't even vaguely resemble the beginning? This puts a different light on what we havta do. I gotta advise HQ about this right fast. That might change supplies and other stuff. Gonna request some choppers to give this site a low-flyover to see if there's anything suspicious remaining out here. Maybe even some satellite activity as well. Also requested more Marines to safeguard this area."

ORDER OF SUCCESSION

"The last part should already be underway right now."

{Smitty's brain, scolding: "YOU better hope the word was sent over to NRO. Since nobody else from the Secret Service has shown-up yet, maybe you've been hung-out to dry all by your lonesome self. Yeah, you woulda been hung-out like a raggedy-ass shirt on the line. What ya think of that possibility, Smart Ass?" "Brain, shut-up, will ya!"}

Rhodes: "You mean the birds are already . . . SAY WHAT! This is a helluva lot bigger than we were told. When? They see anything yet?"

Smitty: "Well, I can't tell you when, but if they spot anything in your area of responsibility, you'll be among the first to know. Now, let's hobble over to the bridgework, or deck, or whatever the hell it's called. We can walk and talk on the way. You might wanta bring some enlisted Marines along so they get a better lay-of-the-land because they're gonna havta do all the grunt work, aren't they? Bring that Gunny Cornell along; I like him. We think much the same. Oh, by the way, if the Army from Irwin wants to get involved, I want you to know, I did not ask for them. But, if you need additional support from, say, Pendleton, or the USMC Air Ground Combat Command at 29 Palms, or even from Air Station Yuma, well that's certainly up to you, isn't it? And, by the way, I requested the Marines because you were nearby with the muscle and attitude to do what I think needs to be done to properly to secure this site. I want to cooperate with you in that respect and to keep prying eyes away from here for a while – especially, the media. I am not going to personally tell you who is in charge of this site, but the Secret Service is going to claim responsibility for obvious reasons. That is, if they ever get here. You all can argue about the finer points of areas of responsibilities, but this is going to be way, way above both our levels and pay-grades."

Rhodes weighed what Smitty had just said before responding, "Understood; we, you and I, sort of think alike, too – well, maybe a little bit. Oh, and thanks for the heads-up on the rest of the politics."

During Smitty's tour, over on eastbound I-8 near the rest area parking area, additional troop transport helos began arriving carrying more Marines until there was a full company plus one platoon on the site.

As the group neared the remains of the cars and the overpass, Smitty began describing how the motorcade was laid out, attempting

Order of Succession

to point here and there while balancing on unfamiliar crutches. "This pile over here used to be Lead Car-1; we just call it 'L-1'. That pile of burned out car used to be L-2. I have no idea if the four agents in L-1 and L-2 got out; my best guess is they didn't. That's two agents in each car." Smitty purposely skipped past the limo, "Chase Car-1, C-1, is on the other side of where the bridge used to be; same about those agents." Then motioning toward the mangled, burnt ruins in the dirt near the on-ramp, Smitty indicated, pointing one of his crutches, "That used to be C-2; ditto about the agents. That's my car, C-3, over there on the other side of the bridge where the on- and off-ramps meet the road underneath all of this mess. Only one agent in each C-3 to C-8. I think it's the only car still on its wheels. Just my luck, I guess. C-4 and C-5 are further up the off-ramp over there. I heard what I think was ambush firing up the off-ramp as I bailed-out of my car; almost sounded like a light machine gun. Unfortunately, I don't think the agents survived through it. By the way, this motorcade left Calexico with three more cars, C-6, C-7, and C-8. I could not see them after this assault began; I don't know where they are. Just something more to think about.

"Back to the beginning of the motorcade. L-1 was blown higher than the bridge; it disappeared completely from my view. Don't know how high it was, but it was clean outta sight. The same thing happened to L-2, C-2, and C-4. Way up, and then crashing back to the ground. Looked like C-1 was too close to the limo; it was blown into the underside of the overpass decking. But, the deck did not collapse right then; there was another hellish explosion that brought the deck right down on top of the limo. Sort of a *coup-de-grace,* I guess. After that explosion and my ears stopped ringing, everything sorta turned quiet around here – real quiet, even no birds.

"About the explosions, the first thing that came to mind was film footage about those IEDs used over in Iraq and Afghanistan. These bastards had this thing planned to drive us off I-8 at this off-ramp. Either that or possibly blow us up if we decided to try to force the issue by trying to outrun them on I-8.

"And, that brings up another point. From what I saw, there were a lot of explosives buried around here. I don't know if they used-up all of their mines and IEDs. There could still be some more buried out here. Have you all got any gear which can be used to locate any more of them with? Watch your steps – for a couple of reasons, okay?

Order of Succession

"Here's one of the crazy things that's still fixed firmly in my mind. I think I also saw a couple of sniper's aiming sticks with cradles on their tops. One over there on the I-8 shoulder and another on the downward off-ramp over there. They look almost like they are camouflaged to look like mileage markers or roadside reflectors. I can't say for sure 'cause I haven't been up there to look at them yet. But, I know that they had shrubs near them. Know what I mean?" Smitty swept his right arm pointing-out the general areas. "Look but don't touch; leave them in the ground for the forensics boys. But I would like you to get your snipers to best-guess what they are, what the approximate field of fire would be, how your Marines would use them, and how many casualties your snipers could inflict the way they are set up. And anything else your men can figure out about them. Hell, they will probably know more than the Forensics Team does. Take pictures, lots of pictures; catalog them, and don't lose track of them – ever. Oh, yeah, there are about 3, maybe 4, slugs in east end of the dirt berm in front of the limo. See if your snipers can find them and dig'em out to see if they can figure-out what type of weapon was used to shoot at me. And protect the slugs and their locations, too, okay?

"Oh, please get somebody to check the buildings in the rest-area for booby traps, IEDs. God only knows if anything else was planted in there, and He ain't talked about that yet – at least not to me. Besides, I gotta use the facilities pretty soon for their designed purpose.

"I'll show you everything I can think of, and then I want to sit down with you and your Gunnies so you can tell me how you think it was done – exactly done. I lost some good friends and the President here, and I am pissed-off about all of it and intend to do something about it."

Smitty briefly scanned the devastated area again, and then quickly returned his gaze to his car, C-3. "Hey, any of you guys got better eyes than mine. Does the trunk of C-3 look like it's open? I didn't have time to open it. If somebody opened it, they got some important stuff out of it. When you get there, get me an inventory of what you see in C-3 and where it was found. Okay?

"In the meantime, I am going to be stretched out on one of those tables over there, if you don't mind having a medic come over to check-out my leg, I would really appreciate it."

Order of Succession

Rhodes yelled an order toward the two corporals, "Get Medic Gannon over here to help Smitty, NOW! We ain't gonna have anything happen to this Marine! GOT THAT?" Toward Smitty, "Gannon may not be much to look at, but he has the hands of a Johns-Hopkins surgeon. Hell, he's even consulted with those docs back east in Baltimore about battlefield-type wounds; he is that good! We'll take care of you and the scene. If you agree, we'll begin on I-8, looking for obvious disturbances and oddities out of the ordinary. And work our way inward down the banks. In the meantime, I got the word to HQ; we will have gear for detecting IEDs sent out here ASAP. We don't want to go walking around with those underfoot, and I know you certainly don't either. They are going to contact CalTrans for detailed maps, electrical drawings, and all the stuff they have about this rest-area."

Cornell to Smitty: "Gannon's on his way. I know he'll take good care of you."

After the first-person guided tour of the site, it was time to lock it down. Tight. With his next breath, Rhodes took charge of the site, and addressed his Gunnies and sergeants, "Listen up. I-8 is primarily an east/west highway; however, in this short stretch, I-8 is actually aligned sort of north/south. We are going to continue referring to it as east and west because we Marines know where Pendleton and Yuma are, that is west and east of here. We are going to search east and west of this rest-area. Is that clear? Gunny Johnson, take your Marines and sweep and secure the area from the rest-area west toward Pendleton at least two (2) klicks out. Use the mileage markers on I-8 as a guide. Choose your own search pattern as you recon the area: out on eastbound I-8 and back over the full width to westbound I-8 or reverse. Gunny Layton, your Marines will sweep and secure the area between this rest-area and east toward Yuma. Gunny Cornell, your Marines will sweep and secure the rest-area itself, overpasses, and the wreckage itself. Gunny Vernor, your snipers and the other support squads will report to Gunny Cornell. Make sure your Marines DO NOT disturb any evidence and DO NOT get blown-up by left over-explosive mines or other munitions. Questions? None? Good. Report back in 60 minutes. Dismissed."

Another Marine catchphrase, "Improvise, Adapt, and Overcome", was immediately implemented. The four Gunnies instructed (no, rather

ORDER OF SUCCESSION

ordered) their Marines about what was now going to be their responsibility, and they were gone – just like that movie *"Gone in 60 Seconds"*.

The two platoons (Pendleton sent five in addition to the special squads) went east and west respectively, taking care to take pictures of everything that looked out-of-place. And, hell, now everything did look out-of-place. The close-in platoon, Gunny Cornell's, conferred amongst themselves, decided who best could do what, and divided themselves up.

One squad commandeered one of the idle medics, PFC Chuck Berkeley, and put him to work on the five corpses. Chuck started photographing the scene, victims, everything – as if his life depended on it. "Hey, Gunny said they brought some body bags out here along with the rest of this stuff; one of you all go round-up five bags and some medical gloves – a whole box of them. And make it snappy. The rest of you stop eating, go wash your hands; you're going to help fill the bags, and I don't want any bodies or bags screwed-up. Any questions Marines?" Chuck's accent marked him as coming from the South. His insignia showed he was still a PFC, but this was his MOS [4], the one he had been trained in – and the one nobody else wanted. So, they figured he knew best and gave him no lip, not even Lance Corporals. He took advantage of that to the max. "Hey, one of you go tell Gunny we are going to have to have some sort of cold storage for the bodies, otherwise they're going to cook in the bags in this heat. A refrigerated truck of some sort will do. Well, git going; these boys ain't going to last much longer. Git!"

The remaining squads spilt up checking over the parking areas, grounds, plaza area, and the buildings. They were angling for a first look at the wreckage over by what used to be an overpass. As Marines, they were fast to realize the way to the wreckage was to do a fast, but efficient, good, thorough search of their area, then they . . . they would be ready to go look 'over there'. And, so they did their assigned job – correctly and fast.

The rumor-mill was already hard at work: "Hell, the President was supposed to be under the overpass in his limo; must be a damned strong car." "It's crushed isn't it?" "I gotta see it and get pictures; they'll never believe this back home. Wow!!"

---

4   MOS = Military Occupational Specialty. This is the specialty in which the person has received specialized training.

ORDER OF SUCCESSION

3 – Somebody Doesn't Want Us Here

Late evening, Friday, 13-July: Westbound I-8, Exit 51, at Buckman Springs Rest Area, Mojave Desert, California

TIME: 17:55 PDT

If there were a way to take pictures of air, there would have been 1,000s to look through. The platoons spread-out – half on the eastbound roadbeds and half on the westbound – taking care to note everything on the shoulders and down the dirt banks. Each marched out a little over two klicks (about 1-1/4 miles) checking-out everything as thoroughly as human eyes could possibly do. Once satisfied that the perimeter of their assigned area was clear, they joined ranks across the median between the two roadbeds about 1/4 mile wide and then proceeded back toward the rest-area, checking-out every grain of sand and leaf on all of the shrubs.

Gunny Jack Layton's Marines found nothing of interest east of the rest-area – not counting the lizards and litter thrown from cars. They returned to the rest-area first and headed for the water taps to refill their canteens.

Cap'n Rhodes was becoming impatient that Gunny Barney Johnson's Marines failed to show-up for some time. Impatient, until a radio call on their scrambled combat gear got his attention. He knew of nobody out in the field who had that freq, not even his Gunnies – just the HQ back in Pendleton as far as he knew. He answered, and the cadre around the table made assumptions on his 1/2 of a conversation. Rhodes, "Who am I speaking with?" Rhodes sort of rolled the handset to the side so his coms sergeant, Sergeant Williams, could also hear part of the call.

The caller responded, "Lt. General Mansfield, Emergency Response Officer?" (No one recognized this general as a USMC ERO – certainly not out of Pendleton. Rhodes motioned to his Communications Sergeant to check who this light General was.)

Order of Succession

Rhodes continued, "Pardon me, sir, but how can I help you? I'm way east of your position as you no doubt know. You're on the ground? Where? No, sir, I've been advised by the surviving Secret Service Agent that I-8 was supposed to be closed in both directions until this incident has been investigated. And, I agree with him. Closed at Alpine on the west and El Centro on the east. Yes, we know that is a long piece of I-8. No, sir, I'm afraid I cannot permit you to drive past the road blocks on the eastbound roadbed. Not just yet. We haven't even checked it yet for IEDs. We are waiting for my Gunnies to notify us of the status. No, sir, we can't do that just yet. The Agent has advised us that military helos could be permitted only in the rest-area parking lot. Let me check with the Gunny who is doing the work; I'll git back to you. Sir, sit-tight, remain where you are, sir, we're taking live incoming fire. Out!"

This was not a ruse; shots were being fired out on the western side of the rest-area. "Get a hold of Gunny Johnson NOW!" Rhodes yelled toward no one in particular. Sgt Williams, the Coms Sergeant, jumped for the radio. Now Rhodes was listening to one-side of the radio call.

Sgt. Williams: "I-8 West, Over. We're hearing shots fired. Any casualties? One. Whazzup? Need I-8 East to reinforce? Which side you want them on? Okay, you got'em coming toward your position from the eastbound side. What are we facing? Three bad-guys above the westbound roadbed. Armed with? You said 'sounds like civilian hunting rifles; one semi automatic; don't think it's fully-automatic, right? Copy that." Rhodes had already signaled Gunny Layton to get over here NOW to decide how he and his platoons were going to reinforce Gunny Johnson's platoons. They were both taking mental notes of this side of the conversation. "I-8 West, I-8 East on the way. Going to stop by the armory to draw something to bring smoke on 'em. Any preferences? Extra ammo for the smokers. Got that. Out."

Hunting rifles huh? Probably .30-Cal. Gunny Layton's Marines already heard the gun-fire and had been mentally improvising what they would take if they had to go forward. Rhodes attached the snipers temporarily to I-8 East, and those boys jumped at 'live practice'. And for themselves, I-8 East chose a little more firepower than hunting rifles. One each: M-240 medium machine gun chambered for 7.62x51-mm; M203 Grenade Launcher (in 40x46-mm); an ammo-box of M67 Grenades; and finally, two full ammo boxes – 5.56x45-mm NATO

Order of Succession

ammo for both the M4s that I-8 West carried and the weapons they were bringing to the party.

The sniper squad unlimbered their weapons: two M40s, both bolt-actions chambered for 7.62x51-mm, one M110 semi-automatic also in 7.62x51, and one semi-automatic Barrett M82 in .50-Cal BMG and their own ammo specially loaded for this work. One sniper had a new rifle chambered for .338 Lapua Magnum [5] and brought it out here for 'practice, too, just to get used to it'. "Gunny Layton, we're locked and loaded. On our way to the objective; ready to 'light 'em up'."

As he departed, Gunny Layton yelled at Sgt. Williams, "Radio I-8 West, we're on our way double-time; should be on his 6 in about 4 minutes. We'll let the Cap'n know if we need air-support when we get there. If push comes to shove, have him ask that Lt. General to have the fly boys pick him up for a hot ride before he gets to land. Got that?"

Williams, "Roger that, all three of 'em."

I-8 East arrived, bringing-up their supplies to the front line. "Hey, Barney, good buddy, whatcha stumble into here? These Marines here are our snipers. They're now attached to our effort. Can one of your guys point-out where the bad-guys are. We'll put their skills to work."

Johnson: "Well, glad to see you, too, Jack. Best we can tell there are three of 'em up there by those trees – shrubs, I should say – at about 2 o'clock spread across to about 10 o'clock on the west – about 350 meters out. We gauge it about only 150 meters east to west. Sure feels like a big-ass damn screw-up somewhere to be pinned-down here in the U.S., know what I mean, Jack?"

Layton: "Yeah, Barney, I know, but they don't cover that situation in any training, do they?"

A couple of PFCs from West drew a diagram in the sand for the newcomers. PFCs, Lance Corporals, and Sergeants, worked to put

---

5 (INFO: .338 Lapua Magnum is a center-fire cartridge developed to hit long-range targets. Its design was proved in Afghanistan and Iraq War. While the .338 Lapua is a proven round in sniper-combat, it is not as powerful as the .50 BMG's projectiles. The .338 uses bullets nominally weighing between 250 grains (gr) and 300 gr, delivering nominal muzzle velocities ranging between approximately 2,700 and 3,000 feet per second. Nominal muzzle energy is approximately 4,800 foot pounds (ft lbs). Effective range extends to approximately 2,000± yards.).

ORDER OF SUCCESSION

a plan together. "Hey, Gunny, do we plan for air-support?" "What's your assessment so far?" The Marines decided to try to flush-out the bad-guys for the snipers – or at least so they could sort of see where the fire's coming from.

They placed a few rounds around where they thought they had been a couple of minutes before. And, in response, the westbound I-8 roadway exploded in front of them – asphalt, concrete, dirt, guard rails, and crap all over everywhere. The decision was made for them.

Barney: "Cap'n, West here. Bring in the helos – loaded with hot shots. I say again, this is not a training exercise anymore; bring hot smoke."

Rhodes: "Roger that. They are already monitoring; airborne now; coming from Yuma. Copy?"

Barney: "Copy. Advise when 2 klicks out, we'll lay-in smoke grenades if they want. Copy?"

(New voice): "Yuma copies. Three hot shots already on their way; 30 klicks now. Out."

Barney: "Corporal, three hot shots on the way; get the smoke grenades ready to shoot the spot for the helos."

Corporal Simmons: "Gunny, how about some real ones? West wind picking-up through the canyon; don't want to blind the jockeys."

Barney: "Good point, Simmons, light 'em up with real ones on Gunny Layton's order; gotta check on PFC Wilson's wound; see if we need a medevac or just a slow walk to the rest-area. Jack, can you take over with the grenades and helos?"

Layton: "Roger. Got the stick. Coms, get a hold of Cap'n and advise of new plan. Tell'em whatever he wants to do with that Lt General, go to it; we hope to have this wrapped up by the time he could get here anyway. Definitely going to be noisy up here shortly. Copy?"

Coms: "Roger. Out."

The bad-guys fired at the Marines a few more times. Excellent screw-up for the benefit of the snipers and spotters. Range estimated at 370 meters, slightly uphill, scopes zeroed for that range, deep breathing, spotter ready. On the next incoming shot, the Barrett M82 replied twice outgoing – very loudly, especially if you are looking straight down the

Order of Succession

muzzle at this short distance – very loudly, indeed [6]. At the estimated range of 370 meters, there's not much time for a bad-guy to react. Plus, there were two of those bullets coming his way about one second apart. Not a healthy diet for anybody who wants to live much longer; it puts way too much lead in one's diet way too fast. The spotter marked his maps where the bad-guy used to be so the remains could be policed-up afterwards. The sniper with the .338 Lapua was also locked and loaded just itching for an opportunity, but used his own scope to glass the area as the Barrett laid-in its rounds.

Layton: "Helos 10 klicks out; ready with the grenade launchers for spotting. 5 klicks. 3 klicks. 2 klicks. When you here the rotors . . . FIRE." Two spots on the hillside exploded followed closely a fusillade from the air. Before the helos let loose, there had been a couple of shots from the hillside. Now, afterwards, no responses to probing fire.

Barney: "Corporals, lead flanking squads up both sides. See if we have any more resistance. Be careful for other planted IEDs." "Roger." "Roger." "Roger." "Coms, advise Cap'n. Suggest recalling helos to rest-area after fly-about recon looking for more bad-guys. Copy?" "Got it. Goin' out now."

Rhodes: "Gannon, how's Smitty? Can he make it over here?"

Smitty: "Already behind you. Can't rest with all of this noise. What's up? You guys hear from my head-shed yet?"

Rhodes: "Ain't heard any news from your folks; we're probably not on their pushes [7]. I sense you gotta problem larger than this mess out here. You thinkin' 'bout that ain't cha? I, ugh, we Marines ain't got a personal need to stir that chili yet. You let me know what's going-on on your side when you hear, okay?

"Now, on to other things. Seems there were at least three bad-guys west of our position out along westbound I-8. Maybe supposed to attack the limo if it passed the rest-area exits; had IEDs under I-8 and set'em off a few minutes ago. So, this stretch is gonna be shut-down permanently for a while. Wasn't before; will be now. Well, those guys could have

---

6   (INFO: Nominally speaking, depending on the loading, the .50-Cal. bullet at a nominal 3,000 fps (feet per second), brings between 10,000 and 15,000 foot-pounds of energy to the party.)
7   (Slang: A 'push' is 'an assigned radio frequency. 'Pushes' are the radio frequencies assigned to an agency/department/ etc.

Order of Succession

gotten clean away, but, no, they decided to pick on us with what we think are hunting rifles yet. They ain't got no respect. You got any ideas why they would stick around and pick a fight they were bound to lose, any ideas at all? Let me know if you do.

"Sorry 'bout the noise cutting your nap short. Our snipers had at one of them. We also brought in three helos from your buddies at Yuma. A little fire and brimstone on the north side of I-8 about 1 klick west of our position. Choppers will be taking some recon runs to see if they can see any more. Be landing soon in the parking lot over there." Rocky motioned toward the lot.

"Gunny Cornell, how you coming with this area? Going to be ready to look over the wreckage soon, are ya? Oh, yeah, what about the refrigerated van; any news from the motor pool on that?"

Cornell: "Cap'n, we're done with the buildings and the parking lot. Lot looks okay; didn't find anything. Five bodies in the bags; moved them over there under the shade from the tarps, but they're getting warm. Know what I mean?"

Rhodes: "Gunny, you forget about the buildings and the plaza?"

Cornell: "Sorry, Cap'n, I didn't exactly forget. Just didn't want to get Smitty here too concerned out loud. He and we, are some lucky Marines. There were some explosives in there all right; pulled the fuses and left them in place for the EOD and IEDD boys to handle. Good thing none of the terrorists were still around here manning the triggers. Where do ya think they got military plastique explosives? This stuff is still in military wrappers wearing military markings. Our, OUR OWN damn military! (Toward Smitty) You know, you're one lucky Gyrene. One was behind the information counter you were leaning against. Come to think of it, I'm a lucky guy, too; I was on the other side of that counter. Whew!"

"About the reefer truck, the motor pool is gonna try to get one from the commissary or the exchange. Still gotta top it off and drive on the shoulders all the way out here. There's one hellacious traffic jam that's already on the news. Those news choppers are gonna be out here like white on rice. Cap'n, what do ya wanna us to do about the overpass or the hole where it used to be and all of the debris on I-8? Tarps? Or keep our helos up to scare 'em off? We could shoot 'em down as a lesson to stay away when you're told to? Nah, I'm just jokin' about that last one.

ORDER OF SUCCESSION

"Cap'n, we don't know who these terrorists are or how many of them there are. The sun is moving west; pretty soon this ravine is going to get real dark. We better establish a security perimeter and post guards every 50 to 75 feet if we got enough Marines for that. Have Pendleton send over generators and flood lights for the wreckage so we can work under the tarps. Also, some night-vision gear might provide very useful since we don't know who or how many. And fuel for ... well, everything."

Rhodes: "Give your list to Coms. The Quartermaster may be earning overtime for the duration. Gunny, you think the parking lot can safely handle a cargo chopper? Traffic is going to be a big factor out here. Man, I hope Margie, my wife, isn't caught in it. Coms, find-out if we can get our supplies on a cargo chopper. Gunny will work-up a list with you. All, make it happen."

Smitty: "Cap'n, can Coms get linked into any network so I can try to find out where the hell our agents are?"

"Smitty, you and Coms try to work it out. But, I have got some gut feelings about this mess that are getting stronger. Know what I mean? You do, too, I'll bet."

Time: Friday, 13-July, 19:16 PDT

{Smitty's mind (wondering): "Why no contact with the head shed? WTH is going on here."}

Smitty wandered over to Coms, "Say, it's Sergeant Williams, isn't it? Have you heard anything out of the ordinary over the civilian news channels? You know, news from the rest of the country. I'm just curious if anything is going on elsewhere, and if we could be involved in it somehow?"

Williams: "No, sir, haven't heard anything weird or hinky out there. I'll ask around. Carefully, if you don't mind."

Time: Friday, 13-July, 21:43 PDT

Smitty: "It's gonna be a long night."

Voice in the dark: "Blades from the east." With two helos from Yuma still on the ground, the pilot of the expected re-supply chopper

ORDER OF SUCCESSION

would have to be a tad more careful of cross-drafts and the size of the rotors. Didn't want to get close enough to clip the others. "Marines, put out some marker lights for the LZ and make it snappy."

Rhodes: "Coms, did you receive notice of the cargo chopper's ETA? Is it supposed to be here already? That would be a magic turnaround."

Coms: "Cap'n, haven't heard back from Pendleton Flight Control yet."

Rhodes: "Coms, something's damned funny here; try to raise the inbound chopper ASAP."

Coms: "Tried already. Got no response."

Rhodes, yelling: "Gunny, that chopper may not be ours. CLEAR THE LZ; kill the lights NOW! Be prepared to bring that chopper down if necessary! SPOOL-UP THE HELOS RIGHT EFFING NOW!" To no one in particular: "Can anyone get a visual on the chopper." Response from over near the snipers: "Visual, sir. No Marine markings on it. NO MARKINGS AT ALL, SIR. Sir, we already got two .50-Cals and the .338 on it. Just for practice, sir."

{Rhodes' brain, nagging: "What do you do? Which way you gonna err? Take it out and the crew is toast. Don't challenge it, and Marines on the ground go home in a bag. Okay, your choice. BUT, DO SOMETHING NOW."}

Rhodes: "Coms, any response from the incoming chopper?" "No, sir" "SNIPERS, fire two tracer bow-shots across chopper's path."

Sniper: "Aye, sir. Two tracers away." And then they quickly moved to their backup secondary positions.

The visible tracks clearly crossed in front of the chopper; there was no change of path. Wait; there was a change – an aggressive one. The bird dropped lower, altered its course to the direction from which the snipers had just fired, and hit the switch for a Nightsun® [8] searchlight, an intense, blinding light at this short distance. Definitely, not friendly.

{Rhodes' brain: "Let's see, now. No markings plus aggressive actions equals TAKE IT OUT NOW. You got the gonads for that? Do something"}

"MARINES, BRING IT DOWN NOW; SNIPERS, TAKE IT OUT ASAP!"

---

[8] Nightsun is a Registered Trademark of Spectrolab Inc, A Boeing Company

Order of Succession

The chopper swept the area with the Nightsun® and again pointed toward where the snipers had been and launched a small missile – its last hostile actions. And the rest-area erupted into another firefight. The chopper didn't clear the area fast enough; the pilot hung around to see the results. Too long. So-long. Too bad. The snipers (and a few other riflemen) fired for real this time. The chopper's fuselage was hit repeatedly and hard – especially by the .50 Cal. Somebody hit something vital and flammable.

It dropped from where it had last fired. More wreckage. Marines tried to put the fire out, but failed for the most part. Two more bodies for the growing collection of body-bags. Hours later, the chopper was identified as resembling an AgustaWestland SW-4 – resembling, only because of the twisted and melted metal.

Rhodes: "Gunnies, somebody really doesn't want us out here very much, do they? WE ARE NOT GOING TO BE PUSHED OUT. Establish that security perimeter ASAP! Nothing gets in or out unless it is smaller than this ant. Any questions?"

"NO, SIR."

"Coms, if we are not cut-off from the rest of the world, get us some reinforcements – armed to the teeth – how about another company to start with. With dogs if that's all that's available. And airborne surveillance. And anybody who can provide flight data on that chopper – FAA, satellites, local airports, farmhands, hitchhikers, anybody!"

Rhodes: "Agent Smitty, we need to talk RIGHT EFFING NOW."

ORDER OF SUCCESSION

4 – Digging for the Truth

Nightfall, Friday, 13-July: Westbound I-8, Exit 51, at Buckman Springs Rest Area, Mojave Desert, California

TIME: 22:27 PDT

Time for a one-on-one conference.

Rhodes and Smitty walked over to a more-or-less 'private' table on the plaza – Smitty, hobbling, brought-up the rear.

Time: Friday, 13-July, 22:37 PDT

Rhodes: "Agent Smitty, you got us Marines into this plot with a single, very convincing word, 'Avalanche'. Hell, I even got a call from some Lt. General Mansfield, who claimed to be 'OUR' Emergency Response Officer, supposedly straight from Pendleton, calling me on a scrambled push directly on our secure coms. Know what he wanted? He wanted to know how he could get past the roadblocks on eastbound I-8 and drive out here to this very rest-area where we're sitting right now. Oh, FYI, I told him to wait right there where he was because that little fire-fight with the three amateur snipers had just broken out.

"First of all, Emergency Response Officers are responsible for notifying troops about immediate field operations. They usually do not take a personal interest in visiting the site. However, I can also understand him wanting to visit this particular site because of the historical interest.

"I had my coms, Sgt., Sergeant Williams – you already talked with him – make some calls. And, guess what. That Lt. General Mansfield, Emergency Response Officer, does not exist, at least not at Pendleton or anywhere else that we could check in very short order. Our Emergency Response Officer, Pendleton's Emergency Response Officer is a Major Joseph Graham, not a Lieutenant General Mansfield. Then, I requested Major Joseph Graham, whom I know personally, by the way, to dispatch some Marines to the roadblock area to talk with this Lt. General

Order of Succession

Mansfield. Would you like to guess what they discovered? Never mind, I'll tell you. They found a Lt. General, or somebody dressed in an older Army uniform! Can you image that – in an Army uniform no less! But, he was sitting in an official-looking car. When our Pendleton Marines approached the car from all four corners, this dumb bastard pulled-out a 9-mm pistol and fired at two of our Marines. That bastard wounded one of them. Well, before we could return fire, this so-and-so, whoever he was, ups and offs himself. Flat-out commits suicide in the open in a damn traffic jam of all places for all of the civilians to see.

"And now, there's the matter of that small, unmarked chopper last night.

"Then you added in the fact that the Secret Service is so friggin' secret, they don't even show-up here. Not so much as a friggin' phone call.

"And, finally, now, when we start adding these things together, do ya wanna guess who I find is the common character at the center of all of this? Don't bother guessing, I'll tell ya. I come-up with YOU. Do ya understand where I'm comin' from and how I got there?

"I think it's time for you and me to have a 'confessional' meeting, dontcha? Oh, I don't really care at this point about being polite and asking you anymore. Sit your ass down and let's talk, shall we?" Captain Rhodes felt he had enough facts to either get to the bottom of all his concerns right now or hold this 'Smitty character' on ice until his commanding officer appeared on-site to make some command decisions. Captain Rhodes had turned all business. The invitation was no longer an RSVP, but now it was a mandatory-participation, command appearance.

Rhodes: "So, tell me, just who the hell are you? Who are you really? What is 'Smitty' anyway? Your last name, an assumed name, or what?"

Smitty: "Fair enough, I can understand how you got to this point; I would probably have come to that same conclusion, too, if I were in your shoes. Smitty is my real name – slang for Smith. My whole name is Willis Hargrove Smith. Smitty is just a whole lot easier. Would you like to see my Secret Service ID badge? It has my full name on it."

Rhodes: "Also fair enough. I'll continue calling you Smitty, if it's still alright with you. What we Marines need is a whole hell of a lot more information about what this whole mess is all about, wouldn't you agree? Considering that we got at least one-and-a-half companies

Order of Succession

of Marines out here and support Marines scattered around California doing whatever we are asking of them, but no one, and I mean NO ONE, seems to know who the bad-guys are. We are putting some very low-level personnel in harm's way for what appears to be somebody's very high-level political coup. Or whatever this mess really is.

"I can understand that you, the Secret Service, and/or everybody on your side of this mess are supposed to be all 'friggin' super-secret'. But right now, I think we are on the same side, don't you? You're the only one who seems to have any personal interest in this mess; your superiors apparently are too busy to even call you, not to mention having anyone show-up here with a company of cavalry to save the day. My opinion right now is we, we Marines that is, have a very real and legitimate right to know just what the hell else is on your plate. How about reading us local Marines into whatever you know about this. Either that, or I'll have Coms contact the CO of Pendleton to hop a chopper out here and decide if we still belong here. That's not a friggin' threat, Smitty: it's an effing promise. As the OIC out here, I am also concerned with the safety of my Marines in addition to whatever the hell your problems are. Have I made my situation clear? Is there anything that I left hazy?"

Smitty: "Abundantly clear. I fully understand your feeling of being between a rock and a hard place. I really want to help you out, but I am unable to. I am not refusing to fill you in. I am just as confused as you are about what is happening, maybe more so. I just do not know anything about this thing that is playing-out all around us. Hell, after seeing C-3 again, I'm lucky to have just a leg wound. I'm just lucky to still be here. Nothing about this makes any sense to me either. I'm still trying to figure this out along with you, Rocky. May I call you Rocky? We had no rumored threats against POTUS, and not a whisper of any planning for a fire-fight out here at a rest-area called Buckman Springs. Honest, I am not holding back anything on purpose. I am as much in the dark as you."

Rhodes: "There's a hell of a lot of friggin' destruction our here. Why are YOU still alive? Got any ideas? I mean, for example, look at the limo. As flat as it is, chances are good that no one is going to come out of it alive. Probably need very flat and wide coffins. Pizza boxes, if you know what I mean."

Smitty: "Since we are in this together, believe me, Rocky, I have no idea why I am still alive. I was assigned to C-3 just this morning – sort

Order of Succession

of on a rotating basis, maybe to keep us sharper and not become too relaxed in any given position. Although, the President can choose which agents he wants in the limo, the rest of the unchosen agents are rotated. This was probably simply the luck of the draw for me."

Rhodes: "Okay on that – for now. But, I personally find it interesting that the 'sniper' who shot at you after you were all armed-up actually missed you at least three times. At close range, no less. We started looking over the site without you; our snipers found three very-recently-fired, brass .30-06 hulls. We estimated that your 'sniper', if that's what he truly is, was probably no further than maybe 80 meters away. Your description indicated that he may have been firing a semi-automatic weapon could be correct. You're bigger than a deer, and he still missed you at least three times without drawing a drop of blood. Conveniently so, don't you think?"

Smitty: "The way you're describing your search sure makes even me think I'm guilty of something, but I am not lying about this – not in the slightest. I don't know where he was or what weapon he used. Look, everybody in the motorcade appeared dead to me, leaving me as the sole survivor; I felt I was fighting for my life."

Rhodes: "Okay on that one for now, too. What the hell was that small chopper up to, the one with the Nightsun® on it? Got any ideas about that one? Why the hell would that pilot and passenger just decide, just off the tops of their heads, to attack Marines, with missiles no less? What's your relationship to them? Were they still looking for you to kill you off, too? So they could get rid of a loose end?"

Smitty: "Rocky, you're beginning to paint a really ugly picture here, and I don't like where this is heading – not one bit. Look, I've been in the Secret Service for a number of years, actually eight next month. I've been on the security details of two Presidents, including this one. ….," Smitty's voice trailed-off. "Well, you know what I was going to say, dontcha? But, back to the chopper. I have no idea who was flying it, what it was about, or who is behind it. Absolutely NOTHING!"

Rhodes: "Which sort of brings-up one really big unanswered question in my mind. Here's the deal: We've always been fed the line that the Secret Service is Johnny-on-the-spot if anything happens to the President – from stubbing his toe to assassination attempts. You have to agree with that – that hovering protective umbrella.

ORDER OF SUCCESSION

"And now, with all this destruction – which has all the looks to be a successful assassination – nobody's even heard from the Secret Service – not once in oh, (glancing at his watch) over six hours – not even a peep. Smitty, my man, you got any explanation for this inaction by the Secret Service? Right now, at this point, they're so secret, nobody knows if they even exist or not. When we dig that limo out of the rubble over there, and WE ARE GOING TO DIG IT OUT' . . . YOU CAN BET YOUR SWEET ASS WE ARE GOING TO DIG IT OUT BEFORE WE LEAVE. And when we do, are we going to find any bodies in the car? Is there anybody in there that we know of? Is the President in it or a stand-in substitute? The real question in this whole thing is just 'WHAT THE EFF IS GOING ON HERE'?"

Turning serious, Smitty began, "Captain Rhodes, let me reiterate: I DO NOT KNOW WHAT THE HELL IS GOING ON. I am in a bigger black hole than you are. I don't know why the Secret Service has left me hanging out like this. My communications gear, cell phone, Service radios, Sat-Phone, nothing works here. Wait one. I wasn't able to try the Sat-Phone; I couldn't get to it before I left C-3. It was in the trunk of C-3 before I left C-3"

Rhodes interrupted, "My Marines gave your C-3 car a real good looking-over. I don't know what you thought we would find, but the inventory of the trunk includes one spare tire, full-size with barely-legal tread, a jack, and its jack-handle/lug-wrench. There is nothing else in there – certainly not a Sat-Phone. What else did you think was in there?"

This detoured Smitty, "There should have been one Sat-Phone, one fully-automatic M4 rifle in 5.56-mm, one bolt-action M40 in .30-06 and four boxes of ammunition for a variety of calibers. There should also have been a longer vest and a Plexiglas-style shield large enough to protect the President. And a special, secure radio that . . . that should have been able to get out of this ravine. And you're saying all of that is gone?"

Rhodes: "My Marines didn't find anything besides the tire and jack – all car stuff. We also looked through the rest of the car. Nothing but maps, empty water bottles, and wadded food wrappers. Are you positive that the stuff you think was supposed to be in there was actually there when you were assigned to that car, when did you say, this morning? Did you actually see the stuff, handle the stuff?"

Order of Succession

To Smitty, the Marines answered the question about what was in C-3's trunk; that was not good. Now, trying to return to the main question from this detour, "I really don't know what the hell is going on. I understand your points about how it's beginning to look. I'm just as bewildered as you are. I can only guess we, you and I, all of a sudden are now involved with some sort of plot, but that's all I can guess at."

Rhodes was mulling over what had been covered in this conversation up to this point, stood-up, turned, and walked toward his coms Sgt.

Time: Friday, 13-July, 23:23 PDT

A voice out of the dark: "Hey, Smitty, Cap'n wants you over at Coms; got a call for you."

His first thought, "A call, finally a call, what a break!" Smitty roused himself off his bed, a picnic table in the rest-area plaza, got his crutches, and tried to get to Coms as fast he could. "Got your wake-up call and got here as fast as I could. Where's the call?"

The voice: "Grab that field-phone; I'll patch it through."

Smitty: "Hold it a moment; can you conference-on Cap'n Rhodes, silently, if possible?"

Coms: "Conference, yes; silent conference, no."

Smitty: "Cap'n Rhodes, I want you on a conference call with me; they're waiting."

Rhodes: "Right behind you."

Smitty: "Coms, I think we're finally set. Let's talk."

A hollow voice on the phone: "Is this Agent Smitty? Sorry for taking so long to finally get down to you; we had other priorities."

Smitty wanted to scream, "WHAT THE HELL IS MORE IMPORTANT THAN THE PRESIDENT, ESPECIALLY SINCE HE IS DEAD," but did his best to hold his voice cool and level. "Out of curiosity, what could have had a higher priority? What have you got for me?" signaling both Rhodes and coms Sgt. with index finger over his lips.

Voice: "Are we secure?"

Order of Succession

Smitty: "Well, yeah, as secure as we can get out here at a torn-up rest-area in the middle of the Mojave Desert with burned-out cars, a flattened limo, with more dead bodies lying around, increasing each hour. Go ahead. Who are you?"

Voice: "Here's the deal. I take it that you haven't had access to commercial news networks. There's been quite a bit of, how shall I say this, activity in several areas of the U.S." At the sound of this, Rhodes, motioned to Coms to see if he could find out anything to substantiate what the three of them just heard.

Smitty: "Considering what we have been through, what was more important?"

Voice: "All in good time. Right now, we have to establish the status out there."

Smitty: "What did you say your name was?"

Voice: "I believe I did."

Smitty: "Well, then please repeat it again, okay? And what agency are you with?"

Voice: "Agent Smith, all in good time. What is the status out there?"

Smitty: "That's sort of one-sided, isn't it? I mean, you have me at a severe disadvantage. After all, you called for me by name, and I don't know what to call you. Dontcha think I should know who I am talking with?" Smitty could see that Rhodes was becoming very irritated with this caller, whoever he was.

Voice: "Agent Smith, I already said all in good time. We need to know the status out there."

Smitty: "Who is the 'we' you mentioned, and 'who' are you. I think 'we' need some verifiable identification before we go any farther. Whadya say?"

Voice: (the answer): "My call was to YOU, not for Captain Rhodes and the Sergeant standing there with you. Got that?" Followed by an audible click when the line went dead.

Rhodes: "Coms, what the hell just happened to the call?"

Coms: "Disconnected from the other end."

Order of Succession

Rhodes: "Coms, did you get any incoming Caller ID on this bastard?"

Coms: "Call came in on the secure scrambler line. No ID possible; one of the reasons it's called secure. Sorry."

Rhodes: "Smitty, any idea who that guy is? How did he know we were on the call, too? And how does he know me by name?"

Smitty: "I ain't got any ideas who that guy is nor who he's working for. Nor anything else, for that matter. And as to how he knew you two were on the call – well, I think he's sitting out on that hill over there or the one behind us, just sittin' and watchin' us with night vision gear." Smitty motioned to both hills with his right arm, his left clutching his crutches. "Any gear to find him in the dark; heat sensors or some such crap?"

Rhodes: "Sorry, no. We didn't have time to go shopping at the 'We Own the Night Depot' emporium of secret-stuff. Know what I sayin'?"

Smitty: "Sorry from this side, too. Cap'n, does this help answer some of your suspicions about me? Does this restore some trust in my claims of ignorance in this mess? Maybe just a little, huh?"

Smitty and Rhodes wandered back to their conference table, whispering in low voices.

Smitty: "As much as I hate to admit it, I am coming over to your way of thinking much faster than I ever thought possible. I believe you're right about something bigger than all of us put together."

Rhodes: "And you're beginning to look like you're truthin' me about you not knowing what the heck is goin' on."

Smitty: "Wow, truthin'; haven't heard that in a 'sunth of Mondays'. You sure you're not from down around home. Now that we're sunk into this mess this far, what are we goin' to do, now? Any thoughts?"

Rhodes' turn now: "Well, certainly an interesting turn of events, isn't it? Okay so now that I'm leaning toward your truthin', let's talk about what we, and the Marines, can do before we get shut-down, which I do believe is gonna happen damn fast. Let's put our heads together right fast. Your ideas?"

Smitty: "Yeah, a few. If that guy is snoopin' on us, let's not give him any targets. I don't know about you, but I don't look good dressed

Order of Succession

in a bull's-eye. Let's try to put together a more secure place for your command post and the coms gear."

Rhodes: "Sergeant, tell all of the Gunnies to meet over between the main rest-area and the out-building just to its west. Advise them of the possible observer."

Smitty: "Next idea, the limo. Screw waiting any longer; can we excavate the limo right effing now. Under tarps, right now. You got troops, sorry, Marines, who can tarp the area and lift the, what do ya call the bridgework again? Are those EOD and IEDD [9] techs still here? Get them to look over the wrecked overpass right now and tell us what they think could have blown the bridge that way. First, get them over to the bridge that's still standing over on the eastbound roadbed so they can see what our side used to look like. And HURRY! That's what I think we can do. That, and track and identify all outside people who call in with orders to stop. We gotta try to identify who else is involved with this. Your thoughts?"

Rhodes: "Basically . . . right on. Let's go."

(After assembling his Gunnies) Rhodes: "Marines, we have a challenge before us. There is something really fishy going on with this whole screwed-up situation. Both Smitty and I believe we and all the Marines here, should investigate and document as much of this site as possible. Here is what we believe we should do." Rhodes briefly outlined the joint thoughts. There was not a dissenter in the lot. "But first, we gotta build us a secure command post."

Rhodes conferred with his Gunnies about creating a secure command post. Two Gunnies scrambled to get their Marines to fill what sandbags they had and begin building a couple of walls parallel to the two hillsides.

Smitty, who had been taking notes, told the EOD and IEDD experts what the Cap'n and he planned to do with the limo. Anxious to get into the action, they high-tailed it over to the still-standing overpass. They had it psyched out in no time.

Gunnies had Marines unloading the tarps as close to the site as possible. They, too, wanted to get into the action. They were preparing themselves for the memory of their lives.

---

9   EOD and IEDD = Explosive Ordnance Disposal and Improvised Explosive Device Disposal

ORDER OF SUCCESSION

All Marines with the slightest understanding about heavy construction were detailed to see how the twisted decking could be lifted with the tools at hand.

Rhodes: "Where's Chuck? Get him over here ASAP."

A minute or so later, Chuck Berkeley: "Cap'n Rhodes, PFC Berkeley reporting, sir."

Rhodes: "Any and all official plans are all screwed-up right now, so we're improvising new plans right now. You get any news about that refrigerated truck yet?"

Berkeley: "Sir, last word I got was that it had gotten to the roadblock coming this way, but there was some sort of suicide or something; some guy in a military uniform – something like that. Well, our truck shows-up driven by a Marine, and somebody commands the driver to load-up and take the victim back to Pendleton, so he does it. The dead guy had more brass than he ever saw, so he does it. Now, our driver had to refuel and start the trip over again. Still on his way. Sir?"

Rhodes: "Thanks, Private. Let me know the second that truck shows up. Make sure the driver is a Marine, and he better be the same driver who checked the truck out. And, Berkeley, you better make sure he is one of our Marines from Pendleton. Ask him questions about Pendleton that not everybody would know. Do you have a sidearm, a loaded sidearm? If that driver is hinky in any way, you draw your 9-mm and hold him in a seated position on the ground until one of the Gunnies shows-up. DO YOU HAVE THAT? In the meantime, see if you can gather any evidence from the bodies – bullets, pictures of the entry and exit wounds, everything. Get Gannon to help if necessary. Git on it and make it fast but thorough. Any questions, now's the time to ask."

Berkeley: "On it right now, sir."

Time: Friday, 13-July, 23:56 PDT (Just about 10 hours now).

Fortunately for the families of the five local sheriff's deputies, the reefer truck finally showed-up, arriving on the eastbound lanes. It was driven by a guy who looked like a Marine. It was cleared-through by the guard at the off-ramp, who also directed him to PFC Berkeley's area. A radio

Order of Succession

message announced his presence and destination. Chuck met him at the turn for parking area, had him turn the truck off and hand the keys over to another Marine, who drove it to yet another area of the parking lot where five Marines were waiting to give it a thorough inspection. The driver was directed to walk over to still yet another inspection area – his interrogation area. Chuck followed about two steps behind. Two Gunnies and a Sergeant were waiting for him. Chuck, just a lowly PFC, stepped outside the circle of questioners. He felt like he had just led the driver to his execution – a real Judas goat.

Gunny #1: "PFC Berkeley, do you personally recognize this driver?"

Berkeley: "Not personally, Gunny, but I think I've seen him on Pendleton a few times. But, no, I do not know him personally."

Gunny #1: "PFC Berkeley, stand over there by the Humvee," and then turned his attention back to the driver.

Between the two Gunnies and the Sergeant, the driver was asked approximately 40 questions. They were satisfied that the driver was a Marine from Pendleton. However, they were not satisfied that his orders said to deliver the five bodies to the local Medical Examiner in El Cajon instead of to Pendleton's. They insisted on an armed escort for the truck back to Pendleton.

PFC Berkeley was recalled to escort the driver, also a Marine PFC, over to where the bodies were being temporarily stored. There were obvious, awkward feelings between the two. The usually cool night air was rapidly turning hotter than the noon-day temperature. Captain Rhodes was notified of the findings. He marched over to where the truck was being inspected with a definite purpose in his step. The Gunnies told him the truck seemed to be okay. One of the Gunnies drove it over to bodies, with Rhodes in the shotgun seat. He introduced himself to the driver, and then gave both the PFCs orders to collect as much evidence as possible, meticulously document all of it, and load each of the body bags into the refrigerated compartment of the truck with as much respect as possible. Rhodes then ordered Gunny Layton to detail four Marines and one vehicle as an armed escort back to Pendleton, all the while muttering something that sounded a good deal like, "Those bastards are not going to get this evidence. Not on my watch, they're not. Those SOBs.". The four Marines were to be fully armed, including one M-240.

Order of Succession

PFC Berkeley showed the driver the five body bags. They went about their gruesome tasks – tasks that neither one had been prepared for. The temperature between them became less heated, but still not quite cordial.

Rhodes: "Gunny Cornell, how's the new command post coming?"

Cornell: "Just about ready for move-in. Didn't have enough sand bags or sand, so we improvised a position using the trees and shrubs over off the back parking lot as additional cover. Say, didn't Smitty say that those five deputies were supposed to have cleared the parking lot? How come there's still a semi parked back there? Just sayin."

Rhodes: "Let Coms know when they can move in, and get a table or sumpthin' set up for his gear. After that phone call, I'm getting a little antsy using one of those open picnic tables on the plaza. Gunny, you said there's a truck back there; where's the driver? Find him and ID him."

Cornell: "Yes, sir. Truck is turned off, but the reefer trailer is still running."

Gunny Johnson assumed command of the Marines trying to figure-out how to lift the bridgework off the limo.

Johnson: "Hey you EOD and IEDD specialists, whadya learn over at the other still-standin' bridge, huh."

{Johnson's brain: "You are one sorry ass. It's deck, not bridge!" "Yeah, yeah, I'm trying. It's all new terminology to me. I'm tryin'."}

EOD Sgt. Winthrop: "Assuming that both were built the same as the standing one, the construction is a piece of cake – if you got a crane or two. We guesstimate that the standing deck weighs somewhere near a whole lotta tons, maybe upwards of 150. And that's just the steel work; the concrete and asphalt paving are extra weight. We know we don't think we have any gear out here that can move the deck off the limo in one piece. However, what we can do for you is make smaller pieces out of it with some special packages in our bag of tricks. We might be able to move 15-ton pieces with the equipment on hand. How soon you want that done? How soon could we expect cranes-on-wheels?"

Order of Succession

Johnson: "For makin' small pieces out of that deck, done by yesterday. And, portable cranes, well, figure on that right after we pull out. Those two don't mesh together well, do they? By the way, there's still a semi truck in the back parking lot. Don't know where that driver is; Gunny Cornell is tryin' to find him. Put your minds back to work. It's a semi tractor and a reefer trailer, both stark white, no markings. Maybe it's a tool we can use along with your bag of tricks? Half of you go see Gunny Cornell about lookin' the truck over; the other half go to the site and figure-out how to move that crap off the limo. Also, figure-out what else is gonna havta be moved to get at the limo. Make it snappy; we got Marines just itchin' to get to work, and we don't wanna keep 'em waitin', do we?"

About 15 minutes later, Sgt. Winthrop reported back: "After looking the site over, we found piles of rubble on the decking on top of the limo. We think this is how it all went down: Looks like they dropped the deck first to get the maximum effect of all that weight dropping about a little over 20 feet or so. Then they blew the concrete abutments inward, that is, toward each other, so their rubble is also on top of the deck and piled-up against the sides of the limo. That just makes it longer to dig the limo out. It also makes it more difficult to get to the heavier deck for us to blow it with our charges. But here's an interesting observation. It looks like those berms front and rear of the limo were caused by charges buried in the roadway. It appears that they were shaped to dig a ditch, or a moat, not sure which yet, around the limo so it could not move. If the wheels were in the ditch, then the bottom of the limo was sitting flat against the ground, and the tires, probably run-flats, had nothing to get traction from anyway. They couldn't drive outta there. Period. Squashed limo. Nice plan. That's what we think happened just by lookin' at it, but we can't tell for sure 'til we dig it out.

"We don't know what they used for sure just yet, but it was some pretty powerful stuff. And their timing was pretty good, too. Somebody had their act together; we gotta give 'em that much credit. However, judging by the charges we found in the buildings, we think it may have been some type of military-grade plastique in shaped charges to cut through the steelwork under the decking. Then the concrete abutments could have been just regular old explosive shots used for quarry work. Maybe some of it on timed electric fuses, so it all comes down in the proper sequence. Or, maybe two separate sets of timers or even manually.

Order of Succession

Hell, after the limo is sitting there with no way to move, it really doesn't matter too damn much, does it? Boom. Boom. It's done one way or another, isn't it?"

Johnson: "Remember – by yesterday. Time's awastin'. Make your plans happen. What about the semi? Any use to us?"

Winthrop: "Might be able to use the tractor to move the bigger pieces. We were thinkin' about driving it up to the I-8 westbound roadbed – on the Yuma side. Back it up to edge and drop a cable or chain down into the hole above the limo. Tie-on and pull; let's see what happens. If they let us move some of those cars, what are they called, Leader and Chase, maybe we can use the tractor to pull the rubble that's on top of the roadway deck out of the sides of the overpass. If they want to keep the cars in place, well, then, it's all gotta go straight up and out the top. We guess that's youse' guys' call. Let us know which way you want to pull – stuff straight up or stuff out left and/or right sides. Makes no never mind to us; we just wanna see if it works."

Cornell to Rhodes: "We searched the rest-area grounds, the buildings, and latrines. Can't locate the driver of the semi. Maybe he left in another truck and couldn't get back through the roadblocks. Anyway, we're gonna try to use the tractor to clear the debris off the limo. Any problems with that, sir? And the EOD boys want to know if they can clear the burned-out cars away from the lower roadway so they can start pulling debris straight out the sides of the overpass. Either that, or they gotta lift all the stuff up and out. Seein' we don't have any cranes out here, they plan to use some of their charges to cut that deck into lotsa smaller pieces, and pull those pieces out."

Rhodes: "I've been speakin' with Smitty. Ya know, Gunny, I almost feel sorry for that poor bastard. Anyway, we both would like to preserve as much evidence as possible; however, with the way things have been going . . . well, dig the limo out the fastest way you Marines can. I'll worry about the heat later, and I expect there will be more than just a little HEAT. Take pictures of everything first. If you find any human remains, call PFC Berkeley ASAP. Carry on, Gunny."

"Yes, sir."

Gunny Cornell passed the 'go-ahead' and 'fastest way' commands to the other Gunnies and, subsequently, to the Marine grunts just bidin'

Order of Succession

their time until the word came down. The condensed version was, "Here's the word: let's go dig it out NOW the fastest way possible."

As Smitty requested, pictures were taken of everything again, everything was documented, and everything was – finally moved. Marines drove their Humvees up to the burned-out hulks of the cars on the rest-area side of the overpass and hooked-up some tow cables, but, unfortunately, there was not enough space to stack stuff neatly near the downed deck. So, the group decided, "We're pulling out on this side all the way over to the parking lot. The deck is in the way to pull the C-cars this way. We're gonna leave where they are for right now. We can pull the deck pieces into the rear of parking lot and leave 'em for somebody else. Hook-up an' do it now."

Voice, somewhere: "Hey, what do you want us to do with the chopper's carcass?" Another voice: "Pull it over there near those cars, but keep it away from the cars. Don't want to mix parts, do we? I guess 'parts aren't necessarily just universal parts' are they? Make sure you get all the human remains outta that thing before you tow it. Check that out with PFC Berkeley."

Marines attached tow-cables to the burned-out hulks of L-1, L-2, and C-1 and then to the Humvees. Within 15 minutes, the roadway was cleared-out all the way to the berms. And now the real challenge became readily apparent. The deck was even larger than expected. Now, the EOD squad guesstimated that it was about 35 feet wide (two travel lanes and two shoulders) and about 3-1/2 feet thick, top to bottom. "You mean there's a limo, a whole damn limousine, under that deck. You gotta be kiddin' me. And we are gonna DIG IT OUT? BY HAND? Is somebody smoking something?"

Cornell: "Okay, Marines, let's clear the debris off the top of the decking. Hook the Humvees up to the bigger pieces of concrete if you can and see if you can drag them over there in another pile," motioning toward the spot.

Cornell: "Sergeant Winthrop, you got the go ahead. Go ahead and cut the hell outta that deck. Slice and dice it; whatever it takes. Use some of the charges you found in the buildings if you have to. We'll bring the semi tractor down here to help pull-out the pieces. And by God, you better make them small enough to pull."

Order of Succession

Winthrop: "Given enough powder, we can make 'em small enough to sweep out. We are going to cut the deck down both sides of where we believe the limo is, then cut those pieces parallel to the where the abutments used to be."

Cornell: "Let's hear your work instead of yammerin' about it. The semi-tractor's on the way. You don't wanna make it wait."

Winthrop: "Don't YOU be late for the party. RSVP within 3 minutes or you'll be too late for the appetizers!"

True to his word, the ground shook 2 minutes and 37 seconds later. Just as they had planned and described, both sides of the deck were cut. "Son-of-a-bitch, there's the limo! Bet it didn't come from Cadillac that way!" Next, they cut each side into smaller pieces, each with a hole for the cable, which was tied-off and wrapped around the tractor's 5th-wheel. Pulled-out slicker than anything – after the bewildered driver figured-out how to use the automatic/manual transmission [10] on the Mack tractor so the tires didn't spin. The Marine driver, a PFC Barnes, found the bulldog hood ornament a convenient aiming device – just like a set of sights on a rifle – good enough to get the long-nosed, bright white Mack to move where he wanted it to. "Pull 'em over there. Now cut the other side."

Cornell: "Sgt. Winthrop, a good show so far, but how are we gonna get the center slab of deck off the limo?"

Winthrop: "Same way. First, we whittle it down to size, front and rear of the limo. But, the piece of deck that's on top of the limo is gonna be larger and heavier 'cause we don't wanna take the chance that any of the charges will also cut into the limo itself. So, what we are planning is to use the tractor to pull as much crap out of the overpass as possible on the east side, toward Yuma. Then drive it up to the edge of the remains of the abutment on that side, or as close as possible to the edge, and pull the deck off toward that side. Basically, just dump it on that side of the road. Done. Then we can get a clear shot at the limo – oops, maybe a poor choice of words, but you know what I'm sayin', right?"

Cornell: "Damn straight. Sounds like good Marine improvising. Make it happen."

Cornell to Rhodes: "Cap'n, sir, EOD's almost down to the limo. Pretty slick use of explosives, if you ask me. Almost magical."

---

10 (INFO: Mack mDrive Transmission – as in Mack Trucks)

Order of Succession

After Barnes cleared the side pieces, he drove the tractor up onto the Yuma side of the old overpass and backed it into the position the EOD boys thought best. But he couldn't get as close to the edge as they wanted; the crumbling dirt just wasn't that safe. They threw down the cables; EOD hooked them on to the remaining slab of deck and gave the signal to pull. Tires squealed, and the air smelled of burning rubber. But gradually, the slab moved; moved until it slipped-off the limo and onto the lower road. There sat the limo – just as squashed, but no longer buried under tons of roadway decking. They had dug it out successfully. But, now what?

Rhodes (to Smitty): "Well, Smitty, there it is. Now what do we do with it?"

Smitty: "Check-it out. Take loads of pictures. Find out how those bastards did this. Find out why the hell they did this. That's what we do, damn it."

EOD and several Sergeants recon'ed the area around the limo as carefully as they could – not sure if there were still other buried IEDs. PFC Barnes turned the semi-tractor around so its headlights could cast some light over the scene below. Likewise, the Humvees now faced into the former overpass – two on each side. An eerie scene, indeed.

Smitty: "Can we obscure the site from prying eyes somehow. Can it be tarped over. Can that hole be concealed before tomorrow morning? How can we stretch tarps that far? Anybody?"

Rhodes: "Yeah, I think that's possible. Gunny Cornell, can that tractor drag a couple of smaller pieces of decking up to the top of the road on both sides? We have some rope and cables. Can we stretch them across the gap and hang tarps from them? How about if we lay the ropes out on the ground first, tie the tarps to the ropes down here, and use the tractor to pull them up that way already tied together? Give them the task; they'll figure it out. Make it happen."

Cornell gathered the other Gunnies and described the plan. All agreed: doable. And so the work order went down to the grunts.

Barnes got with the program and dragged a couple of pieces of cut-up decking up to the top of I-8 on both sides of the gap. He was happy with where the rope anchors were situated. He went down and hitched-up a third piece for each side. This was turning into fun – sort of like a 10-wheel dune buggy. Dust in the air, smoke, burning rubber, and it's not even his buggy.

Order of Succession

Okay, lay-out the ropes and tie the tarps onto them. He threw the cable down and some sort of a 'grabber thing' he found in the tractor's collection of tools. (He found-out later that it was a type of 'come-along'.) He figured if that grabber could be attached not to the end of the rope, but farther up from the end, the Marines who were going to tie-off the ropes to the broken pieces of deck – well, they would have some slack rope to make the tie-off. "Okay, hitch it up, and let's get this thing overhead; I'm gonna need some shade when the sun comes up." The ropes on the first side toward Yuma pulled into place as planned. No resistance to speak of. The other side proved more difficult; now, there was a lot of weight on the ropes. All he needed was more throttle, a gentle touch with the tranny in manual mode, and smoking tires and the ropes were tied-off.

Rhodes: "Lots of good planning here. Now let's take a look at the limo, shall we?"

Everybody wanted to get his own look at that limo – nosey, history, curiosity, whatever. The Marines walking their guard outposts were just as curious as the others, but they had to wait until they were relieved by replacement guards.

Rhodes to Smitty: "Would you care to describe what we are looking at in this pile of bent metal or should we guess?"

Before Smitty could respond, Sgt. Winthrop spoke: "We were partially wrong with the sequence of explosions; we now have to correct the sequence. We now think there was a difference sequence: The first was the IEDs under the limo to immobilize it, keep it from moving.

Winthrop finished explaining EOD's theory of that overpass was dropped from 'up there' to 'down here' – a total of four distinct explosions.

"Still don't know for sure what they used, but they were pretty damned effective."

Rhodes: "Anybody. How do we get the limo out to level ground and still keep it under the tarp? Ideas, men? Smitty, any idea how much that thing weighs?"

Smitty: "Well, the exact weight is a classified specification, but a rough guess would be around 8 to 10 tons. I sorta think."

Order of Succession
5 – The Post Mortem

Early Morning, Saturday, 14-July: Westbound I-8, Exit 51, at Buckman Springs Rest Area, Mojave Desert, California

TIME: 02:15 PDT

Just about 12 hours now.

Rhodes: "Smitty, I have to bring you up to speed on some other things you are probably somehow involved in – things I've purposely kept from you. Remember that ambush up on the west side of the rest-area, those three shooters? Well, the scouting squads found all three positions, the ones we took fire from. But, they only found one casualty – an automated gun mount platform, complete with the weapon – we don't know exactly what the hell it is. It's stamped with something that says 'M2HB by FN Herstal'. This monster is chambered for, are you ready, 12x99 NATO! This bruiser is a .50-Cal machine gun fed outta an ammo box – actually, two of 'em!. At maybe 200 rounds to the box, I'd hate to be down-range when this sucker goes into action. Hell, you'd be in range over in the next county, and we got some damn large ones out here!

"You know what else? It ain't got any sights mounted on the gun itself. Nosiree, it's got its own camera feeding into some sort of interface box with an antenna on it. This is damn near the same friggin' set-up that was in the movie *Vantage Point* – you know, that remotely controlled rifle up in a window. I guess if it's been proven to work once, why reinvent it. The EOD boys think it'll fire between 500 and 700 rounds per minute. That's an awful lot of firepower to have set-up out here on the side of a hill. It sure the hell's not out here for deer. This is one mean bitchin' gun for just sittin' out here in civilian territory. Know what I mean?

"And you are really going to love this. This platform has got a couple of missiles strapped to it, too!"

Order of Succession

Smitty: "Say what? You just said MISSILES, didn't cha?"

Rhodes: "Aye, that I did, laddy. Two. Not one, but two of 'em! One is a Stinger missile, but the other one, are you ready, is a Hellfire missile, if my Marines ID'ed it correctly."

Smitty: "Stingers are surface-to-air, but the Hellfire was developed as an anti-tank weapon." A long pause, followed by, "Where did you say these were discovered? And where were they pointed?"

Rhodes: "Over on that automated gun-platform on the hillside north of the westbound I-8 roadbed where we had that little fire-fight yesterday afternoon. My Marines said they were pointed – or aimed – directly at westbound I-8. Why do ya wanta know?"

Smitty: "Let's just say the limo is sometimes described as 'built like a tank'. And how do you stop a tank? If the driver tried to get past the .50-Cal machine gun, these missiles are probably fail-safes. What do ya think about that? Whoever these bad-guys are – they didn't want the limo to get away, now did they?"

Rhodes: "Are you mad serious about that? Holy smoke! Who's screwin' with us here? Whoever set this up has gotta have access to a lot of big bucks; this gear ain't cheap. And they also have access to more than just the bucks; they also have access to the gun as well as the necessary support matériel, too.

"They must have some real hard feelings against their target. That gun'll reach-out and put his ass in a big world of hurt. That guy would be in a real bind even in a tank – especially, considering they had missiles homed-in on him, too. My Marines sure want to try-out that gun on one of our ranges.

"Well anyway, we didn't find any bad-guys at either of the other two positions. Yes, evidence they had been there; but no live people, or dead ones either for that matter. They even had deep fox-holes, actually more like pits or parts of a trench. We think they fancied themselves as untouchable by our snipers and helos. Damned if they weren't right. But our snipers wiped-out the rifle and the mount with both .50-Cal. rounds. Smashed the hell out of that set-up. Damn good shooting! Don't know where they went; probably high-tailed it when our snipers returned fire with equal weapons. I know I would."

Order of Succession

"**Next Item.** Remember that call yesterday? Like, who the hell can forget it? Our Marines found a tree-mounted camera out there where you waved your arm. Field of view covered the area where the command post used to be. Internet-capable, too, no less. You said you were told this area was supposed to be without radio- and cell-transmission, right? Well, this little jewel had a straight shot to something that had Internet-access. Probably, more big bucks for that setup, huh? We are trying to scope-out this one without raising too much third-party interest. We don't want to blow what little cover we have right now. Say, wouldn't that .50-Cal. gun-mount also need remote control connections, too? I'll bet if we figure-out how they got Internet for the camera, we'll have the set-up for the gun mount, too.

"While all that concerns me, it is followed by this one. You remember how you wanted know what was happening out there in the rest of the world, right? Well, we didn't have to do too much digging for that. Got an e-mail from God-knows-who that there were some 'unfortunate accidents' yesterday. Seems some Cabinet Secretaries were attending a conference of some sort or another when a fire broke-out. Seems the following were 'victims of a tragedy'. Do any of these ring any bells to you – they don't mean that much to us except for the third one: Secretaries of Education, Commerce, Defense – that's the one I know – Interior, and Labor. What do ya think about this?

"Oh, yeah, my final concern – so far – is about that small chopper, the one with the Nightsun®, like how the hell can we forget that pipsqueak! Well, it was tracked from Mexico. Can't tell you exactly how we got this data, okay?"

Smitty: "Yeah, I guess so."

Rhodes: "Well they tracked it from around Tecate, Mexico. I'm told this bird went almost straight for this here rest-area, passing right over Lake Morena, which is about 9.6 klicks from here – at about a 7-o'clock coordinate from here. Went straight cross-country; didn't follow roads. Also went dark just before Lake Morena and straight here until they turned-on that blinding spotlight. Sure was a bright SOB, wasn't it. I'd like to have that thing mounted on my pickup for freeway driving, know what I mean? That'll never be legal, but it's still a fantasy of mine.

"Back to reality. The trackers think the flight may have actually originated somewhere east of the Jacumba Airport and slid down south

Order of Succession

across the border for a little extra cover flying west before hoppin' back north across the border. Jacumba is about 40 or so klicks east on our side of the border, but just barely in the U.S. They couldn't give us any more info; I think they gave us all they have. I do not think anybody's got to our source about this stuff yet. Catch my drift, Willis? Hey, I sorta like Willis; okay if I call you that?"

Smitty sat with mouth slightly parted, but obviously stunned. "Yeah, okay, Rocky, that last one puts us past the formal stage. Do you really want to hear my conclusions, or were you being polite?"

Rhodes: "Go ahead. So far, this whole thing is some pretty weird stuff to us. We're so far removed from stuff like this, we wouldn't know what to make of it way out here anyway. Another point of view could be useful. What's your take?"

Smitty: "Okay, just remember that you invited my guess. This may sound like I'm smokin' wacky tabbacky or just blowing smoke, but here's a scenario that's almost too far-out to be believed. You ready? Okay, here goes nothing.

"To me, this sounds like the beginning of a coup, or an overthrow, or a take-over, or something like that. Of the Government of the U.S."

Rhodes: "That IS an awful lot of smoke you're blowing, but, you have my attention. Go on. Why?"

Smitty: "Those Secretaries are all part of the 'Order of Succession' to the Presidency of The United States. In other words, if something happens to the sitting President, somebody is supposed to take over right away. Right? Well, all of those Secretaries are in the 'batting order', so to speak. They make us understand this kinda stuff once we get assigned to the Protective part of the Secret Service. Well, back in 1947, Congress passed a law that included a listing of 19 positions in the Executive Branch and ranked them in ... in other words, drew up their batting order by their order of importance at that time. We all accept that the President, Vice-President, the Speaker of The House, and the President Pro Tempore of the Senate are at the top of the batting order. But the remaining 15 positions are, basically, members of the President's Cabinet, so they just happen to be at the bottom of the order. It was pointed-out, that, while the top four are elected positions, those lower in the order are appointed to their positions – 'appointed' is the operative word here. These Secretaries are appointed. They are not elected by the people.

Order of Succession

"Those five Secretaries, sorry, five FORMER Secretaries represent one-third of the appointed ones. That's 5 out of 15 who aren't coming-up to bat anymore. 33%, and all at one time. Bam, gone, on the disabled, or dead, list. And, we, that is, you and I and all of the Marines at this site, really don't know anything about the President, who we assume is still in the limo. Do we? No, we don't because not a one of us have seen him. Have we? No, we haven't."

Rhodes: "Wow, that's still a whole lot of smoke."

Smitty: "But let me add some other observations to the mix. Everything that's happened since yesterday is . . . is downright eerie. Try looking at it this way: Just who the hell knew the President's exact route for yesterday, the week before he left on this trip? And I emphasize the EXACT route to get here. Also, considering all of the stuff and munitions we found out here so far, who knew about this trip even several months beforehand so they could acquire, install, dig, and put together all of this stuff out here? If these terrorists built all of the IEDs and planted them, do you think they would be betting on the come that the President would just happen to be out here and just happen to take this route, on this specific day, at this exact hour – or any other particular day for that matter? There would be a whole lot of preparation and money just sitting out here, unused. Right?

"I don't know about you, but I'd say that some of this stuff is difficult to come by. I mean you can't just pick this stuff up down at Home Depot, Best Buy, or Wal-Mart. And you can't bid on it on eBay, or you shouldn't be able to. So, where did they get all of this stuff on short order assuming yesterday was going to be their one and only real attempt? So, where did it all come from? Who provided it? Who installed all of it? Why were some of the charges still in military wrappers from OUR own military? Who has access to this stuff on such short-order?

"Are you still with me so far? I got a little more, I think. You wanna hear the rest?"

Rhodes: "Go on; this is turning into quite story. Maybe 'plot' is a better word."

Smitty: "Okay, who could get access to a Lieutenant General's uniform and car – ready for the next day? And out here instead of, say, San Francisco or St. Louis?

Order of Succession

"Follow me on this one. Why would that Captain Torgelson want to get some Army buddy involved? For glory? Maybe I am just suspicious or even paranoid, but I don't think so.

"Where did they get the remote-controlled rifle and platform? That platform probably is a special order from the manufacturer. So, how far in advance was it ordered? Not even the NRA would even think this one is being covered by the Second Amendment for civilians!

"Assuming that that Internet camera is sort of readily available, who could establish the necessary Internet connection, which sort of looks like a satellite link was required way out here, on such short-order?

"Why with all of the technology available, and in use on this job, why did they have to drop the bridge on the limo? Except if . . . if . . . ," Smitty's voice faded.

Rhodes: "If what?"

Smitty: "If . . . If . . . I don't know yet. Is the limo dug-out yet? Let's go look if we can raise it up a bit or flip it over. Is there some sort of flat-bed truck around here?"

Rhodes: "Gunny Cornell, how soon can we get to the limo?"

Cornell: "Right now if you want to. Walk on up to it and sit on the flat roof; it's only about 3-1/2 feet high now."

Rhodes: "Gunny, meet Smitty and me over at the limo after you figure-out how to move it, maybe load it on something."

Smitty, already having limped over to the limo: "Your Marines did an excellent job clearing the dirt and debris away from all four sides. I've been kicking tires; they're still inflated because the limo just sort of settled down with its floor flat on the ground between the front and rear tires after the dirt was blown out to create sort of a moat around the limo. Sorta like sitting there on top of a southwestern mesa isn't it? Get the picture? The limo simply couldn't drive away anywhere even if the agent-driver wanted to. If we could get it out of the moat, I don't know for sure, but maybe the tires will still roll."

Cornell: "Cap'n, got it figured-out I think. We were already kickin' it around and think maybe we got it figured out how to move it."

ORDER OF SUCCESSION

Smitty interrupted: "Gunny, what if you built a long ramp out of the moat around the limo, can you hitch the semi to the limo and just drag it out? What if we dug enough of the dirt out from under the limo so its floor-bottom isn't sitting on dirt? Would that help pullin' it out?"

Cornell to both Smitty and Rhodes: "Great minds think alike. We already thunk that one up. So, you all want to try it now or later?"

Smitty and Rhodes in unison: "NOW."

Cornell: "Marines, we're goin' drag that limo out of the hole it's in. We need to dig a ramp from the bottom of the ditch around the limo to about here," as he paced off about 25 feet. "And the dirt's too high under the limo; somebody make it shorter. Watch yourselves."

"Where's Barnes, the semi driver? Get him over here with that truck."

"Barnes, back that tractor over near this ramp that's being built. Stretch the cables down to limo so you can pull that bad boy out. Got that? Drag it just out of the hole about 10 feet past the end of the ramp for now. Got that? Fine, make it happen."

Less than half-an-hour later, Cornell: "Cap'n and Smitty, the limo is out of the hole and is sittin' over there now. Go look it over. My Marines need a break. And the outer-guards need to be relieved. They sure wanna see what's been going on over here. Cap'n?"

Rhodes: "Fine job, Gunny. Dismissed."

Smitty, not from beside the limo, but from over at the hole where it used to be: "Hold on, Gunny, if you don't mind, Cap'n. Could both of you come over here ASAP and bring a tarp. Thanks." Ten seconds later, "Cap'n, except . . . except for this. This is one of those big 'excepts'."

They were all looking at a concrete-lined hole in the ground that had been concealed beneath the limo just a minute ago – smack dab beneath the President's compartment – all reinforced to withstand all of the explosions and destruction that had been going-on around this overpass. It was rectangular and about twice the size of the top of office desk, with a ledge on each side about five feet down and a deeper, concrete-lined hole, about 30-inches in diameter through the box's bottom – dropping-off into dark emptiness. This box looked like those large, underground

Order of Succession

utility vaults that contain underground electrical gear – except for the hole through the bottom that looked like one of those you see in movies about chases through city sewer tunnels. Suddenly, as if participating in one of those geo-caching games, the ones where you try to find hidden 'treasures' using only GPS coordinates, all three of them realized they were already at the cache site. They began searching for the covers to the box at their feet. With all of the concrete rubble on top of everything, the area under the limo was the least littered. And that's where they found the clean, manufactured edges and corners sticking out of the rubble. Moving the debris in the area that had been under the limo revealed at least two reinforced metal lids that looked like they could fit the utility-box structure.

While all three of them studied the hole and digging-out the lids, only one of them took charge. Gunny yelled toward the Marines who were resting a bit, "MARINES, TURN THAT SQUASHED LIMO OVER OR ON ITS SIDE; WE NEED TO LOOK AT THE BOTTOM IN 10. AND THE CAP'N WANTS TO SEE IT WHEN HE GETS THERE." "Cap'n, they're a bit tired; give 'em a couple a minutes, will ya?"

Rhodes: "Gunny, the three of us still have to cover this hole with the tarp. Will that be enough time?"

"Yes, sir. Thank-you, sir. Here's the tarp for the hole." So, they put the lids back in place and stretched the tarp over the hole and weighted it down with some debris from the road. Meanwhile, the Marines hooked the cables up to the limo, and Barnes repositioned the tractor. They flipped that limo right over onto its left side, with the cables still tight – just in case the Cap'n wanted it on its top.

{Barnes' day-dreaming mind: "Driving this tractor is sort of fun; maybe I'll change my MOS. The bed behind me looks even more comfortable than my bunk. Hell, there's even a TV back there and a satellite dish, too! What a deal! What model is this Mack anyway? Hey, you saw a sticker that said Pinnacle; maybe that's the model. Find-out later, Marine; you got junk to move."}

The three of them walked briskly over to the limo, now with its underside exposed. Smitty, arrived first (he began sooner than the others), "You'll find the most interesting hole under here. Hey, any of you EOD guys still here?"

Order of Succession

A familiar voice from the dark, "Yes, sir. Whatcha need?"

Smitty: "Can you tell us how this hole was cut – from inside or outside? Torch or a shaped charge? Anything and everything else you can think of?"

Sgt. Winthrop: "Lads, look that hole over. Answer their questions, if possible." Four Marines ran over to the limo and began examining the hole, with low voices amongst themselves, coordinating their thoughts.

From the group: "Sergeant, from what we saw in and around the hole, this is strange, really strange, and weird, too. First, we didn't see any bloody parts or any body fragments. If there were people inside when it was flattened, we thought there should have been a lot blood or something still dripping. Okay, back to the hole in the limo. It appears somebody flame-cut a hole about 26-inches in diameter through the bottom of the limo and then ground the edges nice and smooth; no jagged burrs left to cut anybody. And then drilled eight holes around its edge with nice chamfered holes. Screws were welded in-place and then ground level to the inside of the floor. The covering plate was bolted to the bottom of the limo from the outside. A coupla guys in the pit under the limo could have removed the nuts and dropped the plate in less than a minute if they had a coupla high-torque battery-powered drills equipped with sockets. Anyway, the plate was removed from the underside of the floor. A sharp box cutter could have sliced through the limo's carpet. Sergeant?"

Rhodes, who had been listening: "Thank-you for your analysis. Dismissed. Gunny Cornell, ask the other Gunnies to assemble over here; show them that man-hole over there and the hole in the limo. Then, we need some volunteers to search that man-hole and what looks like a tunnel at the bottom. Sort of like the 'tunnel rats' in Vietnam we've all heard about. We don't have any fancy fiber-optic, spy-under-the-door gear like you see in movies. But we do have a gadget we picked-up from quartermaster that lets electricians and plumbers look inside walls. The QM guys called it a ProVision™ something or other; they said it's got about 20 feet of fiber cable on it. We were gonna use it to look under the rubble when we got near the limo. Maybe they can use it; don't know for sure, but, what the hell, let 'em try it. We still need those volunteers!"

Order of Succession

Time: Saturday, 14-July, 04:27 PDT

Cornell: "Cap'n, volunteers standin'-by. We got too many, and had to weed them out. Just sayin' almost all volunteered, 'cept those Marines on guard duty out there," motioning toward the perimeter around the rest-area. There was almost a full company of Marines standing at the ready. The really eager ones had already shed their equipment too large to let them get through the man-hole; already, they were down to just LED flashlights, side-arms, M-4s, night-vision gear, radios, gas masks, and damn little else. But they sure wanted to try that fiber-optic whachamacallit.

Cornell chose the first five that looked dressed for their roles – the lucky (?) few. Reality was setting-in as they marched over to the man-hole, discussing the dark descent into darkness and what might be down there. They descended and promised to 'be careful'.

{Several minds: "What a crock that is. Careful, are you kiddin' me? What if they're waitin' down there to pick us off as we appear? What If . . . "}

After they disappeared, Gunny Cornell returned to the remaining Marines, the unlucky majority. "Listen-up, Marines. Your buddies down in this hole are in a tunnel that heads off in that general direction," (motioning toward the hill on the outer side of the westbound roadbed). "The tunnel is not a 'T' intersection; it is a dead-end under the man-hole. You volunteers are gonna try to follow them on the surface and meet them when they exit. Get dressed for some night exercises – including face camouflage, matching radios, and live fire. Now, Cap'n, sorry for oversteppin', but . . . "

Rhodes: "Gunny, you overstep? Oversteppin' never once crossed my mind. Just make sure the guards are aware of what's goin' on; we don't need a friendly-fire accident out there, do we?"

Cornell: "Cap'n, guards advised 15 minutes ago."

Smitty to Rhodes: "That Gunny has his act together. He should have been an officer. Just sayin', Rocky."

Cornell: "Cap'n, Gunnies Johnson and Layton are leading the rest of the volunteers out thataway. They have intermittent radio contact with the Marines in the tunnel; following the best they can."

Order of Succession

Time: Saturday, 14-July, 04:43 PDT

Cornell: "Cap'n, sir. Gunny Johnson's platoon rousted some strange folks out there. Claiming they saw people come out of the ground and get into three small choppers around 15:22 yesterday. Strange in the sense of stinkin' drunk and just plain stinkin' from whatever they were smoking – probably some marijuana. Johnson's bringing them in to sober-up. But on the positive side, sir, Layton's Marines think they may have found the tunnel's end out there. Waiting to greet the tunnel rats. No other reports at this time, sir."

Cornell: "Sir, the tunnel rats have exited the tunnel. They estimated that it is just a bit over an eighth of a mile long; they didn't find any lights in it, but they did find some booby-traps, tripwires. They also found some evidence that people have been through it recently. Very recently. They're bringing the stuff out. Oh, Gunny Johnson's strange folks are over there near the plaza tables, and they are really stinking, for sure."

Rhodes to Cornell: "I don't think we really need any civilian prisoners right now, do we? How about interviewing them over at the mess tent, get the basic information, feed 'em, and transport them somewhere out of this immediate area?"

Cornell: "Some Marines are already escorting them to the mess tent. Gunnies Johnson and Layton will interview. Transport may be the problem – to where – but we'll figure it out. Sir?"

Rhodes: "See to it."

Rhodes to Smitty, with Cornell in the background: "Smitty, do you recognize any of these things? Our tunnel Marines found them down there and brought them out. This looks like a shoe; this, a cell phone; and this, a scrap of paper. Can you shed any light on them?"

Smitty's turn now: "Well, this shoe looks a good deal like shoes the President wears at times, but I didn't see him much yesterday, so I don't really know what he was wearing. This scrap of paper does have part of The White House logo on it. It looks like there was a bit of writing on it, but there's this tear through it that makes it illegible – at least, to me."

Picking-up the phone, Smitty scrutinized it, "Now, this phone might have some clues stored inside. It looks like any other smart-

ORDER OF SUCCESSION

phone, except this one can access a satellite. You all wouldn't have its password, would ya? I didn't think so, but it doesn't hurt to ask. If it were the President's, any ideas what that password it might be?" After about 5 or so guesses, they lucked-out. "Of course, it's his unpublished Secret Service Code-Name! Why didn't we think of that to begin with. StormTide. Yes, Storm & Tide, like his sailing environment. And, no, I don't know how they come-up with those things.

"Outgoing calls: Looks like a lot of phone numbers in the D.C. area, most of them in the local Verizon Government telephone exchange. Received calls: the same. Voice mails: Damn, need another password to get into to see those. Funny, the text messages show only one message, and it's unread. No password required; let's see what it says, shall we. Here goes." (Smitty touched some icons and numbers on the touch-screen.):

So, U found phon. Yep, Prez is ours 4 a time. Smity, already tld U B4: ALL IN GUD TIME. Don't U Lisn?

Rhodes: "Who ARE these guys? Do we know for sure this is the President's phone? What's his number? We'll call it to see."

Smitty: "Try 202-555-1600."

Rhodes: "Coms, dial that number right now."

Coms: "Yes, sir. Ringing."

And, indeed, the phone rang a few times before voice mail answered. Coms, let them listen to the announcement: "Smitty, yes, it is his phone. Now do you believe? All in good time, agent, all in good time. At the sound of the tone please leave your message or press star for more options. BEEEEEP." Coms released the call.

Rhodes: "Coms, call it again. This time we'll answer the call."

Coms: "Ringing, sir."

Smitty: "Hello. Yeah, it's you calling. Bye."

Time: Saturday, 14-July, 05:12 PDT

Smitty, to nobody or to everyone: "I don't know about you all, but I'm beginning to think the rest of the Secret Service has just about has written us off. Right now, I don't know what else I or we can do here.

Order of Succession

Nor do I know who this 'all in due time' guy is, anyway. I need some rest. You need rest. They need rest. But those bastards won't give us any; they're about 20 steps ahead of the rest of us. We gotta close the gap and fast. Or . . . Or, I don't know what.

"This mess stinks to high heaven. Is there such a thing as 'low heaven'? Oh, have I already said that it also sucks big-time?"

Smitty: "Medic Gannon, let's totter over to my picnic-table cot, so you can look at my left leg again. I think the wound is leaking again. Thanks."

ORDER OF SUCCESSION
6 – A Quorum of Minds

Morning, Saturday, 14-July: Westbound I-8, Exit 51, at Buckman Springs Rest Area, Mojave Desert, California

TIME: 06:30 PDT

A voice somewhere in the waking fog, "Coffee's hot; first come, first served." Sounded like Rocky's voice.

After Two Hours Of Rest – Not Sleep. Just Rest.

{Smitty's groggy brain: "WTH?" GET UP? ARE YOU KIDDIN' ME! ROLL-OVER DAMMIT!" "You gotta get down to business today. Today, it's gonna be Captain Rhodes, you dumb-ass."}

Rhodes: (to one of the Privates), "Go round-up Smitty, Gunnies Cornell, Johnson, Layton, Vernor, Sergeant Winthrop, and Coms for a meeting at 06:40 over at the new command post."

"Yes, sir."

Time: Saturday, 14-July, 06:41 PDT

Rhodes: "After the luxury of sleep, gentlemen, let's talk about the past 14 hours or so, shall we? We need to put our heads together and try to understand just what the hell happened at this site, and if possible, why. Forget about all the military protocols; we need to figure-out how many bad-guys would be required to pull this shit off. Any questions so far?" No responses. "Good. Chow is MREs, coffee pot is over there, and latrine is over in the visitor information building. We start for real at 07:15, so get your breaks now. See you back here in 30. Dismissed."

Order of Succession

Time: Saturday, 14-July, 07:13 PDT

{Smitty's mind, rebelling: "Hey are you always going to be on time? What happened to a taking a leisurely cup of coffee in the morning. Oh, suckin'-up are ya, huh?"}

Rhodes, to all: "Okay, now, make yourselves as comfortable as you can for the next few hours. We're gonna bisect, dissect, and scrutinize what we all think went on. By the time all the politically-correct people get hold of this and spin it, even we won't recognize we were ever here. But we will know what's what because you're the on-the-spot, hands-on experts with the knowledge and experience. So speak your minds; no holds barred."

Sergeant Winthrop (EOD): "I'd like to speak first, but not to steal anyone else's thunder. The EOD Marines are probably the smallest platoon out here – really, more like a squad, but that's not really our point. We have been talking about this ever since the first IED went off over on the westbound roadbed, ya know, the one past the rest-area toward Pendleton. We also had a decent look at the deck that was dropped on top the limo, even if it was by flood lights and vehicle head-lights. Here's what the EOD Squad thinks happened.

"The modifications on the limo were, for sure, not done at a regular, everyday oil-change garage. That car had to be up on a lift in a shop equipped with a lift and decent metal and machine shop capabilities.

"Smitty, over there, might be able to confirm, or deny, that the Secret Service provides all maintenance in their own garage; our assumption is that they do. So, our SWAG is the Secret Service has been infiltrated for this effort. Not accusing, ya understand, just sayin'. Enough about the car.

Although Smitty did not verbally confirm Winthrop's supposition, he did give a quick nod of his head so that Rhodes could see it. Rhodes confirmed back with another slight nod. Any other observer who happened to see Smitty's nod had to make their own assumptions.

Winthrop: "We think there are two other areas those guys somehow handled by themselves: the overpass deck and the IED up on I-8. For the IED on I-8, they had to make a hole the full distance across the travel lanes and shoulders. We believe that the purpose was to try to prevent

Order of Succession

the limo from making a run for it and reaching the western end of the road-blocked section of I-8 by creating a big trench that the limo could not get past. That, or demolish it right there. When they blew-it, that IED took out the concrete and paving about twelve-feet wide and a good 4 or 5 feet deep. That whole section is gonna havta be completely rebuilt. We think they set the IED off as a diversion during that little fire-fight. For this effort, they probably would have to use a small boring machine modified to drill sideways under the roadbed.

"So, they need the boring truck with a crew of at least three and an undetermined amount of time from boring to final detonation. In theory, the boring and filling it with explosives could be accomplished in as little as a single day.

"The overpass, now that was cute, really cute. That took some thought on timing the charges. But they had to have somebody in the limo to make it work."

Voice in the audience: "Whadya mean?"

Sergeant Winthrop continued: "Well, that limo had to be stopped EXACTLY on the right spot – to the very inch. Look, with that concrete utility-vault box under the limo, proper positioning had to be right on the money so everything lined-up with the hole in the floor of the car. Off by six inches, and nobody gets out from the car and into the tunnel. That means the driver had to be in on it, too. Of course, that's just my assumption, sir.

"So, once the car is over that concrete box, the lids were pushed up and shoved out of the way, under the limo. Once the limo is in place smack dab on top of that box, with no lids on the vault, some sort of high-torque, battery-powered, portable drills take the nuts off the eight bolts, and the plate drops off. Use a heavy-duty razor knife on the carpet, and bam, you got yourself a president – and everybody else inside the limo, too. I actually mean EVERYBODY who was in the limo because we didn't find any bodies or even a drop of blood. After everybody was out of the limo, that's when their artistry really showed itself. Anyway, once stopped just right, the bad-guys detonated some charges near the edges of the limo, basically, to push the dirt out from under the limo – but just hard enough – so that it piled-up around the edges of the car and formed a small dam all around it. And as a result of the lack of dirt, the limo just plopped down on top of the man-hole – if it was aligned just right, that is.

Order of Succession

"How, so?" another voice in the crowd.

"Bringing down the overhead overpass deck, and 'precisely' is the key here. With the limo empty, there were some small charges placed who knows when, so that when they went off, some of the dirt under the overpass deck was blown outward, away from the concrete abutments. Other charges blew the dirt to the sides, leaving dug-out areas on both sides of the limo. Sort of picture a jigsaw puzzle with two gaping slots across from each other, just waiting for the right piece to drop into place. In our case, that piece is the overhead deck. Then the next to last charges were set off; these were the ones on the underside of the bridge itself. When the deck falls, its ends-up falling right into those dug-out areas near the abutments. This sort of guided the deck into place right down on top of the limo – and kept it there in place.

"Then the final charges blew the concrete abutments on top of the deck, sort of sealing the limo under even more tons of deck, concrete, and dirt. And one final added benefit for the bad-guys: the final detonation threw enough loose debris on top of – and under the ends of – the deck so that any would-be rescuers would have to use a lot of physical man-power to clear the debris before any machinery could even be connected-up to lift it. A lot of rescuers' time would be wasted just digging-out places to hook-up to the major steel for the lifting. The EOD squad figures that it probably took about ten people with three trucks to prep the overpass area.

"Digging the tunnel, however, well that would be a different kettle of fish considering that it stretched-out for about an eighth mile. And, they would have had to study-up on the ground conditions out here. We're guessing that took about at least three tunnelers and drilling machines and trucks to dispose of the dirt. We think wiring this area and digging the tunnel may have taken somewhere in the order of one and a half to two months. Maybe longer, up to three months, if they didn't want to attract too much public attention. But, the real kicker about all of this is that they had to know EXACTLY that the President was going to be HERE and EXACTLY when."

Winthrop said, draining a water bottle. "Any questions, sir? Gunnies?"

Rhodes: "I don't have any. Gunnies? Sergeant, you put this all together since you got here? And in the dark, too?"

Order of Succession

Winthrop: "Sir, we have some damn good Marines in EOD. We take a professional interest in how this stuff can be done, sir. By the way, sir, we also think they had access to, and used, military-grade explosives – some really first-class pieces of equipment, the best Uncle Sam buys."

Rhodes: "Anybody try to figure-out how that camera and the gun-platform were controlled?"

Cornell: "Sir, one of the PFCs is at home on the Internet. I asked him to look it over. PFC Thompson's waiting over there in case he was needed."

Rhodes: "Well, invite him to join us."

Cornell: "PFC Thompson, join us and tell us whacha found."

PFC Thompson: "Sir, Gunnies, Sergeants, the way I see it, these guys had access to a whole lot of money. That and some very high-priced technology to get these links operational. Assuming that no one monkeyed with the camera on the tree, then I sort of figured-out which direction it was transmitting toward. Same goes for the gun-platform. Both transmitted toward the same location over in that general direction (waving his arm, indicating direction). I think that both were equipped with tightly focused directional antennas so transmissions would not be broadcast to all of the rabbits and snakes in the area. Normally, that would include humans like the ones we found at the end of the tunnel. Anyway, I laid-out where both of them were and their cones of transmission on this map. If you want to look at it, I'll lay it out on the table so you can see what I mean." Thompson unrolled the map, and the others gathered around as he gave them the orientation of the rest-area to the camera and the platform. He continued:

"Both cones converged on this zone over here (pointing to the map), so that was the most likely place to look. Notice that it is outside the guards' perimeter – about four hundred meters outside. With Gunny Layton's permission, I got two guards to escort me over there to look it over. Didn't see any vehicles or anybody. We did notice the smell of gasoline, however. We found a small clearing that had fresh tire-tracks and some littered food wrappers – all crumpled, but fresh because the cheese bits and pieces were still pliable – and some cigarette butts. We think the gas odor may have been from spilling fuel from a Jerry can when they refueled whatever they are driving.

Order of Succession

Oh, yeah, the tire-tracks are parallel to our sites; they listened, looked, and whatever else at us broadside.

"Now, either they have sophisticated gear in their van to process and control all of the functions of the camera and platform, or the van was just a concentrator and relayed the data up-links to somewhere else. I cannot tell for sure if C&C [11] was in the vehicle. All it would take is a coupla of PCs for sure, so they can operate both up-links simultaneously, which means at least two people, plus maybe a driver. But if C&C is remote, then we're probably lookin' at a satellite link. C&C could be almost anywhere in the world then. That's way beyond any of the info I've found so far.

"About the camera, in all likelihood this was probably just a one-way video link – that is, camera to operator. Basically, the operator had to both look at the video feed and dial-up and talk to our Coms on the secure radio channel.

"The gun-platform is probably more complex. It provides a video feed from the camera on the rifle scope, which by the way, has night scope capability – all that green image stuff. It also requires remote control of the platform. So, there are at least two interrelated functions.

"Assuming that there was the possibility that both the camera and platform could have been used at the same time, well, there are those operators, too – dedicated to their sole functions.

"I think it is a pretty neat link-up and could be done either way. The determining factor is: whoever is C&C, where does he want to be located, and how much personal, hands-on activity he wants. Oh, yeah, probably a day or two to set-up here in the field after they tried a dry run to get the gun-platform aligned and the camera focused, etc. Any questions? Thank-you, sir. I'll wait over there if I'm needed again."

Rhodes: "No, sit over here in case anything that comes up that suggests there might be a different angle."

PFC Thompson: "Thank-you, sir. May I speak again?" Rhodes: "PFC, go ahead." "Well, I heard Sergeant Winthrop's explanation of how the explosives were detonated. I don't want to argue with these the results; who can? However, I would like to offer the possibility that the charges could have been controlled remotely, too. What I mean is, there

---

11 C&C = Command and Control

ORDER OF SUCCESSION

may have been other cameras and sensors out there which provided C&C with the limo's location, motion, etc. and watched us as we responded. In other words, there may have been only two bad-guys out here – the two 'hunters' on the hillside; the others could have been in the van or wherever C&C is. Just sayin', sir."

Rhodes: "Point noted, PFC. Who's next?"

Rhodes: "What about the deputies? Anybody got any ideas?"

Gunny Cornell: "That area was my platoon's responsibility. We attached PFC Berkeley, who is trained for Personnel Retrieval and Processing Specialist (MOS 0471, that is: dealing with Mortuary Affairs) to handle those bodies – you know, tag-and-bag. I have him waiting over there with the rest of the experts. (Turning in that direction) PFC Berkeley! Come on over here and tell us what you think happened."

PFC Chuck Berkeley:

{Berkeley's mind, in confidence-building mode: "You got a chance to make points with the Captain without interference from a Gunny. Don't go motor-mouth on me and blow it now! Got that?"}

Saluting Captain Rhodes, PFC Berkeley began hesitantly, but gathered enough momentum so as not to stumble over his own words. "Well, sir, those deputies, you know there's five of 'em right? Well, uh, I have a write-up for each of 'em so we don't mix-up the facts for one of them with the others; separate sheets for each is the way I arranged it."

Rhodes: "Great idea, but what have ya got on the whole group of them – anything or nothing?"

PFC Berkeley: "Sorry, sir, I'm not used to this yet. Okay. Okay, now, to me it looks like all five of them were just standing around over there by their cars. There are only three of those cars right now, which is sort of funny, but I'll get to that part in just a little bit.

"The bodies look like they weren't expecting whatever or whoever killed them. Only one deputy had a gun in his hand, his Glock. Oh, yeah, all five had Glocks, and all those Glocks are .40-Cal. The others still had coffee cups and fat pills . . . sorry, sir, donuts and pastries . . . in their hands.

Order of Succession

{Berkeley's mind, admonishing self: "Get your act together, Marine, right now, and that's an order. Or you're gonna get an ass-chewing for all this sloppy work. DO YOU UNDERSTAND, MARINE? Now get with the program. Got it?"}

After a really short attitude adjustment, PFC Berkeley continued, "Here's what I think could possibly have happened, sir.

"To me, it looks like more than one person approached these deputies. We tried – that's me and the other guys helping me – to find all the bullets we could. Got us about six from the bodies and around another six from around the cars that had also been hit. We are saying at least three guns were used on them because we found some .45s and two different 9-mm bullets. I also think the ammo in those 9s is from different batches or manufacturers of that ammo because the cannelure groove around the bullets were at different heights from the base of the bullet. Plus, one cannelure was knurled, while the other was smooth. Couldn't measure from the tops 'cause they were all chewed-up and deformed by whatever they hit, especially those we found in the cars."

Question from the crowd: "Canny-what? Jus' what the hell is this canny-whatever you said, and why is so important, anyway?"

Berkeley: "The cannelure is the grove around the bullet where the top of the brass body is crimped; it helps keep the bullets and brass shells together as a unit in the magazine during recoil. Some people call it a 'crimping grove' or a 'crimping ring'. And one of the reasons it might be important is that it might be possible to tell who the manufacturers of the bullets are. Sorry, I got side-tracked here."

Voice in the crowd: "Well, I'll be; never heard it called a 'cano-lure; thanks. Still sounds like it's used to catch fish though."

Berkeley: "Moving on. Well, there were two different sets of 9-mm ammo used, and since shooters usually load a magazine from the same box or even the same batch of ammo, we think there were probably at least two shooters using 9s. Also, all three bullets, the .45 and both 9s, were hollow-points, not ball. These bad-guys wanted to leave no survivors and used the most effective and least costly ammo doing it.

"This rest-area is usually pretty busy this time of year. People always need to take a bladder break. It's hot out, and it offers a break before heading west for the coast and thicker traffic. There were no

Order of Succession

civilians around here, so our best SWAG is that maybe they had already cleared the rest-area. They probably expected to meet somebody here, probably about restricting access to the rest-area by civilians. Using that SWAG, those other guys probably were the shooters.

"When I began telling you all what we found, I also said there was something funny about their cars; well, this is what I mean. You'd think this assignment was pretty high profile, wouldn't ya? Well, think about this:

"There were five deputies, but there are only three cars. Why didn't each one have his own car? What if they got an emergency call to go somewhere? Why should two guys have to go just because the other deputy has the keys to the wheels? Doesn't make sense to me – especially, on this job.

"Next, there's too much junk on the front seats. Ya know, all the gear deputies take with them when they get in the car in the morning. Ya know, so they're prepared for anything regardless of what they run into during their day. Ya got radios, phones, dash-mounted laptops, laser speed guns, the dash-secured shotgun, all that kinda stuff. Well, in those three cars all of that crap is still in place. Where'd the second deputy ride? In the back seat, behind the screen, like an arrested criminal? Kinda doubt that, dontcha?

"Next, each of the deputies had his own morning coffee stuff. Ya know what I mean? Coffee cups, pastry wrappers, that kinda stuff. Two of them had those breakfast muffin sausage sandwich things – these were McDonald's Egg McMuffins™."

Voice from the crowd: "So what? We all have chowed down on that stuff. What's the big deal, anyway?"

"Glad you brought that up; thanks for helping make the point. Here's the big deal – at least to us Marines who were digging through the cars and all the garbage cans around this here rest-area. Think about this: when ya buy anything like a sandwich at Mickey D's it is individually wrapped all by itself, and then they throw it, and the rest of the edibles into a bag, or at least every Mickey D's I've ever gone to does it that way. Even the fast-food places over at Pendleton do that – all of them – even if you get one donut at Dunkin' Donuts or an order of fries at Burger King. This all leads to the point I'm trying to make: we didn't find any wrappers for any of that stuff for the two deputies that had their Egg McMuffins. Not one fast-food wrapper in this whole dad-gum

Order of Succession

rest-area. And we dumped-out all of the cans, even in the latrines in the Information Center; we dumped the dumpsters; and we cleaned-out the semi's cab. We didn't find any greasy, cheesy wrappers that went with those muffin things – not a one. And we didn't find enough wrappers for the rest of the stuff either – not enough cup holders or those drink carriers you can get at a drive-through. Where's a deputy gonna put all of that stuff when he knows he's coming out here and gonna sit for more than half a day not doin' a damned thing but eat snacks and sandwiches and suck on coffee or soda? And, all of the deputy-work equipment is still on the front seats.

"There's just not enough used wrappers. There were some other bad-guys here, and they took these deputies out.

"My final finding is: car keys. Usually, all five deputies would have keys to their own patrol cars; that makes five cars, not three. My SWAG is that each deputy had his own 'personal patrol car' – one that each deputy sets-up the same way he wants it and uses that same car every day – that way they know EXACTLY where everything is located, how far they have to reach to get anything. And, they usually clip the keys to their gun-belt – or whatever it's now called. There's this piece of leather that hangs down from the belt and has a snap fastener on it; the leather prevents the keys from snagging and ruining the uniform pants. Only one deputy still has keys clipped to his belt, and he was lying on them. We found them when we rolled his body over, and it starts the middle car over there. We could not find any keys for the other two cars. Here's our point: There are three cars over there now, so, at least two sets of keys are missing. To us, this means that there are really four sets of keys missing. Anyway, we think the bad-guys grabbed four sets of keys off the belts of four dead deputies, went to the cars, and tried to start any two they could. Then they just drove away in the two missing cars. Our group believes there were five cars, and we believe the killers drove the two missing cars out of the area – maybe along with the missing wrappers."

"Any questions or comments?"

Rhodes: "I have a question, PFC. You Marines gathered all of this intel in the dark?"

Berkeley: "Yes, sir. We wanted to pop-open that trailer that's parked over there – the one next to the semi, but we didn't have time. Yet, that is, sir."

Order of Succession

Rhodes: "Now I have a comment or two. Glory Be! Not enough cars. Too much stuff on the front seats. Missing keys. But I really like 'not enough wrappers'. Hot damn! We now think there were at least three bad-guys here – well, because three different bullets, but at least two because they had to drive the cars – but maybe more if they doubled-up in each car.

"Say, PFC – Berkeley, is it – I think your squad has earned a little reward. Gunnies, what do you say to having them pop-open that trailer – just to make sure?"

Cornell: "Yes, sir, Cap'n, that's one darn good idea. Just so that we don't have to buy whatever is inside if its breakable. Anybody ever found-out what happened to the driver yet?"

Rhodes: "PFC, you all take 15, and then go open it up. Be careful; we don't know if it's booby-trapped, do we? No. Let us know what you find."

Berkeley: "Yes, sir."

Rhodes: "Everybody, take 15. Gunny Cornell, after the break, we'll discuss what, if anything, the perimeter guards found."

Cornell: "Ready, sir."

Rhodes: "Everybody back? Let's continue."

Cornell: "Yes, sir. The Marines on guard duty observed next to nothing up close. They did not see anything inside the perimeter that appeared out-of-place. Several Marines were detailed to sort of 'wander or roam' inside the perimeter just to give it a good look-see. Nothing.

"However, after dark last night, the Marines on the perimeter noticed – or felt – they were being watched. If you know what to look for and have the equipment to help with the looking, we have a pretty good hit ratio for finding aggressors' night-vision gear. We looked and we found it. However, when we tried to pin it down where we thought it was, they shut it down. Our Marines tried to circle behind the spot. No one was there, but they had been there. Food wrappers. Yeah, more wrappers.

"This morning, the perimeter is going to be expanded to twice the distance. The 'roamers' will also scour the new ground to see if there is anything else out there."

Order of Succession

Voice of PFC Berkeley: "Sir, Gunnies, sorry for breaking in. We popped the doors on the trailer. We are taking pictures and all that stuff, but you all better come over and give a look. It's a tight area, and we don't want to risk destroying anything that might be important to somebody else."

Rhodes: "PFC, what's up?"

Berkeley: "I don't know for sure. But one of us Marines is going for a few more body bags."

Cornell: "Damn! More victims?"

Berkeley: "I don't know who they are. We found another weird thing out there, too. But not exactly like the 'no wrappers' for the deputies, just some ripped-up connectors."

Cornell: "Ripped-up connectors? What the hell are you talking about now?"

Berkeley to Cornell, sort of bypassing Rhodes: "Gunny, may I speak freely, please?" He proceeded after Gunny Cornell gave him a quick nod. "Gunny, there's something not right about that trailer. I don't know what else to say, but we think that trailer is definitely connected to the rest of the mess in this rest-area. (The PFC motioned with his arm at the overpass, the deputies, and patrol cars.) We don't know how, but it is way too weird and spooky not to be. When you all go over there, stop at the front of the trailer first; we'll show you the weird stuff first before . . . before we show you the rest. Sorry, but I've been thinking about what we found, and I gotta heave right now." With that, he turned his back, bent over, and heaved everything he had eaten and drunk since breakfast this morning.

The entire group jogged over to the trailer, an all-white 53-foot Wabash. PFC Berkeley showed-up, still rinsing his mouth, and directed the group to the front of the trailer to point out a couple of things his group discovered. The Marines inspecting the trailer knew the group would become too affected by the scene inside the trailer and then to be pulled to the front of the trailer for a couple of 'finer' points afterwards.

Berkeley: "Let me show you my primary point first. We think that semi tractor we were using to drag all that deck stuff off the limo over

Order of Succession

there and this here trailer may not be the complete truck we originally assumed it was. We think it is possible that there may have been at least two trucks – two semi tractors and two trailers. We are using the tractor from one, and this trailer is from the other truck. Now, how we reached that conclusion: Look at the front of the trailer. Note the trailer's electrical connector still has part of the tractor's cable attached to it, all ripped-up. That should have been disconnected by the driver when the trailer was disconnected from the tractor. That tractor we were using – well, it still has its electrical cable in one piece; nothing was ripped off. Again, back on the front of the trailer, see the glad-hands [12] where the air-brake hoses are supposed to be connected? This trailer's glad-hands are still attached, but the tractor's air hoses were ripped apart when the tractor pulled away. Again, the air-hoses on our tractor are still in one piece. This is why we think we may be dealing with a couple of mis-matched pairs of tractors and trailers. Or, something like that." Berkeley's voice trailed off in preparation for, "But the rear of the trailer is where it . . . where it gets . . . well, where it really hit the fan, sir."

Both rear doors were already held open flat against the sides by the trailer's latches, looking like it had its ears pinned back. The group had ample vision of the dark tunnel of space usually filled by cargo. There was cargo toward the front of the van; hell, the front of the van could not even be seen. But the rear – that's where all eyes stopped – stopped by a bloody scene. Four more bodies lay inside – one on the floor, one propped against a stack of boxes on the left side of the trailer, one against a crate in the center of the trailer, and the fourth sprawled on his stomach across an old broken wooden pallet on the right side. All had deep stab wounds and cuts – some, long, wide, deep, and continuous.

Berkeley: "Not pretty. By the looks of it, we think maybe all four bled-out inside the trailer – all over the inside. I've never seen anything like this. Nothing like this. Sir, excuse me again.

"We looked over the rear of the trailer. We don't know why this went-down, but we have some quick guesses if you want them, sir."

Rhodes: "By all means, proceed, PFC."

Berkeley: "Sir, we originally thought one of the bodies may have been the driver of the tractor we were using, but we don't know which

---

12   Glad hands' are the two (2) mechanical connectors for the air brake hoses on semi trucks. In this instance, these glad hands connect the tractor to this trailer.

Order of Succession

one. Since that time, however, we are sort of leaning toward a different theory that they all may have been associated with the ambush on the limo in some way – like maybe these are the guys who did the grunt work, the expendable ones – but not the big guys. So, they did the work to make the ambush work, and when they finished, they were killed-off. Maybe, to keep them quiet, permanently. One other possibility could be that these guys knew something, maybe something they didn't know they knew. We didn't find any bullet holes in them or the trailer. I mean look how they were killed, all cut-up like that. Those poor bastards, man, they must have really been hurtin' bad all the way!" Everyone turned ashen, and a tomblike silence descended on the group at the rear of the trailer. Nobody would have understood anything about torn electrical wires and glad-hands after seeing this.

Berkeley: "Where was I? The hands of three of them are calloused like they may have been laborers or something like that. That's why we thought they provided the labor to build the stuff for the ambush. Maybe truck drivers. But the fourth guy, his hands are soft with well-trimmed nails. No idea what he could have been doing out here. We don't have anything to take fingerprints with, and even if we did, none of us know how – especially from corpses.

"There's more weird stuff here about these poor suckers, too. We went looking through their pockets and poking around the trailer for clues about who they are – or were. These weren't ordinary guys by the looks of what we found. Each of those 'laborers' had at least three IDs each, with different names, but all the respective pictures matched the bodies. The guy with the soft hands, well, he had four IDs, same as the others, but he had ten, count 'em, ten credit cards, all with different names and account numbers. Like I said, there's some weird stuff goin' on here. Way above my rank and pay grade.

"Our plan at this point is to 'tag-and-bag" all four of them after taking pictures of every last thing in the trailer. Every last thing. Every last damn thing. Then start looking at the cargo. Do we have a go on that, sir?"

Rhodes: "You do indeed, PFC. The rest of us will return to our first meeting site over at the Command Post. Let us know if you all turn-up anything else."

Order of Succession

Everybody stopped at the latrine on the way back. (All shivered as the murder scene replayed through their minds. All washed their hands and faces long and hard trying to scrub the scene out of their heads. It was useless.)

Back at the Command Post, more hot coffee all around.

After a long silence, Smitty was the first to speak. "Has anyone heard from my Secret Service? Like where the hell are they? You, Coms? Anybody? We're approaching a full day and no word. What the hell is going on? Coms, you hear any news from the outside world yet? Anybody know anything?"

Coms: "About the news from the outside world. You better ask Cap'n Rhodes, okay?"

ORDER OF SUCCESSION

7 – News from the Outside World

Mid-Morning, Saturday, 14-July: Westbound I-8, Exit 51, at Buckman Springs Rest Area, Mojave Desert, California

TIME: 09:53 PDT

More victims discovered.

{Smitty's sleep-deprived brain: "Isn't this ever gonna end?"}

Another voice somewhere, "Coffee's hot. Lunch coming up in an hour."

Rhodes: "Smitty, thanks to Sergeant Williams, we do have some news from the 'outside world', as you call it. But to us, it's still sort of meaningless. What I really mean is that we Marines don't really deal with this sort of thing – at least, not at our level.

Time: Saturday, 14-July, 09:54 PDT

Rhodes: "Smitty, if you recall, about seven-and-a-half hours ago, I told you about the five Secretaries in the President's Cabinet who were injured – no, make that, who died – in an accident. Remember that? Well, things are happening faster outside of this rest-area. *Way* too fast if you gather my meaning after hearing this next bit of news.

"Seems that last night or early this morning there were some residential break-ins in the Washington, D.C. area. The first reports speculated that the first two were burglaries; however, after those first two, reports of three more break-ins have since been added. None of the five are now referred to as break-ins. Too much coincidence; now, all five of them are now also referred to as assassinations. These next five include Secretaries of: Veterans Affairs, Homeland Security, Housing and Urban Development, Transportation, and Energy.

Order of Succession

"My sources know some things about our own situation out here. Not everything, but some. I have no idea how they know what they claim to know. And Coms, that is, Sergeant Williams, knows the basics about what everything you and I are talking about right now, and I got this information through him. I do know one thing: that our Coms, uhh, rather, Sergeant Williams, would not tell anyone anything about this location and what's gone on here over the last few hours. I have that much faith in him. No question. Period. So, it makes me wonder what D.C. really knows, if you know what I mean, and how do they know it.

"Well, anyway, these sources say D.C. is really worked up into a real full-blown panic like their hair is on fire while somebody is giving them major wedgies – way more so than usual. They think – rumor, to you and me – your branch, the Secret Service, has more-or-less accepted the fact that the President is no longer under their direct protection and/or possession. But, they did not say they accept that he's dead; no they did not say that. However, they supposedly have their hands full and cannot afford to waste any more man-power on 'our lost cause' out here. Reluctantly, they have called-in the FBI to look into our mess out here. Your thoughts?"

Smitty, still somewhat shocked about these recent developments: "I don't know which is more significant – a President who has been abducted or the assassinations of ten Cabinet Secretaries.

"Let's begin with the President, okay?" Without waiting for agreement, Smitty continued, "I think he's still alive. Remember when we were playing with the President's personal cell-phone and the recorded message said 'Yes, we have him'? I am making the assumption that it would have said 'He's dead' if they had assassinated him already. Therefore, I'm going to keep working like he is still alive and we have to find him and get him back – if we can.

"But, I am positively stumped why the Secret Service is giving up on him and protecting the rest of the Order of Succession. Did your source – whoever it is – think they were trying to do that – protect the others – or were they just investigating the deaths? I mean what the hell are they trying to do? Their main, public responsibility is 'The Man – POTUS', not some damn Secretary of some pip-squeak department. They better not have hung us out to dry on our own, or I'm gonna be one pissed-off agent, and I mean seriously PO'ed here.

Order of Succession

"Let's see: the first five plus these five makes ten. And there are only 19 steps in the Order of Succession. Oh, my God, these bastards have already literally wiped-out over half of the approved alternates to officially governing The Untied States of America. Do you see where this could be leading? Oh, yeah, and the President makes eleven. Those no-good sons-of-bitches.

{Smitty's mind, trying to calm him down: "Hey you're getting pretty worked-up here. Say you're sorry to Rita for being so foul-mouthed." "Sorry, Rita, forgive me, please."}

"So, they've already wiped-out the lower half of the Order; that leaves only the more public figures like the Vice President and the Secretary of State. Those are going to be harder targets. I hope." Smitty's voice trailed-off while a thought hit him hard. "Unless, of course . . . unless one of them is . . . in on all of this. Cap'n, do you think that's even possible? That one of them is somehow involved? Tell me it ain't so?"

Rhodes: "You're leading us into territory I'm not all that familiar with. What are you trying to say here, anyway? That somebody in our duly elected government is trying to hi-jack it? For what purpose? Who stands to gain what by this? This is not any battlefield I've been trained for. What the hell are you saying – that we got a traitor trying to take over the whole damned United States? One guy?"

There was silence while Smitty became lost in scenarios. He had not recently played the same military games that the Cap'n plays daily. But the object of the exercise is pretty damn close to the same.

Smitty: "When kids play King-of-the-Hill, the object of the game is much the same . . . sure it is . . . to capture the flag of the fallen king." Followed by dead silence.

Smitty: "Yeah, pretty much so, maybe. Cap'n can I call you George or Rocky? Your title seems so out-of-place right now." Without waiting for agreement, Smitty continued, "Let's talk through some scenarios running through my head.

Rocky: "Okay on the name for now. King-of-the-Hill, huh? Isn't that the name of the game in which you try to capture the flag of the opposing . . . Holy sh. . ! Are you thinking someone, somebody is trying to capture the United States without a war? You have to be kiddin' me.

Order of Succession

We aren't at war with anybody. Just because some politically-appointed Secretaries of government departments are getting bumped-off, you're turning it into a coup or some other screwy thing. Have you gone absolutely crazy, here?"

Smitty: "You're proving my point. Nobody, but NOBODY would believe it. That's right; no SANE person would believe it. But let's talk about the possibility of why the hell that just damn-well might work. Please humor me here for a while. Okay?"

No objections from Rocky.

Smitty: "Good. Okay, facts we know. We know the President was abducted. I mean he's not here, is he? And I saw him get into the limo this morning – uhh, make that yesterday morning. There was no blood or body fragments in the limo when we dug it out and turned it over, were there? No, there weren't. So, somebody's got him; the voice-mail announcement on his own cell-phone even said they have him. He is the Number One guy in the order of Succession. Numero Uno. The Top Guy. He *IS* the *King-of-the-Hill*. They have to somehow remove the Top Guy in some way. They have to take him out of the game. Incapacitate him in some way. That, or, corrupt his authority and/or power.

"They can't just leave him in office – alone, untouched – can they? No, they have to take care of him during the first opening plays. If they left him untouched, the King, I mean the President, could just keep replacing the new successors when they are also eliminated. Sure, maybe the replacements might become more and more reluctant to accept if his or her fellow Secretaries also keep getting bumped-off. But, hell, status and a title will always find willing recipients.

"So, how's this for a scenario? First, they capture the President, not kill him, but capture him. Why, I don't know for sure just yet. Maybe they have other plans and need to keep him alive for some reason like . . . say, eliminate enough of the Cabinet and have him replace the former Secretaries with the bad-guys' personal choices. Hey, that's not a bad idea, now is it?"

Smitty was gathering steam, "Another scenario. They keep killing-off Secretaries until their choice, already a Secretary of, say, Hand-Wringing, is the lone survivor of the purge. Hand-Wringer becomes President and now appoints the new Cabinet consisting only of the bad-guys' hand-picked choices. Not bad either, huh?

ORDER OF SUCCESSION

"Rocky, the next thing we know is that we have to *assume* the information you received from your sources is also spot-on. I mean what else can we do right now, huh? *Only assume.* Okay, so far the bad-guys have also killed-off ten, count 'em *ten secretaries* in this existing President's Cabinet. Most of these were in the lower half of the batting order.

"Then, we also have to *assume* that the remaining Secretaries – without us hearing any reports about them from outside this rest area – we havta assume that they are still alive. That includes the Secretaries of Health and Human Services, Agriculture, Treasury, and State. Also in the Order, but without a title of Secretary are: the Attorney General, President Pro Tempore of the Senate, Speaker of the House of Representatives, and the Vice President. That should add-up to eighteen, and the President completes the nineteen positions in the Order.

"Followed by: of all the nineteen positions, only the top four are elected. So, if the bad-guys wanted one of the elected positions to be in control, all they would have to do is assassinate the other three to get a clean slate in the Cabinet and control of whatever they really want. The remaining fifteen positions are appointees. What would the bad-guys have to do to get to their desired man or woman into power? How about ensuring all positions above the desired position are deactivated somehow. How about that?

"And, finally, things we don't know yet are why or who? That would really complete my scenarios, but we ain't got the slightest idea about those. Not yet. Rocky, whadya think? Am I completely crazy?"

Silence on both sides.

Rocky: "Not quite crazy. You just think a lot differently than we Marines do – way different. No, I don't think you're 100% crazy, but with those theories of yours, you're getting pretty damn close to that border."

Smitty: "Well, how well can you keep a secret? What level of security clearance do you have?"

Rocky: "Top-Secret. Why are you asking?"

Smitty: "Where's a quiet place around here where we can talk?"

Rocky: "Meet me over by the semi tractor in fifteen. Nobody's using it right now."

Order of Succession

PFC Berkeley: "Cap'n Rhodes, sir, can you hold-on a moment please?"

Rhodes: "Berkeley. More news about the trailer?"

Berkeley: "Well, yeah, sort of. We got a slightly higher-than-normal radiation reading near the center of the trailer. We found a hole in the stacks of pallets. Oh, not a hole like a leak hole. A hole, an empty spot, where extra boxes could have been stacked but aren't there now. The boxes around this hole are all hot. Not inside the boxes. Just on their outsides, the pallet, and a portion of the trailer's floor. Nothing else in the trailer registers . . . well, not as much as this one hole."

Rhodes: "Smitty, our meeting is postponed for a bit; come on over to the trailer after you clean-up. Now it's radiation."

Smitty: "A new wrinkle."

Again, PFC Berkeley led the way over to the trailer. He didn't stop at the front of the trailer this time; the worst was already seen the last time.

Berkeley: "The rear floor is still a mess, as you would expect. We're using the side door to get in and out so we don't disturb the scene in the back. Watch your step on the pallets we're using for a ladder to get in and out. The hole I was trying to describe is about two feet forward of this door."

Voice from the crowd: "What about the radiation? How bad is it? How dangerous is it to us?"

Berkeley: "It's not off the Geiger counter. It doesn't peg the needle if that's what you mean. We don't have dosimeters, so we can't give you a reading. It's just constant noise and swinging the needle around 20% of the scale."

Rhodes: "Coms. Order some dosimeters from Pendleton."

Coms: "Yes, sir."

Rhodes: "Berkeley, you say you all determined nothing in the van seems to be hot, just this hole, right? How big is this hole, roughly?"

Berkeley: "We didn't find anything else but this hole in the load. Roughly speaking, sir, it is about the size of one pallet on the floor and about 30 inches high on the sides, up the sides of the boxes on four sides. Oh, yeah, and the boxes that were above the hole like a roof over it. Like maybe concealing it from all sides."

Order of Succession

Rhodes: "Let me give a quick look at this hole. I am not going to spend too much time at this, and you all shouldn't either." So, Rhodes went in and out quickly. "Coms. Get Pendleton to send some rad folks to gauge this problem."

Coms: "Yes, sir."

Rhodes: "Berkeley, thanks for the update. I think. Anything else?"

Berkeley: "Nothing at this point."

Rhodes: "You all stay out of range of that stuff as much as possible. As long as the Geiger counter reads the way it is now, you all stay away, okay? If you got some warning tape, mark the area.

"Smitty, our talk in 30 where we were going to meet before."

Smitty: "Yes, sir."

Part 2 – Untangling the Gordian Knot

ORDER OF SUCCESSION

8 – Early Background

Almost 11:00, Saturday, 14-July: Westbound I-8, Exit 51, at Buckman Springs Rest Area, Mojave Desert, California

TIME: 10:46 PDT

Another voice somewhere off in the distance, "Coffee's still hot. Chow's in the mess area."

The two men met over at the semi's tractor – with MREs and coffee in hand.

Rhodes, general grousing about the weather: "It's gonna be hot today. I wish we were back at Pendleton with that ocean breeze. Beats this stuff any time; beats Yuma, all the time."

"So, Smitty, what's all this security clearance stuff about? What's so important that we have to be over here? You want it to be as close to a SCIF [13] as possible, is that it?"

Smitty: "Yeah, something like that. Well, right now, I don't know how some reports of our status made it back to your sources. I certainly don't want our next conversation doing the same. I took the liberty of having a couple of your privates bring some stuff over near that somewhat secluded area over there by the end of the bushes – some tarps, boxes, tent poles, and stuff like that. Let's stroll over there and you can help me drape those tarps around to make a sort of room for our little confab. Thanks. It may help keep our little tête-à-tête a bit more private. You know what I mean? Some overhead shade would probably help, too, with the sun heatin' this place up – like you already said."

A makeshift SCIF was gradually born from some tarps, a couple of boxes for a table, and some makeshift chairs – all nice and cozy in a 12'x12' space.

---

13 SCIF = Secure Compartmentalized Information Facility

Order of Succession

Smitty: "Rocky, don't take offense at my next questions. About your clearance, you said Top Secret, right? Any attachments, certs, or scopes – SCI? SAP? CI? Poly?[14] Full Scope, Lifestyle? Look, I got some things that I just gotta talk to somebody about. Considering the mess we're already hip-deep in, I want it to be you. The shit's still rising, and I think it's gonna get a lot deeper. But I gotta be sure who I can talk to about this stuff. Hope you understand."

Rocky: "Yeah, it's Top Secret with SCI and Poly. Are you sure you really want to lay whatever it is on me even if you can?"

Smitty: "Yep, I'm sure you're the one I want to work with. I think I can understand the Top Secret, but how'd you get the SCI?"

Rhodes: "For a company-grade officer – what I am now – it may not make much sense; however, I wasn't always a Captain in this ground-poundin' organization. I got all the clearance certs for a previous position with the Corps. I was in counter-intelligence, but I can't talk directly about that right now. I'm sure you know all that 'If I told you, I'd have to kill you' stuff would apply, right? You do, right? What about yours?"

Smitty: "Okay. Mine's pretty much the same, actually, just a tad better, but that is neither here nor there, right now. We are close enough for my purposes. I'm satisfied; you're my man.

"Here's what I'm thinking. Look, we – you and I – stumbled into some deep crap and didn't know it at the time. That is, until we, make that I, heard about all of those Secretaries being assassinated – all at once. That's when I knew there was something going on under really deep cover. Actually, more than just deep, sinister is more like it.

"To repeat what I said earlier, here's what it sounds like to me. Somebody – be it a person, a group of people, some company, a foreign government – is trying to play King-of-the-Hill with the United States Executive Branch as the prize. To me, we are smack-dab in the middle of something really shadowy and threatening. And, we are unable to figure it out yet because we only know very minuscule pieces of it at this time. You and I aren't supposed to even know it's underway. No one is supposed to know anything about it. We're supposed to be just like 332 million other

---

14 SCI = Sensitive Compartmented Information; SAP = Special Access Programs; CI = Counterintelligence; Poly = Polygraph. These are codes attached to some security clearances.

Order of Succession

ignorant bastards until we wake one morning and it's all over and done with – a real *fiat accompli*. And I'm dead serious about this.

"Sit back and listen to a tale I know you are gonna think is unbelievable – too far-fetched, too far out to be real. Well, since noon yesterday, I would have also thought everything we've been through – you, me, and your Marines – was also unbelievable, too. Oh, I cannot tell you how I know some of this stuff. Don't even think about me telling you anything like that, okay. Got that? Seriously, you got that?"

Rocky: "Yeah, I got that. What else can I say? Oh, hell, here I'm agreeing to something I don't know anything about and not even sure I want to know about either. Before you go on, just what do you think we may have already gotten ourselves into here?"

Smitty: "I already told you what I think is goin' on here. I have no idea where it's gonna lead. What I am planning to tell you is just the prelude to yesterday afternoon. I don't know, and have no knowledge of, where it's going to unfold or how it's even gonna get that far. Shall I continue?"

Rocky: "Well, I guess you might as well. In for a penny, in for a dollar. Or something like that. Yeah, go ahead."

Smitty: "I know you are gonna think this story can't be true, but I swear to you it is; I know it is true. I am at a point that I need somebody to talk it through with to see if my conclusions make sense. Rocky, you are here now; I can reach-out and touch you. I can't do that with anybody else at the Secret Service right now. Plus, I don't know who is truthin' or lyin' right now. Right or wrong, I am seriously concerned and worried about the probabilities of this being the beginning of the end. So, here goes."

Smitty begins a tale no one else has heard before. "Keep in mind that this is true; take my word for that.

"About three and a half years ago, I, uh, make that we, became aware of some underground rumors of a plot on the life of the then-sitting President. These rumors all seemed to involve a town in mid-western Maryland named Thurmont. The area was actually a little bit outside of Thurmont, to be exact, almost straddling the Mason-Dixon Line. It was quite an open secret that the KKK was supposed to have been an active organization up there. Hell, whatever else ya call the

Order of Succession

KKK, it is still some sort of 'organization', isn't it? Well, quite a few ears perked-up when it was rumored that threats could be coming from a town so close to D.C. For cryin' out loud, just drive down US-15, grab I-270 to I-495 to the George Washington Parkway to the Memorial Bridge or even Key Bridge and you're right in the middle of the Federal Government inside of 90 minutes of driving, if traffic is with ya. That's damn close, and close enough for an equally fast return trip back up the road if ya need to make a run for it.

"I spent the better part of thirteen months getting' to know some 'good ol' boys' up there. I used an undercover name of Terry Pedrozo out of Coeur d'Alene, Idaho; that's what we settled on and built the background story around that. If this expands to anything greater than what we're facing out here, you may need to remember that name. Terry Pedrozo. Remember it, but don't write it down. And that's only between us, okay?

"Well, these 'good ol' boys' were not members of the KKK. In fact, I don't know if I actually ever saw or met any Klansmen up there. The rumors just pegged the plotters as KKK because . . . well, probably because it was a convenient, existing, suspect organization, that's all. These fellas never expressed any sentiment for the KKK one way or another. I came to the conclusion that saying the KKK was involved was a knee-jerk reaction. I never found any valid tie-in between these good ol' boys and the KKK if there was even one there. I stopped lookin' for a tie-in after a couple of months. No use lookin' for something that wasn't there; it was a waste of time and effort. Hey, I'm not saying the KKK is good or bad. I just didn't care about them when there was much bigger game to aim at.

"These guys were a bunch of 'Gripers' all unto themselves – griping about this and that, but mostly about the Government. I mean they didn't go out of their way to talk to anybody about any of their plans unless the other guy needed to know. They relied mainly on 'good ol' boy tradin' sorta like: I need something, and you got it, well, you just let me borrow it, no questions asked, because some day you may need something that I got, and I let you borrow it. That kind of code.

"Now, these guys got together every so often – usually every other weekend – to 'discuss things'. Well, at every meeting I was at, the only thing discussed was the 'damned gubamint' and how it's screwing the little guy. And how tired they were of 'being screwed-over by the damned gubamint'. At one meeting, the leader, I'll call him Hal, suggested that 'They take some kinda action to 'fix that damn gubamint once and for all'." That sort of surprised me; it was the first time I ever heard a hint of wanting to actually do something. I was really surprised when the others – there were eight of them, not including Hal or me – voted to 'do sumptin'. I abstained because I didn't have all the facts they obviously did, but I might join-in after I had some time to listen to their reasons for feeling the way they did. Something like that.

Rhodes: "Sounds like you obviously got it."

"Not much happened during the next two meetings. Always the SOS [15]. Know what I mean? Same grousing about the same old stuff as usual. But at the third meeting, I had to put-up or shut-up; vote 'yes' or 'get my ass kicked outta town for good'. I was told they'd see to that for damned sure. Well, I voted '*YES*' just to see where the next step would take us – me included. After that '*YES*', the door opened. Literally. There was a new bunch of boys just waiting out in Hal's barn. Chances are good that if I had voted 'NO', I may not be here right now. But that's another story, isn't it because I'm still here.

"Oh, in addition to what I assumed was Hal's home located off a rural road well past the local high school, Hal also owned a welding shop up there in the Thurmont area – actually, sort of northwest of the high school on another side road off Route 550. Decent size shop for the area, I guess, but not much of a building to speak-of. I mean not much signage, a dirt driveway, nestled amongst some scrub trees – not like he was out hustling for business, know what I mean? But, man, that guy can really turn-out some nice welding jobs – both gas and arc – a real artist.

"Anyway, both of Hal's properties are near good, convenient highways suitable for whatever he needed to transport. But there was always the feeling that Hal pretty much valued being left alone. He didn't want to be bothered by any nosey neighbors. I guess I was quite fortunate to be invited into his circle of acquaintances – not real friends mind you, but just good acquaintances.

"Well, we moved the meeting out to the barn, and there they were. Three, no four, of the best built guys I had seen since I don't know when. Not body-builder bulges, but put together solid. Know what I mean?

---

15 SOS = Same Old Stuff or Same Old Shit

Order of Succession

Like Marines with ten years of combat training. I don't think all of us together could have done much damage to them, and certainly not a single one of us in, say, a one-on-one match-up. Mano-a-mano, my ass. I'd be dead real fast.

"I took to callin' them the U-Team, for 'Unknowns'. I've thought about this long and hard ever since. I believed the U-Team used the Gripers – as I called the original group – just plain used them by playing to their anti-gubamint talk. The Gripers also had lots of personal contacts in those parts. Hell, after spending a lifetime in the area, you bet they knew people. People and places where stuff could just disappear and magically reappear when needed. When the U-Team asked the Gripers to see if they could store some stuff on the sly, I realized the game was a-changin'. The time had come to realign myself with a new target group. I decided to try to get closer to the players on the U-Team.

"The meetings every other week quickly turned into every weekend and some nights during the week, too. Hal wasn't the real leader any longer; he just provided the house for the meetings and the convenient figurehead of the leader. The griping sessions migrated from 'something should be done about that damn gubamint' into sessions about 'here's what we ought to do about that damn gubamint'. From 'here's what we should do' to 'here's how to do it'. To 'can you boys – the Gripers – get us some stuff? We'll pay so you aren't out any big dollars'.

"It was absolutely amazing how this outside group – from outside the local area and being all unknowns – could gradually assume control of that relatively small group of Gripers by simply cozying-up to them by agreeing with their gripes against the gubamint. The U-Team played them just right, like fish after taking the bait. I was positive they had their own agenda, so I found reasons to cozy-up right back. Three of the U-Team went by really weird nick-names to remember, like Cinch, Tex, and Verb. No last names to search on, just Cinch, Tex, and Verb. Their leader, 'the man with the plan', just called himself Bubba. While everybody called him Bubba during the meetings and subsequent planning sessions, I once heard one member of the U-Team refer to him once as 'Reese', real quiet-like. I filed that name away for researchin' later.

"Well, anyway, one day, Hal called my cell-phone. That was a real surprise in itself. The real surprise was that Hal asked if I could come over to his place and help-out with a project he was working on. I had no idea what the hell was going on, but told him I'd be right over – just needed a little time to clean-up and drive over. I really had to hot-foot it up I-270 from down near the Beltway (I-495). I originally told him I lived right there in the same county, but that was a white lie. I had been thinking about moving into Frederick County for this assignment but had not done so yet. So, I had to think of a decent reason on the way. I eventually told him I got tangled-up with a woman, Rhonda, who liked more lights and action than Frederick City provided – not to mention Thurmont. Told him I fell real hard for her, but things started to get rocky, and I was thinking about splitting-up with her. Dear old Rhonda was gonna to be on the train to splitsville real soon if she didn't change her ways. I had no idea who this Rhonda was; never met any gal named Rhonda in my life – still haven't.

"Sure enough, Hal asked what took me so long. I told him Rhonda was getting' tough to deal with. He shook his head and muttered something about being 'something'-whipped. He muttered it under his breath not plannin' to be heard, but I knew what he meant. I changed the subject to apartments and rentals in the area, like maybe anywhere around here or all the way down to Frederick – someplace without a lot of car and/or people traffic. That seemed like a logical place to be from for this assignment. He said he'd ask around and see what he could turn-up. Looked like Rhonda was on her way out for good. That was too bad because I really began to like her the way I told Hal about her. Maybe she could have been fun to be around. Oh, well, back to the business at hand.

"I asked Hal what's up with the call. How could I help him? And what was this project of his? He laid-out a plot, obviously, from the U-Team because the Gripers could never come-up with a plan; they were really 'complainers' not 'doers'. This plot included explosives and James Bond movie-type plans, definitely not from the Gripers. 'Hell, yes, I'm interested! Where are the other Gripers; why ain't they here, too?' That kinda talk.

"Turns out we were moving into an entirely new phase of griping – now it's gonna be action. The other gripers weren't too eager to actually get their hands dirty. Hal said that I just looked like I might be interested. Hell, yes, I'm interested . . . and so were my bosses. Whada we gotta do? Let's get goin' right now. Damn gubamint's getting bigger the longer we keep talking.

Order of Succession

"Hal led me outside around the back of his house to where a trailer was parked. It was not as big as that 53-footer over in our rest-area parking lot right over there – not by a long shot. This one was about the size of the ones drag-racers take their cars to a drag strip in – ya know an enclosed one with a V-Shaped front – maybe 20-feet or so long with a 5th-wheel hitch. It was just sittin' there without a truck to pull it. I asked him where it came from because I had never seen it here before. Turns-out that Bubba's boys pulled it in last night and asked Hal to take it someplace outta sight and unload it so's nobody would see it . . . or what's inside. Hell, yes, it didn't look all that outta place just sittin' there to begin with. I asked him if they 'asked' or if they 'told'. Hal says, 'Sorta *told*, I guess.' Okay, where we takin' it, and where's the truck to pull it? Hal says, 'My boy, Ray, will be along directly, and wondered if I was up for a little work unloading it?' I told him, 'Hell, yeah, a little exercise is always good for a person.' "

"Well, pretty soon Ray drives in with a Ford F-450 pickup – almost brand new. There must be some money in this family somewhere because Hal's place sure didn't show like it could support this new truck. But, what the hell, I'm just along for the ride. Right? Ray backs-up to the 5th wheel of the trailer and hooks right-up like he was expecting it all along. That's when I caught a glimpse of the truck's license plate – local government. What the . . . ? The plate indicated the Ford was a gubamint vehicle belonging to some local county government in the area. What gives with that? None of that made sense, but the irony was quite significant.

"Anyway, I asked Hal where we were going and I'll follow in my car. Hal told me, 'Not quite. Your car won't make it over those roads. Get in the cab and put this blindfold on.' I'm thinking, 'Blindfold, say what?' But Hal continued, 'We trust you, but not quite that much already. No blindfold, you don't go, and maybe you don't leave this place either.' Now it became real obvious the U-Team had converted Hal, and I assumed, Ray to their cause – whatever it was.

"Okay, blindfold it was, not a problem, just surprised. Will my car be okay here, or should it be parked in your barn? Well, I got into the truck, sat down, belted in, and put the blindfold on. You know those stories about kidnap victims counting seconds and crossing railroad tracks – all that sort of stuff – it's all B.S. Underneath that blindfold,

Order of Succession

I was completely disoriented; I couldn't even tell when we left the house yard. But I did get a peek at my watch just before I tightened the blindfold – 23 minutes past the hour, actually 23 minutes and 38 seconds. I don't know why, but I remember that really well. Ray drove over paved roads – slow then faster until we turned-off onto what seemed like a twisting-like road – still paved, but slower. Finally, we were on what seemed like a dirt road for some distance, I thought. We came to a stop; one of them, probably Hal, got out, and the truck moved a very short distance, and then Hal got back in, and they drove a little further, and then stopped for good. Hal told me we're here and to take-off the blindfold and get out. I did as Hal said. Grabbed a quick look at the watch – 2 minutes and 40 seconds past the next hour – about a 39 minute trip from the outskirts of Thurmont. That could mean we were either still in Maryland or just over the border in Pennsylvania. I got out and stretched, doing a quick scan around the area. Hell, there was no area to look at; we were sort of inside some sort of building and still sorta hanging-outside it, too. The F-450 and trailer were just a bit too long for the drive-through part of the building. Grabbing a quick look outside, I saw some sort of an old, red, barn-looking building with a red roof – maybe a metal roof – across a small pasture – maybe 200 meters away. My best guess was we were probably in some backwoods location, maybe hunting camp, something like that. And judging by the way the shadows fell, it was probably to the west of Hal's building.

"I had to go with the flow. Okay, we're here, wherever here is. 'What needs doin'?' Hal says, 'Ray's gonna back up the trailer over near that chute over there which is coming out of the floor, and we're gonna unload it. Okay?' 'Okay? You bet it's okay. Let's get on with it.' So, we helped guide Ray over near the chute. Hal unlocked two doors – one to the chute itself and the other one to a set of descending stairs. None of this made any sense to me, but oh, well, it's not my barn. Ray backs-up the trailer to the opened doors. I step behind the trailer; let's start unloading. Whoa, here. What's all the stuff already down there. And, wait another damn minute. The walls of the barn formed a concrete-block building with walls, maybe, 8- to 10-inches thick and painted all white. Electricity, too. What the hell is this place? I kept my mouth shut, and swallowed all my questions for the time being. I did tell them that it was a nice enough place, though.

Order of Succession

"Hal told Ray, 'This trailer gets unloaded into Bunkers 3 and 4.' Say what? Bunkers? Aren't those usually for explosives and ammunition? The trailer doors are swung open to shed some light on the load. Exactly the kinda stuff that bunkers are built for – explosives and munitions. Never in my life did I see so much stuff, for blowing-up all kinds of stuff, that wasn't in a Government bunker. That enclosed car trailer had a whole lot of stuff that goes KA-BOOM in it, and we were going to carry the load down to Bunkers 3 and 4. Then it struck me: Does 3 and 4 mean there's a 1 and 2 and maybe a 5 and 6, too? Now I understood why Hal insisted on the blindfold.

"I asked Hal about Bunkers 3 and 4: 'Where are they and how do I get my boxes to them?' Well, you ain't gonna believe this: there's a small conveyor system. It's installed down a slanted shaft in the chute and along a tunnel-of-sorts extending out from the 'barn' about maybe 100-feet long and maybe 15-20 feet underground – that's how Hal described the bunker system down there. Everybody has to stay grounded, electrically-speaking to avoid static-electric discharges and stuff like that. Hal told me he designed and built everything in there himself.

"Some of the boxes in the trailer still had US Army markings on them. Most of the boxes were high-explosives – plastique, like Semtex and/or C4. A few boxes were marked as containing DEMEX – an explosive available in sheet format primarily used for demolition, sometimes underwater demolition. There were also boxes of fuses and detonators. All went down the conveyor. Hal stayed with me topside, while Ray worked the lower end, where Bunkers 3 and 4 are. Even though Hal was supposed to be helping unload the trailer, his main job was watching me do the work; I understood that. That was not a problem right then.

"Before Ray came back upstairs, Hal asked me if I wanted to take a little recon trip. Sure, why not? Now, this group was getting interesting. But with all of this stuff – the barn/ammo-dump, explosives, car trailers, gubamint plates on the pick-up, all of this stuff and some other subtle hints at more plans – well, now the question became 'Just who is the leader of what?'.

"There's a hellova lot of money just in that so-called barn building, not to mention all of the explosives in those bunkers. To this day, I still don't even know how many bunkers there are down there. Now, Hal's wondering if I want to take a recon trip. The trip it is.

Order of Succession

"For the trip back down the mountain – we were on some kinda mountain somewhere in Maryland, I think – Hal had me put the blindfold back on again. The car trailer was dropped-off at Hal's place again, along with me, too. Ray disappeared in the Ford F-450 – that gubamint F-450. And, yes, my car was still okay just sitting in Hal's yard. No problems."

ORDER OF SUCCESSION

9 – Ridin' His High Horse

Nearing 11:45, Saturday, 14-July: Westbound I-8, Exit 51, at Buckman Springs Rest Area, Mojave Desert, California

TIME: 11:34 PDT

Smitty: "Say, do ya mind if we take a short break?"

Rocky: "Sounds good. Besides, I gotta check-up on some things with Coms. Meet you back here in say 15, then."

Time: Saturday, 14-July, 11:45 PDT

Smitty: "Thanks for the break; I really needed that. What'd Coms have to say?

Rhodes: "Nothing. He hasn't heard any more from our source. You're right; it does sound like a James Bond movie. By all means, please continue."

Smitty: "Where did we break-off. Oh, yeah, Hal had mapped-out three recon trips down to D.C. for us. I'm gonna condense these because they take a lot of talkin'.

"Well, the next day, Hal made arrangements to meet me at a local restaurant up there in Thurmont for what I thought was a small breakfast meeting, but Hal walks in with the whole damn U-Team and Ray in tow. The table for two is now much too small for the seven of us; so, we moved to a larger table in a smaller room in the back. However, now Bubba seems to treat Hal as the leader-of-the-pack so-to-speak. Now, I'm still just as confused about who's who in this zoo. But, I went with the flow.

"Hal led this planning session. The members of the U-Team just kept nodding their heads at everything Hal said. Things like his favorite rants:

Order of Succession

"Hal's standard rant was about, 'This here President's the worst liberal bastard of all those other liberal bastards elected from back in the '80s all the way into the early 20-teens. Now we're all damn broke, stuck paying for all those wonderful benefits for others that we don't even qualify for ourselves. That first bastard ruined the middle class, and this last liberal bastard put the finishing touches on it so now all we got are just two classes – the rich and the poor. This damn President screwed all us 'true' Americans.'"

"Hal just carried-on right into his next rant, 'That first bastard flat-out bought the election that put the country on the downhill slide to bankruptcy. And he didn't even have to spend any of his own campaign money. He just promised the gubamint would give everybody all the bennies he said they were entitled to. And now . . . Now, us suckers gotta pay for his promises then, and we still gotta pay for even more of them added by all 'dem bastard liberal presidents – up to and including this here president. We gotta fix all this crap before we're all flat-broke commies. Crap, we're socialists now; being a commie is just one more step down that road. And our home-grown bastards didn't even remember that even the real, red commies from the 50s on into the 90s couldn't make communism work. So, now we gotta try to prove them wrong and show them how they shoulda done it? Give me a friggin' break.

"Back in the presidential elections back in the 1940s, now, there was a true Socialist in the running. Hell, he was a loyal member of the Socialist Party and everything; he wasn't even ashamed to admit it. I got summa his quotes right here, always keep 'em with me – for inspiration. Here it is – And I quote:'

> "The American people will never knowingly adopt socialism. But, under the name of 'liberalism,' they will adopt every fragment of the socialist program, until one day America will be a socialist nation, without knowing how it happened." And "I no longer need to run as a Presidential Candidate for the Socialist Party. The Democratic Party has adopted our platform." And "The American people will take socialism, but they will not take the label." (from his 1934 Speech?)
> -- Norman Thomas, U.S. Socialist Party presidential candidate 1940, 1944, and 1948

'Ain't that some crap, from way back in the '40s; that's over 80 years ago, closing in on 100 years. I keep it close to me for inspiration.'"

Order of Succession

{Smitty's aside to Rhodes: "I'm gonna digress here for some background. As a side note to Hal's ranting, he usually carried a whole deck of these cards in his shirt pocket just for his inspiration. He even handed-out copies of his favorite ones. I still have mine somewhere as souvenirs."}

"Hal was on a roll by the time he got to his last rant: 'It weren't bad enough that those thievin' illegal aliens were given amnesty once back in the 80s – even with the promise that was the first and only time. Those ferin-ners just kept comin' across the border to El Norte, the good ol' U.S. of A. Hell, you know we – you and me – would do the same damn thing 'cause there ain't no punishment. We suckers are afraid to shoot those trespassin' bastards. We feed'em, give their kids citizenship, schoolin', and every damn thing just like they belong here. We all know that crap ain't right. And why? Because our elected politician bastards down there in D.C. want to keep suckin' every teat they can find so they can keep feedin' from the public trough – the one you and me keep fillin' every friggin' year. Well, those bastard politicians decided that the first time was so friggin' successful, they up an' did it again in 2014 through into 2024, too. 'Hell, they're already here, so let's just let another 12 million more illegals in.' I don't think anybody in this room wouldn't help anybody who needs it, but they gotta be here legal-like, not sneakin' in across the border just for the bennies. They ain't earned nothing here, why should they get handouts from our hard paid taxes. I'll betcha, those politicians ain't gonna want to support any of dem ferin-ner trespassers in their *own* damn homes. How'd they like to havta pay them squatters' medical bills outta their own pockets? And give'em food off'n their own tables, and send their kids to school, and all that other crap they wanna give 'em paid for outta their own personal bank accounts? I betcha they wouldn't stand for none of that crap if'n they had to pay for it themselves; no, sir, not one bit. I'll betcha that fer damn sure! Can you tell me why we should then, huh? We gotta stand-up on our hind legs and tell'em 'NO FRIGGIN' MORE'. With our good ol' boys right here and some of their contacts, we gonna show'em down there in D.C. We gonna show'em real good, ain't we?'"

"There were noddin' heads all around the room. This was the most worked-up I ever saw Hal. Later in the project, Hal got even more worked-up to the point of pounding on the nearest table, machine, car, you name it, and spittin' and droolin' as he continued. Sorta like he worked himself into a real verbal lather.

Order of Succession

"Hal just kept going on. 'And I got me another adage right here from even further back than that other one – over 250 years ago, too. It's another one I also keep on me at all times. It's from one of the founders of this here country, and he oughta know how this damned country should be run. Damn straight 'bout that.'

"When the people fear the government, there is tyranny. When the government fears the people, there is liberty."
- - Thomas Jefferson

"Note that Hal also had lots of Jefferson's quotes framed and hanging on the walls in his house and the barn. Guess he wanted to have his motivation surrounding him all the time. But the one he kept repeating, really sort of like a mantra of some sort under his breath was:

"An armed person is a citizen.
An unarmed person is a subject."
- - Unknown

"All three were also posted in that disguised, concrete, mountain barn – probably, more properly, Hal's armory or ammo dump.

ORDER OF SUCCESSION

10 – 2 Recons of the Primary Target

Nearing 11:45, Saturday, 14-July: Westbound I-8, Exit 51, at Buckman Springs Rest Area, Mojave Desert, California

TIME: Saturday, 14-July, 12:45 PDT

Smitty: "Say, do ya mind if we take a short break?"

Rocky: "Sounds good. Besides, I gotta check-up on some things with Coms. Meet you back here in say 15, then."

"**Well, Hal** finally slowed down to take a drink of water and then continued: 'Well, here's the plan, boys. We're gonna recon all sides of that friggin' White House to see if we can take it down – right down to the damned ground, boys.'

"I know I had a disbelieving look on my face. The White House? Are you outta your ever-lovin' mind? All right, now, exactly how are we gonna do that? What's the plan?

" 'The plan was sort of simple, really. We all go down to D.C. and walk around like tourists taking pictures of all sorts of things – especially, good ol' Number 1600.' "

"Hal provided brand-new digital cameras to everybody. We were supposed to take pictures of everything out to a radius of two city blocks from the WH. This included: addresses, buildings' names, storm sewers, fences, man-holes, pictures from each subject lookin' toward da WH – he liked using 'da WH' – with a slurred 'The'– instead of saying the entire name, 'The White House' or 'TWH'. Stuff like that, but especially, parking lots and structures, and buildings with rentable spaces looking toward The White . . . , oops, da WH. Stuff like offices and hotels; that type of stuff. Oh, yeah, large, but squat buildings. That kinda stuff.

Order of Succession

Here's our first trip

"**Next Monday,** I rode DC's Metro's Red Line from the Shady Grove station down to the Metro Center Station. I got off there so I didn't have to wait to transfer to another train for just a short distance; I just walked a few blocks and done. All seven of us met Monday at 09:30 in Lafayette Park right across from the front of da WH.

"Yeah, so, off we went, all seven of us; that's the four U-Team guys, Hal, Ray, and me. We took all sorts of pictures and wrote all sorts of notes about distances to da WH. The other local Thurmont boys in the Gripers group couldn't afford to take-off from their jobs during the week to go taking trips all the way down to D.C. They stayed back home in Thurmont – workin'.

"There was some sort of method to Hal's madness; Hal split us up into four groups in order 'to cover all four quadrants surrounding our primary target' – as Hal repeated every once in a while – like he was really focused on da WH. He had marked-up our respective maps with our designated quadrants all outlined by a heavy red line. A 2-man team was assigned to Recon Area 1: the area north of da WH. But Hal left Lafayette Park out of Recon Area 1 and assigned it to Team 4.

"The second 2-man team was assigned to Recon Area 2: on the west side of da WH. This quadrant is adjacent to the Eisenhower Executive Office Building.

"My U-Team partner, Bubba, and I were assigned to what I call Recon Area 3 on the east side of da WH. This quadrant abuts the Department of the Treasury Building.

"The remaining team member was assigned to Recon Area 4, which was actually, two areas: Lafayette Park on the north side of da WH, and The Ellipse and Constitution Avenue on the south side of da WH. Basically, most of this quadrant lies between da WH and The Ellipse and the National Mall. "We all split-up and hustled off to our assigned Recon Areas. We were supposed to meet back in Lafayette Park at 16:00 – a little irony there. So, off we went to take pictures and make notes about this, that, and the other. In our quadrant, we quickly discovered that almost half of it was gubamint buildings of some agency, jurisdiction, or another – gubamint buildings with guards at the entrances who wanted to see some ID and a reason for going inside. The federal gubamint

Order of Succession

has the Department of Commerce, National Oceanic and Atmospheric Administration, National Telecommunications and Information Administration, USAD, and the Ronald Reagan and International Trade Center Buildings. The District of Columbia also has offices in our area: District of Columbia Government and the Mayor's Executive Office.

"Physically, the Department of the Treasury Building acts as a wall between TWH and a good portion of Recon Area 3. That cut our area down by about half. But we went about taking pictures and taking notes anyway.

"At the end of the day, Hal collected all of the cameras and notes for 'safe-keepin' he said. Hal said his team will go over the pictures and notes, and we should meet again on Friday evening at his place in Thurmont to review the results.

"**Well,** four days later on Friday, we met in Hal's barn. He used several 4'x8' sheets of plywood to fashion a large table supported by wooden crates and saw-horses. A big map was laid-out on its top – a map of the four Recon Areas surrounding da WH. This was going to be our review of what we had documented four days earlier. Hal called on each of the Recon Teams to explain what they found and observed. Since this was the first meeting like this, no one was really sure what they should be reporting, so, it was all just a lot of 'hemmin' and hawin'.

"Hal had to lead the teams to pull out what he said was necessary 'tactical data'. Recon Team 1, the team that had the north side of da WH said they really didn't see too much with a direct line-of-site of da WH. That is, with the exception of two blocks on H Street, directly across from Lafayette Park – H between 15th and 17th. These blocks pretty much faced da WH with Lafayette Park in between. Team 1 thought that the prestigious Hay Adams Hotel might be a possibility as well. The Hay Adams looked to have about eight floors including the roof, which was supposed to have an open-air area that could be reserved for private parties.

"The rest of the photos and notes detailed these and a coupla others. But we think the buildings we noted seem like the best ones for our purposes."

"**Team 2's turn.** If you recall, Team 2 was supposed to recon the west side of da WH. Basically, da WH is sandwiched between The Eisenhower

Order of Succession

Executive Office Building [16] (EEOB) and the Treasury Of the United States Building, both of which basically shield da WH from everything else on its east and west sides. 'The EEOB is one long building, and even though it is only 5 to 6 floors high, da WH sits neatly behind it. However, the former Corcoran Gallery of Art sits on the intersection of 17th Street and New York, and it covers the block down to 17th and E Street, NW. Now, it might be possible that we could get an unobstructed line-of-sight from the roof of the Corcoran straight to da WH by going around the south end of the EEOB. Don't know for sure about the trees, but a straightedge on Google Maps seems to just miss the southeast corner of the EEOB. Nothing else in our quadrant seems to have any possibilities.'

"**Hal announces,** 'Well, Recon Team 3, it's your turn; you had the quadrant to the east of da WH.' So, now it was our turn to describe what we found on our recon. Which wasn't really all that much, but we laid-out our findings, trying to make things look brighter than we thought they actually were. We, just like Recon Team 2, have an obstacle blocking our quadrant from da WH – in our case, the Department of the Treasury building, to be exact.

" 'However, the two buildings on the intersection of 15th and F Streets, NW may hold promise. Oh, yeah, this is a 'T' intersection with the Treasury Building crossing the 'T'. The building on the south side of this intersection is a hotel, the Hotel Washington; it's about eight floors tall; Treasury is 'four floors plus its roof' tall. The building immediately behind the Hotel looks to be about nine floors; it's still another hotel named the Willard.

" 'Metropolitan Square, that's the name on the building across F Street from the Washington Hotel. It's about 12 stories to the roof. Don't know what's inside – office or shops; not enough time to recon the inside now.

" 'Going north up to the southeast corner of Pennsylvania and 15th, NW, The Washington Building may also offer some sort of line-of-sight over The Treasury Building. Would have to get access to that roof to make sure.

---

16 The Eisenhower Executive Office Building (EEOB) is frequently referred to as The Old Executive Office Building (OEOB) because that was its name before 'Old; was changed to 'Eisenhower' during President Bill Clinton's administration. On May 07, 2002, an official rededication ceremony was held, which was attended by President George W. Bush.

Order of Succession

" 'The line-of-site is the issue, what with the Treasury Building situated in between the hotels, The Washington Building, and F Street and da WH.'."

"**Recon Team 4** was only one guy, namely Hal. He laid-out the story of his recon. He covered the area around Lafayette Park north of da WH and the Ellipse to the south and along Constitution Avenue. Apparently, Hal had begun on the south side of da WH. I wondered why, but, oh, well, right now, doesn't matter much, I guess. Well, anyway, Hal had done some work in his area. He suggested that the building on the northeast corner of 18th and E Streets, NW, there's a building that's about 8 floors, and it sits on a raised plaza that adds about another story above E Street at that corner. It's bordered by New York Avenue on the other side. And it's right behind the Corcoran Art Museum, and it's a couple of stories taller than the Corcoran Gallery. Supposedly, the prime tenant is a labor union. He glared at Recon Team 2, apparently for missing this building in their report. Like someone else said, a straightedge sort of works – directly to da WH, but as we all observed, it's the friggin' trees. Success lies in getting' around all those friggin' trees.

"Walkin' up and down Constitution didn't turn-up any decent locations. Too low, too open, that kinda crap. Decent lines-of-sight seem to be oriented on the north-to-south axis of da WH. That should have been anticipated even before going down to D.C.: The east/west axis runs right through the EEOB and The Treasury; there's no unobstructed position to even view those ends of da WH. Just look at how da WH is sandwiched in there; Google Maps clearly shows that.

"North to Lafayette Park provided more interesting opportunities. Not even going to worry about Blair House for our purposes, unless of course, somebody important visits during our exercises. Crap, that'd be impressive any way it's done.

"Along the north edge on the Park on H Street, I think we've already identified most of the possible sites. The Hay Adams probably offered one of the best lines-of-sight, but, again, it's the trees.

"The east side of the Park also has some interesting possibilities. Not directly on the street, but adjacent to the Park are two bank branches, a national bank and an international one – quite fitting if you stop to think about it – the thieving bastards have set-up shop right across the street

Order of Succession

from the U.S. Treasury and within spittin' distance of da friggin' WH, where they plot how to spend our money on their pet projects, killing-off the middle class to expand the poor class. They're all thieving bastard socialists not even afraid to break socialist doctrine by taking capitalists straight from the capitalist's Treasury – straight from The U.S. Treasury. Come to think of it, maybe it really is socialist doctrine. They ought to just install a vacuum pipe so they can suck the money right out of The Treasury. And right across 15th Street is another damn branch bank, a much smaller regional bank chain. Beautiful old building, but the trees screw-up the line-of-sight.

"Then there's a nice older building, the Washington Building, across New York Avenue, that's about 11 stories, plus roof. Might have a line-of-sight right over the top of Treasury. I think Team 3 mentioned all these buildings in their report.

"Hal announces his plans for next week. We are supposed to meet again in D.C. the following Monday at 09:30-hours. This time, not in Lafayette Park, but over at the Vietnam Memorial on the south side of Constitution Avenue just inside The Mall. See you then. Then he dismissed us by telling us he has a conference call coming-up in 15 minutes about some money for this project. 'Til Monday then. Bye, bye.'

Smitty: This is good time to take a break.

Here's the second trip
Time: 13:47 PDT

Smitty: "Break time, okay?"

Rocky: "You bet."

30 minutes later

Smitty: "You should have sort of the flavor of the stuff Hal was lookin' for – or was it what the U-Team was lookin' for.

"Anyway, here's the second recon cut down to size.

Smitty: "So, the following week, we made a second trip down to D.C., acting like tourists again – cameras, note books, and all – the whole ball of wax.

Order of Succession

"Our second recon trip began at the Vietnam Memorial right on the National Mall. This time, Hal wanted us to widen our recon perimeter to include some monuments around the National Mall. Go to the top of the Washington Monument like regular tourists. Take pictures toward da WH – especially at da WH. All sounded simple enough. And I hadn't even been a real tourist in D.C. yet, anyway, despite having to visit some 'offices' down near The Mall. This time, Hal split us up into three groups, juggling some of the Team members so that we were not with an earlier member. I think happenstance stepped in again; Hal put Bubba and me together again as a team. Hal also provided us with the same cameras and note books again. He also provided some hand-held radios that looked like small walkie-talkies; coulda passed for old-style cell-phones. Hal made a point that these walkie-talkies are old enough that they didn't have any GPS chips for tracking the users. Extremely cautious or paranoid – whichever it was, is anybody's guess.

"Hal assigned Recon Team 1 to the Washington Monument. He told Team 1 to get a move-on because the Washington Monument takes a lot more waitin'time to go up in the elevator, 'Ya know, day let only so many tourists up there every day. Don't miss it.', and off they hustled.

"Recon Team 2 was sent to the National Mall for more tourist-like gawking. Team 2 was facin' a whole lot of walking from the Lincoln Memorial up Constitution Avenue to the Capitol Building – and returning back using Independence Avenue on the other side of The Mall.

'Bubba and I were Team 3 again and were assigned to recon the Jefferson Memorial on the other side of the Tidal Basin. I didn't really understand why Hal made our assignment way over there. Jefferson is way the hell and gone outside the perimeter around of da WH that we were told was so important last week. Seemed like such a screwed-up detour; it made no sense to either of us. But what did we know; it was Hal's plan. And I didn't want to complain too loudly with Bubba walking right there beside me.

"That 'walk' over to the Jefferson Memorial is a real schlep. We walked-up Constitution Avenue just getting the 'lay-of-the-land'. We continued on Constitution to 15th Street and turned right toward the Memorial. What a friggin' mess the streets and roads are in D.C.! That city is really built for cars, not pedestrians; plus there were a lot fewer cars back then when it was built, too. But, hey, as tourists, we fit right

Order of Succession

in; we had no idea if the maps lied or not. We finally got to the Jefferson Memorial and wanted to take a break on the steps. Bubba wanted to poke around the building and grounds; he settled for taking a short break – into the basement area to hit the latrines followed by 10 minutes sitting on the steps outside.

"On the way over, Bubba deflected questions about who he was, what he did, etc. Nothing personal left his lips, and I reciprocated. I got the impression that he had some sort of military or high-security training, though. But nothing concrete to confirm my suspicions.

"Back to playing tourist. Bubba reminded us that we were supposed to be taking pictures in relation to da WH.

"Bubba asked me, 'So, where the hell is da WH from here anyway?'

"I pointed as I said, 'Over there, on the other side of the water.'

"Then while he's holding the map, he asks 'The river is way over there to the left, what is this water right here?' as he points to it right in front of us.

"I point to the map and tell him, 'Bubba, that's called the Tidal Basin.' He doesn't sound like he was too sharp with the intel side of his training – especially, since he was looking directly at the map.

"Well, there's da WH right off there in the distance – due North by my reckoning. Hey, what a deal! Can you believe the trees on the other side of the Tidal Basin about half-way to da WH are even cut-down.

"We took pictures and spread-out maps and brochures just like other tourists. We also made a quick pass around the inside of the Jefferson's Rotunda. Circled the statue and read the inscriptions on the walls. We found the gift shop on the river side of the memorial, mainly to use the rest-rooms again.

"Time to schlep back to the Vietnam Memorial. This time, however, we decided to take a route up the west side of the Tidal Basin past the Franklin Delano Roosevelt and Martin Luther King Memorials. Back in the early 20-teens, right when the MLK Memorial was to be officially dedicated, somebody noticed that one part of the carved-in-stone verbiage seemed to make MLK sound like a cheerleader, one of those sports-like cheerleaders, which did not project the appropriate symbolism of his life, so, they wanted it fixed. Well, we walked

ORDER OF SUCCESSION

around and through the Memorial, like tourists, and 'the fix' shows. Guess it didn't work-out the way they hoped. Say, did you ever hear that, according to the news stories at the time, the stones for the MLK Memorial statuary were reported to have been carved over in China and shipped to the U.S. on a Greek ship, no less. If that's true, ain't that a hoot to have the Memorial for MLK, an American hero of a bygone era, carved in China! Can't believe that one!

"We angled slightly west and passed the Korean War Veterans Memorial and then on toward the Lincoln Memorial. We crossed the National Mall between the Lincoln Memorial and the west end of the Reflecting Pool, ending-up back at the Vietnam Memorial. Took pictures along the entire return route; none a straight, clear shot toward da WH along this route – trees, highways, and other monuments in the way.

"We met the other teams at the Vietnam Memorial as they straggled in from their assignments. Again, Hal collected all of the cameras, walkie-talkies, and our notes. He told us he'd contact us within three days.

Order of Succession

11 – Meet at the Gun Platform

Nearing 11:45, Saturday, 14-July: Westbound I-8, Exit 51, at Buckman Springs Rest Area, Mojave Desert, California

TIME: Saturday, 14-July, 13:54 PDT

Smitty: "Say, do ya mind if we take a short break?"

Rocky: "Sounds good. Besides, I gotta check-up on some things with Coms. Meet you back here in say 15, then."

Time: Saturday, 14-July, 13:56 PDT

PFC Berkeley intruded: "Cap'n Rhodes. Sir, sorry for interrupting like this, but I thought maybe you need to know about something. I think we may have found the source of that slightly high radiation over in the semi-trailer. Maybe,"

Rhodes: "Hold that thought, PFC. We'll be with you shortly – over at the trailer."

Berkeley: "Sir, could you make that over at the remote gun-platform instead?"

Rhodes: "PFC, you did say the remotely-controlled gun-platform over on the west hillside, right? Instead of the trailer, right? Okay. Get a Humvee; we're taking a break from this right now."

Rhodes: "Smitty, I like your background so far, but let's take a break here and go check this out."

Berkeley pulled-up in the Humvee. He asked Rocky, sorry, Cap'n Rhodes to hold the Geiger counter that was on the floor of the front passenger seat. Despite his bum leg, Smitty maneuvered himself into the rear seat for the short ride over to the platform – only about a mile or so.

Order of Succession

Berkeley: "Sir, me and the other squad members were over here to just look this gun-platform thing over, not to touch it or anything like that. It's just that we have never seen one of those before. It's just like in a movie; if you know what I mean. Well, I had the Geiger counter; didn't want to just leave it lyin' around over at the trailer. I didn't realize it was still turned on, and it starts clickin' and beepin' and stuff. Not all that loud, but it was more active than when we were walkin' over here. We were right close to that platform, so I waved it around a bit, and it kept clickin'. So, we sort of kept our distance a bit. But I think there's something in at least one of the ammo boxes, maybe both of them."

"Rhodes: "Damn it all! That's all we need out here – a radioactive site. Okay, PFC, how hot does this thing look; how dangerous is it? Give me a guess."

Berkeley parked the Humvee near the gun platform , but not too close to it.

Berkeley: "Wellllllll, it's just a little hotter than the trailer, but it's still hot, hotter than normal air. I'm not really trained in this radioactive stuff yet, but I'm willin' to pop the lid on the ammo box just to find out what's inside. Know what I mean? Hell, let's do it; I wanna' know what to report when we call this in. Here, Cap'n, you can even hold the counter, and I'll open that box up. Write down a couple of readings off the counter before we do that, will ya, sir? Write down the clear-air reading, say, about 10 feet away or however far 'til it looks normal. Then get the reading right next to the box. When I pop it open; I'm not gonna leave it open very long, get the reading, and then we slam this shut. Okay, ready, Cap'n?"

Captain Rhodes recorded the first two readings, then nodded toward Berkeley.

Berkeley: "Here we go." And he undid the latches and pulled the top away from the body of the box. Rhodes got the reading. They were pretty fast; in fact, too fast for any bystanders to see anything inside the box before Berkeley quickly closed the box. Rhodes and Berkeley conferred, and Rhodes handed the counter back to Berkeley. Berkeley carefully set it down on the ground over 15 feet away and said he'd be back shortly, got into the Humvee and left.

Order of Succession

He returned shortly with a wooden branch maybe eight feet long, some plastic tie-wraps, some sort of vehicle mirror, and a digital camera; said he saw them in the trailer – the mirror, he got off the L-1 car since the car was useless and un-drivable now anyway. As an improvising Marine, Berkeley fastened the mirror to one end of the branch using the tie-wraps and then fastened the counter's sensor/pick-up on the branch very close to the mirror. The body of the counter would have to be set on the ground as near to the ammo box as possible.

Satisfied with the way the branch handled, Berkeley handed the counter to Captain Rhodes and the camera to Smitty. Smitty couldn't figure-out WTH Berkeley was up to. Okay, his plan was to have Rhodes stand back from the ammo box and scan the outside edges and seams of the box; maybe there was crack or something. Rhodes performed the scan as Berkeley described, but the readings were pretty uniform across all surfaces, edges, and seams. So, they recorded the readings and assumed the box was not broken anywhere.

The next part of Berkeley's plan was to have Rhodes position the mirror over the open ammo box so Smitty could take a picture of the mirror showing the contents when he opened it once again. Rhodes and Smitty practiced the procedure with a canteen sitting on the ground. It took a little practice to get the mirror just right so Smitty could focus on it and get a decent picture. They took quite a few pictures and looked at them on the camera's screen until they got a few they liked. Now they were ready to try it for real over at the ammo box.

They all got into position. Berkeley opened the box and quickly stepped away. Rhodes positioned the mirror over the box, trying to hold the stick and mirror as steady as possible. Smitty took pictures, mostly close-ups of the mirror. Thank goodness that the sun was bright enough to get decent pictures. Rhodes gave Berkeley the signal, and he slammed the lid back down on the box, fastened the latches, and skedaddled away as quickly as he could.

Berkeley drove the trio of experimenters back to the rest area parking lot. Rhodes laid the counter and the branch down on the ground beside a shady table. Rhodes kept the camera while he went and found Sergeant Winthrop and had him bring his EOD guys over.

Rhodes, addressing the EOD Squad: "Marines, we got another problem you might be able to help solve. You probably already heard

Order of Succession

about the radiation in the trailer. Well, PFC Berkeley happened to find more radiation over at the remote-control gun-platform."

He explained what we did and why we called on Sgt. Winthrop. "We need to draw on your knowledge to figure-out what we got. Here are the radiation readings we recorded over there at the ammo box. Here are the photos we took. We need to know what you all think we are dealing with." Rhodes handed his recorded notes on the readings to the nearest EOD member and the camera to Sgt. Winthrop. "We'll let you look at this crap and be back here in 10 for your best guesstimates." Rhodes, Berkeley, and Smitty walked briskly to the information building so they could wash their hands and at least feel cleaner – as if that did any good.

When we returned, Sgt. Winthrop led the discussion, "Sir, we think what you all stumbled on is . . . is ammo loaded with depleted uranium (DU) bullets. We don't know why the bad-guys are using that shit, and we have no idea where they got it either."

Rhodes: "Are you kiddin' me? What the hell would you need that crap for in an operation such as this one?"

Winthrop: "Well, sir, we don't know the 'exact-why' of having DU ammo at this site, but we have a guesstimate about that. After we figured-out what could have happened out here, we think we may have an idea about the 'why'. Since the limo pulled-off where it apparently was supposed to, maybe there was no need for this DU ammo. But suppose the driver didn't want to take the exit off I-8; that's the 'maybe variable' in this idea.

"Please try to follow this theory of ours. Okay, suppose the limo driver got cold feet about whatever was planned for the President – and maybe for himself, too. Now suppose the driver kept driving west on I-8, the kidnapping plot at this rest area goes in the crapper big time – not to mention all of the money and personnel labor wasted. Okay, the limo passes the exit, and the driver thinks he did a good deed. However, the planners didn't tell the driver every little aspect in the plot – including back-up 'what-ifs'. The remote-controlled platform is located about a mile, plus or minus, further west on I-8.

"The bullets on the DU ammo are heavier than normal for the caliber, and it also has some armor-piercing characteristics. DU ammo is used in tanks, the big, heavy-duty stuff – just not in this smaller caliber. Here's what we think may have been in the ultimate plan.

125

Order of Succession

"So, the limo keeps on I-8, and the remote gun's camera watches the road. There's not supposed to be any traffic at this time because all of it's supposed to blocked, so the remote's C&C wouldn't have any problem figuring-out which car to target. So, the driver doesn't turn-off at the exit. Here comes the limo, the camera picks-up the limo, C&C focuses on the limo, and the remote gun is set to go. When the limo is within effective hitting range, C&C fires and keeps firing. Hell, there were two whole ammo cans full of this DU crap up there, if your pictures are right and the cans were both full when this plot started yesterday.

"Here's our best guess about the why the DU stuff is out here. The DU ammo is, theoretically, armor piercing, and the limo is an armored car. We think the planners were hoping this smaller caliber DU ammo – well, smaller than tank-vs.-tank stuff – would take-out the limo or at least stop it if the tires could be shot-out. Remember, that gun is .50-Cal., which can also be used on tanks, maybe not as effectively as a larger caliber weapon or an anti-tank missile, but it can still give a tank a big piece of its mind. If it doesn't penetrate the main body of the tank, those poor tankers on the inside will surely know they've been thunked; they sure as hell don't like being a target.

"And then there's the matter of the IED arrangement under the westbound lanes of I-8. We think both of those, the remote gun and the IEDs were supposed to be sort of fail-safes if the limo didn't turn off for the rest-area. In other words, 'We gotcha one way or the other'.

"Sir, one more thing from our observations. The contaminated area inside the trailer is considerably larger than what's needed for the two ammo cans for the platform gun we found at the gun location. Long story short, we think it is possible that there may have been some other radioactive cargo sharing that space with the ammo cans. Please note that we are saying 'possibly' not 'probably' because we don't have any evidence one way or another – just the hole in the cargo area in the trailer is larger than necessary. Any questions, sir?"

Rhodes: "Smitty, you were in the Presidential motorcade. Does the sergeant's theory make sense to you? Do you think it's a doable plan out here?"

Smitty: "Well, yes and no. Let's assume the purpose of all of this is to actually kidnap POTUS, then the first part of the plan – all that planning to drop the bridge on the limo – that makes sense for the kidnapping part. But the rest of the theory – the part about the remote gun and the IEDs – that probably wouldn't work for kidnapping. But, if those, what did you call them, DU bullets were actually armor-piercing, then I think the purpose and intent changes from kidnapping to assassination. Just kill POTUS outright and be done with it. What I don't understand, though, is if they could kidnap him out of the car, why couldn't they just kidnap him from the limo out in the open on I-8. I mean there is a relatively short distance from the IED to where the tunnel from under the bridge surfaced over there. But I think the ultimate purpose was to assassinate him if the limo got past the exit off-ramp – pure and simple."

Rhodes: "Maybe if they tried to kidnap POTUS in the open on I-8, there may have been a fire-fight. One that maybe they didn't have enough people on-site to take-on. Say, Smitty, doesn't POTUS usually have one or more choppers circling overhead when he travels? Were they up there today – sorry, yesterday?

Smitty: "With all this stuff that went on, I completely forgot about them. No, they were not available to the best of my knowledge. Replaying yesterday's events in my mind, I don't recall seeing any helos from inside my car, C-3. I can't t tell you who or why they were pulled off."

ORDER OF SUCCESSION

12 – 3rd Recon of The Primary Target

Almost 15:00, Saturday, 14-July: Westbound I-8, Exit 51, at Buckman Springs Rest Area, Mojave Desert, California

TIME: 15:18 PDT

Back in their makeshift SCIF, Smitty continued filling-in Rhodes about Hal's group.

"**Hal kept his word.** Three days later, he contacted us and arranged another 'recon mission' in four days. We were going to D.C., again at the Vietnam Memorial. However, this time, we were supposed to be dressed like workmen – laborers, tradesmen, or contractors. He'd fill us in when we meet-up. All of us were present at 08:30 as Hal instructed – all, that is, except Hal. Ray was there, but he was dressed in a coat and tie, not at all like a laborer. Must have been some last minute change by Hal that we weren't told about. By 09:12, several recon'ers were looking for rest rooms. We agreed to split-up, find relief, and return by 09:45. We left one of the U-Team there just in case Hal showed-up. Just as we feared, Hal showed-up right after we left; he was peeved when we got back at 09:43.

"Hal assigned the teams their recon areas: 'Okay now that we're all here, today's assignments are to check-out the insides of some buildings. Same teams as before when we walked around the quadrants around da WH.'

" 'Since we won't be able to get into the Treasury or the Eisenhower Executive Office Buildings, Team 1, see if you can find-out anything about the insides of the Commerce Building at 15th Street between E and Constitution, NW. Also the Ronald Reagan Office Building right behind the Commerce Building over on 14th Street, also between E and

ORDER OF SUCCESSION

Constitution, NW. Here are some ID badges and licenses for an HVAC and electrical contractor; memorize your names and addresses. This clipboard has some service requests for the top floor. Once up there, see if you can get access to the roof on the west side of either building – Commerce Building is preferred because it's closer to da WH.'

" 'There's not enough people here for a complete team for Team 2; Ray's coming with me. (Now addressing the sole remaining member of Team 2) Hal told him to, 'Go over to the former Corcoran Gallery of Art on 17th Street over on the west side of da WH. Look like you're taking in the art.' Only at the Corcoran, Hal wanted him to find out if there was an easy access to the roof on the east side of the building. 'Here are your IDs, licenses, and clipboard. Not any current 'service requests', but checking-out expanding facilities for a new art exhibit supposed to be opening in nine months or so. Easy job for one guy.'

" 'Team 3, go to the Hotel Washington with the same assignment – see if you can get to the top floor and see if you can get to the roof to see if there's an unobstructed line-of-sight to da WH over the top roof of the Treasury Building. Then go north to the buildings just north of the Hotel Washington between F and G, in the odd-numbers of the 600 block of 15th Street, NW. Scope-out the same thing. Here are your IDs, license, and clipboard with service orders. Any questions, any of you teams? Good. Then be on your ways and meet back here – let's see it's 10:30 hours now – be back here in five and a half hours at 16:00.' "

"Somebody asked, 'Hey, Hal, what are you and Ray gonna do?' "

"Hal responded that, 'We're gonna recon the north side of da WH around Lafayette Park. Paying special attention to the taller buildings. Shouldn't be too difficult for y'all. And you got your radios, right? Call and let us know if anything needs special attention, okay? Good, then be gone.'

"I found-out later during our subsequent review meeting that Hal and Ray actually seemed to concentrate on the Hay Adams Hotel – especially the top floor rooms and the watering hole on the roof that's reportedly only open during the warm months. The Hay Adams certainly offers a line-of-sight directly in line with the North Entrance of da WH – right smack-dab right up to the friggin' front door. They also checked-out the AFL-CIO Building on 16th Street directly behind St. John's Episcopal Church on the corner of 16th Street and H, NW.

Order of Succession

"Later, when I laid-out these buildings on my own map, damned if da WH wasn't in the center of a really ominous-looking box. I had to call this in to higher authorities at my earliest convenience."

"**Everybody** met-up again at the Vietnam Memorial right on the money at 16:00, so Hal wouldn't get all PO'ed again – at least, not in public. Hal again collected the cameras, radios, notes, and the false IDs and clipboards with the fake work orders and handed them to Ray, who piled everything into a touristy-looking carrying bag. We were advised to expect a call about another review meeting in about four days. Hal and Ray walked-off together; the rest of us split-up and faded into the tourist foot-traffic. I took DC Metro back to the Shady Grove Metro station, where I picked-up my car and high-tailed it home so I could use the secure phone in private, without any prying eyes and ears.

"**If Hal was anything,** he, again, was a man of his word where calls were concerned. Four days later, we all got a call advising us of another review meeting for the following Monday at 17:45 out back in Hal's barn. Actually, the phrasing was more like a 'planning meeting', which was different than any previous invitation. It was time to advise my head-shed.

"We were all there Monday at 17:45. This time, the improvised table had been rearranged; instead of a more-or-less square, it was now a distinct rectangle. The map on the table had been re-sized to fit the new table. The east-west axis was shortened, while the north-south axis was lengthened. It now included the Jefferson Memorial on the south-side of da WH and the Hay Adams on the north-end of this axis. I guess whatever Bubba and I had reported and taken pictures of gave somebody a few new ideas.

"Again, the reviews were first. Team 1 reported on what they had found at the Ronald Reagan and Commerce buildings. Basically, the reports were almost identical for both buildings. First, they tried to look like they knew where they were supposed to go inside the Reagan Building and went directly to the elevators to ride to the top floors. However, the lobby-guard stopped them before the elevator-call button was even pressed. They tried to convince a lobby-guard to either take them where they needed to go – like the work order stated – or

Order of Succession

call a building maintenance man to take them there or give them a key to let themselves into where the work orders said. The guard paged a maintenance supervisor. While waiting, they also noticed that all of the doors in the lobby area were equipped with access-control card-readers.

Well, the maintenance supervisor eventually appeared at the guard desk almost 20 minutes later. He looked at the work orders and told them he didn't know anything about this work-order and no-way was he or anyone else going to take them around inside his building. He told them that their visit was not on his schedule for today and that they could not ride the elevators anywhere without an escort from the department/office they were supposed to do the remodel for. That department said they had no knowledge of any remodeling work. Sorry, come back when you get more information. End of discussion. They apologized for the mix-up, said they would let their bosses make the arrangements, and thanked everyone for their time. And they left. So, basically, the recon ended in the lobby. Sorry.

"Maybe the lobby-guard over at Commerce wasn't as dedicated to security, or whatever. He looked over our work-orders and called somebody, who confirmed they were expecting somebody to scope-out some remodeling work. So, he let our team get on an elevator and instructed them to go to the 4th Floor to meet that agency's guide. That guide met them at the elevators and took them to the area that was supposed to be renovated, and then left our team alone.

"They hand-drew a small floor plan of the halls marking the stairs, elevators, and utility closets as well as the room numbers on the side of the floor facing da WH. They tried the door knobs to the utility and janitorial closets; none opened. These also required keys and/or access-control cards. The staircases led down from the top occupied floor, but not up to any attic or roof access. Even armed with the clipboard with the work orders, no one loaned them a key so they could let themselves in.

"However, while up on the top floor of Commerce, they were able to see out the windows toward da WH. Our team didn't think there was a clear line-of-sight. The agency employees sort of let them look around a little because the work order looked sort of like something they were expecting anyway, but not quite. So the team took pictures of the work area they were expected to be remodel. Fortunately, it was near the windows, so they also got some pictures

Order of Succession

toward da WH. Those were in the camera and didn't show anything exceptional about meeting our needs.

"**Team 2** was supposed to concentrate on the old Corcoran Gallery. Remember, today this was just a one-man team. He reported in to the lobby-guard that he was supposed to check on some HVAC equipment, emphasizing humidity control. The unit to be inspected was on an upper floor. He had to go to the top floor, where a maintenance man was supposed to meet him near a certain door. He waited and waited for about 45 minutes for the maintenance man to appear. Must have been his lunch time – an early one. Our man must have been lucky; this guy says they were, indeed, having problems with that unit, but didn't realize somebody called in an outside company. He showed our team member the unit and said the compressor unit was through another door, which led to the roof. Then he said he had something else to do, and to just close the door and tell the lobby-guard when our man was finished. How great was that!'

" 'So, through the next door and he was out on the roof – along with a bunch of AC compressors – located in between raised portions of the roofs over different parts of the gallery. However, this bank of equipment led to an adjacent part of the roof on the rounded northeast corner of the building. And from there, he could see only portions of the east side of da WH building. The line-of-sight passed by the southeast corner of the EEOB, which shielded the western part of da WH. There was also a bunch of trees along the visual route. Although, he didn't know what the ultimate plan was, he thought maybe this one small area might be usable.' "

"**My Team, Number 3,** was supposed to go to the Hotel Washington and then across the street to a couple of buildings in the odd-side of 15th, NW. So, we went into the Hotel Washington. We simply walked to the elevators and rode to the top floor. Since it was already past mid-morning, the maids were cleaning and making-up the rooms. We just walked down the hall to the west end of the floor and found one of the rooms being cleaned. We told the maid we were supposed to check-out the HVAC unit. She thought about it for a few seconds and said okay – as long as the door remained open and she was in the hall. We tried to

Order of Succession

look like we were inspecting the fan and filter. Took some pictures of the HVAC unit. On the way out, my partner blocked the maid's view while I took several pictures out the window. From what we saw, we think you can see over the top of The Treasury Building, but not down to da WH on the other side. We could see the EEOB, but not da WH. So, we thanked the maid for her assistance and tried to locate any way to the roof. We even asked the maid if she knew of any way to go up there. She said no, but go ask the maintenance department. We checked the obvious doorways, but no soap. But there was a freight elevator that had an extra floor on its floor indicator. We called it, no problem. But it required an access-card to go any higher. We went down to the ground floor and the exit.

"Our next stop was across F Street. There were about three 'main' doors along the block. We tried each of them to get access to any rooftop. 'No way; they said they can't do that because they have contracts with their own maintenance companies, and they didn't have any notice we were showing-up today. Go work it out with them and come back when we get it straightened out. Then they might be able to help us.' Again, we left.

"Well, we had a couple of hours left before 16:00. So, we started looking around the area. You know, looking for something higher than The Treasury Building. And what do you know, right behind the Hotel Washington, there was another building, and wouldn't you know it – it was also another hotel. Considering the ease we had getting to look over a room directly opposite The Treasury Building, we decide to try the same routine in that hotel, too. So, we rode the elevator up to the top floor, but there weren't any maids working up there – maybe because it was getting late in the afternoon. Since we had nothing to lose, we decided to just ask if we could look at one of the rooms. So, we rode down to the lobby, walked-up to the front desk, and told them a dear aunt of ours was planning to be visiting from out of town. And, we wanted to get her a room on a top floor that had a nice west view at night. And we wondered if there was a vacant room that was available to look at now so we could send a picture or something to our aunt. The clerk looked in the computer and found a room, but a bell-hop would have to handle the key. We nodded in agreement. Greg, the bell-hop (it was on his name tag) picked-up the key and off the three of us went to the top floor.

Order of Succession

"Greg let us in and started telling us all of the features of the room – including the view toward da WH. Granted that all you could really see was a corner of the da WH. But, it was the southwest rear corner – the West Wing area of da WH. So, we took pictures of everything, especially the view so we could show our aunt how close she would be to da WH. We told the front desk we were sure she would be particularly pleased. And, we tipped Greg $10 for his courtesy and knowledge of the area.

"That was about all we had to say. We turned the meeting back to our dear aunt, Hal.

ORDER OF SUCCESSION

13 – Where are Those Missing Cars

Nearing 16:30, Saturday, 14-July: Westbound I-8, Exit 51, at Buckman Springs Rest Area, Mojave Desert, California

TIME: 16:24 PDT

"Rocky, we need a break. Say, did you ever hear anything about the two missing Deputy Sheriff's cars? The ones with the missing wrappers in them? I'd really like to hear what happened to them; we know what happened to the deputies – all five of them. But, I'd like to learn who has their cars; make that, I really need to know."

Rhodes: "Haven't heard anything yet. I'll get a hold of Coms and check on it during our break."

Rhodes: "Smitty, Coms says he hasn't heard about those cars specifically, but a contact of his at CHP reported that a CHP officer spotted two Sheriff's cars about half an hour before all this crap began over here. They were driving hell-bent-for-election eastward toward Calexico, passing everything in sight. He thought maybe they were supposed to be part of the President's motorcade, so he didn't flag them over. Besides, you know there is sort of professional courtesy in things like this, so the CHP officer just scribbled a note to himself about the cars' IDs and continued on his own patrol."

Smitty: "Nothing untoward happened in Calexico, at least that I know of. So, what the hell was their hurry? Hold that thought a second. C-8, the car at the end of the motorcade mentioned that there were two county-Mounties directly behind him and he wasn't aware that there was supposed to be any county deputies at the ends of the motorcade of our cars. But since they were deputies, I guess he ignored them. Which brings-up a point: in all this confusion, how many follow cars did you

Order of Succession

count, Rocky? I know where C-1, C-2, C-4, and C-5 are; they're friggin' smoking hulks right here at the Rest Area. My C-3 is sittin' over there, too. So, where are C-6, C-7, and F8? That's what I don't know. Have you seen any of them, Rocky? Have your Marines seen any of them? If they're not here, where the hell are they?"

Rhodes: "We, that is, all of us here, had no idea that there were more cars. Oh, shit, this mess just keeps getting' bigger, wider, deeper, and stickier as the hours tick off just like a sucking puddle of quicksand filled with molasses. Okay, now, what kind of cars are they? How can they be identified? Etc.? Etc.? If I get choppers, again from Pendleton how do they hunt for them? You got any ideas about this? Some really quick ideas?

Smitty: "Yeah, sure, I do. Two Suburbans and a sedan like the one I used to drive. All black. Each one has a GPS unit that continuously transmits its location on a couple of frequencies, one of which is in the dedicated military band. Call the helos and have them tune to the frequency on this piece of paper. If they can't hear the GPS transponders, maybe the batteries have run-down. Have the pilots put their 'hunting' radars and lasers to work scanning the roofs of anything like our vehicles parked in strange areas. The lasers should turn-up some interesting markings on the roofs and rear windows. The pilots will know right away if they found our cars; they'll be so surprised, you'll hear them from here. If the helos are equipped with FLIR [17] units, they can check to see if the cars are occupied. You know, Rocky, I am very ill at ease about what those deputies' cars may have been involved in, and it ain't all that nice. Ask Coms to get those helos involved and give them that radio freq and tell them that laser option works best after dark. Also, please tell, them good hunting, literally. If they find them, mark the spot, radio the coordinates, and you and I will bring a coupla squads of Marines to the spot. Yeah, you could say I have some quick ideas.

"Just had another brilliant flash of insight right now! Since somebody, maybe in the know, thinks that small, attack chopper may have come from, what was the name of that small airport right on the

---

17 (INFO: FLIR is an acronym meaning: Forward Looking Infrared Radiometer (for, Thermal Imaging Heat Sensors). FLIR units are thermal imaging systems for surveillance and force protection [in military applications]) FLIR Systems, Inc. manufactures thermal-imaging equipment for airborne applications, and its product spec sheets were referenced for this book.

Order of Succession

border, ask the Pendleton jockeys to sweep that area too. And all the back roads nearby, as well. Make sure nobody strays over the border line. Jum, or Jack something, or other. Try Jacumba; yeah Jacumba. Strange name. By the way, this is all Ultra Top-Secret technology we're talkin' about here; we gotta keep it that way, okay?'"

Rhodes: "You're serious about that laser thing, right? I never heard of it. 'Hey, Coms, over here right now."

Sergeant Williams: "Cap'n Rhodes, you called?"

Rhodes: "You bet I did. Smitty here has reason to believe we are missing two, maybe three, vehicles from this motorcade of cars somewhere between here and Calexico. He has information you have to listen to so you can transmit to the helos at Pendleton. This is the freq they are supposed to use to listen for a GPS transponder – sorry, make that two or three transponders. Smitty is also going to tell you about a wild laser option for finding those three cars. At least two Suburbans and one sedan like his over there used to be. Coms, pass the word to Gunny Cornell to prepare to mount-up maybe a coupla squads of Marines if the helos find any of the cars. And Smitty just came up with, what did he call it, a flash of brilliance. Ask the helos to sweep that small airport on the border, Jacumba. Stress that nobody gets so much as a rotor tip across the border.

"With the information we have, Cornell will be headed toward Calexico; he should have at least one sniper and one EOD expert. Coms, I forgot to tell you to have the helos loaded hot and ready-for-anything like last night – 20-mm mini-guns and missiles, door gunners – whatever they feel is right for this mission. We do not know if the cars are being watched or if there are any IEDs. Smitty, Coms will be interested in your tale. Go for it."

As Smitty told his tale, Coms was taking notes and asking questions, obviously not wanting to screw-up giving instructions to the helo pilots.

ORDER OF SUCCESSION

14 – 3rd Recon (Cont'd)

At 16:40, Saturday, 14-July: Westbound I-8, Exit 51, at Buckman Springs Rest Area, Mojave Desert, California

TIME: 16:40 PDT

Back in their makeshift SCIF, Smitty continued filling-in Rhodes about Hal's group.

Smitty: "Now, where were we about Hal and company? Oh, yeah. Back in Hal's barn. Well, moving onto the planning stage.

"Hold on a second. I'm sidetracking here for a second. Rocky, back almost a day ago now, Gunny Johnson described the semi and trailer, right? We both saw it, didn't we, you and I? But, we just assumed it was normal. Think, now. How did he describe them? White and no other markings, right? Oh, man does this plot thicken."

Rhodes: "Okay, I'll bite. Just WTH are you talkin' about now? This is really a sidetrack, if you ask me; oh, wait, you didn't ask me. You're telling me something, aren't you? Something more in line with your conspiracy theory, right? I guess, in for a penny, in for a dollar. Go ahead, spill."

Smitty: "Gunny said they are both WHITE with NO OTHER MARKINGS. That's how he described them, WHITE with NO OTHER MARKINGS. But, now that we have some quiet time, so to speak, his observation just popped-up in my head.

"Here's the thought. The U.S. Government has fleets of unmarked vehicles, cars, and trucks. What is interesting, some of the trucks are used to transport some very important stuff that the civilian population isn't supposed to know about. Stuff that could be dangerous like ammunition, bombs, missiles, nuclear stuff; that kind of stuff. And still other stuff that's valuable, like bullion for the U.S. mints. Then there's really dangerous stuff like nuclear fuel and contaminated stuff. And what's so special about those trucks? Typically, they are WHITE with NO OTHER MARKINGS.

Order of Succession

"Sorry, my mind is working overtime in overdrive. So, suppose this truck and trailer are ours – well, ours as in the U.S. Government's. Who has the juice to pull all of this off? He's gotta be damn high in the government somewhere.

"I really wonder who the real owners of these vehicles are, regardless of what the plates say about the owners."

Smitty: "Well, getting' back onto the mainline once again. Hal's barn still had the big plywood table on crates. Hal asks us, no, make that, told us to sit down – on the stools around the table. I guess he used stools this time so we could see the places he was gonna point out. This time, Hal had an assistant for this show-and-tell, Bubba. Like, who coulda guessed who else it would have been. Well, anyway, they have decided how they were gonna take down da WH. That's what he said: TAKE DOWN da WH. Well this meeting got really serious that very moment. Most of those local Thurmont boys looked at each other wondering what they had gotten themselves into. You know what I mean? Planning to do something is one thing and could even be sorta fun. But executing that plan puts all of them in a much different category. These boys had just been reclassified and that reality settled-in fast and heavy.

"The U-Team guys were not in the least unsettled about what had just been said. In fact, they seemed to be gauging the effect on the locals, figuring this one over here and that one over there would best be leaving this gathering, willingly or forcibly. I was busy making mental notes about everybody else, too.

"I had to stop for coffee right after the meeting broke-up so my notes could be coded as scribbles on paper napkins. My head-shed guys would be very interested in them that night.

"Anyway, so, Hal gets on his high horse and gets to ranting about 'how we havta do sumpthin about this here damned gubamint'. And his able-bodied assistant is busy layin' out enlargements of the pictures we all took so we would have some reference points to look at while the rant continued. This time, each team did not have to report on what they saw; the teams were all relieved. But they did have to answer questions about the pictures, how we got them, who may have seen us taking them, etc.; the team members had to confer a couple of times about who may have seen them.

Order of Succession

"It soon became clear that Hal and somebody else had already decided that da WH could 'best accessed' just as it was laid-out on the table – the north/south axis – because that line-of-sight had the fewest obstacles in the path. After all, why complicate the plan by having to enter more dang gubamint buildings and risk settin'-off some rent-a-cop or building manager about why all this equipment is necessary. This is the plan, and we're stickin' to it.

"Right after they laid-out the overview of their plan, one BIG error in their planning reared its ugly head – as it usually does. These smart-ass planners assumed. Ya know what happens when you assume, dontcha, Rocky? Ya make an ass out of u and me. Well these planners, probably professional planners who just assumed they were supposed to solve a problem because they got called-in, they assumed that everybody around the table had already agreed to do whatever they were told. Well, one of the locals, I think a Gene Somebody or other, ups and says, that he has doubts about these meetings now that all of the fun and games are ending. Ya know like going down to Washington, D.C. and sort of playing spy, taking surreptitious pictures, and all that. All of a sudden, the room gets quiet, real quiet. So, now the leaders call a break, and they go into conference. Just Hal and the U-Team, no one else, including me. I really wanted to listen-in but did not get that opportunity. Damn.

"The smartasses decided that Gene and anybody else who had similar problems should leave at this point. And that a report would be written-up and sent to the appropriate authorities if they ever said anything. Like what else could they do? Shoot them right there? With some good ol' boys, you can't really tell who's armed anyway. So, let it lie in peace for a while and clean-up loose ends afterwards. So, Gene and three others, 'Pops', Ernie', and a 'Sparks', left the meeting mumbling to each other. This left Hal, the U-Team, Ray, and me – that makes seven – and two other locals to carry-on.

"This single assumption on the smartasses' part could have derailed our entire infiltration. But we discovered one important fact: they were also dumbasses."

Rhodes: "Break time."

ORDER OF SUCCESSION
15 – The Plot Begins to Gel

Just past 17:25, Saturday, 14-July: Westbound I-8, Exit 51, at Buckman Springs Rest Area, Mojave Desert, California

TIME: 17:28 PDT

Rhodes took advantage of the break to consult with Coms. Sergeant Williams had some news, both good and not so good. The not so good news first. Pendleton's Commanding General was beginning to get some heat for having his Marines on-site for over a full day at a scene that was supposed to be under the control of civilian agencies. On his own initiative, he, too, tried to hand it off to the Secret Service. So, after getting the run-around from the Secret Service, the General called a buddy over in the FBI. He finally convinced somebody that the FBI should take-over the scene on I-8. Following quite a few 'covered handset' conferences, reluctantly, the FBI would have some agents out to see the General's soldiers (make that, MARINES, SIR) on Tuesday, 17-July, about 10:30 hours. Well, it is a drive from San Diego, and then there's morning rush hour and all. That was good news for Smitty; the general also ran into the very same problems he did – to wit, there was no one in charge of anything right now, and not even the lowest-ranking agent in the Service acknowledged there was even a problem with the Presidential detail. The complete absence of a responsible agency out at the rest-area was now personally confirmed and experienced by someone not directly involved with it.

Coms: "And now for the better news. The helo pilots from Pendleton are having fun playing with all of their toys – radar, lasers, FLIR, and stuff. They think they found five cars: two black Suburbans, one black car – described as a government-looking vehicle – and two county-Mounties' patrol cars, complete with lights and numbers on the roofs. But they are not all in one place. The helo-jockeys are real proud of their work on this. I wrote down the locations on this paper for you, sir."

Order of Succession

Rhodes (a little tongue in cheek): "Since they have all this technology, could they tell us if the county deputy cars have enough fast-food wrappers inside them?"

Smitty: "Coms, any news from my Secret Service. That agency seems to have dropped off the face of the earth? Also any news about presidential activities from the commercial news shows?"

Coms: "Sorry, sir, nobody acknowledges any problems, particularly ours. Even my usual contacts have gone high-and-dry, if you catch my drift. It's almost like they don't even want to acknowledge they know me, and I know some of them for over 15 years. Smitty, I haven't heard anything about the President from the civilian side of the house either. Short story: no news from nowhere about nothing. (Addressing Cap'n Rhodes) Permission to add something personal to this lack of news report, sir."

Rhodes: "Of course, Sergeant. Permission granted."

Coms; "Well, only because of the communications traffic I hear, I would like to offer a suggestion that, since the FBI is supposed to be here at 10:30 Tuesday, we all – Marines and Smitty, here – have about two and a half days to keep working this scene before the powers that be are going to shut us down and ask for all of the evidence. So, shall we see how much we can find-out while we are still running the show before we have to pack-up and go home? Sir?"

Rhodes: "Point well made. Point taken. Sergeant, get a hold of the Gunnies for a meeting over at our little SCIF. Smitty, you had best be there, too, of course. Coms, in 15."

Time: Saturday, 14-July, 17:45 PDT

Rhodes: "Gunnies, oh, I'm including Smitty in this form of address for the duration. We have either an opportunity for some sort of success or an occasion for preparing for retreat. Here's what has been placed on our plate." Rocky, laid-out what Sergeant Williams told us just less than a half hour ago.

Rhodes: "Considering that our role seems to be coming to the end in this mess, I propose we go for success. We can pack for retreat at will, but as I see this, we have only a short time, until Tuesday at 10:30, to do something worthwhile with this damn mess. Comments, Gunnies?"

Order of Succession

Cornell: "Since we are the only ones already in this mess so far already, why abandon our work now. Where are these cars are located, the ones the Pendleton pilots found? I'll take two squads to secure the sites and some flood lights to start our inspections and take pictures tonight, sir."

Rhodes: "Here are the locations, but I read these as miles apart. First site is located down near the Jacumba Airport. Hey, somebody guessed pretty close on that one! From the airport go about a klick ENE on Old Highway 80. Turn left on Corrizo Gorge Road for about half a klick, and turn right on Corrizo Creek Road into what looks like desolation dunes. Looks like about another klick to three vehicles on the south side of the road. Probably tried to hide them as best they could, maybe up a dry wash.

"The second location is further east on the north side of I-8. Our locator thinks it's behind some sort of equipment rental company on that In-Ko-something Road. There's supposed to be two vehicles there. The maps show it's less than 10 klicks past Corrizo Gorge Road, but you gotta cross-over to the other side of I-8 before you get to the equipment site.

"Smitty, the pilots said that deal with the lasers picked-out your three cars slicker than greased lightning. Read the info right off the roofs; spot on. They also said to tell everybody their FLIR gear did not pick-up anything larger than a coyote out there; their best guess is that there were no bad-guys around while they were there."

Gunny Johnson: "My Marines are packed to move-out now. Permission to proceed on the mission to one of the locations, sir."

Rhodes: "Both of you mount-up and get going. Advise Coms of your arrangements and responsibilities when you iron them out. Sorry, Gunny Layton, your Marines will secure this area around this Rest Area and post guards as required."

Smitty: "Gunnies, all three of the Secret Service vehicles were fully loaded with arms, ammo, and radios when we left yesterday morning. Try to inventory what's still there – if anything. Cap'n Rhodes, thank the Pendleton crews, but also let them know we may need them again since we are gonna stay until 10:30 Tuesday. Never know what or who will show-up by then."

Rhodes: "Wilco. Coms got that?"

Coms: "Yes, sir. Already on the horn with their CO.

ORDER OF SUCCESSION
16 – 3rd Recon (Conclusion)

Almost 17:50, Saturday, 14-July: Westbound I-8, Exit 51, at Buckman Springs Rest Area, Mojave Desert, California

TIME: 17:48 PDT

Back in their makeshift SCIF, Smitty continued filling-in Rhodes about Hal's group.

Smitty: "Rocky, with two and a half days left, do we have time to listen to the rest of my tale?

Rocky: "Go for it?"

Smitty: "So, with the wimps gone, Hal and Bubba get all worked-up about their plan and how they're gonna take down da WH. Come to think of it, I don't know if all of the U-Team were included in the planning or if this was their first introduction to it right here at this meeting. Anyway, after the unexpected interruption to deal with the wimps in the group, Hal gets all wound-up again, directing our attention to the maps and diagrams on the table right there in front of us. He says their research shows that the least obstructed line-of-sight is that north/south axis between the EEOB and The Treasury – the one da WH sits on. He's really a bright one for pickin'-up on that analysis. Duh!

"On the south end of this axis, Hal's got a small array of some of the photos that Bubba and I took looking north from the Jefferson Memorial. There's also a small array of pictures we took from the treeless area just south of the Washington Monument looking north toward da WH. These all show a fairly unobstructed lines-of-sight toward his target.

"Over at the other end of this axis, the north end, there is a small array of photos looking south from the far side of Lafayette Park, from right about the Hay Adams Hotel. The biggest difference between our sets of photos from the south-side of da WH and the north-side photos were immediately apparent, at least to me. The south-side photos were primarily from street-level, with the exception of a few from the top steps

Order of Succession

of the Jefferson Memorial. On the other hand, the north-side photos were primarily from the roof of the Hay Adams. Now, if you recall, this was the area that Hal and his son recon'ed. I don't know if they lucked-out getting to this area or if it was already pre-planned on their part. And, I'd also like to know who they talked to over at the Hay Adams and what they told him/her. I also don't know if anyone else around the table observed that finer point and if they made a mental note of it.

"Anyhow, with a few follow-up questions and some discussion, Hal's proposed line-of-sight was proposed, seconded, and accepted as the most logical delivery route of whatever he was planning for da WH.

"Somebody checked their watch and said it was closing-in on 2 P.M. and his stomach was a-growlin'. So, we took a break and decided to go to a late lunch before the afternoon planning session. Bubba said that he had already been down at The Treadle Country Inn down in Thurmont a week ago. He said they had a cold salad bar and a hot buffet as well. He said he could call ahead and ask for the room off the main dining room so we could have some privacy. That sounded reasonable, but it also offered Hal and Bubba some control over this group of ours, as well. Regardless, off we went in a small caravan of personal cars, each with a U-Team member. That was probably a sign that they thought we were entering a new phase for these plotting meetings.

"We drove through downtown Thurmont, turned onto Water Street, made another right onto Frederick Road, passed the city park, and turned right into The Treadle's parking lot. I didn't know there was even a small museum about Camp David inside the restaurant; sort of interesting from a local perspective. Well, we made our way up the narrow corridor to the reception podium – about 11 of us. Indeed, they sat us in a quasi-private room right off the main dining room. I say quasi-private because there wasn't much privacy what with those pull-out room dividers and no doors to speak of. Our waitress, Daisy, took our drink orders while we looked over the menus. Before Daisy left, she asked, 'Separates or all on one.' Hal, spoke first, 'Daisy, you know me. I treat when I come here. Put it on my bill, okay?' 'You got it, Hon,' and she was off.

"Everybody chose the hot buffet, which included the salad bar, as well. Daisy reappeared through the doorway across the entrance corridor from the bar. She carried-on what seemed like a one-sided conversation as she passed-out the drinks, 'Okay, now, who gets the iced tea? The

Order of Succession

water? Coffee? Decaf? This beer goes to Hal. Did I miss anybody? Did ya all choose the buffet? Apparently most people did. Anybody ordering off the menu? No? Okay, the plates are out by the serving lines. Go right through that doorway there and turn left. If there's anything you need, just let Daisy know, okay?'

"Everybody ate-up and then it was back to Hal's barn. The lunch down there at The Treadle was a pretty good choice for our group. Maybe too good; we were all sort of too relaxed on the way back. Unfortunately, too many people down there knew some of the locals in our group. So, even though we had sort of a private room, we couldn't talk too much because of all of the extra ears. As a result, it was an eat-up-and-let's-go lunch, not really a working one. But, the depth of recognition across the small community was extremely good to know about, and a must to remember."

Sergeant Williams: "Cap'n Rhodes, some updates, sir. Gunny Cornell called in about 7 minutes ago. He said he had taken the location with the three vehicles, and Gunny Johnson got the location further east. Gunny Cornell said they found one Secret Service sedan, one Suburban, and one Deputy Sheriff patrol car. All three of them had been stripped of all equipment Smitty said should be in the Secret Service cars, and the bad-guys had tried to set the two Secret Service vehicles on fire. Must have been lousy boy scouts because they didn't burn completely. He also said to tell you, Cap'n, that the Deputy's car does have lots of wrappers in it, just so you know, sir. He said you'd know who to tell about that. Gunny Cornell and his Marines are taking pictures of everything and recording whatever they find. No bodies reported by Gunny Cornell. So, one Deputy's car and one Secret Service Suburban should be at the second location. Still waiting to hear from Gunny Johnson to confirm that.

"Smitty, about the civilian news reports of presidential activity. My friends on that side of the house said they haven't heard anything from The White House since the motorcade left the Calexico area yesterday – in quotes, 'Absolutely nothing.' In fact, the strangest part from their side is that The White House also cancelled the daily news briefings – temporarily. They will be advised when those will start again. VERY STRANGE, they said."

ORDER OF SUCCESSION

"Sirs, I have nothing else so far."

Rhodes: "Thanks, Coms. We'll let you know if we have anything else."

Smitty: "Say, Coms, would you please try to find any status on this, say, during the next three or four hours? Thanks. Really appreciate it." as he handed Coms a small scrap of paper.

Time: Saturday, 14-July, 18:10 PDT

Smitty continuing his story about the developing plot: "Back in Hal's barn, we took our seats again. Hal began getting' his head of steam up again. However, Bubba kept pointing-out this part or that part of the plan. How I wished one or the other would just take over and the loser just retire from trying to get a word in edgewise. The gist of their plan – and it really was their plan because they never asked any of the rest of us if we had any ideas. We were told what's what – and that the north/south axis was the path we are going to use. Period. However, they did ask us if we thought we could make it happen and precisely how our 'resources' could best be used. Resources, hell! We had not yet been told exactly what 'resources' we had, or, more precisely, what Hal and the U-Team had in storage out at the bunker or had access to. So, we talked in hypotheticals. You know: If we had this gear, how could we use it to make it happen.

"But, when we unloaded – make that, when I unloaded – that trailer, a God-awful lot of high-explosive crap went down that chute. Note that up to this point, I still had no clear idea where that enclosed barn was actually located. So, we discussed hypotheticals. Here's where the merging of minds sort of began to show. A few still outstanding points were brought up. For example:

Manned or unmanned:

"Frank Eugene Corder, stole a Cessna 150 and crashed it onto the lawn on the south side of TWH on 12-September, 1994 at 13:49 hours. From the looks of the crash, it was assumed that he wanted to actually hit TWH. He was the one and only casualty and died in that attempt. The story goes that he was picked-up on radar at Ronald Reagan Washington National Airport several minutes before the crash. Most local people still say just plain old 'National', and everybody still knows what they are talking about.

ORDER OF SUCCESSION

"Well, at that time, everybody thought TWH was equipped with missiles – or that some of the rooftops around TWH had missiles on them. You know, the surface-to-air type of missiles. Well, Frank proved the point either way. Either there were no missiles on TWH itself or surrounding roofs, or the missiles were just plain too slow to recognize the threat from Frank, because no missiles were fired at him.

"Our discussion on this point proved sort of a no-brainer. Nobody wanted to be just hanging-around with a serious weapon in his hands just waiting for the Secret Service to show-up. So, the hands-down winner was an unmanned remotely-controlled device of some sort.

Should our strike be from a distance or up close and personal:

"Well, this was also a no-brainer if there ever was one. Why would anyone want to attack TWH close-up and personal and get caught. There was not one vote to get close.

What to use:

"Again, the choice was unanimous – missiles. Nothing big like a cruise missile launched from 100s of miles away; that would be way too obvious, especially, at the launch site. Rather, the vote was for using some small shoot-and-forget missiles. At least that way, we could be high-tailing it and blend-in with rubber-necking crowds."

Time: Saturday, 14-July, 18:25 PDT

Coms: "Cap'n, sir, Gunny Johnson reports the other two vehicles are in decent shape. The Suburban had some burnt tires, but looks to be drivable with new wheels and tires. Oh, yes, the Deputy Sheriff's car also has wrappers in it, too. They are taking pictures and inventory, but Johnson says there's not much in the way of equipment left. No radios, cell-phones, Sat-Phones, guns, ammo, etc. – nothing to speak of. Except for a weird-lookin' bracket in the back of the Suburban – something to hold maybe a missile or something like that. No names or labels of any sort on it.

"Smitty, no further news about civilian news stories. Sorry."

Smitty to Cap'n Rhodes slightly under his breath: "Cap'n, he got the missing gear right. Just so you know what may be loose out there now."

Order of Succession

Rhodes: "Thanks, Coms." At which Coms started to retreat to his radios."

Smitty: "Coms, I just had another quick thought for both Cornell and Johnson if you can. Did they see any semi-trailers with anything wrong with its glad-hands on the air-brake hoses. Remember that was pointed-out in our parking lot here, Someone thought there may have been two trailers and/or tractors? Maybe there's an orphan trailer or even a semi tractor that could belong to us?"

Rhodes to Smitty: "Are you telling me these bastards may now have a missile of some sort out there? You're telling me that seriously, aren't you?"

Smitty: "Well, not quite 'a' missile, Rocky."

Rhodes: "I know I'm not gonna like your answer to this but just maybe we need to know for our own safety. If it is not just 'a' missile, just how many missiles are you gonna tell me are out there loose in somebody's hands?"

Smitty: "Well, let's just assume that the deputies' cars didn't have any on-board. Then we might be looking at between six to eight of 'em out there that are NOT under our control. I don't think we have too much to worry about where we are right now because the bad-guys have had them for close to a day and a half, and they haven't fired any at us yet. I think they are already on their way to some other location – a lot further east from here. A whole lot further east."

Rhodes: "It's getting damn difficult to keep listening to all your bad news. Do you have any good news?"

Smitty: "Well, Rocky, now that you asked."

Rhodes: "I'm not gonna like this am I? Not one little bit, am I?"

Smitty: "Probably not. You are right – not one little bit. Let's take a break and meet back here in 15. Okay?"

Time: Saturday, 14-July, 18:52 PDT

Rhodes: "Okay, let me have it, all of it."

Order of Succession

Smitty: "As much as I can tell you is this. I never did finish the story about Hal and the U-Team, did I?"

Rhodes: "I don't know, did you?"

Smitty; "No, I didn't because it is still playing out right now as we speak. The story I told you was current up to about eight months ago. My manager pulled me off the case at that point because they were gettin' ready to bust 'em. I told Hal that I had family problems out west; my real boss set-up the cover story over in Coeur d'Alene, Idaho. But, for whatever reason, they haven't busted 'em yet. So, the truth of the matter is that Hal and the U-Team are still out there plotting. And I'm afraid this may be part of their primary, central plot going active.

"Now the real spooky part is that this operation, the one we — you and I — are in right now, is pretty much what we — Hal, the U-Team, and company — talked about back then. Basically, I am looking at that plot unfolding in front of me right now. The first exception is that the original one was supposed to take place down along the Mexican border in New Mexico and over into the El Paso area. The results were supposed to be the same; however, just the location is different."

Rhodes: "The first exception? You tellin' me there are more exceptions?"

Smitty: "Well, yeah, kinda sort of. What I haven't told you is who is behind it. And, I can't tell you that because I just don't friggin' know just yet. I was pulled-out too soon — before we got down to discussing the weapons for this project, the money to pay for it, and who might be the driving force behind it.

"But, if it is of slight comfort to you, this mess right here is playing-out almost according to their plan back then. They have POTUS, radios, arms, and now six to eight hot, shoot-and-forget missiles. You bet they had to spend some big bucks for kidnapping POTUS, but I guess that was already in their game plan. The questions that keep running through my mind have been compressed into just a few right now.

"Since it doesn't appear they want to assassinate POTUS, at least not right now — they kidnapped him from inside the most protected civilian-looking vehicle in the world this side of a tank for God's sake. They want to keep him alive for some reason, which I think leads to the next question.

ORDER OF SUCCESSION

"Why go through this effort? To what end? What is the reason for all of this?

"And finally: Who is behind this? Who stands to benefit the most from not killing POTUS outright? Who has access to all of the agencies and power structure within the U.S. government? Who can coerce them into participating on the sly? Covertly? Who?"

ORDER OF SUCCESSION

17 – Still Unanswered Questions

Just past 18:30, Saturday, 14-July: Westbound I-8, Exit 51, at Buckman Springs Rest Area, Mojave Desert, California

TIME: 18:43 PD

Returning from the latrine, Rhodes and Smitty stopped by the mess area, and each grabbed a cup of coffee and a sandwich – probably some sort of mystery meat. They wandered over to one of the shaded rest-area tables – albeit as close to the trees as possible – to catch any evening breeze. Both thought of other places they would rather be and other people they would rather be with. But, right now, here and now, they shared a vexing problem – one that those other people in other places could not begin to comprehend.

Smitty: "Rocky, I'm in a bind, a real bind, and you know it, too. I have been cut-off from my support group for situations such as this. And I don't know why the link was cut – on purpose or just coincidental fall-out from all that went on here the past day and a half. I suspect it is intentional. But . . . ." And his voice trailed off into nothing.

Rocky: "I understand your problem, but, obviously, I don't have the contacts, the background, the intensity you do. Because, well, because I am still in my element; this is what I – we Marines – train for. But not for what looks like a game of political one-ups-manship, however. Well, maybe not this exact SNAFU, but ones like it, but just not in our own country. When all is said and done, this might even be turned into a training exercise, what with all of these weird elements. Who knows."

Smitty: "I don't know about you – but I think you'll agree – we don't like having these invisible unknown persons pulling our strings. We don't like being puppets jerked around by some unknown and unseen master puppeteer. So, first we, you, I, and whoever else belongs

Order of Succession

in our group, should try to figure-out what their game plan is, what's happening, and why. And, who is trying to pull this off. We can't play this game if we don't even know what the game is. It's like we think it's crossword puzzles so we bring pencils to an ice hockey game; we are going to get creamed big time! Know what I mean?"

Rocky: "So, what game do you think we are playing, and what game are they playing?"

Smitty: "That's just it; I don't have the slightest friggin' idea. But, it's beginning to feel like these bad-guys are playing real, serious *King-of-the-Hill, Beta Release, Infinity-dot-zero*. And, we are way behind them at this point. We are so far behind, we can't even see their dust. I think we better start leveling the playing field a little bit, and damned fast, too. Amongst all of us Marines out here, maybe we can assemble a coaching staff that can point us in the right direction. Are you a gamer or a spectator? If you're a gamer, call in the Gunnies and whoever else you think might be useful or thinks outside the proverbial box. Like that PFC who decided there weren't enough food wrappers. Wasn't that PFC Berkeley? You and I can lay-out the shortened version of what we were talking about over in our so-called SCIF. We'll just make it bigger so we can all gather with coffee and chew the fat and come-up with our own scenario that makes sense. What do ya say? And by the way, there may be some more clues to this in some stuff I didn't have time to tell you yet about Hal and the U-Team." Smitty's brain was still working all the background chores.

{Smitty's admonishing mind: "Watch your language, agent Smitty. You know Rita doesn't like it when you swear, so knock it off. Clean-up your act. Get your shit – oh, okay, sorry, Rita – stuff together for this meeting you're talking about. Get your mind thinking straight and for God's sake, stay on subject."}

Rhodes: "Coms, over here on the double. (After Coms ran over) Coms, I need you to get the word out to all of the Gunnies, including Johnson and Cornell, that Smitty and I are putting together a think-tank of our own. We want all of the Gunnies and a few others like you, the EOD Sergeant, and PFC Berkeley to join-in. Here's a list I wrote down while listening to Smitty. Let's call it 18:55 now, tell 'em to be here in an hour at 19:30. If Johnson and Cornell are late, we are starting without them; their squads can keep clearing the scenes without them. That'll

ORDER OF SUCCESSION

get 'em moving. Also tell the mess sergeant to have coffee and chow throughout the night. Any questions, Coms?"

Coms: "Not really a question, sir. Smitty, I got a call from a buddy of mine back in the Pentagon. He told me he noticed there had been a lot of traffic about repositioning satellites out in the southern Mojave Desert. He wondered if I knew what was going on. I told him I didn't have a clue about that. Then he said all of the civilian and military heads of the services – you know, the Secretaries of the services – had been called into an emergency meeting about 17:00 their time – and on a Saturday yet. I asked him if the Commandant of the Marine Corps was also notified. He said that, to the best of his knowledge, the USMC would be represented by the U.S. Navy. I took that to mean the USMC was being left in the dark on purpose, sir. I'll go start notifying the folks."

Rhodes: "Very interesting, Coms. If you're not on that list, add yourself and come on over at 19:30. But make sure somebody's on the radio and phones. Roger?"

Coms: "Roger that."

Smitty: "Cap'n Rhodes and Coms, if it's not too much trouble, I'd like to get two of those helo pilots to attend our little meeting – or at least one of them. Preferably, a jockey with combat and air-to-ground missile experience, if that's not too much to ask. I got some ideas floating around in my head, and I need somebody with experience to gel my thoughts or tell me I'm all full of it. Besides, I know they'd love to get further involved with us; I can just feel it. Coms, ask them if a Major Phillip Jenkins is still at Pendleton and if he and his second are available. If, yes, as that old song goes, 'We got us a convoy lookin' for bears.' "

Coms: "Yes, sir. Sorry, yes Smitty. On it as we speak."

Rhodes: "We are underway, and may God look favorably on our undertaking. Let's go enlarge our SCIF, shall we?"

Smitty: " Roger that, Rocky. Oops, gotta start using military titles, sorry, Cap'n."

Time: Saturday, 14-July, 19:22DT

Smitty heard the helo approach and land in the rest-area about five minutes ago. He figured, correctly, that if Jenkins and/is second were

Order of Succession

in the area, they'd make sure to show-up. Jackpot! Both arrived on the same chopper – just in time to pick-up a bit of chow and coffee before our 'think-tank' meeting began. They greeted each other in the mess area. Jenkins introduced him to Captain Brian Hauser, a new second Smitty had not met yet. After the preliminaries, all three made tracks toward the makeshift SCIF. Smitty, still hobbling, sort of led the group.

Almost everybody had found the latrine and chow line before our start time. At least, it promised to be interesting just to be invited to participate. Or just a big bust, depending on your point of view. Regardless, almost every Marine out here, officers down to privates, would have given his eye-teeth to just eavesdrop on it outside their SCIF.

Rhodes: "Grab your coffee and chow or whatever you need, and our SCIF, such as it is, is over there where you can see sort of a dull glow."

When they were all seated or standing in our SCIF, Cap'n Rhodes opened the meeting by introducing Smitty and turned the meeting over to him.

Smitty: "Thank-you all for coming over here on such short notice. All of you Marines from Pendleton who recognize each other and me, we have a couple of guests, guests whom I know from previous training over at 29. The Major is Major Phillip Jenkins and his co-pilot is Captain Brian Hauser, who is a new player to me. Both are pilots of those helos out of Pendleton. They are whiz-bangs with choppers and live for airborne combat. They are going to tell me if what I think is probable is really doable or if I'm just plain full of it – as some of you may already be thinking right now. It's good seeing both of you as reps of Marine aviation, and I am gonna pick your brains as if you're bad-guys. Get ready. Anyway, welcome to Conspiracy Junction. The next items are a few ground rules for this here meeting – and all subsequent ones, too.

"Let me be clear about this: THIS MEETING IS NOT A CONSPIRACY FOR THE PURPOSE OF PLOTTING ANYTHING. We are trying to understand what or who created this mess in which we are now mired. In other words: WTF happened here; why is it continuing to happen; who's behind it, and; who's going to profit and how. There are lots of dots out there, and we need to figure-out how to connect them, who drew the pictures, and how we bring Marine ability to improvise, adapt, and overcome to prevail in this fight.

Order of Succession

"Next one: Inside this makeshift SCIF of ours, we are all equals. We are gathered here to understand a situation and to solve a problem. For the duration of this effort, we cannot afford to get hung up on titles or rank. No one, I repeat, NO ONE, can pull rank. We need to talk this mess through with candor and imagination. I think everyone can understand why. After the ground rules, we can introduce ourselves and get right to work.

"That one is followed by: While in this SCIF, at least, I may tell you some things that may be considered Top Secret or higher. Therefore, we are going to assume that everyone, I say again, EVERYONE will have the same clearance, so we will all be bound by the rules of at least a Top Secret with a Sensitive Compartmented Information certificate (TS/SCI) and any other damn abbreviated certificate which may also apply. AND THAT APPLIES ONLY TO MEETINGS IN THIS SCIF. When you step outside this SCIF of ours, your clearance reverts to whatever you currently hold. And you may not speak about this discussion to anyone else outside of our little group. Does anyone have any questions? No questions, good. Then consider yourselves 'read-in' to the purpose of this special meeting.

"And finally: If any of this does not sound correct to anyone here, you are free to leave. But leave right now before we get started." No one left.

{Smitty's sarcastic brain: "You didn't seriously think they would, did you? What a dummy. Do ya need a handbook for that, too, huh?"}

"So that we all have the same baseline information, Cap'n Rhodes will bring all of us up to speed on what has happened so far on the Marine side of this mess. I will follow the Captain with what I can provide from the Secret Service side and an undercover operation I was involved with a while back. Following all of that, our plan is to have all of us brainstorm who, what, why, how, etc. I believe we have a very small window before all hell breaks loose back in Washington, D.C. I'll be back shortly after I check on some news. Cap'n Rhodes, you're up."

Captain Rhodes introduced himself and had all of the others do the same. Rhodes started when he was first ordered to go out into the Mojave to see what some Secret Service agent was talking about. A flattened limo of all things. Sure it was, right? He filled them in for the better part of half an hour.

Order of Succession

The pilots, Major Jenkins and Captain Hauser, were most astonished, "... with the missiles strapped to what – a .50-Cal automated gun-platform. Did we understand you correctly, a Stinger and a Hellfire. Are they still hot and alive? Who's got control of 'em now?"

Rhodes: "Major, yes, those missiles were strapped to the .50-Cal gun-platform. Yes, they are a Stinger and a Hellfire. And, yes, they are warhead-equipped, but they are not actively seeking targets now. But, we have no idea who was controlling them at the time this mess began. And we still don't know."

ORDER OF SUCCESSION
18 – The POTUS Phone Rings

Just past 20:10, Saturday, 14-July: Westbound I-8, Exit 51, at Buckman Springs Rest Area, Mojave Desert, California

TIME: 20:10 PDT

A voice from outside the makeshift SCIF: "This is Corporal Knight, substitute coms; I'm sorry to interrupt, sir. Sergeant Williams, I need to speak with you right now."

Williams: "Be right there. Captain, I instructed Corporal Knight not to interrupt us unless it was most important. Let me check this out real fast."

Rhodes: "Sergeant, I'll continue while you're gone." Sergeant Williams made his way toward the draped entrance. Rhodes continued filling-in the rest of the listeners.

Williams from outside the SCIF in an urgent tone: "Captain Rhodes and Smitty, if he's in there, out here on the double please." Rhodes instinctively knew something must be terribly important. He headed for the entrance without a word – except for signaling Cornell, Jenkins, and Hauser to follow him. Smitty was still outside somewhere checking on something. All four left without another word.

Time: Saturday, 14-July, 20:16 PDT

Coms, with a finger across his lips: "Cap'n, PFC Knight here says, there is a guy holding on that cell-phone we found in the tunnel. You know, the one that supposed to belong to POTUS." (Jenkins and Hauser immediately looked at each other, both with an 'ARE THEY FRIGGIN' KIDDING US – POTUS? THAT'S A BIG OOPS HERE; WE GOT OURSELVES INTO A WHOLE HEAP O' TROUBLE' look.) Knight says he asked for Smitty, but he told him Smitty wasn't right here right now but he'd go find him for the call. We still have to find Smitty. Cap'n, you want to talk to this guy or shall I?"

Order of Succession

Rhodes, in a steady voice: "You sure he's still on the line?" Knight nodded yes. "Okay, I'll see if I can stall him until you all find Smitty." Picking-up the phone and placing it to his ear, Rhodes thumbed the 'Speakerphone' button as he did so, while motioning with his other hand for quiet, "Sir, this is Captain Rhodes of the USMC, we are trying to find Smitty as we speak. Is there anything . . . "

Voice on the POTUS cell-phone: "I don't want to speak to you, you piss-ant. You're a Captain; I outrank you." (Another 'OOPS moment', immediately followed by the kind of dead air right after you said something you shouldn't have.) Emphatically, Rhodes put his finger across his lips again. And motioning for somebody, anybody, to write notes about this call, PDQ. "I want that pain-in-the-butt Secret Service guy, the one who calls himself Smitty." The group clustered around the coms table straining to hear every word. Hauser was also taking notes.

Rhodes: "He is not here right now; we have five people out looking for him right now. Is there anything I can do for you while we wait for Smitty? Can I have him call you back or anything? I'm sure Smitty wasn't expecting your call; can you call back at a specific time, and I'll make sure he's here waiting?"

Voice: "I'll call back in 30, you piss-ant. It's getting' late; already dark. You better make sure he's there, or I'll have your . . . make that, I'll make a whole passel of trouble for your little piss-ant group out there. Got that? In 30, then." And the line went dead, really dead.

Rhodes: "Coms, can that be traced?"

Coms: "Already working on it with Corporal Knight as we were listening. I'll be back to your SCIF meeting as soon as I can."

Rhodes: "Gunny Cornell, go back to the SCIF and tell 'em to take 10. And get a whole bunch of privates to find Smitty and get his ass back here in 20. Take a break gentlemen; briefing continues in 9."

Time: Saturday, 14-July, 20:24 PDT

Smitty, sticking his head into the SCIF: "You lookin' for me? I was just gatherin' . . . "

Rhodes: "You bet your ass we are! Get over to coms right now for a call on the POTUS phone from somebody somewhere. Cap'n Hauser, read him your notes on the way. I'll catch up. And tell him to turn on the speakerphone so you all can take more notes."

Smitty: "I found these in an office in the Information Center building; somebody take 'em. I'm gone." He shoved a small whiteboard and some markers into a pair of empty hands and was gone as fast as he could on crutches. Rhodes, Cornell, and Jenkins hustled out of the SCIF, in hot pursuit.

Smitty: "Coms, whacha got?"

Coms (Williams, trying to inject a little humor, while waiting for the rest to show-up): "Oh, the usual, Smitty, some guy calling in on the POTUS phone. Maybe a wrong number or an order for take-out – pizza and beer. But, seriously, some bad-guy called the POTUS phone from a number that won't display on the phone. I'm trying to get a caller-ID by tracing the call in reverse, but that is taking time. From his wording, the call probably originated back east – 'getting late', 'already dark', 'little piss-ant group out *there*'. We're also guessing that this guy is still in one of the services and is used to being obeyed – 'outrank', and 'piss-ant'. Also, we think the use of 'piss-ant' means the caller is not from this neck of the woods because it is not commonly used out here in California, but possibly from the south. If his wording means anything, we're expecting his follow-up call right around 20:46 hours, give or take. Please make sure the speakerphone is turned on; we're gonna try and record this guy. And stay as calm as you can, too."

Still a few minutes to go. Smitty and Hauser were huddled over the earlier notes trying to get a better feel of this caller.

Coms: "Time's approaching."

Time: Saturday, 14-July, 20:44 PDT

Coms: "Incoming call's early. You're on whenever you pick-up." All conversation stopped dead in mid thought. It was suddenly quieter than the desert air – not even the breath of a breeze.

Smitty: "You all keep it dead quiet," motioning with finger across lips.

Smitty (taking a deep breath): "It's show time. Recorder on?" Picking-up the POTUS phone and pressing the speakerphone button, "Hello, Smitty here."

Order of Succession

Voice (gruff, raspy, a hint of a nasal problem, not to mention authority, and a slight accent): "Our time is valuable here. Where you been at? Visiting the latrine, you piss-ant?"

Smitty: "Yeah, you could say that! Can't drink coffee for two days and not take a break; even generals don't have that big of a bladder. Know what I mean?" Smitty motioned to Hauser to scribble a note about this. "Say, I don't suppose you have a name, something I can call you, do ya?" Silence on the other end. "Well, how about I call you . . . call you Calvin. That okay? Okay, Calvin it is then." (Motioning to take notes.)

Voice (sensitive nerve): "NEVER MIND THAT, piss-ant. You ain't even close. What the hell are you trying to do out there? You sure as hell ain't gonna solve anything; right now, he's ours. Hell, piss-ant, he was ours before you got to the top of the dirt bank around the car – you know, where three rounds hit the dirt at your feet. Let this thing go. Go home." (More motioning about notes.)

Smitty: "There's nothing I'd like better than going home, but you see I don't have any way outta here. Your boys killed all the cars and drove the others away, and the limo is a useless pile of junk. But you know that already, dontcha? Interesting way you all got him out and then buried the car.

Voice: "Thank-you. A lot of planning and money went into that."

Smitty: "Say, just what is the purpose of this anyway? Say, you know what, it's dad gum hot out here. You know what I'd really like? Some case-quarters to get me a soda or two." Some of the others in the cluster wrinkled their brows and gave Smitty a questioning look." (Get that down in your notes.)

Voice: "You play your cards right, piss-ant, and you just might get your Coke® [18]." (Take *that* note. And mouthing to keep writing, damn it.)

Smitty: "You didn't call back just to shoot the breeze, so let's get-on with it, okay? Say, just what is the purpose of this exercise anyway?"

Voice: "Dream on, you piss-ant agent; you ain't read-in on this here undertaking. We want you all to start folding-up your show out there and take the rest of the weekend off. Got that, piss-ant? We've

---

18 (INFO: Trade Mark of the Coca-Cola Company)

Order of Succession

made arrangements for you to turn it over to the FBI on Tuesday morning. You'll be contacted by FBI Special Agent Howard Phelps and his team leader Agent Pat Tobin for the official transfer." (Put the FBI names into your notes.)

Smitty: "That's really interesting. What about involvement by the Secret Service . . ." (Cut-off by the 'Voice'.)

Voice: "That ain't gonna happen, son. (Get that note.) The Secret Service has been read-out of this operation. I'm so sorry to be the one to tell you this, but you're one lucky sonovabitch. You weren't supposed to make it out of there alive, more-less get to 9-1-1 and get all of does Marines involved. Now why dontcha just sit back and enjoy the fact that you're still alive instead of makin' all our lives more difficult than need be? If you keep goin' like you are, you . . . well, piss-ant, let's just say you better have your life insurance paid-up so Rita doesn't have to worry too much. Capiche, piss-ant?" (More notes.)

Smitty's face and neck immediately flushed. *{Smitty's irate mind: "That no-good friggin' bastard. He brings Rita into this damn plot and thinks that's okay. We'll see about that. He and the rest of those bastards are going to pay for that." "Brain, get control fast."}*

Smitty (as calmly as possible): "This brings-up another question. Are you the one who left the messages about ' . . . all in due time. . . .'? Look, if the FBI is supposed to be taking this site over mid-morning Tuesday, what am I, or we, supposed to find-out in 'due time'?"

Voice: "Astute of you, little piss-ant. Again, more information all in due time.' I'll call you back tomorrow same time, same phone. And tell your Marine buddies to stop trying to trace this call. It is untraceable. Out." The POTUS phone went dead. (Didja get that note?)

Time: Saturday, 14-July, 21:02 PDT

Smitty: "Anybody got some water? Cornell tossed him a sealed, 16-oz plastic bottle of water. Smitty emptied it. And then his white knuckles crushed and crumpled it into a much smaller lump. All recognized how the 'Voice' naming Rita affected him; they let him be for a half-minute.

Rhodes: "Smitty, you okay enough to continue?"

Order of Succession

Smitty: "Let me walk to the latrine in the Information building. Be back in 10." And he turned on his heels and left, crutches under both arms.

Rhodes: "Let's get some other stuff taken care of. Coms, did you get that recorded?"

Williams: "Yes, sir. You want to listen to any particular part of it, sir?"

Rhodes: "Not right now; hold it for later – when Smitty's back. 'Rita' must be someone really important to him. Let's make sure he's calmer when he returns. Any of you have any observations?"

Hauser: "Smitty used at least one peculiar phrase, at least to me. Anybody know what Smitty meant with 'case-quarters'?" No one responded. "Then we'll have to wait for him."

A few minutes later, Smitty rejoined the group without any greeting. And began with: "For your information, Rita is my wife. And, now I am really pissed-off that these bastards for brought her into this plot. Really friggin' PISSED OFF. If I ever find-out who these maggots are, I am going to BRING SERIOUS SMOKE ON THEIR ASSES – UP CLOSE AND REALLY PERSONAL. (Smitty's voice changed to deeper and more measured.) Not a threat; a promise.

"I'm okay enough for this effort of ours. Now, let's get down to the matter at hand. I think I detected an ever so-slight southern accent. So, I used a couple of words just to find-out a few things. I tried to egg him on about some other things, too. Let's break this down back in the SCIF so we get more minds working on this intel [19]. Coms bring the recorder so the others can hear."

The Group re-entered the SCIF with a newly-found purpose.

Smitty: "Marines, they presented a challenge to us. We have new clues and a time-frame. Yes, we have firmly established that this is a plot, but we still do not know who is behind it or who all is involved. We need to pick our collective minds so we can get a grasp on this plot. I believe we are up to this task, so here goes. Is everybody still in?" Not a murmur of opposition.

Smitty: "Thanks to Coms' ingenuity and a smart-phone – not the POTUS phone, we have a recording of the call. You all, make notes of anything that piques your interest or curiosity. We'll use the whiteboard during the follow-up discussion. Coms, please play that recording."

---

19 (INFO: 'intel' = Intelligence)

ORDER OF SUCCESSION

Following the playback, Smitty opened the discussion: "Okay, let's quickly dissect this call. Cap'n Hauser, I can read your handwriting, so would you please work the whiteboard." Hauser, moved and set-up the whiteboard so most could see it. "What are your questions? Anybody? Remember, no rank in here. Anybody? Go? Remember, you really have to pay attention to the caller's voice, accent; that's all we have. Every little nuance helps."

A voice from the crowd: "What did you mean by 'case-quarters'? What are they?"

Hauser started to write, but Smitty answered right away: "They are regular 25 cent, quarter-dollar coins. I thought I heard the slightest southern accent in the caller's voice. The only place I ever heard 'case-quarter' used is in the southern U.S. It simply means a quarter coin that was used to buy a soda from an older iced case holding chilled soda bottles – usually, Coke® bottles. The Voice on the phone bit on the question. He must have known what it meant because he answered using Coke® in his answer. It also sort of pinpoints either where he was born or where he was stationed. Hope that answers your question."

Group discussion:

Smitty: "I also think the caller is now in or was in the armed services. He used 'latrine', which is not common in the civilian world."

1st Marine: "He also took mild offense to a 'general's bladder' being larger than mine."

2nd Marine: "He also knew about the three slugs we found in the dirt berm near the crushed limo. He knew how many and that they were low."

3rd Marine: "He confirmed the planning and money – lots of it."

1st Marine: "He likes the word 'piss-ant'. He uses it as an insult."

4th Marine: "He also confirmed, at least in my mind, that there is some sort of conspiracy in this plot. He already knows who the FBI agents are who are supposed to show-up on Tuesday at 10:30 to take over this investigation. But, at least, now we know it, too."

3rd Marine: "For whatever reason, he or his group does not want the Secret Service involved in this investigation. We've already seen how the Secret Service has been hog-tied out here – no contact, no nothing. Just hung out to dry."

Order of Succession

Smitty: "He feels all powerful because, basically, he sort of threatened to have me eliminated."

2nd Marine: "He also feels some minor attachment to Italian. He used 'capiche', which is also not used widely any longer."

Smitty: "He also brought my wife, Rita, into the plot; I am really pissed-off about that. Don't let me lose my cool about this part; tell me to cool it if I start to get carried away about it."

1st Marine: "Either he is the leader of the plot or a major part of it, which I suspect may be not be the case. Or he was also compartmented-out by the higher-ups. Because of the use of the phrase 'all in due time'. I suspect he doesn't know enough to know what's what with that, but that he's heard it used by others."

Smitty: "Coms or anyone else, do you know if it is possible for this call to be untraceable?"

Coms: "We are working on it now, but we have not been successful so far. Don't know if we can get into their switching servers since we don't have official access to civilian systems. Know what I mean? Say, what would you say if a known three-letter 'spy agency' got involved? I got a buddy at such an agency; I could call her if you want me to."

Smitty: "That is an interesting angle. I'll get back to you about that. I don't want to get too many outside people involved with so little time left just yet. Cap'n Rhodes any ideas about chasing rabbits down this path?"

Rhodes: "It's my turn to get back to you. I got some checking to do to see if this is doable."

Smitty: "Cap'n Hauser, please keep the whiteboard current. Y'all write on it as you see fit. Break time; take 15."

ORDER OF SUCCESSION

19 – Forming A Brain Trust

Approaching 23:00, Saturday, 14-July: Westbound I-8, Exit 51, at Buckman Springs Rest Area, Mojave Desert, California

TIME: 22:55 PDT

Smitty: "The Mess Sergeant has coffee and snacks available. I suggest that we take advantage of that and make a pit stop. Back in 15."

Time: Saturday, 14-July, 23:05 PDT

Smitty: "Glad to see all of you again. Plan to break for the day at about 01:30. Let's begin."

"Coms: "Smitty, about that note you asked about status of a certain event: PFC Knight's note says, and I quote it, 'That bird flew the nest Saturday @ approximately 21:43 wheels-up, San Diego,' unquote."

Smitty: "Thank him for me. Back to our meeting."

"Cap'n Rhodes briefed you on most of what's known. There are still some things that I did not have time to tell him about before I was pulled-out and transferred to Coeur d'Alene, at least on paper. The first few are really sort of airborne questions and are intended for the Major and Captain from Pendleton.

"I still don't know where Hal's secret barn with the underground ammo bunker is located. Phillip, Brian, I'll let you mull over if there is any sort of ground-penetrating radar that can search from an airborne platform and is readily available.

"Next: These folks, Hal and the U-Team, were chatting among themselves about getting a hang-glider into some target area using radar stealth gear. Do you know if a hang-glider can be built to be 'radar transparent'? Do either an Israeli company named Nanoflight or something called Signaflux, or something like that, mean anything to you? They mentioned all of these in really hush-hush whispers."

Order of Succession

"Same more questions from some more eavesdropping: Do either of you know what some regulation called 'P-40' means?"

"Finally: All, put on your bad-guy, black hats. From all of you, your collective military experience; we need some idea how they could take-out The White House. With unlimited access to military armaments, which these bastards apparently have, how would YOU do it? Then how could you defend against that solution, or is it so spot-on that THEY can actually win?"

"Those are my top questions. Does anyone have others?"

Hauser: "Speaking about our assigned projects, we, that is, the Major and I, think we would like to chew these down to size before too many are put on the table. To that end, we have a couple of possible solutions. If you want to hear them now, we're ready. I'll write on the whiteboard so we can all see where we are all headed."

Rhodes (beating Smitty to the punch): "Times a wasting. Go for it. We'll chew 'em over and keep on movin'."

Hauser: "Movin' on, then. Your first concern requires some refinement if you actually want to do this from the air. Ground-penetrating radar already exists; however, in its basic application, the antenna is generally in contact with the ground. Or, at least, very near to the ground – sort of like on those *CSI*-type TV shows on which the techs push a lawn-mower-looking device around on the grass. When you take that airborne, you gotta figure-in the altitude, available power, soil type, dry/damp, etc. Wouldn't it make more sense to try to find a strange-looking barn out there someplace first instead? You estimated the approximate travel time to that barn and the road conditions, right? So, maybe first scanning or searching for above-ground buildings meeting certain parameters that you can specify might work. Basically, look through satellite pictures for likely areas and see what pops-up. Then a chopper flight with the right scanning gear might be able to show you what the insides look like. Just sayin'."

Smitty: "You say this is sort of doable. Good enough for me. Comments, anybody? No comments. Write it on the whiteboard."

Hauser: "Both the Major and I think your second and third concerns are related to each other. We'll address both together. At first, the hangglider with radar-evading stealth technology made no sense because

Order of Succession

we couldn't figure-out a target that could be used against. However, the reference to 'P-40' sealed it for us. Just for grins, we looked it up in a special aviation database we pilots use. What we think they were discussing is an attack on Camp David."

Cornell: "Camp David? Are you guys really serious? What you all been smokin'? Sorry about that phrasing, sir."

Jenkins: "Gunny, no offense taken. When Hauser and I found P-40 listed, we were also dumb-founded. Cap'n Hauser will explain how we got to this conclusion. Cap'n."

Hauser: "Okay, as they say, here goes nothing.

"Why would anybody want to use a hang-glider in this operation? We think the bad-guys want a quiet approach.

"Why the quiet approach? They don't want to be heard. Make sense so far?

"And then why mention radar-transparency? They think their target has radar to protect it. Or, they want to approach at night to enhance their approach. By the way, we cannot verify, one way or the other, that Camp David has radar. If it does, it is not documented in any database we have access to.

"Fortunately, Smitty, you must have a photographic memory for names; I never pictured you with that. But, the name Nanoflight rang a bell; Signaflux will require more research. Nanoflight is, indeed, an Israeli company that specializes in a special paint they claim will 'turn any aircraft into a radar-evading stealth plane'. We don't know if it really does or not, but they claim it does.

"We checked our resources about such a hang-glider and couldn't find a specific reference to one or a contract to develop one; however, apparently, there is lots of interest out there. We speculate that maybe one of the SEAL teams or one of the three-letter agencies may already have one.

"Okay, here's where Camp David comes into the picture. As I said, we looked-up 'P-40' in our database. What we found is that the airspace around Camp David is usually designated 'R-4009', meaning RESTRICTED. However, it is re-designated as 'P-40' when the President is at Camp David; the P now means PROHIBITED.

Order of Succession

"Here's how all of this ties together. At about 10:30 on a clock face from Camp David, there is a local hang-glider jump-off cliff named High Rock. It is located in a public, county park located in Pen-Mar, Maryland, almost in Pennsylvania. Pen-Mar itself is on the west side of old Fort Ritchie, with a mountain between them. Fort Ritchie, in turn, lies to the north of Camp David. So, when POTUS is at Camp David, the airspace now turns R-4009 into P-40, the airspace is expanded to include at least High Rock. As a result, all hang-glider flights are supposed to be forbidden when airspace is classified as P-40.

"All of this really begins to make sense if you believe any, or all, of the rumored protection in the terrain surrounding Camp David. In addition to the usual fences and such, some of the rumored gear include: ground vibration sensors, camouflaged audio and video sensors, 'shake' sensors on the fences, armed troops, and the like. Of course, none of that is ever confirmed or denied by any of the agencies involved with presidential protection. I assume that the Secret Service is one of those agencies. Right, Smitty?"

Smitty: "Brian, as you said, I can neither confirm nor deny the breadth and depth of the presidential protection detail. After all, even this detail right here at the rest-area failed."

Hauser: "Smitty, I know, I know. But you asked for a certain depth of analysis about how this stuff fits into this plot. So, we, the Major and I, just laid it out for all of you. Basically, if we were going to take-on Camp David, this may not be such a bad part of the plan. I mean, look, you keep your boots off the surrounding ground mined with sensors and stuff. So, you have to rely on some sort of aerial violation of airspace. If you are going this far, that's the least of your concerns. But stealth becomes paramount. This hang-glider approach may be what they're looking for as a secondary component of the plan.

"The one thing we, the Major and I, cannot tell you is if this part of the plan is their primary, secondary, or a diversion plan. Maybe after we hear more thoughts from this group, we can all agree on the most likely primary plan. But, with the amount of manpower they have invested in recon down in D.C., my guess is that they probably want to make some sort of political statement by actually taking-out The White House – that is, razing it all the way down to the ground – maybe as a major symbolic statement. That's all we have for you so far. Smitty, the meeting is yours again."

Order of Succession

Smitty: "Thanks Cap'n for your insight. You know, I was once over at High Rock, but it never dawned on me how close it was to Camp David. It all makes a lot more sense now, especially, the significance of P-40. Break time. The meat of this meeting begins in 10."

Smitty: "By the way, Brian, you mentioned checking a database a couple of times. Is that a local database? One you have in your laptop or wherever?"

Hauser: "Nope. As far as I know, it's on servers back at Pendleton."

Smitty: "Why didn't you say so hours ago! We can't get out to the outside world; we've been isolated here ever since this mess started. We were told this is a 'radio-free' zone. How do you do it?"

Hauser: "See that helo we flew into here? It's got a gizmo in it that shoots to a satellite, clear and everything. Drop by and we'll get you hooked-up."

Smitty: "How about we send Coms over? He might get more benefit than we would."

Hauser: "Be glad to. Any time, no sweat. Done deal"

Smitty: "Coms, what would you say to a SAT-link? Go see Cap'n Hauser about a SAT-link off his helo."

Coms: "Roger that. Corporal Knight is on his way as we speak. He took off when we heard 'SAT-link.'"

Time: Saturday, 14-July, 23:52 PDT

Rhodes: "By my watch, we have about one and a half hours left for this session. We already have a lot of information, but for the sake of discussion, we will not be getting any more. And as far as the last concern goes, can we build a respectable plot with what we know? But, can we defend against it? Anybody want to go first?"

Cornell: "I'd like to layout what I think about this plot. I think The White House is the primary target – maybe even the only target. I think they want to do as much visible damage as possible regardless if they take-out the president at the same time or not. I think they mean it to be the most massive, impressive, visual political statement ever. Considering that The White House is in downtown D.C., they won't try

Order of Succession

a direct frontal ground assault. They want something that is hidden and out of sight until it is actually well underway – and the public can see it is already a done deal. The more undercover, the better. No trucks, no tanks, no armed soldiers. If TWH falls, that would be just the final demonstration of what their plot has already accomplished."

Smitty: "But, everybody in D.C. is already used to seeing choppers out in the open; they ain't a big deal anymore, what with, medevac, TV traffic, police birds. They're all commonplace now. So, if I were planning something like this, one or two choppers would work for me.

"Assuming this is a doable approach, how would you deliver the 'packages', Major, Captain? Is there a way to do the job and limit collateral damage?"

Smitty: "Gunny, down to basics. Has anyone thought, however, what the purpose of this plot could be? And, by extension, the plotters? Or, vice versa? Just saying, let's not forget the political aspect while perfecting the plot-execution. Sorry, poor choice of words."

Jenkins: "Agreed with Smitty; however, from my perspective, we've already been chasing this rabbit down the armaments path. I need to mull the politics around in my mind some more. In the meantime, why don't we try to figure-out an aggressor's mind-set for delivery. Anybody have heartburn with that approach?"

Rhodes: "Not here. Anybody object? No comments. Carry on, Major."

Jenkins: "The Cap'n and I ran some scenarios during the break. If any of you were looking at us, that's what all of the hand-gestures were about. Just so you know, we were not playing like we were doing loop-the-loops on a roller-coaster. We would like to offer a possible plan to do this.

"We agree with Gunny Cornell that a ground assault on The White House would not be doable in downtown D.C. So, this plan is for an air assault using one chopper, maybe two. The Cap'n and I like our birds. We're comfortable with them and what we can do with them. But, no matter how much we like them, they still look military. But people get real curious when our helos are seen where they are not expected. We came up with three scenarios."

Order of Succession

Jenkins and Hauser led the discussion about their ideas of using helicopters to accomplish the objective as they saw it, laying out the pros and cons of each of their variations.

Jenkins: "This is not a 'capture and occupy' mission. It is a flat-out 'destroy it to the friggin' ground' operation. As they say, 'Here goes nothing.'

"Oh, by the way, all of them assume to target the south side of The White House because air-space is considerably more-open – no buildings and trees on The Mall side of TWH. However, if they have access to a second helo, well, then the buildings on the north-side could certainly act as a screen. They could knock on both doors simultaneously with missiles meeting in the middle of the first floor."

The first plan they came-up involved too many other 'players' to control the secrecy of the plot.

The second option also proved to involve too many 'what-ifs' and too much area over downtown D.C. to control – although, it would have been an impressive show of force.

Jenkins: "Our vote goes to our third variation as being the most likely because . . . Well, just because we like it and would run it that way. So, moving on."

Smitty: "Hold that thought for a moment. Just a bit ago, you did mention 'Agusta', didn't you? Right? We have a wrecked chopper we think is an Agusta. You can look at it later if you'd like. So, we know they can get those, too.. Sorry for the interruption."

Jenkins: "We'll look at it in daylight, if that's okay." Gesturing toward his Captain: "Brian, did we forget anything we dreamed-up here?"

Hauser: "Sir, how about those diversions prior to launch?"

Jenkins: "Oh, yeah, right you are. This is where we want to invite the other Marines to join in this exercise. We welcome your thoughts about one or more diversions on the ground to divert attention away from the skies for only a minute or two. You guys are a lot closer to ground action than we are in our helos. Any ideas for the group?"

Smitty, turning toward the Pendleton Marines: "Can you Marines hold on to that thought for a moment. I've got a question for Phillip and Brian. You both probably heard Cap'n Rhodes filling-in most of what I told him about my under-cover assignment, right? When we were

Order of Succession

on those recon walks around the TWH area, we took a lot of pictures. Brian, if you can pull-up that map area off the Internet, I can show you what I'm talking about. Hal and the U-Team spent a good deal of time on the pictures around the Tidal Basin."

Brian: "Okay, here's the map of the Tidal Basin I think you are talking about. This is a satellite shot; where do you need to be?"

Smitty, moving to Brian's display: "Here's a piece of paper for a straight-edge; just lay it between The White House and the Jefferson Memorial. Look at this spot right here (pointing to the spot). Looks like you're using Google Maps, right? Pull that little guy down to street level and plant him in the area right about here. Make him look north and south along the paper's edge. You will probably be able to see in both directions at roughly eye height. There! See what I mean?"

Brian with Phillip and others clustered around the display. "There ya go. See what I mean! It certainly looks like a straight shot! Major, what if the bad-guys had a . . . something or other along this line-of-sight? Can you see what I'm talkin' about? Hal and The U-Team have lots of pictures of this alignment. I think they could be using this for a game of 'Target acquired; target hit; target gone'.

Hauser: "Max distance along the line-of-sight is only about one mile. Oh, my God! Major, we just discovered a whole new dimension to this game!" This is the first time Brian, the computer-game player, was this excited playing a new game.

Smitty: "I believe you can now see what I have been thinking about. Take 10. Marines, we still need your diversion ideas."

Time: Sunday, 15-July, 00:46 PDT

Smitty: "Welcome back. I'd say we ended on a high point before break. Marines, any ideas about one or more diversions to distract from the bad-guys placing their main plan into action?

Rhodes: "We were talking this over during our break. We came-up with a few diversions that might work for a few seconds. Sgt. Cornell, you're nominated to open this round of discussions."

Gunny Cornell led the discussions about the diversions they thought would or would not work well in the streets within half-a-mile or so of

Order of Succession

TWH. Most of these dealt with confusing the civilians in the area. A few were planned to confuse first responders and their respective agencies. But, all were supposed to cause a degree of panic and traffic grid-lock in the area.

Smitty: "Phillip, Brian, if you were flying a chopper, intent on harm, could you use anything we brought-up here? Or can you think of something else to make your flight-mission work better?"

Jenkins: "I think Brian would agree that a couple of these diversions would probably be just the ticket. From the perspective of wearing a black hat, that is, the more time we have to approach and acquire the target means the better chance for our success. We both like three of them and a fourth one to distract the guards in their shacks. Three of them could all appear to be random events caused as the results of the first one. Might work well enough to keep TWH guards off balance for a little while – maybe just long enough. Plus, the panic and gridlock might be a reason for one of the choppers in our scenario to get quite close, even if they would be flying into restricted air-space. I think in real life, they might want to take the chance that crossing that line would be overlooked as a spur-of-the-moment incursion. Might work very well for just the few seconds that they would need and not look too obvious, finished-off with the diversion at the guard shack. Might work-out okay."

Smitty: "We're pushing right up to 01:30. Shall we call it quits and meet here again later this morning? What time? How about 08:30? Done. Meeting adjourned."

Order of Succession
20 – More for the Brain Trust

Around 06:40, Sunday, 15-July: Westbound I-8, Exit 51, at Buckman Springs Rest Area, Mojave Desert, California

TIME: 06:42 PDT

Corporal Knight: "Smitty, sir? Should I be calling you something else, sir?"

Smitty: "No, Corporal. Smitty is just fine; it's a lot better than some of the names I've been called before. How can I help you this fine desert morning?"

Knight: "Well, Smitty, sir, last night 'bout 22:30 or so when you all were talkin' over there in, what didja call it, your SKIP, well, some Marines from those platoons searchin' for deputies' cars and whatever . . . Well, some Marines stopped over here and said to tell somebody that they found a truck and trailer out by some equipment rental place. Does any of that make sense to you? I'm sorry, Smitty, sir, but I haven't done this too much and I didn't want to screw-up too bad, but I thought it would keep 'til this morning. Coms, Sgt. Williams, that is, wasn't around to confirm what I should do, so I decided it could wait and not interrupt y'alls' meetin'. I hope that's okay, Smitty, sir."

Smitty: "Two things, Corporal. We just decided that you should call me Smitty. No 'sir' is necessary. Second thing, at 22:00 hours, we could not look that trailer over too well in the dark, now could we. So, no harm done on that one. You do remember who told you, right? Go find him after coffee and ask him to come see me. We need a squad to go look at it and go over it with a fine tooth comb. Make sure PFC Berkeley is notified to join me, too. I want Berkeley and his Geiger counter to go with the others, too. We needed daylight, so don't worry about this delay too much. Next time, make sure you take notes like a newspaper reporter: Who, What, When, Where, Why, How. Is the coffee hot over in the mess tent?"

Order of Succession

Knight: "Thank-you, Smitty, sir. (The 'sir' trailed off.) Sorry, but it just don't seem right without the sir, sir."

Smitty: "Smitty will work okay for now. Eventually, all this will work itself out okay. Oh, before I forget, did the squad leader say what color the tractor and trailer was?"

Knight: "Well, now that you ask, yeah, he said they are both white. Is that important?"

Smitty: "Just go find him and ask him to find me or Gunny Cornell. PDQ!"

Knight: "Smitty, Sir, do you know who I'm supposed to tell that there's gonna be a Marine Chaplain flying out on today's supply chopper? They want to know where he can set-up for a Sunday non-denominational service. Actually, I think they said maybe up to four services to cover everybody out here. Who would be the best person to direct him to?

Smitty: "Work on no 'sirs' for me. First-off, I guess the Cap'n. Second, probably Gunny Cornell. Third guess, set-up shop in a corner of the mess tent. But that's just my guess. Make your best guess."

Smitty ran into Gunny Cornell in the mess tent. "Gunny Cornell, just the person I need to see. Do you have a few minutes?"

Cornell: "You betcha! This desert is gonna get warm in an hour or two. Whacha need?"

Smitty: "Two things, and you're the first Marine that came to mind. Just spoke with Corporal Knight. Seems one of the squads that were searchin' for the trucks and cars yesterday thinks they found the semi-tractor and that trailer with the ripped glad-hands over by the equipment rental place. Could you put together a squad to go check it out – a real thorough check with pictures and stuff – just like you all did here? Don't need a Gunny to be in charge 'cause we should continue brainstorming in about 90. Okay?"

Cornell: "Got just the Marines in mind. What's the second thing?"

Smitty: "Make sure the PFC with the Geiger counter goes along. Berkeley, right? And make sure he takes it along. If ANYTHING is rad-hot out there, they back away from it, call us, and turn it into a 'secure-the-site' mission. Okay? Call us anyway."

Cornell: "Got it."

Order of Succession

Smitty: "How about a couple of specialists to go, too? Like somebody from EOD and a sniper. I just got another really peculiar feeling about that trailer. Like why did it have to be moved way over there and stuff like that. By the way, Corporal Knight said the squad leader said they are both white. How's the coffee and Sunday brunch?"

Cornell: "White, huh? Well, ain't that just what you expected, isn't it? Coffee's hot. Sunday brunch? Brunch, my ass. When was the last time you Gyrenes were in a field mess? Still looks like SOS [20] to me, and tastes like it, too! Time's awastin'; got things to do; a squad to assemble; jobs to assign."

Smitty: "Thanks, see you in 80 in the SCIF. Oh, Corporal Knight says a Chaplain is supposed to be arriving on the supply helo. He wants to know who needs to know and where he can set-up shop for services today. Can you help him out?"

Cornell: "Yeah, I can help him out. I'm going right past his table."

Smitty: "Major Jenkins. There's a seat over here with your name on it."

Jenkins: "You all really eat well out here? All the amenities – sunrise, fresh air, smell of diesel and avgas [21]. How ya doing?"

Smitty: "Where's Brian? They think they found the second semi-tractor and trailer last night after 22:00. There's a squad going out there to check it out. The squad leader says it's white. But, I got a really bad feeling about this. I hope it's nothing more than the breakfast mystery meat. Phillip, is that helo of yours loaded . . . "

Jenkins: "For hunting big, bad badasses? You better damn well believe it. Ever since this little exercise started out here and Pendleton got called-in, our CG didn't want to lose any of his choppers over here without defensive arms until this is settled. If anybody is flying around this area, we are to be fully armed to bring smoke, hell-fire, and damnation on the bad-guys. Yes, we are fully armed. Why do you ask? You know something we should be aware of?"

Smitty: "Nope, Phillip. I don't really know anything about this. I just got a really bad feeling in my gut. That's all; a really bad feeling. Hope that's all it is – a really bad feeling. Maybe just an upset stomach?"

---

20 In this case, SOS means 'Shit On a Shingle', slang for 'Chipped Beef on Toast' (or some other meat).
21 Aviation-grade fuel

Order of Succession

Time: Sunday, 15-July, 08:07 PDT

Time to reconvene the meeting of the minds. All of the participants brought their coffees.

Smitty: "In case you haven't heard yet. (The morning chatter turned into silence.) One of the squads reported that they had found what looks like our missing semi-tractor and trailer over at that equipment rental place. Cap'n Rhodes, just so you know, I asked Sgt. Cornell to assemble a squad to return out there and give them a thorough inspection, take pictures, etc. Sgt. Cornell, are we still on track with that?"

Cornell: "Yes, sir, squad left about 30 minutes ago."

Rhodes: "Smitty, I was aware of the find out at the rental place last night. You beat me to that same decision."

Smitty: "Just so you all know, I have a real bad feeling about that site. Don't know why, but my gut doesn't like it one bit, and I haven't even been out to see it yet. Gunny, are they loaded hot?"

Cornell: "Well, now, I don't know how hot you mean. But, they are armed with two extra ammo boxes of 5.56-mm [22], and the Sniper took along one of his favorite rifles, a .338 Lapua, I think. What's up?"

Smitty: "Just a real bad feelin'. That's all."

Smitty: "Cap'n Rhodes, does anybody have any possible ideas why that truck had to be hidden over there?" Silence. "Does it make any difference if I told you they are white?" Murmurs, but nothing spoken out loud. Phillip and Brian, any ideas about how to defend against an airborne attack in downtown D.C.? Like we don't want an all-out air battle with civilians in the middle, but if that's the only way . . . Well, maybe I'm just thinking out loud too far into the future."

Phillip: "Brian and I did some brain-storming way-earlier this morning. We got some ideas, but nothing firm because of a few factors:

"We don't know the probable battle-field all that well yet. Sure, everybody knows what The White House looks like, especially the South Lawn where Marine-1 lands. But the rest of that area – well, that's a big unknown to the two of us.

---

22   5.56-mm = ammunition for the M-16 and M-4 rifles.

Order of Succession

"And second, we don't know who the bad-guys are. So, we don't have a good idea how they think.

"Their choice of assault vehicle is another unknown. We know how we would do it, but that doesn't mean they think the same way. We know what our helos will do, and I'd say we will beat theirs unless . . . Unless, they have access to another armed military helo and a fully-qualified combat pilot to fly it. Then it could turn-out to be aerial combat for real – one for the history books. Frankly, that sort of makes my blood run cold.

"And the timing is all in their court. We good-guys could wait until hell freezes over, and then we assume that it'll never happen. We fold our tent, and they seize that opportunity to fully activate their plot. How long can we wait?

"Basically, we, that's Brian and I, think it's doable, but not with the intel we have right now. I know that's not what you want to hear, but those are the roadblocks we have come to right now."

Smitty: "Coms, are you here? Is it possible to have somebody try to raise that squad out at the rental place? I still am not comfortable."

Coms: "Roger that. I'll go do that myself." Sgt. Williams excused himself and left the SCIF.

Smitty: "All, Phillip and Brian weren't the only ones playing mind games last night – or rather, very early this morning. Here's a what-if for this brain-trust:

"Suppose we are dealing with not one, but two plots? Suppose that the one out here is being run by one set of bad-guys. And the one I was undercover for is an entirely different plot? And suppose that they are unaware that somebody else is plotting something else on their own? How does that affect your thinking? Anybody?"

Rhodes: "Okay, what weird stuff did you put into your coffee this morning? Isn't that pretty far-fetched – to have multiple plots against the same target, running at the same time?"

Smitty: "Almost agreed with you, except:

"The White House is a building. It is not mobile; it's not going anywhere. At least, not that I know of. This area right here where we are sitting looks more like a kidnapping to force some changes in the President's cabinet.

Order of Succession

"So, if you are trying to take-out The White House, why would you eliminate ten members of the batting order in the Order of Succession? No matter how I look at it, what I keep coming-up with none of this makes any sense. I cannot think of a good reason to get rid of all those Secretaries just for the sheer hell of it. Can anybody here help me with that?

"Then on the other hand, if you have all of this money, time, and effort to kidnap POTUS, kill ten Secretaries, and sort of harass us lowly Marines out here in the desert, why would you want to destroy The White House? Maybe I'm just looking at this as a conspiracy, but to me, this operation that started out here looks more and more like a forcible change of government. In other words, a coup! But, without a change of leadership at the POTUS position – just those people who report to POTUS, and what government Departments will they manage for him. Of the eight still-remaining positions in the Order, three are elected; these are: the Vice-President, The Speaker of the House, and President Pro Tempore of the Senate. I think these could be 'convinced to retire for 'personal reasons'. The other five are presidential appointees and are the Secretaries of: State, Treasury, Attorney General, Agriculture, and Health and Human Services. These are the ones I am concerned about. Can anyone explain how killing-off all of these Cabinet members fits in with taking-out The White House? Anyone? (No answers.) Neither can I. So, I don't understand how either plot correlates with the goals of the other. Which brings me back to the implausible: two simultaneous plots unknown to each other. Let's think about this new angle over coffee, shall we?"

ORDER OF SUCCESSION

21 – The 2nd Trailer

Just past 08:50, Sunday, 15-July: Westbound I-8, Exit 51, at Buckman Springs Rest Area, Mojave Desert, California

TIME: 08:54 PDT

Coms: "Cap'n Rhodes, Sgt. Cornell, and Smitty. ASAP. NOW!"

Rhodes (with Cornell and Smitty in hot pursuit): "Coms, wassup?"

Coms: "Two messages. Smitty, this just in from a personal contact: Secretaries of Agriculture and Health and Human Services have been involved in a crippling auto accident in northern Virginia. And the Secretary of State was taken hostage in one of the 'stans. And the Attorney General resigned, effective immediately."

Smitty: "That leaves one appointee, the Secretary of the Treasury, and two elected officials – three if you count the Vice President on the elected side – remaining. Now we're down to four remaining members of Friday's original batting order. The bad-guys' pitcher has taken-out 14, not including POTUS. Wow! A major league record if there ever was one!"

Coms: "Cap'n Rhodes, the other message is from the squad out at the rental place. They said they found both the tractor and the trailer. They started inspecting them, and then they took some incoming fire from at least two locations – still incoming. One Marine is injured; didn't say how. Waiting for instructions. Sir?"

Rhodes: "Gunny Cornell, mount-up two more squads and get out there ASAP. Loaded hot."

Smitty: "Cap'n, mind if I ask the Major and Captain if they can join them?"

Rhodes: "Hot damn! I knew you were good for something. You betcha. Git on it!"

Order of Succession

Smitty: "Phillip and Brian, that squad at the rental place is taking incoming fire, and . . . "

Brian (over his shoulder, already trotting to the helo): "Major, on my way to the helo; gonna spool-up now. Smitty, who knows where it is? We need coordinates. Oh, wait, is that that big equipment rental place right along I-8, on the north side? We know exactly where that is; we use that for a landmark. Tell Coms to tell that squad to set their ears to Combat-2 freq. Tell them we will already be in hunting mode when they see us. Out." Both pilots were already running to the helo. Rhodes chased after them and hopped in.

Smitty: "Coms, relay this to the squad. Switch to 'Combat-2 push'. Look for a chopper from our location. And stay out of their way; they have their hunting license."

Coms: "Roger that. Corporal, transmit that ASAP."

Squad Leader Sanchez: "Coms, roger that. We are on helo Combat-2 now. Located on east end of the yard just outside the fence. Look for the 53-foot white trailer – only one there. We think two bad-guys are firing from further east and two more from behind the back fence of the rental lot. Sounds like a .30-Cal. hunting rifle. Not on auto yet. Sniper has his .338 aimed toward the bad-guys on the Yuma end of the yard. We are trying to keep both sides pinned down until helo arrives. Over."

Knight: "Roger that. Helo already gone. Out."

Smitty: "Gunny, should we be on our way with more Marines? And how soon are you leaving."

Cornell: "Damn straight we are going. Two more squads are mounting up now. When you hear their engines, we're gone. Hop on board anything if you're going. Don't worry about a side arm; we got extras especially for Gyrenes. Better git moving; the first Humvee's already gone."

Smitty: "Race you for the seat over there."

Time: Sunday, 15-July, 09:25 PDT
All the vehicles took I-8 eastbound as the fastest route to the rental lot.

Order of Succession

Cornell: "This could take a while; we have about 30 klicks to the off-ramp. Cap'n will probably have it wrapped-up by the time we get there. Right now, it's that old 'Hurry-up and wait'. Not much we can do but that."

Time: Sunday, 15-July, 09:43 PDT

Cornell was right about the Cap'n being there first. Phillip flew the helo above I-8 until he was about five klicks from the off-ramp. Not much else he could really do because the route was quite mountainous. Now he had Brian arm their weapons systems and went high for a better look-see. They saw the white trailer and turned on the FLIR system just to see if there was enough thermal difference to 'see' human bodies in the desert heat. Not much difference, but there were two figures behind the fence along the rear of the rental lot.

Brian: "Sir, two tangos at our 11 o'clock. Just on the outside of the fence about 200 meters from the white trailer. 'Squad leader; this is Pendleton helo. Confirm you see us.' "

Sanchez: "See you above the lot's office building. Your nose is pointed in the correct direction. We think two bad-guys off the port side outside the fence. All our Marines are at the white trailer. Over."

Brian: "Roger. Keep them there. Out."

Phillip: "Okay we know where two tangos are located, but how do we verify they are bad-guys and keep the other two from turning us into a target? Cap'n, grab our binoculars and see if you can identify our tangos as targets or civilians."

Rhodes: "Okay, focused on their location. Can't see any firearms from here; must be their angle to us. Can we poke them to see if they move so I can see rifles or something?"

Phillip: "Roger. Brian, on three, fire a burst in front of them. Rhodes, keep watching. Brian, two, three." Followed by a short burst.

Rhodes: "They didn't like that. One raised a rifle toward us."

Phillip: "Brian, we're gonna try to flush them out. Radio Sanchez to look for possible runners in his direction but keep an eye on his six for the other bad-guys. Then on three, another short burst behind them and walk it in for another short burst. Brian, two, three." Sand erupted about

Order of Succession

20 meters behind the targets. That got their attention right fast. They decided to vacate their cover and make a run for it.

"Rhodes: "Both are armed with rifles. Looks like a hunting rifle and maybe an M-16 or a look-alike."

Phillip: "Brian, the targets are confirmed. Can we herd them toward Sanchez?"

Brian: "They are not cooperating; they are angling away from Sanchez. They don't want any part of us or him."

Phillip: "Brian, put a short burst ahead of them to see if they will turn." Sand erupted ahead and to the left of the fleeing targets. They continued to run away from Sanchez. Phillip again: "Brian, Rhodes, either of you see any way to turn them?" Two negatives. And then both runners stopped, raised, and aimed their rifles toward the helo. "Brian, you have our hunting license. Tag them and we go for the other two. Roger?"

Brian: "Roger. Two tags coming up." And the side pod-mounted 7.62-mm machine gun spoke with authority. "Two tagged. Land forces to collect. Next targets at location approximately 200 meters from the white trailer. Reference I-8. There is a frontage road along the front side of the rental lot between it and I-8. Approximately 150 meters toward Yuma on I-8, there is a small building that could be a house. There appears to be a gulch behind the house. Tangos in the gulch. FLIR does not pick-up too much heat-differential. Wait one."

Brian (On radio): "Squad Leader, over."

Sanchez: "Squad here, over."

Brian: "Put sand in the air where the other targets are? Over."

Sanchez: "Roger that. One magazine for effect coming-up. Out." And the sand erupted behind the house. And the bad-guys returned fire.

Phillip: "Poor bastards; just couldn't resist, huh? Brian, did you acquire targets?

Brian: "Roger. And roger on those 'poor bastards', too. Should we try to get them to surrender and herd them toward Sanchez?"

Rhodes: "Well, I have a lot invested in this mess so far. It'd be real nice if we could talk to them. I vote to give it a try."

Order of Succession

Phillip: "Brian, radio Sanchez and tell him what we are planning to do. We're gonna try to drive them to him if they let us. Otherwise, two more tags. If they raise rifles toward us or fire at us, we are not gonna screw with them; tagged and done. Roger?" The Major spun his helo into position for one way or the other. He mumbled something about, "Please don't be poor stupid bastards again, okay? You'll leave me no choice."

Phillip: "Sanchez rogers. Short burst to begin with. On my three. Brian, two, three." And the 7.62-mm spoke again. The targets also decided to make a run for it. However, this time, they both raised their guns over their heads with both hands – not aiming, but holding them in surrender mode. They kept moving toward Sanchez, but tried to sidestep into another gulley. Another short burst convinced them of a wiser direction. They were gathered-up by Sanchez's squad and surrendered.

Phillip: "Brian, notify coms in the rest-area that we have resolved the problem. Two body bags and two prisoners. Cap'n Rhodes, you got some time for a little trip; we'll be back for dinner."

Rhodes: "Yeah, I guess so. What didja have in mind?"

Phillip: "Trip to Pendleton for refueling and top off the ammo. Brian, call Pendleton with requisitions and a car for three passengers. Need to notify our CG of our status."

Brian: "Roger that."

Rhodes: "The Exchange has a good stock of suds and soda. Can we get about 20 cases, mixed, any brand and transport? My treat to my Marines for being fired on here in the U.S."

Brian: "The credit receipt will be at the pad. Transport's free; our treat."

Order of Succession
22 – Relief from the Heat and an Old Buddy

Approaching 15:00, Sunday, 15-July: Westbound I-8, Exit 51, at Buckman Springs Rest Area, Mojave Desert, California

TIME: 14:56 PDT

On the return trip from Pendleton, Brian radioed Sanchez for a status update. Sanchez reported that the Marines in the Humvees showed-up about 20 minutes after we left. Gunnies Cornell and Johnson took charge of the two prisoners. Secured them to the fence posts, with two Marines guarding them. With the additional Marines, the trailer was opened-up, and inspection and inventory underway. PFC Berkeley said there's another hole in the cargo area just like the other one. His Geiger counter clicks the same way as in the first trailer. He thinks maybe they just split the load.

Brian: "Squad, we are about 5 from you. Need two Marines to offload 'matériel' transfer en-route to the home base. Out."

The Major landed the helo a safe distance from the white trailer. Brian slid the cargo bay door open, and two Marines just gawked at the cases of 'matériel' they were supposed to off-load.

Rhodes: "How many Marines are out here? Take enough to wet their whistles. Your choice. I hear driving on I-8 can be hazardous; you all drive safely on the way back. I hear that Smitty is out here, too. Is that right? One of you scout him up; we got a vacant seat in here with his name on it. ASAP."

Off-loading Marine: "Yes, sir. Right away, sir." His web gear rattled as he made tracks back to Sanchez. Arms motioned toward the trailer. More rattling.

Rhodes made a mental note about 'rattles can get you killed'. Brush-up training on keeping Marine gear silent will be scheduled soon. Two

Order of Succession

Marines carried Smitty in a 'chair' made from their rifles, and a third Marine ran alongside with his crutch. All pulled and pushed Smitty into the chopper; said 'thanks' and saluted Cap'n Rhodes. They turned smartly, grabbed their cases of drinks, and ran like conquering heroes to whatever shade they could find. Even before the Major had spun-up and lifted off, pop-tops were spewing suds and soda into grateful mouths.

The Major wasted no time as he headed his helo for the rest-area following westbound I-8. Rhodes and Smitty were already in animated conversation. Neither Phillip nor Brian could hear them – not that they were whispering; the chopper was just plain too noisy.

Major Jenkins landed the helo back in the rest-area. They knew the water-cooler rumor would spread fast from the inspection squad, but they didn't expect 20 Marines waiting to off-load 'matériel' here, too. Rhodes: "We need a couple of you to pull Smitty, and his crutch, out of this here helo and take him to some shade. Marines, this cargo is supposed to be kept cold. You know what to do with it after we get our sorry asses out."

Voice in the crowd: "We already got him and his crutch. Why are you all taking so long; the ice is melting." Laughter all around.

Rhodes: "Sorry, but when we get rank, sometimes we get slower. We're clear. Handle the cargo careful . . . oh, hell, go for it. And thank the Major and Cap'n for transport. Now, git."

Because the SCIF group was now scattered between sites, all parties headed for the shadiest area with a table. A couple of Marines followed them carrying some 'cargo', set the bottles and cans down on the table, saluted, turned and left. Pop tops and twist-off caps sure were appreciated. All clinked glass or can, and settled back to the business at hand. "Thank God for the invention of refrigeration."

Rhodes: "Smitty, did you find-out anything out at that trailer? Anything about our situation here? Anything about the greater plot? Anything?"

Smitty: "That trailer was just about the same as we have here. Same hole in the cargo area. Same slightly elevated radiation around it. PFC Berkeley's guess about splitting the load between two trailers may be spot-on. The big difference is there were no corpses in that one. Maybe his other guess about all the victims in ours were the crews from both might also be correct – except for that guy with the multiple IDs. I don't know anything about him for sure yet, though.

"Those two bad-guys haven't said a word yet. But that heat out there by the fence might cook some sense in them. Rocky, (at which, both Phillip and Brian raised their eyebrows, then they got it) is there somebody at Pendleton that's an expert at enemy interrogation? Here's what I'm thinking – another gut feel of mine, you might say – we're supposed to hand all of this over to the FBI, right? Before that happens, I would dearly love to get some of OUR pros to see what they can find out. Why? Well, nobody, and I mean NOBODY, seems interested in us out here right now. Except for the plotters, right? And once we hand them over, I don't think we are ever gonna see any bad-guys again. If we can keep the FBI lads running in circles for a couple of extra days, maybe we can get some information. Like if the four sets of fingerprints are blocked, well, then we know somebody else is involved, which we already know, but maybe we can get a clue who that somebody is. Ya follow my line of reasoning? Whada ya think?"

Rhodes: "Know just the Marine, but he's up at 29 Palms last time I knew. Just got to get somebody higher-up in the food chain to okay it. Want him out here, too?"

Smitty: "You said you thought he was at 29 already, right. That would be just perfect. I got the feeling that the Base Commander at Pendleton is not too interested in our operation out here anymore. But the Air Commander at 29 wanted all of his helos armed on flights in this direction. So, how about we airlift them outta here to 29 and store them up there? Phillip, is that possible? Before you answer that one, can you make a run to Pendleton for any reason such that it may have been possible that the prisoners could have been on that flight so the FBI will have to run rabbits trying to find them? And then can 29 hold them someplace other than the 'official' brig?"

Phillip: "I like the way you think a lot, but I didn't know you were this devious, too. Let me make some calls. But I know it is absolutely doable. Just gotta git some brass on-board. Hold that thought. Maybe just some Gunnies I know. Let me pick-up the prisoners – and two armed guards – at the trailer and let them see us head for Pendleton. That sets the story at the trailer end. Then turn north when we're out of site from the rest-area. Everybody knows where we were headed. How's that sound?"

Order of Succession

Smitty: "I like it a lot. Rocky, your thoughts?"

Rhodes: "Sounds like a plan to me. Let me get a hold of my buddy at 29. He used to do this for a livin' when he was in Afghanistan. Ought to be right up his alley."

Brian: "Might his name be Major Erwin Rollins? Rollins is supposed to be one convincing interrogator."

Rhodes: "Right on! Wow, his reputation certainly gets around. Is he still up there?"

Brian: 'You bet he is. He runs the Marine school on this crap."

Smitty: "This is comin' together, folks. If he runs the school, I'll bet he also knows how and where to store our bad-guys incommunicado for a few days. Not to mention throwin' the fear of God and the Marines into our new-found friends. I'm up for this. If the big guys running this plot can't find their minions . . . maybe us little guys can stop this before it gets too far. Nope, I didn't forget they already got POTUS. Great plan, let's do it!"

Rocky, Phillip, Brian: "On it!"

ORDER OF SUCCESSION

23 – Sleight of Flight

Just past 16:00, Sunday, 15-July: Westbound I-8, Exit 51, at Buckman Springs Rest Area, Mojave Desert, California

TIME: 17:04 PDT

Everyone returned from making their contacts through the SAT-hub at the helo. All loose ends were tied down. Now to tie-up those loose ends still out here.

Group decisions:

- Phillip and Brian make arrangements involving the chopper.
- Rocky got his buddy Erwin up at 29 on-board (enthusiastically).
- Smitty and Rhodes to be the armed guards on the helo.
- Windows on the helo are blacked-out.
- Nobody at the rest-area or the trailer sites needs to know what the game plan is (to keep them in the clear if it all bellies-up)

Time: Sunday, 15-July, 17:23 PDT

With all arrangements made, Rhodes and Smitty belt-in in the helo. And the Major lifts off and follows eastbound I-8.

 Phillip: "Brian, give Cornell a call to get the bad-guys ready for travel in 5. And two bottles of whatever's left over."

 Brian: "Roger. He's getting them ready for travel. And those two bottles, too."

 Brian: "There's the trailer over on the port side about 11 o'clock. The off-loading LZ still looks like the best spot. Looks like Gunny thinks the same; the prisoners are waiting."

Order of Succession

Marines guarding both prisoners loaded them on-board and belted them in inside the blacked-out cabin, and the bottles were transferred to Major Jenkins. The prisoners were handcuffed to the floor, with the new guard detail, Rhodes and Smitty, sitting on canvas seats.

Phillip (in a louder voice): "Off to Pendleton; hang tight."

Brian (playing the role): "Flight plan cleared right up westbound I-8."

Brian (as they neared Buckman Springs): "Coms, overflight passing your location in 2. Over."

Coms: "Can hear you; can't see you yet. Hold that. There you are. Enjoy the ocean breezes. Out."

Smitty (loud enough for the prisoners to hear): "So far, so good. They all saw us headed for Pendleton." The rest of the flight was normal, just a little buffeting from thermals when they transitioned to cooler coastal air.

Phillip: "Brian, call this number and ask for Ajax. He'll know what to do."

Brian: "Permission to land on marker nine. (quietly) This will be a touch and go, right?"

Phillip: "Almost, but not quite."

The Major set his helo down as gently as possible on Number 9, unfastened his belts, and headed to center door – where the two bottles had been stored. He slid the door half open, jumped out, and closed the door from the outside. While he waited in as much shade as possible, Phillip pulled a half liter bottle of water from a pocket on his flight suit. In less than 90 seconds, a car pulled-up and a female Marine got out and walked toward him. They kissed for what seemed like a long time to Brian, who was watching from the cockpit. Phillip handed over both bottles, and they kissed again before he turned toward his chopper. She got into her car and left the area. Phillip followed her car with his eyes, watching until even Brian couldn't see it. Phillip got back into the helo, secured the door, and belted himself back-in. Phillip: "Brian, we're done. Call air-traffic and advise of next destination. We're gonna be late for chow at 29 if we don't lift off right quick."

Brian: "Cleared to go, sir."

Order of Succession

The Major applied power, and the helo lifted-off and was airborne in seconds. He pointed the nose toward 29 and hastily cleared the air-space.

Brian (whispering): "Ajax, sir?"

Phillip (also whispering): "I know you are wondering. When you called that number, you didn't talk to a woman, did you? You spoke with Ajax. She is not Ajax."

Brian: "Well, then, who is . . . Never mind; you don't have to tell me. You're just gonna say I don't have a need to know, aren't you?"

Phillip: "That's a big Roger. Besides, indeed, we delivered two 'packages' to Pendleton, didn't we? (Now much louder for the benefit of the two prisoners) Okay, now lay in the course correction. We got appointments to keep."

The taller prisoner: "You all said Pendleton. What the hell you mean by 'course correction'? Where does that correction take us.?"

Smitty: "That's a good question. I'd have the same question if I were in your shoes. But it's too late now. Sit back and enjoy the flight; might be your last one."

Other prisoner: "Whacha mean with that 'last ride' crap? Where you takin' us."

Rhodes: "As the commanding officer of the Marines who responded to the kidnapping of the President, I decided that this was an act of war. You are now our prisoners. Furthermore, it has been decided that the initial destination could not provide adequate security for such criminals as yourselves. Therefore, your flight has been diverted to somewhere that can provide adequate security."

Tall prisoner: "Jes wha the hell is going on here. Hey, those guys never said anything about the President being involved. We were just supposed to sorta guard that trailer. Ya know, just keep snoopy people away from it, 'til they come back for it, ya know."

Rhodes and Smitty looked at each other. Maybe they found the weakest links in the plot right here in this chopper.

Smitty: "You sound like you might be truthin' us; but it's too late for that now. Both of you are already in it up to your lower lips. Sorry 'bout that. Keep your story for 'Hard-Ass'; he's gonna want to hear it first-hand."

Order of Succession

Tall prisoner: "But, we weren't told nothin' 'bout none of this. We were just supposed to watch over that damn trailer. Nobody was supposed to get hurt. Just keep people away from it; that's all."

Rhodes: "Tell that to your buddies on the other side of the trailer. You know they didn't make it, right?"

Short prisoner: "Whada ya mean Hoss and Lefty didn't make it? They wasn't doin' nothin' wrong. Just keeping people away; that's all."

Brian: "Say, buddies, you remember this chopper firing a short burst behind you? Do ya? And you didn't point your rifles at our chopper, right? Well, now, that was right smart of you. And do'ya know why? Well, ya see, if this here pilot just happened to have an itchy nose and twitched that stick in his hand, you wouldn't have had time to surrender. Got that? But Hoss or Lefty – don't matter much to him or me which one – pointed his rifle at us. And both got tagged by at least a 7.62-mm bullet outta this here little Gatling' gun we got hangin' off the side of this chopper. Or, maybe you understand a '.308' bullet better. That's why they aren't on this chopper, and you are. They're in body bags heading for a morgue. You gotta remember that chopper crews don't take kindly to being screwed with by people on the ground pointing rifles at us."

Smitty: "Y'all heard the man. Don't screw with choppers."

Taller prisoner: "Man, they didn't say nothin' about this. We was just supposed to keep people away from that effin' tractor and trailer; that's all. Really, that's all we was supposed to do."

Rhodes: "What did ya think those Marines were? Don't you recognize damn uniforms? How screwed up are you that you don't recognize uniforms of these United States?"

Short prisoner: "Hell yes, we recognize the uniforms. One of the guys who paid us to watch over the semi and trailer was wearin' one. Ya think we're stupid or sumpthin'?"

Smitty: "One was wearing one of these uniforms? Are you tryin' to screw around with us? One of these. Oh, sure they were!"

Tall prisoner: "They look all the same to me; but it was a uniform that looked a lot like yours. Man, we were just supposed to keep people away from that friggin' tractor and trailer. That's all. That guy didn't say

Order of Succession

nothing' about helicopters and machine guns and shit like that. What are we supposed to tell Hoss and Lefty's families."

Rhodes: "Brian, if you can get a message to Gunny Cornell from here, advise him to look at the tractor and trailer very carefully. Very thoroughly 'cause I think I got Smitty's gut problem. Something's not ringing true here."

The question and answer session suddenly struck a sticking point. Now it's beginning to look like somebody in one of the services may be involved up to his lower lip, too.

Smitty: "Brian, what's our altitude outside?"

Brian: "Probably, oh about, 2,000 feet above the mountains below us. Why?"

Smitty: "Just curious. Got some thinkin' to do real fast."

Rhodes (whispered): "Remind you of Hal and the U-Team?"

Smitty (whispered): "Yeah. Something like that, but can't put my finger on it."

Time: Sunday, 15-July, Says: 18:46 PDT

Silence ruled the rest of the flight. As they neared 29, Brian radioed ahead and advised Major Rollins of his new nick-name, *Hard-Ass*.

Brian: "Destination site dead ahead. Phillip, Hard-Ass should be waiting about 12 klicks at 2 o'clock."

Rhodes: "He said to set the helo down behind the concertina wire. There's supposed to be an LZ with a regulation marker. Call his number and he'll turn on the lights. Additional guards will also surround the LZ."

Brian: "Phillip, Hard-Ass said to continue on your present course for 3 and watch for the lights to come on."

Smitty: "Well, boys, we are on final approach. Hard-Ass just loves new meat. Good luck."

The lights popped on about half a klick away. The Major found his target and set the helo down. The side door slid open. The prisoners had to adjust their vision because of the bright landing lights surrounding the LZ. They now wished they had never ever

Order of Succession

heard of or seen whoever that guy in the uniform was. They were looking straight at five Marines with their rifles pointed directly at them, and they were still cuffed to the floor of the helo. They could see the rifles had magazines in place. This was definitely not a situation to screw-up.

Rollins: "Gentlemen, welcome to Little Afghanistan. Isn't it nice here? Oh, I forgot; you won't see any of this for a long time. So, let's begin with one simple ground rule, shall we. 'If you try anything threatening, they will shoot for center-of-mass – your center-of-mass. There is no second order. Got that? Only one standing order.' "

"And, please don't make me live-up to my nick-name; that will not be pleasant for you. And since I am told you are prisoners of war, well, don't expect any POW treatment because I consider you to be terrorists as well as traitors. Do you understand your positions? No questions, so I guess you do. It's lovely that we understand each other so quickly, isn't it? Sergeant of the Guard, escort these prisoners to their cells – one in Cell Number 2 and the other in Cell Number 5. Doesn't matter which goes where. And no talking between them.' "

Hard-Ass sounded convincing even to Rhodes who had lived with Erwin in Kabul. Actually, if Rocky didn't know him, even he might be a bit concerned.

Smitty: "Good luck, boys. Sleep tight. And, I really mean that, too, if you can."

As Taller and Shorter were unloaded from the cargo area, Major Hard-Ass stopped by and greeted Rocky. "Was that hammy enough for you? Haven't done one of those in years. Has something to do with instilling the fear of God or something like that."

Rhodes: "You know, Erwin, I think we almost believe them. They said a bad-guy in a uniform that looked a lot like ours paid them to watch a semi-tractor and a trailer – both all white with no markings. Just to keep nosey people away from them. Two of their buddies, Hoss and Lefty, didn't make it; got tagged for pointing a rifle at the chopper. I think we, Smitty here and me, stumbled right into the middle of some sort of plot. As near as we can tell, POTUS has already been kidnapped. Smitty, can you fill-in, Erwin, about your theory about the Order of Succession?

Order of Succession

Smitty (all business now): "Sorry for this Captain Rhodes, but Major Rollins, I need to know what your clearance level is. I'll make it easy for you, is it TS/SCI or higher?

Rollins: "I understand completely and would be disappointed if someone didn't ask. Yes, it is TS/SCI or higher along with a couple of other certs as well."

Smitty: "Okay, for the purposes of this discussion, you, Major Rollins, cannot speak to anyone about this plot unless they are already involved with resolving it. The four of us in this chopper are already 'read-in' for this purpose. And so far, there are only about ten of us – all in the Marines and me – who know the full extent of this plot so far. You would make eleven. Do you understand what I am telling you, sir?"

Rollins: "Yes, I do, and I agree to your stipulations. I would have to if I am supposed to find out anything important from those two guys. It sounds interesting; please continue."

Smitty: "Sorry I had to be a hard-ass on you, sir. Here goes nothing in a nutshell. Friday afternoon the President was kidnapped at a rest-area on I-8." Smitty continued his story including his theory about the (very) recent deaths of almost all of the people in the Order of Succession hierarchy – so far 14 out of 19. He also related the breakdown of all communication in all of his chains of command. Smitty's final description was of the 'Voice on the phone' – good old 'piss-ant'.

Rollins: "This guy sounds most interesting. How do you know about him?

Rhodes: "When the President was kidnapped, they left his cellphone in a tunnel. This guy knows what the number is, and he called it several times already. He wants to speak to Smitty, but we listen to it on the speakerphone. Oh, before I forget, the FBI is supposed to take-over this Agent Howard Phelps and Agent Pat Tobin are supposed to contact us to take over the investigation on Tuesday at 10:30 hours at the rest-area. Whoever this caller is, he must be wired into a lot of agencies – all the way down to Agents' names. And finally, nobody but the four of us in that helo and you know where these boys are. Please be careful, Erwin."

Erwin: "It's getting deeper as we speak isn't it? I think we can provide decent security here. You both be careful, too."

Order of Succession

Phillip: "Up and out. Gotta refuel. And talk things over with the CG. And don't forget, we still gotta put in an appearance at the mess hall."

As Smitty recalled, Phillip wasn't that much of a chow hound, but a couple of 29's mess halls had late hours because of late-night training, and they put out a good spread for the 'midnight' Marines. As they got out of the Humvee, their hunger was almost sated by the cool breeze fanning the aromas across the mess hall parking lot. They were not disappointed. They rode back to the helipad in silence, each thinking their own thoughts about what lay before them and the country. And if they would ever find out any truths about it.

Time: Sunday, 15-July, 21:34 PDT

Both man and machine were full and satisfied, with 'all systems go'. The Major lifted off toward the rest-area, airborne again in the dark of the desert. Smitty finally broke the silence, "Guys, let me know if this sounds crazy. I'm seriously thinking about going undercover again. I'm fixin' to pull what strings I know and trust, and see if I can get back into contact with Hal and the U-Team again. Am I nuts to do that? Wait, before you answer, there's more to this plan going around in my head about this.

"I was thinking – just trying to put pieces of the puzzle together, you understand – if I could find out anything more about this from the inside of at least the plotters that I know of, well, maybe we could learn something about the other group – if there is still one. What do ya think? But, wait, there's still more.

"I'm not sayin' I have any pull left, but some folks I worked with in the past trusted me on some important projects, and, I repaid their trust on those. We got our guys. So, here's the last piece in my puzzle. If push comes to shove, and I discover an honest-to-goodness plot, would you all mind if I tried to get you re-assigned to fix it? On a TDY basis, of course. We would need good-guys who know what the hell they're doin' as well as improvising some possible solutions. And, Rocky, I like how some of your Marines work on challenges. Now that they are known Marines to me, I would like to include some of them, too, in what I'm thinking about. Okay, I'm finished; your turn."

All three answered: "You're on." "You bet." "I'm in, but as for my Marines, I'll ask at that time. Okay?"

Order of Succession

Time: Sunday, 15-July, 23:43 PDT

The Major set the chopper down at the LZ in the rest-area, and the landing lights were quickly extinguished.

Corporal Knight (coms): "Sergeant Williams been lookin' for ya. The POTUS phone rang again. That guy was all bent out of shape you weren't here. Coms is waiting for ya over in the mess area. I gotta get back to the com gear."

"Smitty: "Well, I guess we – make that I – screwed-up. First time today. But, hell, there's less than 30 minutes left, so that's a pretty good score. Gotta hit the head; meet y'all in the mess tent."

Brian: "Roger all of that." And he followed Smitty.

Rhodes (to Coms): "We heard the POTUS phone rang again, and the guy is really ticked-off. Any clues about his problem this time? And don't ask about what took so long. No need to know, okay?"

Coms: "Understood, sir. No, we didn't get anything from that guy's call, unless you call colorful cussing informative. He has a vocabulary like that Sergeant Snorkel in Beetle Bailey. Wow, is he salty!"

Rhodes (across the tent): "Hey, Gunny, can I see you over here?" Now, to Gunny Cornell up close; "Did ya find-out anything out at the trailer? And, no, we can't tell ya anything about how come we were away so long."

Cornell: "There's blood back in the ass-end of the trailer, too. But no bodies, just blood, but I don't think it was from a complete bleed-out. Found some packing material with foreign writing on it; sort of German, I think, but not quite. Maybe that's from the automated gun-platform, ya know that Fabrique Nationale Company. Oh, yeah, you already heard about that radioactive spot near the middle of where the load would have been, right? The tractor, however, did have some documents in a briefcase – some packing slips, more ID Cards, and order-sheets that look like TDY papers, but we didn't have time to make sense of them out there. Brought the case back here for safe-keeping.

"We policed-up the two bad-guys that didn't make it; they're in body bags in the refrigerated truck over there in the parking area. Too bad they didn't listen-up; they had upwards of $3,000 in folding money each. Maybe that's what the bad-guy who hired them paid them. Bet their families could have used it, even if just to bury them."

Order of Succession

Smitty: "Gunny, where are the others? I know it's late, but I'd like to have you all meet over at the SCIF for about 10 minutes. I want to bring you up to speed on some things. Okay?"

Cornell: "I'll round them up. Be there in 10."

Time: Monday, 16-July, 00:05 PDT

Smitty: "Remember we are still using the TS/SCI rules in this SCIF.

"Here's an update for you. Those two bad-guys are in a very safe 'undisclosed location' – as the politicians say – where we hope the bad-guys' leaders will have a really tough time tracking them down. Because we don't know who's who in this screwy zoo, and because that guy on the POTUS phone sounds military, and because a lot of the explosives out here appear to be from our own ammo bunkers, and all sorts of other crap. I am gonna try to protect you here all by not telling you anything else. Make sense? End of update on that item.

"During the return trip, I came to the conclusion that I am going to try to go back undercover again so I can find-out if these bad-guys and my bad-guys are related in some way. I mean, maybe it's just a coincidence that two groups want to do harm to the President, but I'm beginning to think they are connected somehow. I'll have some more news if I find-out anything, but that's about it for now. Monday's already here, so we have one day to clean-up and preserve whatever we can. I spoke to a new friend named Hard-Ass who might be able to store some sensitive material for a while. More on that later in the morning. I think I'm about done with this update. Anybody have any question that I can answer? None. Great. Most of us need to catch some zzz's. How about the mess tent at, say, 07:00?"

ORDER OF SUCCESSION

24 – Cleaning-up the Rest Area

Around 06:30, Monday, 16-July: Westbound I-8, Exit 51, at Buckman Springs Rest Area, Mojave Desert, California

TIME: 06:32 PDT

The changing of the Marine guards had the mess hall pumping-out coffee by the gallon, or that's just the way it seemed. And the returning guards kept the chow-line moving by devouring eggs, bacon, sausage, cereal – you name it. Smitty joined the rest of the Marines for his usual breakfast: coffee with cream, diced fruit, and an egg & sausage sandwich on dry toast. He started chuckling to himself.

{Smitty's mind, replaying earlier events: "Who was it now? PFC Berkeley, I think. Yeah, PFC Berkeley; he's the one. Berkeley even had that theory about the cannelure grooves and that 'not enough wrappers' thing. He's one weird dude for dreamin'-up all that kinda crap. But he was ever so right, too; that's the really weird angle. And here you are eating one of those breakfast sandwiches without a wrapper. How weird is that?" "Okay Brain, cool it for now."}

But, it all tasted so right this early morning in sunny southern California.

Time: Monday, 16-July, 06:45 PDT

Corporal Knight (running and breathless): "Smitty, sir, the POTUS phone! It's that guy again! Whacha want me ta do?"

Smitty: "Is he on hold?"

Knight: "Yes, sir. I don't want to be responsible for hanging-up on him."

Smitty: "Good. Catch your breath, grab something to drink, and find as many of our guys and have them meet us at the phone over at coms

Order of Succession

ASAP. I'm gonna walk over there to give the rest of them time to get there." And, he, indeed, walked, with his crutch in tow, over to the coms table.

{Brain: "Hey, it is a beautiful morning after all!"}

Time: Monday, 16-July, 06:55 PDT

The POTUS phone was still on hold while the team assembled.

Smitty: "We don't want to keep this guy waiting too much longer; he'll really be pissed-off at me. Okay, Brian will you take notes again and somebody help back him up. First couple of questions may be important. Let's keep it as quiet as possible. I'm going live on the speakerphone in 3, 2, 1." To the POTUS phone: "Morning to ya. How can I help you?"

Voice on POTUS phone: "Considerin' the circumstances, you're pretty damn difficult to git a holt of, wouldn't cha say, piss-ant?"

Smitty (signaling to the note takers to write): "Nah, I wouldn't go that far. We got work to do out here getting' ready to hand this scene over to the FBI. Ya know that neither Special Agent Phelps nor Agent Tobin have even tried to call us yet. What's up with that, huh?"

Voice: "Geez, I'm sorry about that. How the hell do I know why they haven't called ya, piss-ant? And I don't even friggin' care if they do or not. What the hell am I, piss-ant, your babysitter and their mama?"

Smitty (not giving the Voice a chance to say another word): "Well, I'd think it should be important enough that all of you try to keep tabs on your supportin' cast, dontcha think so, too? By the way, it's just about 07:00 out here. What time is where you are, and I'll set an alarm for your next call?"

Voice (caught somewhat off guard by feeling on the defensive): "It's 10 – *wait-one*. Belay that. Let's just say it's not 0-dark 30 here. And, we – rather I – don't control the FBI agents, you dumb bastard." (Smitty makin' frantic writing gestures about the 10 o'clock screw-up.)

{Smitty's brain: "Too late you dastardly bastard. [Hey, that sorta rhymes. Aren't you the smart one!] We heard that '10' you just said. You got caught. Hope the rest of your effing group is just as smart and have egos to match."}

Smitty: "Hey, I wasn't sayin' anything about them. Hell, I was just sayin' that we hadn't heard from them yet. How are we gonna know who

Order of Succession

they are when they show-up here? Can you describe them for us, huh? Oh, by the way, you do know that I-8 is still shut-down, dontcha? Oh, of course you know that; how silly of me. But, anyway, how are they plannin' to get here? I mean, after all, with the security we have here, we wouldn't want to mistake them for some local yokels guarding a semi-tractor and trailer, would we? How would that look?"

Voice: "Whadya mean local yokels guarding that truck? Whadya talking about? They were just . . ."

{Smitty's brain: "Gotcha again, you dastardly bastard! [Hey, I like that rhyming.] Doesn't this dummy know when to shut-up? Oh, well, keep him talkin' and pretty soon we'll have all their names, ranks, and social security numbers, too. What a dummy!!"}

Smitty's still making scribbling gestures; two more listeners start taking notes. "Yeah, we know they were just supposed to watch the tractor and trailer to keep snoopy people from pokin' around them. Isn't that right? Well, of the four of them, two got it in their heads to screw with us by raisin' hunting rifles at us. Can you imagine how terribly stupid that was! And to make matters worse, both of them were carrying around $3,000 apiece – in folding green. You got any idea how these local yokels got a hold of that much money and were still carrying it? The really pitiful thing is, now that they didn't make it, their families are not even gonna see that money. No way because that's evidence of a conspiracy – at least. And how are their families gonna even bury them? Ain't that a bitch; their husbands and fathers think they struck it rich and simply sit around that all-white trailer and end-up in a 'flyin' hot-lead' confrontation with US Marines. Not in my worst nightmare would I want to be them. There's just no way those poor bastards struck it rich." Smitty's finally poking and prodding the Voice and gave 'the Voice' an opening to get a word in edgewise.

Voice: "Sorry 'bout that. What about the other . . ."

Smitty didn't miss the invitation to butt-in: "Oh, you must mean that other two yokels, huh? They were much smarter; they surrendered."

Voice: "Whatcha mean 'surrendered'? You mean they just up and gave-up?"

Sometimes, reality sort of bites – hard. Smitty: "Well, yeah, pretty much. They were pretty ticked-off to hear their buddies were in body

Order of Succession

bags. Until they realized they weren't. Just kept mentioning they were only supposed to keep snoopy people away from the WHITE tractor and trailer. But enough about reports from the front; I'm sure you already knew that crap, huh. So, what else is still on your agenda?"

Voice (silence for a while, then): "Say, ya know we're down to three. Numbers 3 and 4 will retire. Number 6 is effing feckless; he'll be taken care of by friends in the Middle East." At this, Smitty makes really frantic scribbling gestures.

Smitty (although he knew who the Voice was referring to): "Numbers 3 and 4 and 6? Say what? Whatcha talkin' about? Is the fix in on a horse race? Hey, if it's already in, what track and race is it? I'd like to get some of the action on that one. I'll be the one bettin' against ya, though."

Voice (with renewed composure): "What am I talkin' about? Give me a break. The rest, well, all of the rest in due time. I'll call you back tomorrow morning. Be there this time, piss-ant."

Smitty: "What time should I set the alarm for? Oh, tomorrow morning. I forgot to tell ya I might not be here; I might havta catch an early flight out of here." (Giving a look at Phillip and Brian about the 'flight'. They shrugged and nodded in agreement.)

Voice: "Whadya mean 'an early flight'? Who said you could go, piss-ant? Your boss didn't . . ."

{Smitty's brain: "Another big OOPS. When will this bozo ever learn to just plain shut-up! When?" "Brain, you got that right!"}

Smitty: "Well, as you probably know, we have sort of been isolated out here. Through no fault of ours, that is. So as the Marines say, we 'Improvised, Adapted, and Overcame' those obstacles. Gaining a lot of insight in that process, however, I might add. Anything else I can help you with?"

Voice: "Yeah, what happened to those yokels – as you called them – the ones who surrendered? Whatcha do with them?"

Smitty: "Oh, those two locals. We were thinking about handing them over to the FBI, but ya know we haven't decided that yet. Well, we have a meeting to attend. Talk with ya tomorrow if I'm still here. If I'm gone, Cap'n Rhodes will havta do, okay? Well thanks for calling. Bye." Smitty hit the mute button on the speakerphone just to listen to the Voice's reaction.

Order of Succession

Voice: "Smitty. Smitty. SMITTY!! That sonovabitch hung-up on me. That bastard is gonna pay for that. Wait'll Bubba hears this."

Smitty (to no one in particular): "There's the biggest OOPS yet. Bubba. Could this be the same Bubba plotting with Hal. Maybe I won't be going undercover back in Thurmont. Gotta reconsider this some more. But, at least we have more clues."

Rhodes: "More and more, this sounds like it's all the same plan to me."

Smitty: "Yep. Okay, now what clues did we gather from this call?"

Group discussion:

1st Marine: "One mistake: he's three hours ahead of us. That puts him in the Eastern Time Zone."

2nd Marine: "He knows about the four 'yokels'. But he didn't know about the fire fight and surrender."

3rd Marine: "And he REALLY wants to know about the two live ones. Probably to keep them from talking."

1st Marine: "He uses the word 'holt' instead of 'hold'; frequently heard in southern speech."

4th Marine: "He's used to being in-charge. Not comfortable when his agenda is not followed. And he's careless using modern technology. Forgot or didn't realize his microphone was still live."

5th Marine: "I think he knows that you know what WHITE means on tractors and trailers."

2nd Marine: "He thought his bad-guys had isolated this area. He didn't like 'a morning flight out' one little bit. Their control was not as complete as they thought. Do you really have a flight out?"

3rd Marine: "The Secret Service higher-ups are probably involved"

6th Marine: "He thinks those two yokels are still here at the rest-area. Say, where are they anyway? Sorry, never mind; shouldn't have asked. I do not want to know anything about that. Forget I even asked."

1st Marine: "He may have some naval experience. The way he used the word 'belay'."

7th Marine: "I still think he's military or, at least, has military experience."

Order of Succession

3rd Marine: "He doesn't like to be pushed and prodded like you did by taking over his meeting."

Smitty added: "He knows number 3, 4, and 6 are part of the Order Of Succession."

2nd Marine: "I know I don't want to buy a used car from you!"

4th Marine: "He's got a better vocabulary than I do. What the hell does 'feckless' mean anyway; sounds X-rated to me."

Smitty: "All good points. Keep them in mind when we have to identify this dastardly bastard."

{Smitty's mind: "Couldn't leave it alone for once, huh. Just had to say it one more time. What am I ever gonna do with you!"}

"Let's grab some coffee or left-over chow. Say we report to the SCIF in 45 and give this place a really clean sweep."

Time: Monday, 16-July, 09:22 PDT

Smitty: "After this morning's call on the POTUS phone, I think it's time to make tracks, at least for me. Right now, I don't think the bad-guys can assemble a team to harass us out of this rest area if we don't want to go. They may not know what we have here – the chopper and some firepower, now – and the FBI is supposed to be here in the A.M. anyway. I don't think they are going to try anything else now that they apparently have the President.

"So, Cap'n Rhodes, if I am not here in the A.M., can you handle the FBI in a manner to keep them out of our hair for a few days? Can you get a hold of Hard-Ass, say this evening, to see if our guests cooperated, especially after the 'Voice call' this morning and tell him about this call? And can you have a guard posted through the night in case I'm wrong?"

Rhodes: "I think we can manage to inundate the FBI with pictures and tours to keep them busy trying to get their arms around this site. No problem. I'll get Coms involved to bring them up to speed on the 'limited' communications we had out here. Who wants custody of the POTUS phone?"

Smitty: "I'll bet that sucker has GPS tracking, and not the civilian version either. For what I am planning, I do not want it anywhere near me. Maybe the best bet is to simply turn it over to the FBI and let them answer the calls from the 'Voice'. That'll give both sides something to do trying to find out who's who. Or maybe the agents already know. Either way, I don't want it. Too much danger from tracking, if you know what I mean. Phillip and Brian, seriously, any chance I can get a flight out of here first thing in the morning before the FBI appears? I'll tell you where to after we are airborne, okay?"

Phillip: "Anytime, anywhere, we deliver. You want oh-dark-30 or daylight? Just let us know tonight so we can rest up from all the hard partying out here."

Smitty: "Roger. Now, if there are no other pressing issues, let's make this place look like we weren't here, shall we?"

And with that, the Marines took the former SCIF apart and folded the walls back into tarps. Everybody joined in separating-out the items that were going into 'protected' storage and piled them in a few isolated boxes; the rest went into large piles of stuff the FBI was going to take custody of tomorrow morning. Those agents were going to be busy signing hand-receipts for lots of miniscule items, pictures, bridge-deck fragments, the limo, you name it. Everything was going to be handed over with tracking paperwork for each item. Yes, sir, they were going to be swimming in paperwork up to their eyeballs – or maybe even higher. And they could also deal with CalTrans and their decking, the morgues, the county sheriff, all of it. Cap'n Rhodes and his Gunnies were not going to leave with too many souvenirs at all – except the ones that were already packed and shipped.

Part 3 – Recon, Planning, Searching, and Training

ORDER OF SUCCESSION

25 – Getting Back Into the Game

Around Oh-Dark-30, Tuesday, 17-July: Westbound I-8, Exit 51, at Buckman Springs Rest Area, Mojave Desert, California

TIME: 03:46 PDT

Knight: "Smitty, sir, that guy on the POTUS phone is calling again. What do I tell him, sir?"

Smitty (already up and heading for coffee and to meet Phillip and Brian): "That's easy Corporal: You looked, but you couldn't find me. Ask him if you should look in the latrine because you think you saw me headed that way. Okay?"

Knight: "Sure enough, sir."

Smitty hustled over to the mess tent and found Phillip and Brian. "Right now would be a great time to lift off. PDQ."

Phillip: "We were just thinking the same thing. Pack your gear and be in the helo in 10, and we're outta here. PDQ."

Another Changing of the Marine guards, and the mess tent kept the coffee urns filled. The weary Marines coming off guard duty shoveled bacon, eggs, sausage, and cereal onto their trays. Toast was at the end of the line, and the baskets overflowed with slices, butter, and jams and jellies. Coffee, milk, and juice followed the toast. Smitty normally would have found a vacant spot at the end of the guards' line for his usual breakfast. However, today was different; he jumped the line and grabbed an egg and sausage sandwich and two bottles of water. The Marines did not object; they even offered to carry his food for him. He thanked them but declined.

ORDER OF SUCCESSION

Time: Tuesday, 17-July, 03:51 PDT

Smitty: "Rocky, you awake in there?" Smitty was talking to a small cargo trailer behind a Humvee.

Rhodes: "I am now. You making like a ghost? I don't want to really know about this, do I?"

Smitty: "Ya better start callin' me Casper. Remember, you may get a call from me about goin' TDY. Oh, by the way, Corporal Knight says the Voice is back on the POTUS phone. Thought you should know that just in case. If you need to contact me for any reason about this mess, call this number and ask for 'Craig Richards'. I'm gone now." He shoved a scrap of paper with a phone number into Rocky's hand, and Casper was gone.

With that, Smitty hobbled quickly over to the helo and threw his pack, followed by himself, into the belly and strapped himself into his canvas sling seat. As the Major maneuvered the controls, the helo quickly achieved hover altitude. "Smitty, where to?"

Smitty: "East to where they may not think we are. Don't know how safe it is to fly this thing without lights and tracking, but that would be helpful, if possible."

Phillip: "Thought so. Minimum equipment on. Any place in particular?"

Smitty: "Someplace with a commercial airport. If this is what I think it is, I gotta work my way back east somehow. I still have my undercover credit cards; gonna try one to see if they are still active. Doesn't have to be San Diego; that may be too active with too many eyes, but it may work okay this early. Whatever you can get to without causing yourself administrative grief."

Phillip: "May have to be Yuma. We can make a 'training' flight up to 29 with the stuff we loaded last night. And then go back to Pendleton from there. If Yuma's okay with you, that's the plan."

Smitty: "Do it. We'll make it work." And then Smitty began checking his eyelids for holes.

Phillip (about 45 minutes later): "Yo, Smitty, wake-up, your snoring is killing us up here. We're almost to Yuma International Airport. The Marines over here share the airport grounds with civilian airlines. I've got a car waiting for you at the pad. When I touch-down, you hop out, and we go deliver some goods to storage. Got that? Don't want to be on the ground too long with this stuff."

Smitty: "Understood. And remember you and Brian, here, may be getting a call about a TDY assignment sooner than we thought. You two still up for it?"

Brian: "You bet."

The Major brought the helo down on the money, and Smitty bailed-out, grabbed his pack, and made for the car, which was a Humvee. The Major did his' touch' part of the run, and now he began the 'go' part. The Humvee driver headed over to the airport terminal to the Marines lounge, which was equipped with a 'universal' ticket counter. His undercover credit card worked and he was off to Lambert field in St. Louis, flight leaving in 20 minutes. The agent advised, "Right this way, sir, up those stairs to the gates." And Casper was gone.

Smitty flew a zigzag route through Chicago, Indianapolis, Pittsburgh, and finally ending-up in Baltimore's BWI airport. The rental car was from a small, non-descript rental agency off the airport grounds. He began bringing Terry Pedrozo back to life – just in case the fabricated, vaporous agent was needed again. Smitty picked-up a Maryland highway map from a big-name rental company within the consolidated, centralized garage and perused it outside in the parking lot. He easily found Thurmont on the map and then started looking for a nearby town where he could still be close to Thurmont, but not directly next-door to it. For tonight, he settled on Hagerstown, Maryland, because it was screened from Thurmont by a ridge of mountains between them. The highway between them, Maryland 77 (MD-77), looked like it should be a simple drive, with a bonus that it was the closest highway to Camp David. And it would give him an excuse/reason to drive the area trying to find Hal's personal storage arsenal.

Time: Wednesday, 18-July (Early Evening, Hagerstown, Maryland)

So, off he went trying to navigate to I-70 (Interstate 70) from the BWI airport. He found it located as an exit on Baltimore's I-695 Beltway. Easy exit and headed west. Traffic slowed down as it passed Frederick, especially where I-270 poured commuters in by the hundreds during

Order of Succession

the regular workday. The traffic's speed picked-up again after passing an off-ramp for US-15/340 (heading toward – Virginia and West Virginia), but the traffic just crawled up a long hill – three lanes wide and still crawling – and under a bridge painted a fading orange. However, he began to make time on the down-hill side; however, I-70 squeezed back down to two lanes again – so it all turned-out to be sort of a wash. Westbound I-70, however, expanded again back to three lanes where it passed under MD-17 at Myersville. The map showed it should lead him directly to Hagerstown.

Smitty exited from I-70 at Exit 32B onto older US-40 west, which he later learned was called 'The Dual Highway' in this stretch in Hagerstown – descriptive, but not really functionally different from other four lane highways with a grass median between the roadways and stop lights. He drove around the town getting the lay-of-the-land and making notes of motels that looked to be locally-owned. He was prepared to motel-it for a few weeks and then rent an apartment if necessary. His first temporary room was a local, non-chain motel on Pennsylvania Avenue north of downtown Hagerstown. It offered motel basics, but certainly not permanent quarters for his purposes. He'd search for something better for his needs later. Maybe in Pennsylvania or even down in West Virginia – it just depends. But first, sleep. Smitty blocked the door with a door-stop and a chair, sleeping well into early Thursday morning.

Time: Tuesday, 17-July, 04:36 PDT (Rest Area, California)

Coms: "The POTUS phone just rang. Same Voice, etc. He wants to speak to Smitty; what do I tell him?"

Rhodes: "Don't you worry about that. I'll talk to him. Why does this crappy stuff always happen during a change of command?"

Over at the Coms table: Rhodes (after thumbing-on the speakerphone): "Morning to you, whoever you are. Captain Rhodes here."

Voice: "I didn't ask for you, Marine. I want that Secret Service agent, Smitty. Go get his ass over here!"

Rhodes: "Would really like to do that, but we can't. Looks like he left; he's gone."

Order of Succession

Voice: "Whadya mean 'he's gone'? We didn't . . . .ash nobody authorized him to leave. Where the hell is he?"

Rhodes: "He didn't say anything to me either. We woke-up this morning, and he flat wasn't here. Our guards didn't even know he left during the night; he must be really good at buggin' out. He never said anything about having to be released from here. But what can I do for you since you got me up?" Rocky knew this was really stretching things, but the circumstances warranted it.

Voice: "Where did he go? How did he leave? What you got to say for yourself, Marine?"

Rhodes: "I've got nothing to say for myself, but the answers to both your questions are the same – I don't know anything about why, where, or how Smitty left. I repeat once again that he was gone when I woke-up this morning. There's nothing else I can tell you about that. But on to other things. So, tell me again, when are those FBI agents supposed to show-up out here this morning?"

Voice: "Probably still on for 10:30 your time. Those Fibbies are the least of my worries right now. You sure, Smitty never left any clues? Yeah, you wouldn't say anything anyhow, would ya? Oh, shit, Bubba ain't gonna like that one friggin' bit!"

Rhodes (agreeing, but didn't say so): "No, he didn't clue any of us in about his plans. Again, I say again, he was gone when we woke-up this morning.

{Rhodes mocking brain: "Is that guy dense or what! Maybe the third time is the charm for this bozo. But what does he know? Can you find-out?"}

Rhodes (continuing): "Who's this 'Bubba' you keep talkin' about? Is he one of the FBI agents comin' out here?"

Voice: "No, he ain't with the FBI. He's with the . . . (another big 'oops moment' – almost). I gotta go."

Rhodes: "When the FBI agents get here, are they supposed to report into you? What number do they call? Hello? Hello? Hello?" Looking over at Coms, both shrugged their shoulders. Rhodes gave Coms the signal to cut the call off.

212

Order of Succession

Time: Tuesday, 17, 06:23 PDT (29 Palms)

The Major set his helo down behind the concertina. Major 'Hard-Ass' Rollins was waiting for him with mugs of fresh coffee in hand. After the blades spun down to a stop, the Marines off-loaded the boxes of 'stuff' from the rest-area. Major Rollins agreed to store them 'temporarily' as long he could leaf through them. Smitty, Rhodes, and Jenkins agreed that maybe there might be some clues buried in the notes and stuff – so, why not.

Jenkins: "Good to see you again, Erwin. You have the best coffee this early in the morning. You know that, don't cha? By the way, you never officially heard of Smitty. Okay? He's on his way back to where the plot of some of those guys originated. I don't know where he is right now; he didn't even say 'goodbye'. Okay?"

Rollins: "Roger to both. Smitty? Who's Smitty?"

Jenkins: "How are our buddies doin'? Find-out anything interesting?"

Rollins: "Truth is they're probably telling the truth about how they got involved. We're working on descriptions now. I'm a decent 'facial artist'. Got a preliminary sketch; want to see it? Maybe it'll ring a bell if the right person sees it. Who knows."

Jenkins: "Sure, let's give it a look-see. Maybe if Smitty ever contacts us again, he'll recognize somebody. Sure, why not." He and Rollins disappeared into the building to look over the results. Then they 'poked-at' the 'guests' – rattling their cages, so to speak. Jenkins took a picture of the 'artistic' rendering with his phone – ready to send it, if Smitty ever contacts him again.

Stepping back into the early morning air, Phillip gave Brian the signal to get the helo ready for the final leg of their 'training' flight. The Captain operated the controls for lift-off, hovered, rotated to the southwest, and was gone for Pendleton.

ORDER OF SUCCESSION

26 – Finally, the FBI Arrives

Around mid-morning at a little past 09:30, Tuesday, 17-July: Westbound I-8, Exit 51, at Buckman Springs Rest Area, Mojave Desert, California

TIME: Tuesday, 17-July, 09:34 PDT (Rest Area, California)

Captain Rhodes prepared for the arrival of Howard Phelps, FBI Special Agent, from San Diego and Pat Tobin, FBI Agent, also from San Diego. Rhodes and the Gunnies were discussing the FBI over coffee. Coms appeared, and they invited him to join the rest.

Rhodes: "Coms, we were just discussing how we were all surprised to find-out Smitty was gone when we woke-up this morning."

Coms (picking-up on the clues): "Same here. Surprised that we also couldn't find him this morning, either."

Rhodes: "Any word about the FBI agents who are supposed to be showing-up today? Supposed to be sometime around 10:30."

Coms: "Thanks for reminding, sir. We got a call about 10 minutes ago about the FBI. Somebody named Phelps called into Pendleton wanting to know how to get out here. Our Marines didn't know anything about the FBI and our situation, so they took their number and we, or you, have to call them."

Rhodes: "Don't toy with me this morning. Are you tellin' us that the FBI doesn't know how to get out here? And these bright flashes are supposed to be smart enough to take over this investigation? Is that what you're saying?"

Coms: "Well, sir, they know where we are, but the Interstate's shut down. So, 'how are they supposed to get there' is their question."

Rhodes (toying with Coms): "Coms, call'em back and tell them to get in their chopper and land at Pendleton's terminal, go inside, talk with Ajax, advise the tower, and follow the parked cars on I-8, call you on

Order of Succession

the Combat-2 push for permission to land. Were you on leave recently, Coms? Do you need a retraining class after the break?"

Coms: "Negative on the retraining class, sir. I just wanted clarification of what should be done, sir. The FBI chopper is about 10 minutes out, sir."

Rhodes: "Just as I thought. We got ourselves another 'Radar' [23] on our hands, Gunnies, another friggin' 'Radar'. Gentlemen, we have guests to prepare for. You have the plan; let's make it work."

Gunnies (collectively): "Yes, sir." Coffee break was officially over. Now, just waiting for the fun and games to begin.

Time: Tuesday, 17-July, 10:16 PDT (Rest Area, California)

The FBI helo landed in the same paved parking lot where Major Jenkins had also parked his chopper – not like there was much of a choice considering the size of the lot. Four people finally got out. One of them talked with a Marine, who motioned over toward Captain Rhodes' direction. As a group, they all walked toward the mess tent. The first two again spoke with a Marine, who pointed toward Rhodes' table. The other two found the coffee and a couple of snack-type goodies, which they gathered-up for all four of them, and wandered over to the table.

Rhodes (rising): "I'm Captain Rhodes. FBI, I presume? Welcome to the 'Buckman Springs Rest Area'. Which one of you is Special Agent Howard Phelps?"

Phelps: "I'm Phelps; I recognized the 'tracks'. (Gesturing toward Rhodes insignia.) From the air, this looks a lot like a war zone. How'd you get assigned to this hell-hole?"

Rhodes (really thinking about how Phelps and group got their assignment – considering that the Voice on the POTUS phone knew about it before almost everybody else did. *{Rhodes' suspicious mind: "Is Phelps part of the plot?"}*

"Luck of the draw, I guess. And you?"

Phelps: "Got a call a coupla days ago to assemble a team for an important assignment. No clue about what this might have been about until about 19:00 yesterday evening."

---

23 Reference to Radar O'Reilly from the TV show, MASH

Order of Succession

Rhodes: "I'll be darned. That late, huh? We've been out here since Friday afternoon. Oh, well, how about introductions and a tour after coffee and a pit-stop? We were given the names of only two agents. Who's who?"

Phelps: "Sorry, this is Pat Tobin; she's the team leader for this assignment. The other two are Agent Tyrone Peterson – he likes horses and goes by the nick-name of 'Cinch'. The last agent is Ronny Cowell – goes by 'Tex'."

{Rhodes' slightly-paranoid brain: "Son of a bitch, two outta three! Whadya bet the third one's here, too? Verb or Bubba or Reese? That would be one damn fine mess, wouldn't it!"}

"If you haven't seen it yet, the coffee and chow are over in that line. Help yourself while you can. The latrines are in the building over there. As soon as you all take this site over, we are tearing all of this down and heading back to Pendleton. Say, do you also have a nick-name? Ya know, one that goes along with the others, Tex and Cinch, was it?"

Phelps: "As a matter of fact, I do. You can call me 'Verb', you know like they teach in school, an action word."

Rhodes: "Ya, I like that – a man of action.

{Rhodes' now-convinced brain: "Son of a bitch, they're all here! Where the hell is Smitty? Ain't this a bitch! Just gotta find out what that Reese/Bubba fella looks like. Gotta get some information to him if I can. Just where the hell is he?"}

(Turning to look at the only woman at the whole scene) "By the way, Ms. Tobin, do you also have a nick-name? Ya know, just curious so we're on a friendly-name basis."

Tobin: "Nope. Just Pat. That's it."

Rhodes: "That works for me, ma'am. Are you all set with the chow and coffee? We'll be ready for the tour of the site just as soon as I get back from Coms. Sorry, communications. Be right back. Get more coffee if you like right over there (motioning toward the mess tent)." And the Cap'n hustled away, motioning to Gunny Cornell to follow. They jogged over to Coms.

Rhodes gut began to knot-up. He stood so that his back was toward the 'FBI' agents just in case one of them could read lips. "A few items before we take this tour. Corporal Knight, go get yourself some coffee

Order of Succession

or something in the mess tent; come on back when Gunny and I aren't here. That's an order." Rhodes waited until the bewildered corporal left, all the more curious now.

Rhodes: "The three of us are back in SCIF mode right now. Got it? Good. You Marines keep a wary eye over my shoulder on those so-called FBI agents while we talk over here. My gut says there is something seriously wrong here – very seriously wrong.

"Gunny, get a hold of a camera with an empty memory card if you can find one like that. If not, get any one and don't lose the card; kill to keep it safe. Got that?"

Cornell: "Sir? Sir, I understood the words, but that 'kill' part has me confused. Did you mean to really 'ice' somebody who wants to take it, sir?"

Rhodes: "Damn straight! It could be evidence of something goin'-on a lot higher up in this food chain. The three of us must keep custody of that card. Gunny, you and Coms here, got that? Good. Gunny, I want you to accompany us on that tour and look like you're taking more pictures of this and that. But you take lots of pictures of all four of them – just like mug shots – so there's no mistaking who they are – close-ups, whatever to identify them. Got that?

"Coms, don't look at their helo right now, but can you research its tail number to find-out who owns it? And I need a nod from you right now." (And Coms nodded.)

"And, Coms, find-out how to get in contact with Smitty, and I don't care whose toes you crush or whose databases you hack. I don't know where he is, but I think he's going to be someplace in Maryland when you finally track him down. Gut feel. I, make that we, have to send two of the best photos of each of these jokers to him ASAP PDQ, like yesterday, so he can ID them if he can. Coms, keep it as quiet a secret from Knight as you can. I'll leave it to your discretion on how much he knows, but keep it minimal. Okay, Gunny, we have guests to show around our former home; let's make tracks." And they were gone.

{Rhodes' mind (running check lists): You know you're forgetting something dontcha? Want to know what it is? Now or later, doesn't make any difference to me. Well, think on it then, if that's your attitude. Be that way, then."}

Order of Succession

Time: Tuesday, 17-July, 11:20 PDT (Rest Area, California)

Rhodes: "Sorry for the delay. Commanding officers, you know; what are ya gonna do? Gentlemen and ma'am, ready for the tour? If you brought along boots or sturdy footgear, now is a good time to change into them. Please watch your step." The Captain led the FBI agents around the site, followed by the Gunnies. Only Cornell had specific orders, and he started immediately.

They covered everything including: the pile of overpass-deck debris after EOD took it apart to reach the limo, the remains of the limo, the semi-tractor and a white trailer, the ambush site on westbound I-8, the remains of somebody's small Agusta chopper, just everything. They even took a trip out to see the other white trailer near the equipment rental lot. Rhodes was getting ready to turn them loose and get back to packing-up the Marine gear and get-back to Pendleton when the moment he sort of knew was coming finally appeared in extra-strength form. On the way back to the rest-area, agent Phelps said his team had some questions. Rhodes suggested coffee in the mess tent, where they might also find some chow. Gunny Cornell gave him a nod as he slid the camera into his pocket.

Time: 17-July, Tuesday, 14:59 PDT (Rest Area, California)

Phelps: "We heard that there was a Secret Service agent out here – a Smitty or something like that – can we talk with him?"

{Rhodes' mind: "Now, it's gonna get interesting, huh? What are you gonna say, you stumbling motor-mouth?"}

"Got to admit, he would be the ideal witness – what with him being the sole survivor and all, but he's not here anymore. Haven't seen him since late last night. And, no, I don't know where he is right now, either. Wish I did; he owes me some money from a card game" (giving the gunnies a slight wink, covered by a cough). We assumed that he got orders from his HQ and got a lift outta here."

Phelps: "Really, you think he just found a ride outta here – this locked-down site – just up and left? How are we supposed to believe that? Huh?"

Rhodes: "Well, I understand your point. Gunny Cornell, where did we find that missing Humvee? I thought I heard somewhere over near that equipment rental yard wasn't it?" (giving Cornell their own high-sign)

Order of Succession

Cornell: "No, sir, you heard wrong; it wasn't over there. Gunny Layton and I found it almost in Mexico way the hell and gone over near that little airstrip they call an airport. Jack (looking at Gunny Layton), you remember what's the name of that airstrip anyway?"

Gunny Layton (fast on the up-take): "Wes, I swear your memory's already checked-out on ya. Jacumba. Get the mental picture of a Jacuzzi with a couple dancing the rumba. You gotta get your memory checked out, Wes."

Cornell: "Yep, that's it, Jacumba. It's a little dinky air strip without a tower. And if you walk south, in a coupla minutes, you'll be in Mexico; it's that close. The Humvee was parked under a tarp on the north side of the field near Highway-80. Didn't see anybody around there except Mariah."

Phelps: "Who's Mariah? Can we talk to him or her?"

Cornell: "Sorry, you can't, she's gone. Hold on, I'm pullin' your leg. Mariah is slang for 'the wind'."

Phelps: "Guess you're right, the wind probably blew across the border by now. So, no other leads on the whereabouts of this agent Smitty? Any ideas why that airport?"

Rhodes: "Do y'all remember that wreckage of that small chopper we showed y'all over there? (gesturing over to the blackened wreckage). We think that's the airport that chopper probably came from. Maybe Smitty made arrangements to leave from there for the same reason. Maybe security? Any other questions?"

Phelps: "Yeah, at least one more. What happened to those two yahoos your men took into custody out there by that rental yard? Them and the two body-bags?"

{Rhodes (now really suspicious): Now who the hell do you suppose told them about those four guys? Not even everybody here at this site knows what happened to them – or where they are.}

Rhodes: "Last we saw of them, they were on a helo headed to either Yuma or Pendleton. I guess they'd be in one brig or the other. The deceased were put into body bags; they're probably in the refrigerated truck over there, if it's still here. Can't tell you if they're on the top or bottom though. Anything else?"

Order of Succession

Phelps: "Guess not from us. Thank-you for the tour. I can see we have our work cut-out for us. If you're gonna tear this camp down, okay if we go through the chow lines while it still here, or can we make arrangements to keep some of your Marines here to assist us? That would be a big help. You know, one branch of the government helping-out another? All that kinda stuff."

Rhodes: "I see your point, but that's not a decision we can make at our pay-grade level out here in the field. But you got a piece of paper? I'll write our commander's contact information on it. Your HQ can talk with my HQ. How's that?" Phelps tore off a piece of paper from his notepad.

{Rhodes' sarcastic brain: "Boy, you know how to zig an' zag, dontcha. Well make a Marine outta you yet."}

"Okay, this name and number will give your guy a place to start. Ask him to make it snappy because we're supposed to start packin' to-go in a couple of hours. The trucks and the helos are already laid-on to take us back to Pendleton. Even though the mess tent is about the last to be packed, grab yourselves coffee and whatever else you want now. It doesn't take that long to pack when the extra Marines show-up and lend a hand. Nice meeting all of you."

{Rhodes' thoroughly convinced mind and sarcastic brain: "Wonder how you get a hold of Smitty really ASAP. Maybe Major Jenkins knows. How do you get a hold of Jenkins? Hey, dummy, you forgot already, didn't you? Remember that piece of paper with Smitty's number on it? Do I have to tell you everything?"}

ORDER OF SUCCESSION
27 – New Accommodations

Around 18:15,Tuesday, 17-July: Westbound I-8, Exit 51, at Buckman Springs Rest Area, Mojave Desert, California

TIME: 16:16 PDT

Rhodes continued playing the part of guide and led them to the mess tent. While grabbing some coffee and a sandwich, he made a big, noisy deal with the cook about being ready to tear this tent down and pack-up to return to Pendleton tomorrow after an early breakfast. The cook was now completely flustered because they already had this talk. But that talk was for packing it up tomorrow after a light supper. Rocky was trying to put a sense of urgency into those FBI agents – if that's who they really were. He wanted to stay on-site to keep track of them.

Rhodes: "Say, Agent Phelps, you know where everything is; I gotta go take care of some Marine business. I'll see ya later, okay?"

Phelps: "Oh, yeah, sure."

Rhodes hustled over to the coms section. "Corporal Knight, I just saw chow with your name on it over in the mess tent. Take-off; I'll hold down your job here for about an hour. Git along now." Knight took the hint and left – albeit even more bewildered than before and now very, very curious.

Rhodes: "Coms, did you find-out anything about anything? The helo? Contacting Smitty? Anything at all?"

{Rhodes' sarcastic brain: "Did you remember yet? Reach in your secret pocket, will ya, huh?"}

"Coms, I screwed-up big time about contacting Smitty."

Sgt. Williams gave him such a look, and Rhodes knew he had been had. "Well let's take this from the top, shall we? Guess what. First, about that chopper, your gut was gnawing at you that it wasn't FBI, wasn't that it? By the way, we are back in SCIF-mode, Cap'n, aren't we? You were right, that helo isn't FBI; it isn't even federal government. It is registered to a rental company out of Tonopah, Nevada, named Mid-Nevada Aerial Surveying Services that supplies planes and choppers for air-surveys. Their web-site says they can do their thing anywhere in the western United States. But that's all I got on it so far. I couldn't find-out who rented it yet. And we don't know who piloted it into our location because we assumed it was FBI.

"On the second item, Smitty (all in a lowered voice): A few calls to some buddies, who called around to their buddies, etc. produced a phone number and a very, very all-business call. They said . . . "

Rhodes (cutting-off Coms): "Read me your number?" Rhodes pulled his paper out and listened as Coms read-off of his note pad. "The same. Coms, memorize it and destroy that page as well as at least five sheets underneath it. And erase it from whatever logs you may have, either written or stored in memory. Flush all of it out of all memory, and I don't care how you do it, either. These boys aren't gonna get any free clues from us. Got that?"

Coms: "Yes, sir. But do you want the rest or not?"

Rhodes: "What rest? Are you saying you know how to contact Smitty? You are, aren't ya?"

Coms: "Contact him? Hell, sir, I spoke with him. He'd only say that he's not in this state. He gave me a number that's supposed to be some sort of relay line.'

Rhodes: "Can he get pictures if we transmit them?"

Coms: "The relay folks are supposed to handle that. That's all the information he would give me."

Rhodes: "Coms, hold that thought for a second." Rhodes whistled at Gunny Cornell walking toward the head, who immediately veered toward them and quickened his pace. In order to appear to be handling Marine duties, Rhodes waited for Cornell to join the two of them at the coms desk. Gesturing toward different areas around the site to throw-off the 'Fibbies', "Gunny, share the camera with Coms; the two of you review the pictures for two of each FBI agent – including the woman – that's eight photos. Coms, transmit those to that relay service with a question for Smitty: 'Do you recognize these four (4) supposed FBI agents who

ORDER OF SUCCESSION

showed-up at our desert location in a rented civilian helo?' Emphasize the FBI part. Then police-up all of the paper-work and logs about this. Gunny, then safeguard that memory card somewhere; assume we will be returning to Pendleton tomorrow morning – maybe. Any questions about what I am asking?"

Both Coms and Gunny in unison, quietly but emphatically: "No, sir."

Rhodes: "I'm going to try to keep tabs on those agents assuming they aren't already keeping tabs on us. Keep me posted what happens whenever it happens. Let me know when it's sent and what our buddy says when he responds. And remember, this is still in our SCIF mode and sure as hell, they aren't invited in and THEY WILL NOT BE READ-IN EITHER. Oh, Coms, get a hold of our C.O. and sort of tell him all he needs to know about a call he might get from these boys about extending our stay to help them-out. Maybe extend us for a day or two – just so we keep your gear on the air for our buddy on the POTUS phone. And maybe start getting some Corps trucks to haul this stuff outta here so CalTrans can get in here and start repairing I-8; they must be seriously pissed-off with us by now. But, the Corps really needs to control and safeguard all the evidence back at Pendleton. Trucks to be fully fueled for possible diversion to an alternate site." The Captain moseyed over toward the mess tent to update the agents on just a few of what the Marines were working on – but certainly not everything.

Time: Tuesday, 17-July, 17:56 PDT (Rest Area, California)

Rhodes (seemingly) wandered into the mess tent, got a cup of coffee, and 'just happened' to pass the agents, still seated at a table. "Mind if I join ya? It's been a long day. First, the C.O. says get ready to pick-up and move, and now he says hold-on 'til he gets some of his paperwork straightened-out. Can you believe it; more 'hurry-up and wait' crap. Oh, well. How's everything going with you all? Getting your playbook in order? Man, it feels great to sit and take a load-off for just a few minutes. Say, you need anything from the chow line? Ya know, I know the Marine in charge of it," Rhodes said trying to insert a little humor. "Mind if I leave my coffee here while I see what he's serving tonight? Be right back." Not waiting for an answer, the Captain set the cup down sharply with a slight bang, got up, and walked to the chow line.

Order of Succession

Halfway to the trays, his phone rang. "Cap'n Rhodes here. Oh really? When did it ring? Just now. Okay, I'll bring the agents along. Purge the area of you know what." He grabbed a pre-made ham and cheese sandwich and ran back to the agents' table. Grabbing his cup and draining it, Rhodes informed the agents, "Gotta call on the POTUS phone – the phone I showed you. Come on along if you want to." There was no doubt in their actions. All four jumped to their feet and almost beat Rhodes to the coms desk, which had been sanitized long before Rhodes had even been notified.

Coms: "Same Voice, sir. And he's PO'ed about the wait."

Rhodes, turning-up the tension: "Which one of you wants to talk to this guy? I mean it is your operation now, isn't it?" And just left the question hang there for about five seconds while the agents procrastinated who should take it. "Okay, I'll break the ice for y'all. Coms, standard note-taking procedure. Where's Knight? Signal him to take notes, too."

Rhodes, picking-up the POTUS phone and activating the speakerphone: "Evening to you, sir. It's about 18:10 hrs here; what time is it there?"

Voice: "Uh, uh. Not gonna happen. You should know that by now. Don't know who your superiors are yet, huh? Who am I talkin' to again? The same piss-ant Marine Captain again, huh? Don't you ever learn? You ain't high enough in the food chain; I can't discuss anything with you. And you know it. Get me one of them FBI boys, and be quick about it, you piss-ant."

Rhodes: "You got my rank correct. Those agents are around here somewhere and aren't used to getting your calls yet; we're tryin' to scout them up for you. Say, while we wait for them, I gotta question for ya. Do ya mind? (Without waiting for an answer, Rhodes rolled on.) Ya musta heard of a restaurant chain named Waffle House, right? Well, I heard somewhere that FEMA – you know, the Federal Emergency Management Agency outfit – well, that they're using Waffle House as a quick measurement of how much damage has been done during disasters. Do ya know if that's true, or has the public been fed another line of crap about this? I mean how can this Waffle House be better than all the government agents in the field. And Waffle House is only in the south isn't it?"

Order of Succession

Voice: "For a piss-ant Captain, you sure got lotsa ideers, huh? I reckon Waffle House is a suthin' outfit – one of our finest. Seems like we got one almost every dad-gum mile. If'n the areas are really bad-off, Waffle Houses are probably closed-down tight. If'n they're open, well the areas ain't dat bad-off. Pure and simple; it works. Hey where are dem Fibbies, anyhow? Whadya do, park 'em under dat limo?"

Rhodes: "Nah, we found 'em conferencin'. They was just makin' small talk 'cuz I know how y'all hate waitin'. Here they come now double-timing over here. Hold-on a moment. Be right back to ya." Hitting the mute-button, he nodded to the agents and offering the phone in their general direction. Special Agent Phelps finally took the phone. Rhodes quickly pointed-out how to take the speakerphone off mute.

Phelps, pressing the mute-button again: "Special Agent Howard Phelps here. Who am I speaking with?" As he spoke, he also got the hand-signaling going so his agents could also take notes.

Voice: " 'bout time you all get your friggin' act together. And, no, I ain't gonna tell you any more about names than that piss-ant Captain got, neither. What time did ya get there? How'd ya like the work we did out there? Damn straight good wasn't it. You damn right it was. And we got the man; uninjured, too! This is almost as good as our next step. Y'all gonna get a new friggin' gubamint, too! How about them apples!" (Rhodes motioned to Coms and Knight to keep scribbling notes.) "Well, Special Agent Howard Phelps, my boy, you in charge out there now, are ya?"

Phelps: "We assumed control of the site this afternoon. So, yes the FBI is now in charge out here. I just what to . . . "

Voice (interrupting Phelps): "Man, you rubes are really slower than molasses when it comes to the learnin' curve, ain't you, you piss-ants? You don't want to rub me the wrong way, you gubamint piss-ant. You ain't assumed control; y'all was assigned to this case a day or so ago. And the Gyrenes are still there, too, ain't they. You ain't got crap for control. Lissin-up, on paper YOU are in charge, an' that's the only reesin you be privileged to be talkin' ta me. Got that? Good. Here's what you gonna do for us."

Phelps held the phone at a slight angle, grimaced a bit, and shrugged his shoulders – as if to indicate 'what's this guy talkin' about; he must be crazy or something'. "And what would that be, sir – whoever you are. And, what makes you think you can tell the FBI what to do?"

Voice: "Keep that up an' you gonna find-out what's what. You gonna find yourself investigatin' gators and snakes down thar in the Okefenokee. Now, lissin-up, you piss-ant. The first thing is to turn that damn speakerphone off so only me and you can talk. Yeah, I figured you'd have it on 'cause that's what I'd do cause it makes sense. Now turn it off; just press the liddle button. I ain't got all day and neither do you. Click it off now, you dumb-ass." Phelps pressed the 'Speaker-Off' button and put the POTUS phone to his ear and stepped slightly away from the crowd and continued the conversation in a muted voice.

About now, Rhodes gut was really becoming more active. With the separation from the group, both Coms and Cornell really began to understand where the Captain was coming from. Phelps's voice suddenly grew louder: "Whoever you are, that just isn't going to happen; the FBI doesn't work that way. We will not submit to blackmail." "I don't care who you know." "You want to call him? Go right ahead. I'll even give you his number, too?" "First, you kidnap the President, and now you want me to break the law, too? As I already said, that ain't gonna to happen! Hello. Hello." Turning toward the others (all absolutely quiet by now), "That SOB just hung-up on me. He wants us to break some laws so he and his group don't have to release the President until he's damn good and ready". His words exactly: 'Until we're good and ready to remake this here country.' What the hell does that mean, 'remake the country?' We'll just see about that."

Rhodes gut went into overtime.

{Rhodes' analyzing mind: "Captain, my boy, you got two choices: 1) Phelps was real serious about what had just happened; or 2) He was one ham of an actor wanting more time in the lime light. Go with your gut. Whadya think they were talking about before all hell broke loose? Why was he so quiet, all lovey-dovey – betcha, like plotters is more like it. Betcha. Whadya think, huh? These bastards are trying to be oh so clever, aren't they? How do we even know the Voice was even on the phone? Or, giving him orders for the rest of the week? Huh?"}

Agent Pat Tobin spoke for the rest of the team of agents: "Howard, you're absolutely livid; what the hell happened on that call? We've never seen you like this. What's going on here? It's more than the

Order of Succession

kidnapping of the President, isn't it? Come-on now, we're a team; you gotta tell us so we can help you."

{Rhodes' now-paranoid mind: "Give me a break will ya? Are we gonna be singin' hymns and givin' out hugs next. Lissin-up, Buddy-Boy, you just seen a not-yet actor tryin' to play to a house full of theater critics. Tryin' to put on a good performance is what he's trying. Sorry, make that 'they're tryin'. Don't forget what we already know about these fakers: First) Their nick-names match those from Smitty – exactly, I might add – the only fly in the ointment is the woman, Pat. We don't know anything else about her yet. Second) Their white chopper is registered to an aerial mapping company in Someplace, Nevada. So, how many FBI agents fly around in an out-a-state chopper – a rented one from a civilian surveyor to boot? Tell me that will ya, how many? And don't forget, nobody remembers seeing a fifth member on that helo – the pilot. How many times do FBI agents fly their own rented chopper huh? Give me a break. Bigger than hell, these guys are damn fakes."}

The POTUS phone rang again; everybody was looking at each other with WTF looks. Before, anybody could protest, Coms answered it. "Hello?" Yes, sir, he's here right now. Shall I put him on now?" "Just a coupla secs, sir." Phelps held-out his hand for the phone, but Coms walked past him and extended the phone to Captain Rhodes, who accepted it and automatically thumbed the speakerphone on. "Captain Rhodes here. How can I help you?"

Voice: "Say, piss-ant, betcha got that damned loudspeaker on, dontcha? Well, leave the damn thing on for now. Is that friggin' FBI *Special Agent Phelps* still there? Yeah, bet he is. Piss-ant, tell me what makes him so special, huh? You ain't got the slightest idea, do ya. Wall, I know what makes dem friggin' piss-ants tick, too."

Rhodes: "Well, anyway, this is the first time you've called twice so close together. What can I do for you?"

Voice: "That speaker's on, right, sonny-boy? Betcha he's listening, too. Good. I'm gonna tell that friggin' piss-ant that his friggin' fate is friggin' sealed. He's done screwed with the wrong SOB. His boss's boss's boss is playin' in the same friggin' game that he friggin' didn't like. The gators and snakes down thar in the Okefenokee are passin' out da invites to friggin' have him over for

Order of Succession

friggin' Sunday supper. No RSVPs required. YA HEAR DAT, YOU PISS-ANT. YOU'RE ON YOUR FRIGGIN' WAY DOWN THAR TA SEE MY BUDDIES! YOU GOT THAT, YOU FRIGGIN' PISS-ANT PIECE OF GATOR SUPPER MEAT?"

Rhodes: "Well, if that's the case, are YOU relieving him of his responsibilities out here? Do you want to speak to any of the other agents." Rhodes shrugged his shoulders even as he tried to motion for less background whispers.

Voice: "Nah. I like talkin' to you, piss-ant Captain; you'll do for now. You, piss-ant, you'll do just fine. By da way, y'all better git usta dat dare rest-area; you and your company ain't goin' nowhere 'til the end of this damned week. You gonna see I ain't BS-ing none. FBI *Special Agent Phelps*, start kissin' your ass good-bye, you friggin' piss-ant."

Rhodes: "Excuse me, sir, are you changing our orders over this phone? My CO ain't gonna like being out the loop. You know, a lowly Captain just can't tell HQ what to do. It's all gotta go through proper channels. You know that, dontcha? Surely you, of all people, must know about channels, right?"

Voice: "You got that part right, you Marine piss-ant. We know all about channels, chains of command, pecking orders, food chains, all that crap. You damn straight we do. In about four minutes your coms sergeant, Williams, isn't it, should be getting' an order extending y'all's stay all signed, countersigned, initialed, re-initialed, so betta get usta at least another week out there. By the way, where's your buddy, Smitty? We wanna have a nice liddle talk with him – a real serious talk. You find-out, let us know, and we'll take really gud care of ya, ya gud ol' piss-ant buddy. Say, you like Golden Jack? Gooood sippin' stuff. Gotta go. Hey, Fibbie piss-ant, you had yur chance, but you screwed with the wrong people." And the phone went dead.

Rhodes: "Special Agent Phelps I think all of us should sit down and have a heart-to-heart meeting right NOW. Coms, you and Gunny Cornell better join us. In the mess tent in 30."

Coms: "We just received an order from our CO's CO. We have been extended at least one week to next Tuesday morning. Sir?"

Rhodes: "Verify THAT with our CO, and bring it to the meeting. Knight, the coms desk is in your control. Coms, at this point, might as

Order of Succession

well read him into the situation, making it four (4) now, and advise him of what we are looking for and the how to deal with it."

Coms: "Yes, sir; consider it done. In 27, sir."

The agents realized something changed their situation – suddenly and dramatically – and tried to change the Captain's mind. To no avail.

(As they walked toward the mess tent) Rhodes whispering to Gunny Cornell: "Get a hold of Gunnies Layton, Johnson, Vernor, and the sniper team leader and invite them to join our little conference in the mess tent. And tell them to be armed with side-arms. I want them to sorta wander in, get coffee, and take seats at tables to the sides of the agents so we don't have a cross-fire accident. They are now included back in our SCIF group. I want two squads of Marines with rifles and full magazines posted quietly around the perimeter of the mess tent. NO FRIENDLY-FIRE ACCIDENTS. Did I miss anything?"

Cornell: "No, sir. Consider it done." He took-off at a fast trot to advise the other Gunnies. No questions or arguments – just checking the magazines in their pistols and those on their belts, too. Be a little late, get coffee, and quietly take seats to the sides of the FBI, if the Cap'n wants it, he's got it. Done deal.

Time: Tuesday, 17-July, 20:56 PDT (Rest Area, California)

Rhodes (trying to remain calm and appearing hospitable): "Y'all get your coffee and something to eat if ya want. We'll be right over there." He motioned in the general direction of a table near the edge of the tent. Then he and the other Marines took seats on the tent-wall side of the table. The agents would have their choice of seats with their backs to the open, middle of the tent. On his way back through the coffee line, Rhodes spoke with the cook ordering him to 'close the mess tent for cleaning' and to clear the tent of everybody else. Period. Done.

The four agents settled into their places all ready to discuss what's what with that POTUS phone call. The first five minutes went slowly with people settling into conference mode on the agents' side of the table. Rhodes watched his Marines slowly gathering around the outside of the tent. He also watched the four other Gunnies quietly getting coffee and a sandwich so the tent wouldn't look like the trap it was rapidly becoming. Gunny Cornell was already seated at the table; he was the one the others would key-on when the action started.

Rhodes (to the agents): "Gentlemen and ma'am, from our side, we Marines have a couple of problems maybe you can help me with. We Marines are having some trouble identifying you, and by that, I mean we can't make $3 + 1 = 4$ when it comes to the four of you." Phelps tried to speak, but the Cap'n cut him off with his voice now in command mode. "Agent Phelps, I'm not finished yet. We got word that either you, Special Agent Phelps, or someone using your name cold-called Pendleton for directions to get out here. That's not quite SOP, is it? I was told your names, Agents Phelps and Tobin, days before you were supposed to arrive – yet you apparently had no idea where we were. Ever hear of a map or Google for directions?

"And another thing, we didn't get any orders to provide any personal support to y'all except for food, courtesy tours, and briefings. To us, that means y'all were gonna be self-sufficient. I also had my Marines inspect that chopper. We didn't find any sleeping gear. So, y'all planning on sleeping on the ground or sumthin' else out here? Do ya see why $3 + 1$ aren't adding up to 4? Hold on, (holding up his hand, index finger pointed at Phelps) I'm not finished yet; there's more that doesn't add to 4 using our old-fashioned Marine math.

"Which one of you is the chopper pilot? You four got out of the chopper, but a fifth person did not get out of your helo. So, one of you must be the pilot, right? I want to know who the pilot is. Is that too much to ask? Let me ask again. Who flew that friggin' chopper into MY site?"

Agent Ronny Cowell: "I flew the helicopter. I didn't know that was such a big deal to fly a chopper out here on official FBI business. Who should I have contacted?"

Rhodes: "Pilot Cowell, so you flew that bird out here on official FBI business, did you? Well, here's what's got our little neck hairs standing at attention. That helo doesn't have any 'official' FBI markings on it. Ya know, like 'FBI' in big bold letters. It doesn't have any 'U.S. Government' markings on it, either. It is just simply plain friggin' white."

Cowell: "What difference should 'all white' make? We're all one team here, aren't we? I said we're here on OFFICIAL FBI business."

Rhodes: "We heard you jaw-bonin' about all that so-called 'official FBI business'. We aren't sure about that 'all on one team' thing either.

Order of Succession

We don't know which team you are on yet. Because your chopper had no markings on it, we ran its 'tail number'." The color drained from Phelps' and Cowell's faces. "Care to tell us dumb Marines how a helicopter registered to *Mid-Nevada Aerial Surveying Services* out of Tonopah, Nevada, is being used for 'official' FBI business? Is the FBI now sub-contracting helicopter services to a small mapping company in a small Nevada town? Or has the FBI gotten into the aerial mapping business? Got an official FBI explanation for that? Do you sort of see why we are having trouble making 3 + 1 = 4? And your answer better be damn fast, no BS, and, RIGHT NOW."

Corporal Knight had been speaking quietly to Sergeant Williams, both pointing and tracing something on a piece of coms paper.

Coms: "Cap'n Rhodes, an answer to a previous query from . . ." Coms slid Smitty's message down the table to Rhodes, who quickly read it, also tracing rows with his fingers.

Rhodes: "Gentlemen and ma'am, this incoming message is quite interesting. But before I tell you what it says, I need to show you some photos. Sorry, we don't have a color printer out here, so this camera will have to do. Gunny Cornell, share the photos with these agents, but retain possession of the camera. Y'all take a good look and remember what you see." Gunny Cornell showed the agents pictures of themselves.

Rhodes (after the agents had seen the photos): "Agent Cowell, you haven't told us about the aerial survey chopper yet. Try it RIGHT NOW, or you'll really piss me off. My Marines will tell you it is not good to piss-off a Marine officer. Nothing to say?. Okay enough of this jaw-boning."

(Gunny Cornell caught the second 'jaw-boning' comment and knew the Cap'n was nearing completion of the lead-in to completely and totally restrict these agents' personal freedoms BIG TIME. He gave the other four Gunnies the 'get ready' high sign by wiping his brow. Gunnies Layton and Johnson both stood and walked toward the sides of the tent and gave the same high-sign to the platoon of Marine Riflemen. Get ready to go to combat mode and those four are the aggressors in your camp, but just go to the 'Ready, Aim . . . stage.)

Rhodes: "Agents, at this point, we Marines are gonna pretend we are the TSA when you get on a plane. We, like the TSA, want to know exactly who the hell is on the other side of the counter. Now

Order of Succession

is a good time to lay all of your firearms on the table in front of you. I suggest that you handle those guns very carefully with no sudden movements because my Marines already have their orders. Also take-out all of your ID cards and cell-phones, government, personal, and otherwise." At which, Cornell nodded and raised his already-drawn sidearm, cocking the hammer in one smooth, fast motion. If the agents listened fast enough, they would have heard four more hammers being cocked on pistols at both ends of their table as they were also raised and pointed toward the four agents. And a sixth, if they had time to count Cap'n Rhodes' pistol in front of them. If they had looked outside the tent, they would have seen two squads' worth of M-4 carbines aimed at them." Rhodes continued: "Point your pistol up into the air, remove the magazine, and rack and lock the slide open to clear the chamber. Place the pistol, magazine, and the cleared round on this table as far as possible toward my side, grip toward me, and the muzzle pointing toward you. Then remove ALL of your government, civilian, and other ID cards and cell-phones very slowly and lay them next to your pistol. Then place your elbows on the edge of the table directly in front of you with arms extended with palms up. Do not move after that. You will begin in sequential order beginning at my left, your right. Cowell, you're first, ending with your hands on the table; the last will be Agent Peterson, or whoever you are, on the other end of your row of chairs. Start doing it now. Do it VERY slowly."

Discretion proved to be the better option. As directed, each so-called agent withdrew his/her weapons in sequential order, carefully unloaded it, and carefully placed it on the table. Producing their ID cards proved more cumbersome; each was permitted to stand to remove them from pockets, etc. Agent Pat Tobin was very flustered and fumbled her way through the Captain's orders. Coms and Knight policed-up each weapon, magazine, and the round extracted from the chamber, placing each set on respective mess trays to avoid mixing components; they placed the ID cards and phones in front of Rhodes. The Captain looked at each set of IDs as they were produced, frowning longer as each set was placed before him. After all firearms, IDs, and phones had been policed-up, the Gunnies lowered their pistols and de-cocked them, but did not holster them. Cornell, ordered the Marines around the tent to go to 'port arms', but did not 'dismiss' them yet.

Order of Succession

Rhodes: "Gunny, get PFC Berkeley to bag all of these as evidence if we need it as such. He's got the rubber gloves from handling the deputies. And if he needs plastic bags, the Mess Sergeant should have some."

(Turning back toward the agents): "By the way, you are now all under arrest. Gentlemen and ma'am, here is the gist of this message that confirmed our suspicions. Briefly, to the three men here, your pictures have been identified as participants with some people in Thurmont, Maryland, deeply involved in a plot to blow-up The White House. Agents Phelps, Peterson, and Cowell, you have been further identified as men going by the nick-names of Verb, Tex, and Cinch, all participating members in the plan to blow-up The White House. Agent Tobin, you have been identified as going by the name of Daisy, a waitress at a restaurant named The Treadle, also in Thurmont. Anybody here know a Hal, also from that town? Again to the three men here, none of your civilian IDs match your official FBI IDs, which, by the way, are fakes, but you all are no doubt already aware of that, right. Miss Daisy, your IDs are just as fake. The charges just keep piling up.

"Anybody care to tell us how much of our findings are wrong and start clearing this up for us? If you value any part of your personal freedom for the rest of your life speak-up RIGHT NOW. Otherwise, your silence confirms that we are dealing with dangerous terrorists. We will transport you out of this rest-area for 'safe-keeping' and subsequent prosecution. Your opportunity to speak-up is rapidly fading away. Speak-up now or tell it to an interrogator who's already waiting to talk to you.

Daisy tried: "Captain Rhodes, can you hold on just a second? Please, sir? Yes, I am, or was, a waitress at The Treadle in Thurmont. Some guy came in and offered me a lot of money to act the part of Pat Tobin, an FBI agent. I don't even know if Pat is real or not, and I didn't know it was part of any plot. I thought it was for a movie or something. Don't hurt Hal; he's my husband. He's such a motor-mouth always wanting to be somebody important. But he didn't tell me nuthin' about what he was doin' with that guy. Please, sir, this was just supposed to be a part in a movie."

Rhodes: "I assume your real name could be Daisy, right? If it isn't, we'll find-out later anyway during the booking process. I've got some other questions for you later. Ma'am, you are still under arrest because I don't have a choice; I have no leeway at this point. I am not a judge; our JAG officers will take care of that.

Order of Succession

"Alright, now confession is good for the soul; who's next? Anybody know a Bubba and what's his relationship to this plot?"

Nobody else responded.

Rhodes: "Alright then, Gunnies, isolate each of these four terrorists and secure them to something stationary, post a guard on each, and there will be no communications between them. Secure them to a wheel on a Humvee for all I care. The female gets restroom privileges under guard with all doors open. The males can piss in the bushes for all I care. Consider them as terrorists and POWs until turned over to higher authorities. Make it happen now."

A chorus of: "Yes, sir." And the first four conspirators (no longer 'plotters') in whatever this friggin' plot is are now in custody and locked-down.

Rhodes: "Coms, get a hold of the Major and see if three or four more customers can be accommodated by Hard-Ass. That ought to put these guys on ice for a while if they ever get out. Then notify our own C.O. about how fouled up this mess is getting. I mean, we got three plotters, a possible sucker of a waitress, a rented helicopter, a batch of pistols that have finger prints all over them – am I leaving anything out? Go easy on the Hard-Ass part though. Just tell him we're arranging transport to a secured location. We don't want to get him involved and screw it up before we get a handle on it. Also, advise him I'll call him as soon as we get this situation under full control. Thanks, Corporal, that message was timed just right."

Cornell (to the platoons of Marines) "Order ARMS. Dismissed."

ORDER OF SUCCESSION

28 – Resolutions and Clearing the Plate

Just past 22:00, Tuesday, 17-July: Westbound I-8, Exit 51, at Buckman Springs Rest Area, Mojave Desert, California

TIME: 22:12 PDT

Rhodes and the Gunnies met in the mess tent to discuss WTF just happened on their watch. Almost all agreed that the female, Pat or Daisy, was probably suckered into this mess. She probably really thought that this was a simple part in a movie. And that it was probably supposed to be over in a day – because no one brought an overnight toilet kit, more-less a sleeping bag – plus, they were planning to fly out this evening. The lone hold-out was the sniper team leader. He thought she was part of the plot because she should have known this was not a movie because there were no rehearsals, no cameras, and why would a movie company fly her from Maryland out to California, where countless actresses could have played such a simple part.

All agreed the three males were guilty of something, but nobody knew exactly what. That's somebody else's problem for now.

All agreed the JAG must be brought on-board now, if for no other reason than the helicopter. Somebody owns it and probably wants it back, but the Marines now have possession and control of it. Somebody else must investigate if the owner gets it back and when. Or if the owner is part of the plot, but right now, that chopper belongs to the USMC. Period. Let the lawyers figure it out.

Rhodes: "Good points, all. Coms, see if you can get our C.O. on the line. If nobody has any objections, we're gonna invite him out here to discuss our actions right here on-site. Considering how fast that Voice on the POTUS phone got our Marines extended for another week, I don't know who to trust or who might be listening to our radio transmissions.

Order of Succession

Hell, somebody sure as hell used some sophisticated links for the ambush satellite links; they might even control the satellites. I don't think we want to be out here alone by ourselves holding the bag for every friggin' little thing that's happened so far. Anybody got a better idea than involving our C.O.? (No dissents.) Okay, then, Coms, make the call; we'll be ready any time he arrives."

Their C.O., Colonel Michael Gahagen, made good on his word to show-up ASAP. He must have rattled some cages and scrambled a helo crew and the necessary support crew at Pendleton. His chopper hovered overhead at 01:34. Gunny Cornell detailed PFCs Berkley and Barnes to guide the chopper into the LZ, which was getting tight because of the white helo the 'agents' had flown into the rest-area. Rhodes hustled over to greet the Colonel, and exchanged salutes. Good thing that Major Jenkins hadn't flown in, too; that could have been awkward in more ways than one.

Having been previously advised, the cooks in the mess area began breakfast preparations a bit earlier than usual. Already, the coffee was hot and fresh. The Colonel, the Captain, and the four Gunnies settled around one of the rest area tables and began analyzing the hand they had been dealt.

Gahagen: "To begin with, these are some of the questions I have. Where's this Smitty fella now? You sure you don't know where? Could he be part of this so-called plot? He started all of this crap for us, and now he's gone? Nothin' we can do about that here is there? Table that one for now; we'll pick that up later. Exactly what can we do? Y'all got flashlights? Bring me up to speed about this place; take me on a quick tour of this place." And off they went traipsing around in the dark at 'OH-SO-DARK:30' hours. Looking at all of the same stuff the 'agents' had been shown about 12 hours earlier.

When they returned, Gahagen wanted to see the four so-called agents. So, he was shown each of them in their respective areas at least 100 feet from the next. And each cuffed to a substantial item – including Pat, or Daisy, or whatever her name is.

Gahagen: "Now that I know the lay-of-the-land, let's call it quits for now. See you at chow in what, two hours." And that was it for now;

ORDER OF SUCCESSION

more to come when the sun comes up. Except that Rhodes had Coms notify Major Jenkins that their C.O. was here, and that we will notify them again when the LZ is cleared.

Time: Wednesday, 18-July, 07:15 EDT (Hagerstown, Maryland)

To say the least, Smitty had been caught off-guard when those pictures appeared on his cell-phone. Somebody was putting some part of their plan into operation, which to him, meant the rest of the plot was already in motion. He thought he was already near the beast's lair, Thurmont and Hal's place. If the munitions in Hal's bunker were to be used, they might be preparing to move them out into the field. How can that cache be monitored? The better question is just where the hell is it.

Smitty went down to the local AAA office and bought some maps of both Maryland and Pennsylvania, the only states where Smitty thought that stash could be in. He also stopped and bought some drawing equipment from a store advertising a sale on 'back-to-school' supplies. Smitty sort of laughed about that, already a back-to-school sale in July! When do the children take vacation?

Back in his room, he opened the maps showing the area around Thurmont and weighted the corners to keep them in place. Then he took the ruler and protractor and laid-out what he thought was the widest possible circle they could have driven to deliver the trailer of munitions in what was that, oh yeah, about 39 minutes. And drew a circle showing Hal's barn at the center; so, the bunker should be somewhere within that circle – some dinky place inside how many square miles. He could have figured that out, but why worry about that right now.

Smitty still didn't know who in the government agencies could be trusted, so he preferred to do the grunt-work until he was sure. Now that he had the approximate area, it was off to the Fletcher Branch of the Washington County Free Library in downtown Hagerstown to use their Internet access and hope his searches would get lost in the traffic of other library patrons. He brought up maps from both Google and Bing just for comparison. He tried to recollect the twists and turns, railroad tracks, everything that came to mind about that first (and only) day out to the bunker. No matter how many times he re-played them, all the routes led to someplace out along Maryland Route 550 or between it and Pennsylvania 16. That was still quite a large area, but at least 80% of the possible area was eliminated. And interestingly enough, Hal's welding shop was still inside that much smaller area. Smitty thought it would be a hoot if all the driving around was just a fake-out and the bunker is right near Hal's shop? Well, right now, the only way to find-out is to drive it – all of it – beginning near the welding shop.

Smitty finally realized it was high time to check-in and see how Rhodes and Jenkins are doing with transport. Jenkins advised Smitty of the situation out at the rest-area and that transport had been delayed slightly. Then it was Smitty's turn; he told Phillip that he thought the plot was well past the planning stage and beginning the implementation phase. He asked Phillip to seriously think about how to get himself and Captain Hauser up to D.C. in the VERY near future.

Jenkins: "How about in about a month and a half near the end of August for a full week and the weekends on both ends. We're scheduled to be up there for something new for the public, something called *Your Armed Forces on Display*. Let's see, the notice I have here says it starts Friday, 31-August. I don't think we'll have our own helos flown in with us; however, we will probably have access to a helo or two from maybe down at Quantico."

Smitty: "What I'm really concerned about is air-maneuverability in a close-in area like a city – especially, D.C. Can you get a hold of something you may not have flown in a while, something like an Apache with all the weapon mounts for cannons and missiles. And at least a second helo a slightly larger one to carry a special device to induce an aggressor pilot to want to land. Maybe something like a Huey or something. And if you have the spare time, can you think-up a strategy, or strategies, to defend TWH from the south side, the side facing The Mall? And what kind of device could make a pilot want to land on The Mall.

"I haven't heard anything about this *Your Armed Forces on Display*. What is it about, anyway? Is it open to the public or do the visitors have to be pre-cleared ahead of time?"

Jenkins: "Oh, it's supposed to be open to the public. All the services are supposed to have displays of their respective vehicles, tanks, cut-away missiles, Humvees, all that sorta stuff. It's supposed to be on The Mall on both the east and west sides of the Washington

Order of Succession

Monument down toward the Lincoln Memorial. Supposed to be a really big deal. Whacha thinking about?"

Smitty: "Do ya think a news or medevac chopper could fly over The Mall during that time? Would that *Your Armed Forces on Display* make a perfect cover or what? In my mind, it would absolutely be the perfect cover. I think you and Brian and maybe even a third pilot should be prepared for a rogue aggressor to show-up in front of TWH during that show. That's what I think. I'll bet your helos are also supposed to be 'garaged' over at Andrews when they are not needed. That's gonna be way too far away when our unscheduled festivities begin; you gotta be closer, a lot closer. We'll have to work on that one. That and the live munitions."

Jenkins: "Hey, Buddy, you're sounding like you're preparing for full-fledged aerial combat in the streets of D.C. You're jokin' right? Please say you're jokin'."

Smitty: "You're dead-right about where, but I'm not jokin' about it. It's the perfect cover. Think about how you can defend TWH and convince an aggressor pilot to willingly land. All without firing a shot, or the fewest, if it comes to that. I'm going to try finding that bunker with all of the munitions I unloaded from that trailer. Call you later. Come to think of it, I am gonna try to get you and Brian TDY'ed back to the D.C., area about two weeks sooner than the others so we can scout flight-paths and routes both in D.C. and Camp David and possible routes between them. Would the earlier recon work for you two?"

Jenkins: "We can work that in without a problem."

Time: Wednesday, 18-July, 05:03 PDT (Rest Area, California)

Colonel Gahagen had been up for an hour already. "Say, Rocky, you showed me a lot of stuff early this morning. I know you well enough to know there's something else goin' on out here. What haven't you shown me and what haven't you told me? How can I help you?"

Rhodes: "The biggest problem that isn't all that obvious is we didn't know who to trust with any information about this site. These plotters, as we call them, seem to have fingers into everything, including the Corps. We hesitated involving Corps officers until these four fake FBI agents choppered in yesterday. We decided . . . make that, I decided to involve you just because we ran out of options at our level, and things

Order of Succession

just kept compounding themselves. We think our results are the best that could be expected under the circumstances. We think our next steps should include: (as he handed the Colonel a hand-written list of steps)

"Sir, I think that just about covers outstanding issues so far."

Gahagen (who had already been scribbling on Rhodes list): "Yes, I'd say you had a lot on your plate right now. Let's start resolving some of this stuff for you. Where's your coms Marine? Get him over here."

Rhodes: "Yes, sir." And he motioned for Coms to join the meeting. "Sir, this is Sergeant Williams, our communications department."

Gahagen (handing over most of the list): "Sergeant, here are some things to take care of on my orders. Priority one is to get the refrigerated truck taken care of. We need some compassion for the families. Get a hold of Lieutenant Sean Clancy down at the motor pool; tell him we want, how many trucks was that Cap'n, about 18 with tarps and anything else necessary to load them with. The Captain here will tell you what types and sizes. Cap' Rhodes here will also tell you how and where to transport these four apparent terrorists. Get me a line so I can talk to JAG myself. Oh, and our target timetable is to give I-8 back to CalTrans fully by tomorrow at 17:00 hours, but their inspectors can ride out here in our trucks if they want to. But they will not be able to take pictures of anything that is not part of the overpass deck. And advise me where our secured area is in say about 30 days; that should be enough time to sort things out. Captain, anything else I should be aware of at this time?"

Rhodes: "Thank-you, sir. 30 days, yes, sir. And nothing else at this time, sir."

They exchanged salutes, and the Colonel turned toward his chopper, giving the 'wind-it-up-now' signal as he walked to the latrine and a coffee-stop in the mess tent in that order. And he was up-and-out on his way back to Pendleton.

Rhodes was still shaking a bit, but his plate was pretty well cleaned off. "Coms, after we get the 'official' coms out, better get a hold of our buddy from Yuma to arrange 'unofficial' transport."

The Pendleton Motor Pool wasn't used to this much unscheduled requests, but it marshaled a 17-truck convoy, which also had a couple of fork-lifts and one small crane on the flat-beds and pallets of tarps.

Order of Succession

With an ETA in four hours. CalTrans planned to have two inspectors on board, and the JAG was also sending-out a single representative. The Motor Pool also sent an additional fuel truck and two tractors with operational 'glad-hands'. The white trailers were going into storage, too, as well as their tractors.

Coms: "Cap'n, transport is on its way. About 150 klicks out. Should I get the Gunnies to ready the agents, sir?"

Rhodes: "Roger that." At least four more problems off his plate.

Time: Wednesday, 18-July, 07:15 PDT (Rest Area, California)

Cornell, Layton, Johnson, and Vernor (to respective 'agents'): "Get up. Your ride's almost here. The Marine guards will follow you over to the LZ. You will put on your hoods after you are in the helo."

Somebody in the group: "Hoods? What do ya mean hoods? I want to see my lawyer right friggin' now."

Major Jenkins brought the helo into the LZ. "Hey is that the chopper the FBI's renting these days. Nice little bird, but I bet it can't go where we're going."

Another agent's voice: "And just where the hell is that? Where are our lawyers; we want to see them right friggin' now."

Jenkins: "Feisty little devils, huh? You'll see your lawyers after you talk with Hard-Ass. Marines, we gotta be gone in five minutes. Load 'em up, tie 'em to the floor, and hood 'em. Times awastin' unless you want 'em to fall out enroute. Captain, wind 'em up; we gotta go." All calculated to keep them un-balanced until Hard-Ass can work his magic. And true to his words, the helo was lifting-off in 4:50 minutes over the protestations of the three males; Daisy should have visited the latrine before being loaded on-board.

Rhodes: "Gunnies, things are going to work themselves out. Give your Marines a long rest break. Don't forget that gun on the hillside; it goes, too. When the truck convoy shows-up we got a lot of work to do to load-up all of the physical evidence and get it ready to be gone by the time CalTrans gets this site returned tomorrow at 17:00. There will be two advance CalTrans engineers to start figuring-out what is going to

Order of Succession

be required to put I-8 back together. We will also provide three Marine guards, sorry, make that 'guides', for each to make sure they take pictures only of their bridge. They will not document anything else out here or whatever leaves this site while they are here.

"There will also be a JAG representative in the convoy. Try not to tangle words with him or her; leave that to me. You all have other assignments. Capiche? Oh, by the way, I asked the Colonel if we could get a trip to the east coast to help finish this mess. My source thinks maybe in about a month and a half or so. Think about the trip. If you're not interested, let me know. I asked for a company of Marines who are familiar with the beginnings out here. Let me know – within the next two weeks. Okay?"

ORDER OF SUCCESSION

29 – Hunting for the Red Barn

Mid morning approaching 11:30, 18-July: Hagerstown, Maryland

TIME: 11:26 EDT (Hagerstown, Maryland)

Smitty happened to run across a store that sold county maps in books with large-scale pages; he bought four of them including Frederick and Washington counties in Maryland and Adams and Franklin counties in Pennsylvania. Now he thought his final target area was pretty well 'bracketed'; it had to be in one of these books. He grabbed something to eat and several bottles of water at a local convenience store.

The relay folks called, telling him there is a message from a major who said "four packages delivered to Hard-Ass. Does that make sense to you? Any reply?" "Thanks for the message; I've got his number."

Smitty still needed to pick-up some more tools for this little 'tour" of the area: binoculars, digital camera with lenses, distance-measuring scope of some sort, boots, and a handheld, electronic compass to generate the necessary GPS coordinates if he ever found that bunker. While at the library earlier in the morning, he planned ahead and searched for the various gear on the Internet. He found an Internet listing for a camera store right there in Hagerstown over on Professional Court just off Eastern Boulevard. However, when he found the address, the sign said Samuel Parker Contracting, not a camera shop. Sam Parker greeted his query about the difference in businesses, with, "That's what the Internet does for you. It's just like an elephant; it never forgets. The camera shop has been closed for quite a few years now. We got so many inquiries, we even made-up a list of photo stores in the area for folks just like you. Here ya go and good luck taking yur pitchers." Smitty gladly accepted the list

243

ORDER OF SUCCESSION

from Sam. The list was awful short: Best Buy, WalMart, Sam's Club (if you are a member), and something named L.A. Cameras. Smitty's first thought was that this L.A. Cameras must be a local store, but it was way up in Chambersburg, Pennsylvania. Well, that one's not even in Maryland. Then it dawned on him that he had just lucked-out. Chambersburg is also where he planned to buy the rest of his outdoor gear anyway. When he was back in the car, he looked-up L.A. Cameras' address in his maps. For the rest of his gear on his list, Smitty had already decided that The Mountain outdoor store, also up in Chambersburg, offered the best selection of gear. He really lucked-out; the stores were just two I-81 interchanges apart.

So, off he drove north on I-81, first to Pennsylvania Exit 14 to find L.A. Cameras. The store had a good selection of DSLRs. Smitty wanted a camera that could record GPS coordinates just in case he needed to provide them to a pilot. He also wanted a compact, casual-use camera so he would not look too obvious taking pictures around sensitive areas. The knowledgeable clerk was quite helpful and guided him to models of each type that would 'probably do the job for you' – even though he didn't know exactly what that job was. Smitty described the lenses he wanted for the DSLR, and the clerk selected a few out of their stock. And, did they happen to have a bird watching guide for this area? (He got a, "Sorry, not our field.", on the bird guide.) How about a couple of cases for the cameras and an extra battery for each one? Just add them to the bill.

After getting all of the photography gear stowed in the car, it was already about an hour and a half past lunch. Hey, the Interstate is right over there; there's gotta be some place to eat around here. He located a Cracker Barrel restaurant, right near the on and off ramps, and drove around the corner into its parking lot. He grabbed the manuals for the new cameras and took them inside so he could familiarize himself with his new gear while he ate.

After lunch, Smitty got back onto I-81 and drove the six miles to Exit 20 and drove right into The Mountain's parking lot right off Black Gap Road. He also asked about a book on bird watching; The Mountain had one that fit his needs. After selecting his outdoor gear and trying-on the new boots while wearing his new socks, Smitty paid-up and carried everything out to the car.

Order of Succession

He rechecked the maps so he could drive cross-country and navigate from the north side of his search area, hoping to eliminate the early part of the trip and pick-up the trail mid-point. His new path lay down Pennsylvania Highway-316 to Waynesboro, noting motels and rental signs along the way. Yep, he was going to move to this area and monitor Hal's plotters from here.

ORDER OF SUCCESSION
30 – The President's News Conference

Around 18:15, Wednesday, 18-July: Preparations for POTUS's News Conference, somewhere in Hagerstown, Maryland

TIME: 18:17 EDT

The relay service rang Smitty with some news, "The President announced a news event for tonight at 21:00 EDT. Thought you might need to know."

Smitty: "Thanks for remembering. Might be something important."

{Smitty's scolding brain: "Yeah, thanks? For cryin' out loud, say it like you mean it. I know, I know, just what we need right now, huh? Up to our eyeballs in plotters; FBI agents who aren't agents; hang-gliders planning an aerial attack on Camp David; and now a presidential news conference. What else can pile-up just cryin' out for you to fix it next? You know you don't have to fix everything; there are others. You know that, right? Huh?"}

{Smitty, (thinking, back-talk): "Yeah, I know what you're sayin' is all possibly true, but I'm the one who knows all about this one. Me, I'm the one. You know that. Now shut-up, will, ya. I got some serious thinkin' to do right now.}

{Now a sarcastic brain: "Okay, if that's the way you want to play it. Keep it all to yourself; see if I care. You'll come back to me with your hat in your hand. Just you wait and see. Oh, you don't wear a hat, do ya? It doesn't matter. You'll see it my way yet. You'll see."}

Time: Wednesday, 18-July, 18:39 EDT

As expected, Smitty was really curious about just how POTUS would explain his absence from the news during the past six days. What could he

Order of Succession

possibly say about being out of contact with the rest of the world of politics for almost a week, especially from the D.C. scene – and remain credible.

He noticed a Ruby Tuesday restaurant near a shopping center in Hagerstown and bought a 'build-it-yourself' salad and a burger with fries to-go. He needed to be back in his room in time for the Presidential News Conference, scheduled for 21:00 hours tonight. On the way back to his motel room, he ran across a liquor store and bought a six-pack of Yuengling, a local, regional beer to take back to his digs.

Using his special cell-phone, Smitty called Cap'n Rhodes and Major Jenkins to make sure they were aware of the telecast. Following the news conference, all three were going to be in a conference of their own.

Time: Wednesday, 18-July, 20:59 EDT

By the time the news conference began, he had already eaten the salad and had begun working on the burger, accompanied by a beer. Thank goodness, he had Ruby's throw a selection of condiments into the to-go bag; the ketchup went well with the fries, and the mayo helped the burger's toasted bun.

{Smitty's still sarcastic brain: "Well here comes the Big Lie, huh? We're all gonna find-out just WTH happened at a previously unheard-of rest-area out in the middle of no-place in the southern California Mojave Desert. Can't wait to hear the official explanation of what you actually lived through, huh, good buddy, Smitty. And you are proud of protecting his ass? Sure, you are, but does he care or even know you are still alive? Think about it; you're up against some pretty nasty boys playing a vicious game with access to at least all of the military assets of the U.S. government. What makes you so damn sure you are even in the same league as they are? Sorry, Rita, I'm just getting worked up. The show's about to begin. Get back to you later, okay?"}

Of course, all of the major TV and (the remaining) radio networks preempted their normal programming to broadcast this news conference – as if they had any real choice. They all used the same 'pool-feed' from the Oval Office at The White House. The official announcer assumed control with the audio lead-in, and with an appropriately deep voice announced, "Ladies and Gentlemen, the President of the United States of America." Let the show begin.

ORDER OF SUCCESSION

President Avery Jacobson told America a much-edited narrative of what had happened to the members of his Cabinet. Not quiet 'the truth', not exactly 'the whole truth', and certainly not 'nothing but the truth'. Smitty didn't know if POTUS even realized that he, Smitty, had survived the initial attack. That point was not mentioned once during the 47 minutes the news conference lasted. Basically, it went something like:

"America, here's what happened: (Instead of just absent-mindedly clicking his pen, Smitty began scribbling notes about this part of the speech, trying to keep-up with the 'official' story-line. *For future reference, you know.*)

"There have been some unprecedented accidents within the Cabinet:"

Friday evening, 13-July:

"A fire at a conference fatally injured five (5) Secretaries of the Cabinet including the Secretaries of: Education, Commerce, Defense, Interior, and Labor."

{Smitty's unconvinced brain: "Dammit, what was the cause? Why were all of them clustered so one event would get all of them at the same time? Who planned the trip? None of that is gonna make the news, is it?"}

Early Saturday morning, 14-July:

"Tragic break-ins in Washington, D.C. took the lives of five (5) additional Secretaries including: Veterans Affairs, Homeland Security, Housing and Urban Development, Transportation, and Energy."

{Smitty's still unconvinced brain: "They ain't gonna make any announcements about how five Cabinet Secretaries just happened to be burglarized at the same day and time, are they? No, they ain't. What'd you expect an actual line-up of the local 'usual suspects' in D.C.? Get a grip, will ya."}

Sunday morning, 15-July:

"And then just three (3) days ago, additional members of the Cabinet were incapacitated in some manner.

Order of Succession

* These included automobile accidents affecting the Secretaries of Agriculture and Health and Human Services.
* Our Secretary of State was kidnapped in one of the 'stans in middle-Asia and is being held for ransom.
* Lastly, the Attorney General has just resigned."

{Smitty's very unsatisfied brain: "Were 'Ag' and HHS together in the same car? Who was driving the other cars in the accident? Was it hit-and-run, or did the other guy hang-around for the police? WTH happened at the scene(s)? Which 'stan' is it; is it a friendly 'stan' or does it lean away from the US? Why was 'State' even over there? Was there a special reason – like maybe some sort of treaty against Russia or a trade pact? And why did the 'AG' suddenly just up and resign? What's he afraid of – make that 'who' is he afraid of? What does he know about the impersonators out at the rest-area? And how the hell could he approve of a waitress from Thurmont being involved with that little act; hell, she's not even an actress. Or, maybe she is, and we don't know for sure about her yet. Wouldn't that be a kick in the head if she ran the entire operation!"}

Here's what needs to happen:

We have to get our government, yours and mine, working again for the American people. We will do this by replacing the members of the Cabinet with the most capable people we can find on such short notice."

{Smitty's sarcastic: "Hey, Smitty, my boy, have you ever noticed that most times during problem-times like this, the elected officials always keep saying, 'It's time to get back to work for the American people?' Ever notice that when they are taking heat, it's always getting back to working for the American people? Why is that, huh? WTF were they doing when they were supposedly working for us? Not working for us? Sloughing-off? Ya know, it sounds too damn suspicious, if ya ask me. Just sayin'."}

Here's how we are going to accomplish this:

"I will submit the list of names for these positions, which we have been assembling over the past few days, to the appropriate authorities over in the Capitol. I have asked that they streamline and fast-track the approval process so that our government, yours and mine, can resume taking care of the nation's business. While we are wading through the approval process, I will allow these appointees, to begin managing their respective agencies immediately."

{Smitty's disgusted brain: "More of that 'nation's business' stuff. WTF have you been doing before all this crap happened. Takin' care of your own business. I'll betcha that's it!"}

"Thank-you one and all for your understanding during these trying times. Etc. Etc."

Smitty's First Reaction

"Well, it certainly looked and sounded like him. Sure hope this isn't one of those movies like *Dave* or *Vantage Point*."

His second reaction: "Son-of-a-bitch! *{Brain: "Sorry, again, Rita."}* That's what they're planning to do – bypass the approving authorities to insert their own conspirators. Damn slick idea: Cause a big crisis within the government and just happen to have a quick solution. Damn friggin' slick idea."

Time: Wednesday, 18-July, 21:49 EDT

{Smitty's inquisitorial brain: "Hey, good buddy, things are really startin' to pick-up here. So, what's your Plan A? You do have one dontcha? You got a Plan B yet? Better start thinkin' about one? Okay, now, how's this gonna play out? Can you get some eyes in the air, but close-in. How do we do that? Think that through will ya, ya dummy. Plan to figure it out over a cuppa coffee? Better make it a fast one cause it's all comin' together faster than you ever thought it could. Take it with lots of antacid so the acid doesn't aggravate ya too badly, okay?"}

{Smitty: "Yeah, yeah I think I have a Plan A. Hey, it's only three hours difference between here and California. If I were gonna start something involving an aerial assault in downtown D.C., would there be a better time than that public relations show Your Armed Forces on Display? *Hell, hiding amongst your own and lookin' like you belong*

ORDER OF SUCCESSION

there besides. Gotta check for the exact dates near the end of August. About 45 days away. Not much time to plan a strategy and rehearse it, if necessary. And it's gotta be on the QT, too. Better get this thing rolling and call Jenkins and Rhodes. Plan A; there you go. Not ready to think about a Plan B or C. A's gotta do it or we're toast. Brain, out!"}

Smitty dialed Major Jenkins first. "Phillip, didja listen to the President's address? I believe this is how they are planning to take over the federal government. Basically, the President's Cabinet runs the country what with writing the rules, signing contracts, paying the bills – all that mundane 'make-work' business. These bastards are gonna do a wholesale transfer of the Cabinet's power to their own people. And then run the government with their own people in power. I don't think the POTUS I knew would go along with that willingly. God only knows what they're using to make him go along with this plan.

"I think that *Armed Forces* show in late August would be an opportune time for their conspirators to act. I've already begun planning about how I'd do it at that time in my head. I am thinkin' with all that military hardware right there on The Mall, something goes 'terribly wrong', and The White House is a pile of cinders using our own weapons. I'd like to have you and Brian arrive at least three weeks early to recon the area around D.C., The Mall, and surrounding area about 70 miles northwest into Frederick County, Maryland – up and around Thurmont. I think they are also planning something up at Camp David, too, but that's probably their contingency Plan B. So, your recon area would extend up to at least there, too. Phillip, I've been talking pretty fast here; break-in any time you want."

Phillip: "Yeah, I noticed you've been drinking way too much coffee. But what you've been describing makes a lot of sense to me. A lot more than when I heard it the first time, I'll say that much. Let me talk this over with Brian to figure-out our availabilities. I'm thinking a minimum of two helos with the possibility of a third. And we'd need a place to park the choppers that's away from the rest of the show and away from the press, but still close-in so our travel time in-bound is right close to where we think the action is going to be. Any ideas on that yet? Actually, two sites to park the birds so that one counterattack doesn't wipe-out both of us. And both must have access to fuel and mechanics, too. Think about that for a while."

Order of Succession

Smitty: "Already on it. I originally thought of Andrews, but I betcha that's where the rest of the aircraft and choppers will probably be. Plus, it is quite a distance to TWH. So, if you don't mind parking at another service's facility, I've got calls out to park your helos at two, diverse, separated facilities in the area. Fuel, mechanics, and armaments are also being arranged. Plus they are already behind a perimeter fence and guarded gates. But no hangars are available; tents and tarps will have to do.

"Oh, we would appreciate knowing if Hard-Ass found-out anything from our guests. Could you please call him? And I had a hare-brained thought for you to run past Major Rollins. Suppose Daisy is really an actress, and suppose she has some say in this whole plot – up to, and including, maybe even being the leader of the whole damn thing. I know that doesn't sound plausible, but just suppose that it is. Ask Erwin if that makes any sense to him. I did say it's just a SWAG, right now."

Phillip: "As long as the birds are near enough to the action site to be effective and still light-up their asses, we can live with your Plan A. Ahead of you on the last point. Erwin says they were no fun; broke too easily. After being shown the pictures of those so-called FBI agents, our first guests, the locals from that white trailer out in the desert, both picked-out the same two guys, the Special Agent Phelps and that pilot so full of himself, Cowell. Erwin also said the three male agents didn't say much. He thought maybe they seemed a bit too confident that somebody was gonna up and pull them outta there. On the other hand, the female agent seems to be frightened not only for herself but also for her husband, Hal. Erwin's letting her stew for a coupla days before his Hard-Ass alter-ego pushes her buttons. I'll pass along your latest thoughts about Daisy; who knows, maybe it'll be a new angle for Hard-Ass.

"Erwin also said he's heard rumors that somebody's been pinging the Marine brigs in the area about who has our guests in custody. He hasn't said anything; afraid he might tip his hand and have bloody hell to pay for it."

Smitty: "Good man there. Time's a wasting; don't be too surprised if you get TDY orders pretty soon. Gotta call Cap'n Rhodes to invite him to the party, too. Out here."

Phillip: "Roger that."

Order of Succession

The next call went to Rocky. "Coms, would you please get Cap'n Rhodes for me? And, yes, I just left your area just a few days ago."

Coms: "Yes, sir, even if you are a Gyrene."

Rhodes: "Terry Pedrozo, I assume. How can I help you?"

Smitty: "Thanks for remembering my name. I've got an offer for you that I hope is too good to refuse. Have you ever heard about something called *Your Armed Forces on Display*. It's supposed to be a show for the general public scheduled around the end of August down on The Mall in Washington, D.C. I want you and at least three platoons of Marines to be there to help protect TWH. I have already invited two helo pilots you should remember. Are you up for it?"

Rhodes: "Wouldn't miss it; be honored to join you, but that's a lot of paperwork and the orders must come down to us, not up from us. If you know what I mean. And, we're still providing security and clean-up out here at the rest-area. Those FBI agents, well they really screwed over my C&C folks. They've become very leery of non-Marines intruding into their chain of command."

Smitty: "I fully understand that. But these orders will send you and about three platoons from your company TDY to D.C. for about three weeks give or take. I want all of your Gunnies, Coms, and most of your company including Berkeley, Winthrop and two snipers, and Barnes. You can fill-in anyone else you think you need. If you want your C.O., Colonel Gahagen, to go TDY with you all, he will be TDY only as an observer, not directly in command unless the crap really hits the fan and we need a lot more muscle and assets.

"You will have to work with two to four platoons of US Army troops from local facilities I think maybe from Fort Myer. Rocky, we've worked together and you know where I'm coming from, so, company command will be all yours. During the exposition time, all companies will provide roving security in civvies and later, in uniforms. However, when the action begins, you will have command of all companies. The Army will be officially advised, but I've been unofficially advised that they will agree. Orders are being processed as we speak to include everybody I mentioned and up to 30 more, including your colonel.

"An additional Marine company is being moved from 29 to the rest-area to replace you if it takes longer than two more days to

Order of Succession

transfer the rest-area to other authorities. CalTrans engineers will be on-site tomorrow at 08:00.

"Oh, Quantico will be your supply point, and they are stocking for our new mission. Rocky, your time out there is ending. I'm asking you to join the TWH team."

Rocky: "Since you put it that way, how can we refuse – providing the Colonel approves, of course."

Smitty: "Get ready to pack-up. He will be on-board by the time the TDY orders come down – that, or he will be replaced and given command of the motor pool. Yes, we do have that capability, too; not just the Voice on the POTUS phone. Speaking of which, did he ever call back?"

Rocky: "As a matter of fact, he did shortly after the four FBI agents were arrested. I'd say Mr. Voice never expected to hear that 'cuz he hung-up muttering something about 'damn SOBs'."

Smitty: "Good for our side. I assume you agree to come around the middle of August, right? We gotta a lot of places for you and the Gunnies to recon. Better bring some civvies, too; don't need to attract too much attention wearing camo's all the time. And cut back on haircuts, too."

Rhodes (returning to military bearing): "Roger that. Gotta go and advise the Marines about this TDY assignment. Thank-you."

Smitty: "Oh, forgot to mention that your names and units have been changed; whoever has access to the Corps HR systems probably knows exactly which Marines were involved at the rest-area. We don't need to give them too much help if we can help it. Details to follow. Welcome aboard."

ORDER OF SUCCESSION
31 – Searching for the Bunker

Just past 09:30, Thursday, 19-July: Somewhere west of Thurmont, Maryland, near Maryland Route 550

TIME: 09:32 EDT

Late to bed; late to rise.

Smitty stayed up too late last night putting plans together in his mind – Plans A, B, and maybe part of C. He made notes and laid out each side-by-side just to see where the holes might be. Finally, around 02:00 and after the last two bottles of Yuengling, he went to bed – tired, but well-satisfied so far.

He checked-out of his motel, determined to find a new one up in Pennsylvania to be closer to his planned search area. He ordered a fast-food breakfast and coffee to-go at a nearby restaurant. After consulting his maps, Smitty decided to check-out Waynesboro, just across the state-line up in Pennsylvania. They must have something up there in the way of a motel for a lowly government employee. Instead of driving north on I-81 again, this time Smitty took some of the back-roads shown on his maps north to Waynesboro. Might as well get used to the lay-of-the-land, so he took Highway MD-60 to Pennsylvania-316 and ended-up right in the middle of Waynesboro.

He turned left onto Buchanan Trail East (a.k.a. West Main Street and also Pa. Rt. 16) just to see what was down that way. He spotted a motel within a few blocks and pulled-in to see what it looked like. Lady Luck was still in his corner. There was sort of an inner court for the parking area, making it more difficult for someone to check-out license plates without drawing attention to themselves. And another recessed parking area was off to one side of the main parking area. All pluses. Why pass-up an opportunity when it's staring right at you. The office clerk said they still had a few vacant rooms available and offered him the keys so he could look at them. All three met his needs, and all were priced the same. "How about the one on the second floor in front." At least the car couldn't be seen from the street, and he could watch for uninvited visitors if he needed to. He registered using his undercover name and moved in. Like, why wait when there's planning that's gotta be done. He carried his gear into the room and arranged it so he could get to work right away.

He also went down to talk with the Housekeeping staff. He told them he was new to the area and working on a consulting job. And also new to the hobby of bird watching, as well. He talked them up about bird-watching; did they know of any good areas for spotting birds over around Rtes. 550 and/or 77. Any places he could find information about local birds – maybe some that might be rarer than others. He told them he was going to have some maps, pictures, and other stuff laid-out in his room and didn't want them disturbed because they were important for his consulting job – as well as bird-watching. He gave them a $20 tip to not clean his room every day. Just pick-up the trash he would put inside the door and leave fresh towels every three days or so. Would it be okay with them to do their standard clean-ups on Saturdays instead? What's not to like about that? Done deal.

Time: Thursday, 19-July, 12:34 EDT (MD 550 near the junction with Foxville Deerfield Road, Maryland)

Using his best recollection of the turns, slow-downs, bumps, and road noise, Smitty's best guesses put his target somewhere along Maryland-550, the winding highway between Thurmont and old Fort Ritchie. Surely, it was a big piece of real estate, but Smitty was determined to cut it down to size this week – this very afternoon, if he could. That is, if Lady Luck had fallen in love with him and aligned all the stars for success. His old morning coffee was only luke-warm now – actually, sorta luke-cold. He had stopped for a pit-stop and a cuppa coffee to-go at the Mickey Ds in Waynesboro.

He took PA-16, driving mostly sorta east, with some south east thrown-in at the far end to get to Blue Ridge Summit, where he drove over some local back-streets over into Maryland and to Highway-550. And finally, he followed 550 mostly south-southeast toward Thurmont. He was pretty sure his goal lay along this stretch of 550 – well, at least 75% sure anyway, which was a whole lot better than 50/50. Hey, ya gotta start somewhere, and this was his best bet. His nervous energy

Order of Succession

was building so rapidly that he belatedly realized that he shoulda picked-up a sandwich or something else to eat, too, in addition to the coffee.

One thing he knew for certain, he was not going to go down to The Treadle in Thurmont. Who woulda thought that Daisy and Hal were hitched; that thought never even crossed his mind. And, she was now arrested and in the custody of the Marines out in the California desert. Just goes to show ya about the weirdness of life.

Just south of Sabillasville on 550, there was a local, farm-grown, produce and fruit store. Smitty pulled into the parking lot to consult his maps. He decided this parking lot was going to serve as his base for the upcoming search. This would meet his needs to a 'T'. He also found it convenient for another reason: there were fresh fruit, snacks, drinks, and a rest room, all inside. The fact that it was about the half-way point on Route 550 between Hal's welding shop and the farthest he thought he had been driven out to the bunker, sealed the deal. It will do fine for now.

He opened the map books to get close-up views of his proposed search area and wrote down his best-guess route for his first search. He put on a floppy hat and sun-glasses he bought at the Walmart down in Hagerstown (behind a Cracker Barrel restaurant) and then drove south back to the edge of Thurmont, pulling into the Burger King to get a cuppa hot coffee. His 'Plan A': Drive the first part of that trip to the bunker only once and then mark his starting point at the intersection of the road for Hal's shop and 550. He didn't want to be seen frequently down there if he could help it. He hoped the hat, sun-glasses, and unshaven beard (since last Friday) provided enough camouflage to let him drive around without being recognized too readily. He wanted to drive all the side-roads on the east side of the road and work his way back to the produce stand. He figured it would take him at least a week to search south of the produce stand. He hoped that he would be successful without having to keep-up the search on the north side of the stand.

{Smitty's sarcastic mind: "Okay now, when are we gonna start searching? Isn't that part of Plan A? Or did you make it to Plan Z already? C'mon man, get with the plan, when are we gonna start? You ain't got all month, or do ya?"}

And with that, Smitty opened his maps and books and laid-out his first official trip to personally locate that secreted bunker.

Order of Succession

Time: Thursday, 19-July, 13:03 EDT

Now driving 550 and its side roads beginning at the Thurmont end, his goal was to cut the area in half, and then in half, and in half again as quickly as possible – without being seen by anyone who might recognize him – neither Hal and company nor any of the 'Gripers'. To that end, Smitty always wore his beard, sunglasses, and floppy hat when he was out driving around. Back in Waynesboro, he planned to start wearing a different colored cap and differently-framed sunglasses. He drove away from Thurmont, turned off just past the road to Hal's welding shop, and found a wide spot to pull over into and lay-out his maps on the passenger seat. He was now so confident about his bearings that he merged back onto 550 and passed Hal's road again still heading away from Thurmont. And he kept driving until he got to a safe spot to park and check his maps again. Now, the time-consuming part of his plan began. He was trying to overlay his memory of that first and only trip out to the bunker on top of the real roads. To say the least, he knew his real enemies were the lack of time and his impatience to get his show-on-the-road. He just hoped he didn't attract any attention. Then Smitty transformed himself from the searcher into Terry, the bird-watcher, searching for an elusive something or other. Better brush-up on what Terry's looking for; gotta make notes on that. He changed into his boots; too bad he didn't have time to break them just in a little. Oh, well, it was too late now to worry about getting some bothersome blisters.

{Smitty's still sarcastic brain: "Hey, you know there are an awful lot of side-roads, dead ends, and wrong turns out here dontcha? You sure your Plan A calls for all of this nuisance? You sure of your memory about all the turns and what-not? You sure about this? You sure you got time for this before the troops arrive?}

{Smitty: "Hey, brain, if you're so friggin'-smart, you got any better ideas? Shut-up for now, will ya? My Plan A has got a built-in budget of 10 to 12 days of this searching. Just chill-out; I got lots of time built-in. So, just shut-up for now, will ya. Sorry, Rita."}

{Brain: "Okay for now. Don't be so touchy! It's just that this is so mind-numbing. Okay, have it your way. Over and out for now! Just call on me whenever you need some smarts, okay?"}

Order of Succession

Eylers Valley Road appeared on the right. He thought this right turn was not in the correct spot; so, nope, not here. He decided to pass by it for now, but he made a note to return, if necessary. Mumbling to himself, "I better be careful about passing up stuff or I'll be back to that produce stand and have nothing to show for it."

{Smitty (thinking, back-talk): "Brain, you got any better ideas?}

{Brain: "Say, smart-ass, only took you 3 hours and 37 minutes to get back to me; I've been timing you. Didn't think you'd last this long. So, now you want help or directions to the nearest latrine?"}

{Smitty: "Neither of those. How about just a sanity-check? Without a chopper, this is the best way to do this, isn't it?"}

{Brain: "How would I know? Remember back when you took this trip, you weren't talkin' to me. You were way too confident in your own abilities to make small talk with me. Remember that, don't cha, huh? That kidnappin' out in the desert in California shook your self-confidence. Am I right? Sure, I am, and you know it. So, do it your way for 10 to 12 days. I got all the time. Do you? I can wait for you to come to my senses."}

Time: Thursday, 19-July, 18:12 EDT

By the time he got all his points organized and got the lay-of-the-land, daylight was growing short. The roads were beginning to look alike; and nothing felt like he thought he remembered it. Time to call it quits for the day.

Time: Friday, 20-July, 06:15 EDT

A better and longer sleep last night meant Smitty would be up earlier – and with a refreshed sense of purpose. Coffee and pastry rolls down in the hospitality room would tide him over until healthier food was available.

Then it struck him that this episode all began almost exactly one week ago out there in the Mojave Desert. He let that sink-in for no more than 35 seconds, during which time, he quickly ran through those events again, trying to follow the time-line again.

Smitty drove back up the hill and turned right to drive through Blue Ridge Summit and turned left downhill past the Victor Cullen Center turnoff, continuing on 550 through Sabillasville to the parking lot at his produce store Search HQ. Good thing he also stopped at the Mickey D's and picked-up some grub to-go because the produce place didn't open to the public until around 10:00. Maps, chow, and coffee built his enthusiasm again. He didn't want to waste time waiting in a parking lot, so he left wearing sandwich crumbs and a spot of spilled coffee on his shirt, and the DSLR camera with pictures of birds on the passenger seat just in case somebody asked what's up.

The previous afternoon, Smitty tried every side-road off 550 between Thurmont and Eylers Valley Flint Road. So, back down 550 and a left turn onto Eylers Valley again. He drove slowly so he could match the road's turns and meanderings to the map he had sketched from his memory. He drove down the side-roads on both the left and right sides of Black Road and Eylers Valley Road.

Smitty even stopped to read the information board about a small church, the Eylers Valley Chapel, at an even smaller crossroads junction. Just that many more roads to check-out. Eylers Valley Road turned to the left at the church. The other road was Hampton Valley Road; Smitty followed that road to the right. Summit Lake Camp was just ahead on the left; he hadn't seen a lake on his first trip, but you never know. But, nothing seemed to match any part in his memory – nothing yet. He followed another road through the Emmitsburg Watershed; it turned into a dead-end. Back to Hampton Valley to veer right onto Crystal Fountain Road and its side roads. In his map books, Smitty used a light red highlighter to indicate the roads he had already driven without finding anything that mated his memory. Nothing felt right, and that was confirmed by the light red highlights. Their permanence mocked his memory.

Time: Friday, 20-July, 16:32 EDT

Nothing matched. Again, nothing. Around mid afternoon, he crossed over into Pennsylvania on MD 140, which he found off of Annandale Road. Although it was on the maps, Smitty just didn't expect it. He was positive that the bunker was back in Maryland. Time to call it quits for the day – again with nothing to show for it. Well, it was still within his time-budget, so he still had a week and a few days left to find it.

Time to go back to the motel. The maps showed Waynesboro west of his location. Instead of back-tracking over those same back-roads, this time, Smitty took MD-140 to Pennsylvania-16 straight into Waynesboro.

Order of Succession

Time: Friday, 20-July, 21:16 EDT

Smitty: "Phillip, how goes it? I'm back here driving country roads in the Catoctin Mountains searching for the roads they drove me over when I was blind-folded. Nothing looks even vaguely familiar yet. Thought I should give you an update about your helos for that *Your Armed Forces on Display* show. I assumed that you wouldn't be able to bring your own birds, so some mechanics down at Quantico are making a few unofficial modifications to a coupla helos down there – an AH-1Z Viper and a UH-1Y Venom Super Huey already down there. Both are fully-armed along with some special gadgets on loan from some manufacturers for 'test and evaluation' purposes. The shop down there also worked-up a little non-lethal gadget to persuade the aggressor pilot that landing his chopper would be the smart thing to do. Plus, they're also fitting some non-standard armaments to both. You know, a little from here, a little from there. They think these helos are gonna be some 'A-One Mean Mothers' – bar none."

Jenkins: "Sounds very interesting. Brian and I have been trying to figure-out what we would do if we were the aggressors and how to we can neutralize them with those two helos. Our big consideration is that there may be lots of civilians on The Mall when this confrontation starts. They may not all get the hell out of Dodge after the first shot. They will probably gawk at those choppers in a dog-fight and think it's all part of the show; I know I would. They're gonna be, 'Wow, what a show! Can't be for real; it's gotta be all for show.' That kinda stuff. But, you really got my attention when you said non-lethal gadget."

Smitty: "Well, it's non-lethal for the civilians with limited damage to buildings – if you're not directly underneath the confrontation, that is. But if the aggressor doesn't comply, there's always gonna be danger to him. The mechanics are waiting for you and Brian to show up to make sure you'll be comfortable with the mods they are bolting onto the birds. And, they gotta show you how they work, too. When are you leaving for back here?"

Jenkins: "We got orders today. Different names on them, but we were assured it will all work. Anyway, a military transport is supposed to fly us and our gear back east the end of the first week of August. That should give us about three weeks before the real show begins."

Smitty: "Does Hard-Ass have any news about any of the folks out there yet?"

Order of Succession

Jenkins: "Spoke to him just this morning. The boys from the white trailer are just spooked about the deep crap they think they're in; really stewing about it. However, Erwin thinks they're just a bunch of innocent guys caught-up in the money-trap. He doesn't think they are active participants of the plot, but he's just gonna let them stew for a while longer.

"The three fake FBI agents are another story. They are putting up a good front, but they are getting the definite feeling that no one's coming to get them out. Erwin says the probing questions about which brig is holding them as guests seem to have stopped. They now are getting the message that they were considered expendable all along. And Erwin is driving that point home hard and repetitively. Sort of reminds me of you being hung-out to twist in the wind, old buddy.

"He says Daisy is an interesting character. He believes she knows exactly what's going on. Knows a lot more than a naïve waitress at – what's the name of that restaurant again?"

Smitty: "You talking about The Treadle? When all this is over, I'll have to take you and Brian there and the other Marines too. Say, did Hard-Ass get her full name yet; might be interesting to poke around Thurmont to see who knows what about the real Daisy."

Jenkins: "Yeah, The Treadle, that's it. Well as Erwin was saying, he thinks she knows a lot more than she lets on. She's now his prime target now. I think he said her name is supposed to be Darlene Zoe Drixler."

Smitty: "Thanks for the update. Interesting about Daisy's name, isn't it? I wonder how deep she's in to the plot. Well, Drixler matches the name on Hal's welding shop. Betcha she got the nick-name 'Daisy' from people saying, 'DZ, DZ, DZ, Daisy'; that makes sense to me. But wouldn't it be a real hoot if she were running the whole show? Oh well, a different day for that research. Gotta call Rocky and see how he and the Marines are doing. If you have any ideas or need anything, call my answering service. They'll get in touch with me right away. Oh, by the way, they do not know anything about the plot – not even from when I was undercover during the planning stages. Please do not get careless when talking to them; we don't know who they are loyal to at this time. Okay?"

Jenkins: "Roger that; I'll tell Brian, too. Out."

Order of Succession

Time: Friday, 20-July, 21:53 EDT

Smitty: "Captain Rhodes, is this a good time for a briefing?"

Rhodes: "Terry, you bet it is! The Gunnies and I are throwing-out ideas about how we would accomplish the plot and how we would have to defend against that. Oh, by the way, the truck convoy arrived at its destination this afternoon. Some of my Marines rode along as guards; everybody is supposed to be back at Pendleton tomorrow late in the afternoon. Oh, yeah, my company was replaced out at the rest area by that company from 29. The other companies will be relieved next Monday.

"Oh, man, you should have heard those CalTrans engineers after they saw the ruins of their overpass. They're like, 'How'd all this happen. Looks like you guys had a real battle out here. Were you all using our bridge for a training exercise? Just look at this mess; it's gonna take months to rebuild this.' I asked him about a coupla months, really? How long did it take to put a temp fix on the San Francisco Bay Bridge after that earthquake back whenever? And look how big it is and puny this one is. Really, a coupla, months? I'll bet our Marine engineers could make it passable in a much shorter time than that, and it would support a tank, too.' Got no more complaints from them.

"But he wasn't too far off with his training exercise comment. Colonel Gahagen asked us if it wouldn't be a good idea to destroy the tunnel to keep it from being misunderstood and have somebody figure-out what could have happened out there. So, we made one more trip through the tunnel with lights and cameras, recording everything once again. Didn't find any booby traps. Then we invited the EOD boys to plant enough explosives to blow it up all the way to the tunnel exit. So, now there's a big long depression heading away from the site. And the concrete box that was under the limo, well, it is no more either. The CalTrans guys asked about all of that, and we just shrugged our shoulders. Told them that's the way we found it when we got out of the choppers a week ago. We told them they could fill it in if they have to because it's not ours. So, what do 'ya have, Terry?"

Smitty: "I like the idea of wiping out that tunnel and the concrete box; good thinkin' there. And the 'playin' dumb' about what actually happened out there – well, that's really sort of the truth, too, ain't it? We really still don't know anything about it yet, do we? Phillip and Brian got their orders this morning, also under alias names, too. Did you all get yours, too?"

Order of Succession

Rhodes: "Not officially yet. We just got back to Pendleton this afternoon. The Colonel says there's a raft of paperwork waiting for us. Says it looks like TDY orders. That's why the Gunnies and I were shooting the breeze about our task back there."

Smitty: "Here's the capsule view. The Marines will be joined by two platoons from two companies from the Army. I tried to get two full companies, but remainders of these companies could not be released from prior commitments. Well anyway, you'll all start down at Quantico for some joint training about military exercises in a city environment. In other words, Close-Quarters-Battle (CQB) if it ever comes to that. That, and crowd control. The teachers will also be flown in just for this training. You're gonna havta become familiar with the Army troops; I know you and the Gunnies will do just fine. Then we are all gonna plan out our defenses after the Marines, the Army, and I take a little tour of grounds – so to speak. We've got some civilian tour buses laid-on; didn't want to use military buses. I've got most of the sites we need to see laid out – and some that are tourist attractions just to make it look right. We want to blend in as much as possible, so all y'all are gonna need civvies and let your hair grow. Don't worry, it's only for a few weeks. Sorry, but you'll be billeted in an old Army barracks, which is really close to the Major's new helo toy. Take good care of both of them.

"I've been trying to find that bunker – the one I had to wear the blindfold in the pick-up. I'm trying to drive the route I have stuck in my head and no luck so far. Maybe the roads were in a different direction or flat-out in a different state."

Rhodes: "Maybe two minds can help. Describe it to me once again. What kind of truck and trailer was it? How big was the trailer, what was in it, and how much did it weigh? And what kind of terrain do you think it was?"

Smitty: "Okay, let's try your idea. A ginormous Ford F-450 pick-up with duals on the back and big, tall tires all around – I almost needed a step-stool to get in it. It has a diesel engine. I could smell the fuel, but didn't notice any decals about its size. A fifth-wheel trailer looked like an enclosed car trailer – the kind for taking cars to race tracks. I guessed it was about maybe 18 to 20 feet long or so because it had a small compartment up front for quick access to some tools or equipment. I unloaded all the munitions that were in it, so

Order of Succession

I guess maybe the load capacity was maybe five or six tons. Well, we had to drive on two-lane roads and highways leaving Hal's barn. They were winding and hilly. I suspect we were always on something like them until we got near the bunker."

Rhodes: "What was the driver's speed? Did he have to back-up at any place? Did he vary the speed any, and how fast do you think he drove? Did the engine labor at any point? What was the time-duration again?"

Smitty: "About 39 minutes. Okay, I'm guessing a top speed of maybe 30 miles an hour because I think the engine wound-up enough to get up to highway speed, but I didn't feel it was that fast. Sort of like all noise and not enough speed because of the load and the terrain. He only slowed down when he turned onto a different road. I think I got the answer now! I think I gauged the distance by the sound of the engine. I may have been off by as much as 25%. Tomorrow I approach this with a new perspective. Thanks for a different perspective, Rocky. Call you back after I adjust for errors. Bye."

ORDER OF SUCCESSION
32 – It's Gotta be Here – Somewhere

Nearing 06:40, Saturday, 21-July: The Motel in Waynesboro, Pennsylvania

TIME: 06:42 EDT

The sting of the morning shower whetted Smitty's enthusiasm to keep looking for that bunker.

{Smitty's questioning mind: "You sure about this, Huh?"}

{Smitty: "Yep. It's gotta be out there somewhere, and I'm positive I'm searching the correct quadrant. It's just gotta be here."}

After toweling-off, dressing, and starting on another cuppa coffee, Smitty spread-out the map books on the second bed and fastened the larger sheet maps to the curtains with those springy binder-clips he bought at an office supply store just a few days ago down in Hagerstown. For the next hour, he coordinated all the maps to show the same information about his previous day's drive-about. He didn't need to waste precious time retracing his search – especially if he happened to search from the opposite direction. He assumed, that if it wasn't there going one way, sure as hell it won't be there from the other. Would it? Nope, it won't.

{Smitty's sarcastic mind: "You sure about that, huh? You're so turned around out there, you're damn lucky you can find your way back to this motel. You know you're not an outdoors man. You need your coffee and pastry. Gotta admit though, eating fruit from the stand surprised me – in a good way, I might add. But you ain't gonna earn a living wandering around off-road, you wimp."}

{Smitty: "You just wait and see. I am gonna – no, we're gonna find that bunker. Gayronteed! You just wait and see. After breakfast."}

He gave the map books another once-over, then folded both together (interlocking the pages he wanted to concentrate on today) and went down

Order of Succession

to the free breakfast. He filled his insulated cup with fresh, hot coffee and added his favorite flavoring (hazelnut) and one packet of sweetener. As he neared his room, the maids were already heading his way.

{Smitty, to self: "Damn. This is Saturday. Completely forgot about them. Hey, Brain, is anything out that shouldn't be? Think quick."}

"Good morning, ladies. Here, let me open my door for you. I didn't think you'd be startin' this early. I just stopped at the hospitality room downstairs. Pretty decent morning wake-me-ups down there. Especially, this coffee. Here you go (as he opened the door). Thank-you for only dropping by today. I got papers and maps all over the place (which was true). You sure you don't know where I can find any special birds, huh? Let me gather some stuff together, and I'll be outta your hair. Oh, there's an envelope on the night stand for y'all; you can figure out how to share it." (Another $20)

He gathered his maps and his notes about the original trip and waved goodbye. For today's trip, Smitty, laid-out his route up PA-16 to Blue Ridge Summit, and over to downhill MD-550. The produce store won't be open yet, so they won't mind if I use their parking lot for about 30 minutes and plan where to search today

Time: Saturday, 21-July, 14:21 EDT

Smitty pulled back into the parking lot at the produce store, not as chipper as he was in yesterday's morning. Still hadn't found that damn bunker.

{Sarcastic brain: "So what were you saying about finding it today? Did you find it already and just happen to drive past it? I don' think so."}

{Smitty: "I did not say I'd find it this morning. And I didn't. Just gotta work the maps better. That's all. Now, hush, will ya?}

{Attentive brain: "By the way, you've got company. See right over there."}

Smitty was already absent-mindedly walking toward the store for some fruit and a fresh drink. A Maryland State Police cruiser just pulled into the lot and backed into a space that looked directly at his car. Coincidence or what? Smitty continued into the store, used the rest room, and bought some local fruit and a cold water. Then he asked for the manager.

267

Order of Succession

A woman with "Fern" embroidered on her apron approached. "I'd like to introduce myself just so you know who I am. My name is Terry, and I'm working on a consulting job nearby in Waynesboro. And, if I have any spare time, I am also trying out a new hobby. Bird watching. Just so there's no confusion, I stop by your store in the mornings and pull into your lot so I can organize my maps, and then I leave for a few hours. And then I end the day by stopping by again around this time for some fruit and water – oh yes, to use rest room, too. "

Fern: "Yeah, somebody told me about somebody stopping by for several days when we ain't open yet. Maps? Whadya looking for?"

Terry: "Well, you may find this hard to believe, but here goes. I'm trying to get accepted into the Mid-Atlantic Ornithologists' Society."

Fern: "The Mid-Atlantic what? Whatever you said."

Terry: "The Mid-Atlantic Ornithologists' Society is for birdwatchers. And I'm trying to join it. They said I would have to provide some bird-watching records for this area of Maryland in order to be even considered. Hold on will ya, let me go out to the car and get some pictures so I can show ya. I'll be right back." Before Fern could object, Terry ran to the car. The officer was reaching for something – the radio microphone – as he watched Terry run out of the store. Terry headed for the passenger side and grabbed most of the maps and bird pictures and walked quickly back to the store. The officer lowered the microphone. Not a coincidence.

Terry: "Maybe you can help me. See, this is the picture of the bird they were really interested in. Maybe they were stretching the truth a bit, but they think there's a small flock of them in this very area. (Terry gestured toward the area, in the map books, where he had been driving around for three days.) Maybe you've seen one like it? I'd certainly appreciate it if you could point me toward the area you were in if you can remember. That would be most helpful."

Fern: "Bird watching? Well, I never. No, I've never seen the bird in that picture. Bird watching, don't that beat all." Fern waved toward the officer outside; the officer gave her a friendly wave and left the lot to patrol other areas. It was certainly not coincidental.

Terry: "I still have a few days left to find that bird. If you don't mind, would pulling into your lot in the mornings be okay? Just long enough to get my maps organized; that's all?"

Order of Succession

Fern: "Sure. If you promise to show me a picture of that bird if you do find it. Don't that beat all."

Terry: "You got a deal. I'll even stop back in around this time each day I'm out there. That okay with ya?"

Fern: "Sure is. That's what we're here for. Drive safely; these roads can fool you, especially at night."

Terry: "Pleasure meeting you, and if I ever get a picture of that bird, you can have it. My gift."

Terry bought a few more pieces of fruit and a coupla carrots. He headed for the car, but turned around half-way to the door and asked Fern, "Say, do you know any restaurants in the area that you can recommend? The food in Waynesboro is getting a little old – not that there's anything wrong with it. You know what I mean?"

Fern: "Sure do. There's a place a few miles north of the Liberty Ski area, which is closed now during the summer. Here, let me show you in one of your map books." She marked it with an 'X'. "They're only open on Fridays, Saturdays, and Sundays. Sundays they close at 3-o'clock; maybe tomorrow would be better for you – before 3-o'clock."

Terry: "Thanks a lot, Fern, I just need the break. You know, something different.

Time: Sunday, 22-July, 12:43 EDT

Sill had not found the bunker.

{Smitty's ever-sarcastic brain: "Well, where is that little 'bird' located anyway? Gonna give Fern a picture of if when you find it? Say, how much of this quadrant you got left to drive? Sure you're gonna find it; but when? Willya make it soon; I got things to do."}

{Smitty: "Shut-up, willya? I told ya we're gonna find it. Just shut-up for now, okay?"}

The produce store wasn't open, but Smitty pulled-in anyway. Got out of the car and stretched his legs. Carefully crossed-over 550 and ran half-way down the driveway of the school and ran back. A little exercise felt good.

Smitty arranged his search so he could find that restaurant Fern suggested. He leisurely drove following the roads to that restaurant –

highways, roads, and a back-road. He arrived at the Hickory Bridge Farm Restaurant just in time for the last seating at 3-o'clock. There was a larger crowd than he expected waiting in the room directly outside the main dining room. He decided that if he wanted to eat here again, he would call ahead for a reservation. He ate an excellent meal and was back on the highway by half past four. A great way to spend the afternoon.

Time: Monday, 23-July, 15:22 EDT

The bunker remained elusive. Smitty repeated the same conversation with himself, to no avail.

The produce store was open, so, Terry bought some fruit and a coupla veggies. Said hello to Fern and told her he still hadn't seen that bird yet, but that restaurant she had recommended was excellent.

Time: Tuesday, 24-July, 06:47 EDT (At motel in Waynesboro)

Starting another search day, Smitty worked the motel's breakfast buffet line including more coffee, cold cereal, mystery-meat patties, eggs, and pastry. He planned the first stop at Mickey D's for something extra to make it over to the produce lot. He knew it was every-day monotony, but what else is he going to do when he is consumed by the task at hand – finding that damn bunker?

{*Smitty's now-mocking brain: "Hey you did okay with Fern, didn't cha? She sorta likes ya. You know that dontcha? Yes, ya do."*}

{*Smitty: "Knock it off, Brain. We got important stuff to do. Keep focused on finding that bunker, willya?*}

{*Brain: "Sure will. But don't get too involved with Fern. Remember she knows the police; and they know her; and they have your car's ID, too. Remember that, okay?"*}

Time: Tuesday, 24-July, 07:43 EDT (In the produce store lot again)

Smitty laid out his maps once again. He realized he had been hitting all of the roads in his chosen quadrant pretty hard. Most had light red highlighter on them – the color for 'driven and eliminated'; still he had to continue. He still believed the bunker was in this quadrant, but his

ORDER OF SUCCESSION

options were becoming fewer. He simply had to continue to the end because it was already past his point-of-no-return on his time limitation.

Driving slowly downhill on 550, Smitty turned left onto Eylers Valley Flint Road. He'd been on this road before; however, then he had driven the side-roads on the far half, found nothing, and ended-up in Pennsylvania. Those roads had been highlighted in red as 'eliminated', but the near half of Eylers Valley Flint Road was curiously not highlighted. Must have been an oversight on his part. Today, he was going to drive these roads so he could highlight them one color or another, too.

And now the fun began; he had to drive up and down all these side roads, which he did, although this routine was really getting old and monotonous. About a mile and a half later, he turned left on Debold Road. And drove along Debold. Nothing jumped out; nothing. He added more red highlighter to his maps, now eliminating these roads, too. At this rate, none of the maps will ever see any green highlighter.

He had driven these roads so long with no positive results, he decided to try driving the roads on the other side of Thurmont – the ones on the east side – just in case his memory was really, really that far off-base. So off he went trying to find any roads that came close to the pattern burned into his mind. Driving the other direction on MD-550 led him through Thurmont, down to Woodsboro, and on to Libertytown. 550 seemed to just disappear on the outskirts of Libertytown; he couldn't find any continuation. On the way down to Libertytown, he tried driving all of the side roads that looked about right, but nothing seemed to fit his pattern. On the return trip, Smitty again drove all the remaining roads on the other side of the highway that held promise. Nothing. Time to mark the maps with red highlighter, the color of failure.

Time: Wednesday, 25-July, 07:04 EDT (Leaving his motel in Waynesboro)

{Smitty's brain: "Okay, now. East 550 didn't pan out, but that doesn't mean your idea was an out-and-out failure. Just a set-back. Okay, what else we got over on the east side? Get your coffee and let's drive."}

Today, Smitty tried MD-77 on the east side of Thurmont. He followed it from its intersection with MD-550 and found himself over in Keymar at the other end. Again, he tried all of the likely-looking side roads in both directions. No soap. Nothin', again.

Order of Succession

While returning to the motel well after 18:30, Smitty took a little joy-ride to ease his frustration and un-wind a bit. He ended-up stopping at one of those all-you-can-eat (AYCE) buffet restaurants over in Rouzerville. This was not his intended destination, but he just happened to end-up there anyway. He ate at a table far away from the early-birds so he could open his map books while he ate. He realized he probably looked weird to some diners just turning the maps as he tried to make the roads match his memory. But he felt this was the only way he could match memory to reality.

Time: Thursday, 26-July, 06:53 EDT (Leaving his motel in Waynesboro)

{Smitty's mocking brain: "Okay, we tried it your way. Now let's try something different, shall we? How about this? Pick-up your map books and lay out a search grid and start concentrating on smaller segments of the overall picture. Let's not try to eat everything in sight in one gulp. Bite-size nibbles will still getcha the whole enchilada."}

Just like the GPS gadgets, Smitty recalculated his desired search area. Using Thurmont as his focal point, his area became: Thurmont north to Emmitsburg (bounded by US-15), east to a little past Taneytown (on MD-140), south on MD-84 to New Windsor, and southwest on MD-31 to Libertytown, returning to Thurmont on MD-550.

Smitty drove the roads inside the smaller grids the rest of Thursday. Nothing. Friday the 27th, Saturday the 28th, and Sunday the 29th were also equally unproductive.

Time: Sunday, 29-July, 14:24 EDT

Eating dinner again at the Hickory Bridge Restaurant in Orrtanna, Pennsylvania.

However, this time Smitty had called ahead for a reservation for the last seating at 15:00, figuring he would have enough time to do some searching before an early dinner.

He was smarting from failure during the past week of not finding any roads that even vaguely matched the map in his mind. It didn't have to be an exact overlay, but just something similar would certainly help for a damn change.

Order of Succession

When he entered the waiting room, he, just like all the other diners, looked for a vacant seat – chair or bench, it did not matter which – and found one at the far end of the room. He sort of poured himself into the chair, deep in thought about whether his Plan A was really ever going to pan-out okay. His name was called; he acknowledged with his raised hand, proceeded to the podium, and followed the hostess to his table in the newer section of the restaurant. Since the meal was pretty much a set-menu, there was no need to even look at a menu – there weren't any to begin with. After selecting his main course (one of four choices), he also ordered something from the bar.

He needed to clean-up a little from driving around all day in his car. He followed the directions (arrows) to the rest rooms. On his way back to his table, he noticed something red through one of the old-timey windows between the dining room and the waiting area. The red immediately caught his attention. It was in a painting – a painting of a red barn – the one above the same chair he had been sitting in while he waited just 15 minutes ago. He mumbled under his breath, "How could I have missed that? In broad daylight, yet, and I sat right under it! Less than five feet from it, too."

He asked his server, Naomi, if she could change his table to a vacant one near that window; he simply said he like the lighting better over there. She made the arrangements and brought his order from the bar over on her next trip.

It sure looked like his red barn, or was it just wishful thinking. Smitty told Naomi he had forgotten something in his car and that he would be right back. He immediately walked out to the painting and noted the artist's name in fire-engine red in the lower right corner – Rosalie Bergman. The sign beside the painting simply read 'Old Red Barn on Debold Road – Near Sabillasville, Maryland'.

{Smitty's confused mind: "I have been on that Debold Road several times. Where the hell is this barn? How the hell could I have missed it? It sticks-out like a friggin' sore thumb. Where the hell is it that I could have missed it? Oops, sorry, Rita. You must think I'm a hopeless cause. Sorry."}

He continued on to his car and picked-up a camera and one of his map books and returned feeling more enthusiastic than he had been for several days. He caught Naomi's attention and asked if she knew anything about that painting or its artist. "No, sorry, I don't. Did you look at the tag? Maybe it's for sale; there might be a phone number on the tag. Or, maybe you could check with the manager, Mary; she's usually out in the waiting area. She might know something about it." Smitty thanked her. On his way out, he checked the tag. Sure enough: 717-555-1094. He decided tomorrow would be a better time to call than late on a Sunday night.

ORDER OF SUCCESSION

33 – Aha and More

Around 06:45, Monday, 30-July: The Motel in Waynesboro, Pennsylvania

TIME: 06:47 EDTT

The motel's 'Free Hot Breakfast Buffet' was fast approaching monotony. Coffee, mystery-meat patties, cold cereal, eggs, and pastry. Oh, don't forget the yogurt and pre-packaged pancakes and apples and bunches of bananas. Mickey D's for some more coffee and privacy in the parking lot for a phone call or two. It was turning into a really monotonous routine.

Time: Monday, 30-July, 08:15 EDT (From his car in Mickey D's parking lot in Waynesboro.)

Usually, Smitty was up-and-at 'em much earlier that this; however, he delayed calling the artist, Rosalie Bergman, until a more civilized hour. He was working on his second cup of Mickey D's coffee. He felt this was about the right time; so, using his special phone, he called her. And listened to four rings before, "Hello."

Smitty (in his best civilian voice with just a little bit of a southern drawl): "Good morning, ma'am. I'm trying to reach a Ms. Rosalie Berman, the artist."

A feminine voice: "May I ask who is calling, and how can I help you?"

Smitty: "Well, you don't know me, but my name is Terry. Terry Pedrozo. I saw one of her paintings in a restaurant last night over in Orrtanna, a small town north of the Liberty Ski area over in Pennsylvania. I wanted to ask her about it."

Voice: "Oh, isn't that nice of you! I'm Rosalie. You said over in Orrtanna, didn't you? That painting must be "The Red Barn", right? How can I help you?"

Smitty: "Pleased to meet you – at least on the phone, ma'am. Well, I am trying to find that barn. Let me explain. I am trying to join the Mid-

Order of Succession

Atlantic Ornithologists' Society, a birdwatchers' group. I am really trying to find a seldom-seen type of bird that is supposed to live in the area around Sabillasville, Maryland, area. Another member of that society told me to find a red barn in that area, but I haven't been able to find any red barns that even come close to what he described. He thought it is near some fruit and vegetable store located in the Sabillasville area. I found the store, but can't seem to find the red barn. So, when I saw your painting and read the description, well, I immediately thought you might remember where it is. Well, that was a long story, but that's why I called."

Rosalie: "Well, I certainly think I can help you. It's on Debold Road. Hold on, while I try to remember exactly where."

Smitty: "This is the closest I've been to finding it; this is exciting. I have my maps open right now. Do you remember how you got onto Debold?"

Rosalie: "If you're coming from Thurmont on Highway 550, you go past the fruit and produce store. Debold is just a little bit past that store. You turn right and take Debold back up into the hills just a little piece. If you reach Eylers Valley Flint Road, you done gone way too far."

Smitty: "I thought I had driven this section of Debold earlier last week, but I guess I missed it. Ms. Rosalie, after I turn right onto Debold, do you remember which side of the road the red barn is on? Just so's I don't make the same mistakes all over again."

Rosalie: "When you come off of 550, it's on the left-hand side, oh, I don't know, maybe a mile and a half to two miles. On the left-hand side; oh, I already said that, didn't I? But you can't see it from the road. It's several hundred feet down an old farm lane. I had to park and walk-in because of all the potholes and ruts and tree roots. My car almost bottomed-out; guess I shoulda used a 4-wheel drive car – especially if I want to paint more of these back-woods places. If it helps you any, that farm lane meets Debold at an angle. It is not a straight-on 'T'. One of its corners, where it meets Debold, I think it had a small cluster of three or four trees, while there was nothing but ruts on the other corner. I think that's how I remember it. Does this help you? By chance, if'n you meet a man named Hal, tell him hello for me. He was building a concrete barn across the meadow when I was painting the red barn. Say hi to him from Rosalie the painter, will ya? Nice fella' he was."

ORDER OF SUCCESSION

Smitty: "Ms. Rosalie, you have no idea how much you have helped me out! If I spot this bird the guys were saying is down here, I'll be a shoo-in for membership in the Mid-Atlantic Ornithologists' Society. Thank-you a lot. You did say that fella's name is 'Hal', right? If I see somebody across the meadow, you can bet I'll give him a hello from you. Keep-on painting, and please take care of yourself. Thank-you for all your help. Good-bye now."

{Smitty's somewhat mocking brain: "Wow! You did good, real good there, you young whipper-snapper. Go get yourself another cup and let's go see if we can find that red barn, now. Why didn't you go to that restaurant sooner; you could have saved us a whole lot of wasted time. Oh you were there last week, weren't you, and you didn't see it hanging in broad daylight in the waiting room; what kinda intel guy you are, you dummy. Well, let's get on with it, now; go get some more coffee and visit the latrine while you're at it. Come on, git. Let's go say 'hi' to Hal, too. I'll bet he'd be tickled to see you again. Whadya think?"}

Time: Monday, 30-July, 09:41 EDT (In the produce store lot again)

Smitty spread-out his maps again – this time with a specific area in mind. He suddenly realized how badly his own blinders had slowed his progress. Now, looking at the bigger picture, he realized he screwed-up royally because he just assumed that Hal and Ray had driven to the bunker only from the Thurmont end of the roads. But Rosalie's directions had taken him to the 'far' end of Debold and then driven a much shorter route over the unpleasant back-roads.

{Still mocking brain: "You are some kind of dummy! Look at this new route; look at your 'only from Thurmont' route. Jeez, any dummy can see which is the better one. Jeez, and I gotta help you all the time, too! What do I always tell ya about assuming anything? Do ya ever listen and pay attention? Doesn't look like it from this side of the conversation. Why do I even try to keep you straight? Huh?"}

{Smitty: "Yeah, you're right as usual. But, look at it from my side for a change. They live up here; I don't. They knew where they were goin'; I didn't. Give me a break, will ya?"}

He greeted Fern over by the vegetable cases. Selected some carrots, celery, snack bars, and a coupla bottles of water. Paid for them and got in his car for a more-promising hunt.

Order of Succession

This time, Smitty turned right out of the lot onto 550 and turned right again directly onto the 'far end' of Debold – only a couple of hundred feet from the parking lot. It began to feel right. Pretty soon, Smitty was guessing correctly what the next turn should be; he was quickly running out of turns and bumps on his mental map. Was he really getting closer; was his memory still way off; or, was it all just wishful thinking? Two minutes later, he saw what looked like an old farm lane on the left with a cluster of three trees where it met Debold. He slowed and drove past the lane and tried to visually scan for anything through the trees, thinking that maybe he had spotted a small splash of red. He found a wide spot alongside the road to park the car and grabbed the binoculars, GPS compass, the DSLR, and his cell-phone. He also tore-out the best-looking page from his map books and, almost as an afterthought, a picture of a bird he was supposed to be trying to find.

According to the map, the red roofed building should be right over there. He traced the locations on the map with his finger while trying to make the map match the spot of dirt he was standing on. Smitty walked down the dirt farm road that looked like it could be the one to take him to the building.

{Smitty's excited mind: "Boy, was Rosalie right! If you don't have a farm vehicle, this lane is an obstacle course. A road block for a regular car."}

About 125 yards later, there sat the red-roofed barn, on the south side of the pasture. Whoa! There also was an older wooden barn in the trees further from the pasture than the red-roofed one and to its left when viewed from the pasture side. Hal's bunker should be directly across the pasture. He took a GPS reading and stored it in the compass. Still trying to stay in the shadows and tree-lines, he carefully and silently worked his way through the trees along the edge of the pasture. There, on a slight hill across the pasture, sat what looked like Hal's bunker. It, too, was situated in the shadows of its own tree-line. He took some pictures of the trees around him just in case that rare bird happened to be in one of them; he also made sure he got several with the bunker in them. Several more with the red barn to landmark the spot. No need to make himself any more obvious and suspicious; he turned and made his way back out on the farm's road. He walked slowly and deliberately back to the car, taking care not to move too fast so as not to attract unwanted attention if there

ORDER OF SUCCESSION

was anyone around. He was trying to just get to the car, mark his maps about that mysterious bird, and just get outta there for now. He wanted to call in the coordinates from a much more secure place.

As Smitty got into his car, another car (actually, a 4-wheel-drive [4WD] pick-up) drove out of the farm road he had just left. He hadn't seen any cars down there, yet here it was. He tried to play it cool by holding up one of his map books, pretending to be lost. The car turned in his direction and slowed to snail's pace. Now what? Did the driver recognize me from someplace, or what? The driver gave him a slow once-over. Smitty took the initiative; he glanced sideways from his maps and motioned toward the driver that he needed help with the map. The driver stopped directly opposite of Smitty and asked if he was lost. After a coupla minutes of directions and tracing roads on the map, Smitty thanked him in an exaggerated manner and gestured toward the direction the driver had pointed out. Smitty didn't recognize the driver, and the driver continued on his way – slowly. He also hoped that his unshaven beard and floppy hat would make it more difficult to recognize or describe him.

Smitty had originally planned to back-track down the county road on which he had driven-up here anyway. However, in order not to push his luck any further, he followed the stranger's directions on the map, which, fortunately, took him back the way he had come earlier today. Things were finally lookin'-up. Lady Luck must be smug about something.

Time: Monday, 30-July, 11:33 EDT (Back in the produce store's lot)

He turned left on 550 and drove back to the vegetable and fruit store he had just been in about 90 minutes ago. He parked the car facing 550 and went shopping for something to eat. He brought another coupla pieces of fruit and a drink back to the car.

Terry (shouting enthusiastically): "Hey, Fern, I got the pictures of that bird!! Here let me show ya!" Terry handed her his second, back-up camera – the one with the pre-loaded pictures of 'the bird'. "Look at these pictures, will ya. Wow, I'm gonna be a shoo-in to get into the Mid-Atlantic Ornithologists' Society now. Whadya got in here to celebrate with?"

Order of Succession
34 – Hang-Gliders

Almost noon, Monday, 30-July: The fruit and veggie stand near Sabillasville, Maryland.

TIME: Monday, 30-July, 11:56 EDT (Back in the produce store's lot)

With his primary mission completed, Smitty now took on a secondary search – finding that hang-glider jump-off place. He returned to the store and asked Fern if she knew of such a place.

Fern: "Oh, I betcha you mean Pen-Mar. Bring me one of your maps that shows the end of 550 thataway." She was pointing up toward Cascade, Maryland, right outside old Fort Ritchie, on the other side of Sabillasville. Terry brought his map books into the store, and Fern pointed to High Rock at the end of what looked like a dead-end road.

Terry: "Somebody told me that the views from up there are terrific. Thought I'd go up there to see for myself as long as I finally found that bird and got my pictures. What a great day this is! Thanks for the directions. Wouldn't it be something if my bird lived up there, too. Wow! See ya in a bit." And he was off for High Rock, but not for the scenery – that's for certain.

Smitty drove back to his motel to write and prepare a report with all of the GPS location information and pictures. And grab a bite at an AYCE buffet restaurant in Rouzerville before driving up to High Rock. He worked through his lunch, writing reports and coordinates. With those out of the way, he checked-out the maps for a route back to High Rock.

Time: Monday, 30-July, 14:53 EDT (Rouzerville restaurant)

{Smitty: "Hey, Brain, "Let's go take a look at this hang-glider jump-off place. It's just part way back to Cascade; we turn-off on this side of the mountain behind old Fort Ritchie."}

Order of Succession

On the eastern side of Waynesboro is a smaller town named Rouzerville that the maps showed to be north-northwest of Pen-Mar, the gateway to High Rock Road, the hang-glider jump-off road just west of Camp David.

Since he had already written-up his report about the bunker's location, his remaining recon mission was to see what this hang-gliders' rock was really like. The road, although paved, was a 2-lane road with speed bumps and gates that could be closed as needed. Smitty parked his rental car in a far spot next to the trees at the far edge of the rocky, dirt parking area, which was maybe large enough for a dozen cars. Blaze markings on some of the trees indicated the Appalachian Trail passed directly through this area, and he recalled a note on one of his maps that said Pen-Mar was almost the exact halfway point of the trail between Georgia and Maine.

Several hang-gliders were preparing their gliders for launching-off the High Rock overhang, the edge of which is 100s of feet above the valley floor below. In fact, it was high enough that, the locals frequently claimed, on good days, birds also enjoyed the rising wind currents and thermals. People, standing on the jump-off area of the large rock, could literally look down on the birds' backs as they silently glided past without even flapping their wings.

{Smitty's brain, sort of admitting failure: "Okay, you located your target within your self-imposed time limit. Gotta hand it to ya. Good for you. While there's some slack-time today, call-in its location and take that off your plate. Ya know ya got more sessions of plannin' comin' up. Clear your mind for the rest of the day and call it in, will ya?"}

Smitty got the point. He grabbed his notes and the phone, got out of the car, and sat down on a nearby boulder, with his car at a slight angle between him and the jump-off rock. He watched the glider pilots assembling their crafts over near the rock across his car's hood as he dialed into his answering service. When they answered, he asked to speak to a recon satellite operator; he was transferred immediately and began speaking with Larry. He had worked with Larry before – actually, most recently from that California rest-area. Always good to continue the same mission with the same operator you started with; there's less wasted time trying to bring a new one up to speed. It also didn't hurt any that Smitty trusted Larry's abilities.

Order of Succession

Smitty: "Larry, I got some new coordinates for you to look at when you can." He read them to Larry and explained what he should see there. "For the building about 250 meters to the north of these coordinates, could it look like there is a drive-through door directly through it – like in on one side and exit through the door on the side? Does the ground around that building look like it was disturbed, maybe enough to build an underground munitions bunker? Like maybe on the east side of the building as the first choice; the west side as the second choice?"

Just as Smitty just finished reading-off the bunker's GPS coordinates, a big, black 4WD pick-up pulled into the parking area and headed straight to a vacant parking space much nearer the jump-off point. The driver turned it off, hopped out, and began unloading gear on the rock-side of the truck. Smitty assumed there was a glider tied into the bed and it was being unloaded.

The only thing Larry heard was a muffled, "Oh shit; Bubba's the driver. I gotta move quietly. Larry, hang-on; don't hang-up on me. You gotta wait for me."

{Smitty's alarmed brain: "WTF. You just said 'Bubba', right? Ya got your phone and the bunker location GPS coordinates are secured, right? Ya got your floppy hat and sunglasses on, right? What the hell am I thinking; you're not wearing sunglasses because you're in the shade. At least you haven't shaved for several days now; good thinking. Okay, keep it low-key; no sudden movements to attract attention. Wait until he starts moving his gear toward the rock, then sorta ooze further back into those trees. Okay, just play it cool – real cool; got that? Real cool. Good.}

{Smitty: "Thanks for the advice, Brain. Now, just shut-up; we have to concentrate on being quiet so we ain't seen. Get back to me later when I can listen to ya. Back atcha ya later, but right now, it's OVER & OUT to ya."}

Smitty opened his map book and expanded it as wide as he could, hoping to look a little lost. Using that as sort of cover, Smitty watched Bubba unload a dull-looking, black glider that was strapped into the bed of the pick-up. Bubba began assembling it for flight.

Although Smitty had delayed reconning this jump-off point, he also quickly realized there was no 'landing area' way up here.

Order of Succession

{Smitty: "Brain, I'm back. Shut-up and listen and then shut-up and think this through. This is only the launch jump-off point; they gotta land somewhere else, right? And, most likely, a lot lower in altitude. So, Bubba's pick-up will be up here; he was the only person in the pick-up; he can't land here; so, how does he get back up here to get the pick-up? Is the driver for the return trip already up here, too? Who's just hanging around up here looking like a sight-seer? And then, what about the glider? Can't just leave it wherever Bubba lands it. So, who's got a pick-up up here and isn't a hang-glider? Maybe the return driver is down there somewhere waiting for Bubba's jump and will follow his route and landing by radio? Why is Bubba's glider such a dull black that there's not a single shiny spot, not even on the aluminum framing?"}

A few minutes later, the answers to all those questions drove into the parking area – Ray in the Ford F-450 with the gubamint plates. The pieces fell into place. Two pickups and two drivers. Both part of the plot on da WH.

{Smitty's cautious brain: "You still sittin' here, dumb ass. Don't attract anybody's attention, but you better fade into the trees. Git outta sight right effin' now."}

Smitty dropped to the ground on one knee as if looking for something he dropped on far side of the car. Having both Bubba and Ray up here also explained the dull black glider, and, now, Bubba's similarly colored jump-suit. Smitty began mouthing the words very softly to himself, "It all adds-up to 'radar invisibility'. They are trying-out a glider coated with what appeared to be radar-absorbing paint or something like that. And, Camp David is just over there (pointing to an area on his map). Maybe the target isn't TWH; maybe it's Camp David instead. No, it has to be TWH; we spent too much time re-conning the area around da WH. Camp David must be their Plan B."

Larry: "What were you saying about radar invisibility? Whacha talking about, anyway?"

Smitty suddenly realized he was not talking quietly only to himself; now the question is did Bubba or Ray hear him, too. He peeked across the hood. They weren't looking his way, so probably not. As quietly as possible, "Larry, I gotta move; I may have compromised my location. Whatever you do, do not hang up. I'll be right back."

Order of Succession

Using his car as a shield, Smitty now had a solid wall (albeit a low wall) between Bubba and Ray and himself. He duck-walked backwards deeper into the trees around the parking area, being careful not to snap any branches to alert either Bubba or Ray. After about 50 feet or so, he got on his knees to get a better view of the jump-off point. Bubba's turn was next; he was waiting on the sloped-rock approach-area of the rock for the first-in-line to jump. Ray waited on the lower steps near the parking lot. Smitty retrieved the new GPS compass from its belt-pouch and thumbed it on while he removed his special cell-phone from his shirt pocket.

Smitty: "Larry, you still there? I sent you another set of GPS coordinates for you to play with; they're for my present location. Larry, did you get them? Don't lose or delete either set, okay?"

Larry: "Roger. "Hey, you do know that's damn close to Camp David, dontcha?"

Smitty (still trying to be as quiet as possible as he backed further away from the parking area): "Damn straight. I'd have been disappointed if you didn't bring that up. Here's the deal, I'm not too far from the subjects. My location should be a jumpin'-off rock for hang-gliders."

Larry: "Oh, you're talkin' about Pen-Mar and High Rock, aren't cha? While you were quiet or moving or whatever, I was relocating one of my birds. It's almost within range now."

Smitty: "Oh, you know this place? Well, what we're lookin' for is an all black glider that I think could pretty well be coated with radar-absorbing paint. I have every reason to believe the pilot will try to get as close as possible to Camp David. I want to find-out if it is 'radar-proof'. Any way to put radar eyes on him, too?"

Larry: "Wait one; hot-lining now. You can talk to them while I punch-in the coordinates for my bird. Hey, Andy, Larry here. Talk to this guy, Terry. He's got something for you that's more in your bailiwick. Light 'em up if you can; I'm gonna see if my bird can track the target." Smitty quietly relayed as much information about the target to Andy as he could. Bubba had already launched himself, and Ray was preparing to drive back down the access road.

Larry: "Bird's coming-up on targeted area. Black, you say? Nothing on the rock right now."

Order of Succession

Smitty: "Target just jumped; I'll bet he's headed in the general direction of Camp David. His buddy just left the parking area, heading down toward Pen-Mar. He's driving a white Ford F-450 with Maryland local-government plates – if that helps any. The next glider up on the rock is red with white stripes."

Larry: "Going to wide angle. Got the red with white. Going to wider. Got a black glider heading east-south-east. Andy, try looking at these coordinates (as he read them off); that'll put you somewhere near Maryland Routes 77, Stottlemyer, and Foxville Deerfield Road. I think he's not as radar-proof as he thinks he is. If I'm right, he's coming in about 20 degrees west of that road intersection. Just watch for a 'disturbance' from that direction. Still heading toward that intersection. Oops, I stand corrected, heading changing more toward the north-east from that intersection. Sort of puts him on an angle toward Camp David. Andy, you got anything?"

Andy: "You're right, he's a 'disturbance' alright, but he's not completely invisible. Smitty, you want him taken-out?"

Smitty: "Wow, that fast, huh! Don't take him out now. I say again, DO NOT TAKE HIM OUT NOW. Watch where he lands and advise Camp David to approach as Maryland DNR if they can; you know just checking the wild-life, reports of poachers, something like that. Okay. The F-450 should show-up shortly to help pack the glider to take back up to High Rock to pick-up the glider pilot's pickup truck. Like to know where they go, etc. I have to change my position. I'll get back to you in about 30 minutes."

Time: Monday, 30-July, 16:45 EDT (Near the produce store again)

Smitty high-tailed it down the hill down to Pen-Mar and then circled around the northern end of the mountain to avoid delays of driving back toward Waynesboro and then back-tracking to Blue Ridge Summit, which he had just passed. A left on 550 and he was headed down the hill toward the produce store. He found a wide spot to pull-over and redialed Larry.

Smitty: "I changed my position down the road near the produce store on 550; I'm parked up the road from their parking lot.

Larry: "The bird's up and working this area now. Say, that black glider landed in a field next to Sabillasville Elementary School. That's pretty close to these latest coordinates."

Order of Succession

Smitty: "It's closer than you realize; it's across Highway-550 from where I'm sitting right now. It's maybe 200 meters from me right now. Can't see anybody over there right now. Talk about a real small world. Was Andy able to follow it on his radar?"

Larry: "He said he got a 'disturbance' when I directed him to certain coordinates but wasn't able to get a clear image. He stored its characteristics and plans to put into his computers to see if he can clean it up."

Smitty: "Tell him it may be something out of Israel named Nanoflight or Signaflux, or something like that. Maybe that will help him refine his search."

Larry: "Wilco. Well, will you look at this! It looks like there are driveways on both sides of your building, maybe 30 feet through the building. My birds don't have ground-penetrating radar or anything like that. That requires way too much power from way up where they fly. After having said that, however, the plantings on the east side are definitely different than those around the rest of the building. Say, you sound like you've been there. Just an observation; don't really want to know."

Smitty: "Sort of a roger to that, but really can't say, either."

{Smitty's planning mind: "Don't need the search pattern any more. Gotta get some research and recon teams in here. Difficult to break-in; where do ya start. That bunker just has to have an alarm on it, dontcha think; yeah, it should have one. What's the worst that can happen? An alarm transmitted somewhere?}

{Smitty's sarcastic brain: "Are you always this slow on the uptake, old boy. The worst that can happen is that bunker is booby-trapped, and it goes sky-high in a big brilliant flash, taking the burglars with it. That's what I think is the worst case. Biggest friggin flash-bang grenade you'll ever see and hear. Boom. Flash. Gone. A gargantuan hole in the ground."}

{Smitty: "Okay, wise guy. What would you do to recon that bunker? Huh?}

{Brain: "Glad you decided that maybe I have ideas on this that are worth listening to. Ya got your fancy, dial-anywhere phone, right? Divide-up the tasks. Dial somebody who has the expertise you need. Split-off some stuff to the pros. Yeah, I know you feel this is your baby. Sure, it is, but you ain't got all of the know-how for everything. Call in

Order of Succession

the back-up teams, glory hog. That's what you should do. Now get with it; there's more on your plate besides a late lunch. Git-on with it."}

Smitty relented, stopped arguing with himself, and placed the calls for the experts. He requested somebody with ground-penetrating radar to sweep the ground around the bunker – even if they can only get a chopper to fly over, low, slow, and at night. He also requested a small team to visually assess the bunker for security and ease of entry. Smitty also copied his boss, the only one he trusts, on these events. He just happened to omit the other plans he was making for the assault on TWH he was positive was going to happen during *Your Armed Forces on Display*, and he certainly didn't mention any of the Marines from California who were planning to stop it. Let them be heroes afterwards, not fellow counter-plotters before. Just too dangerous because no one on his side knew all of the players on the other side. Yet, that is.

{Smitty: "But we will uncover them. The world will know we took them right out of the air – one way or another. Plucked them right out of the air like a bird – like a sparrow by an eagle – it doesn't matter that much to the head eagle in the forest. You bet we're gonna find-out who they are."}

ORDER OF SUCCESSION

35 – Prepping for the East Coast

Almost dinner time, Monday, 30-July: At the motel in Waynesboro, Pennsylvania.

TIME: Monday, 30-July, 18:15 EDT (Back at the motel)

Smitty decided to turn his attention to the area down on The Mall in Washington, D.C. He determined how he would arrange the display of military hardware to support defending TWH if push came to shove during the assault he was sure was coming.

He placed his status calls to Rhodes first, then to Jenkins.

Smitty: "Rocky, how's everything going for the trip back here?"

Rhodes: "We're packing our gear. We're scheduled to be in Quantico next Monday with CQB training to begin next Tuesday. Supposed to meet-up with several platoons of Army soldiers from MDW down there. Say, just who the hell do you know that can arrange this so quickly on the QT? I don't want an answer, just sayin' you understand. Just sayin' we're amazed."

Smitty: "Glad to hear your portion is comin' together and on time, too. The Army is sending only two platoons from 'The Old Guard' located at Fort Myer, Virginia – one platoon each from Bravo Company and Delta Company. We were also able to get an officer and the Platoon Sergeant from each. I know you will be introduced to their officers; make sure you all work together because their soldiers will be under your command through them. Again, my gut feel is that we will be making decisions on the fly because we've never had to plan something like this in our own country. Just sayin'.

"There are also some veterans from SWA in both of those companies. Use their experience to your advantage because I think our plotters also have similar veterans amongst their number. I also feel

Order of Succession

the action may well be centered along Constitution and Independence Avenues, the major streets adjacent to The Mall, on its north and south sides – as well TWH – and expanding across the Tidal Basin to include the Jefferson Memorial. I do not think we will have to stray too far from that area because I think there are going to be several diversions designed to clear the area around TWH of normal security organizations like the District's Metropolitan Police Department, Park Police, Secret Service, as well as Fire and Emergency Services agencies. We are not planning to respond to those diversions en masse; maybe a gunny and a driver to make our own quick assessment. We're gonna let those other local cops respond with their own show of force.

"Oh, make sure your Marines bring their civvies so they will blend-in while out of uniform. And no haircuts right now either."

Rhodes: "I understand your position on these risks. Are you really all that positive that all of those possibilities are probabilities? You really sound serious that there may be intra-city fire fights around TWH."

Smitty: "Serious as that assault out at the rest-area. Major Jenkins and Captain Hauser will also be down at Quantico at the same time. The three of you and the two Army officers need to get together to discuss possible tactics about how to deal with threats around TWH. Both of the pilots have been advised that, at least when they are on the ground, they are also under your command for whatever needs to be done. However, once the air assault begins, they will be in primary command of their portion of airborne counter-measures. You all work-out the details, but your job is to make it all dove-tail together. I know this sounds like I'm serving big portions on your plate, but I'm confident in your abilities. Before I really forget what's reeling around in my head, I hope you still have, or have access to, the POTUS phone. I think we can use it in our strategy. If you get it to Coms, I'll use him for implementing my plan for it. If you ever have any questions, please contact me directly, ASAP, okay?"

Rhodes: "Your observations are contagious. Coms should still have it; he grew quite protective of it. I'll make sure he packs it to-go with us and keeps it secure. We are gonna make this plan work for sure."

Smitty: "On a different point, have I told you that I found the bunker; passed the word up to higher authorities to have the area checked-out. That reminds me, I gotta get a status update on that. Talk with you later; gotta go."

Order of Succession

Smitty (calling the pilots): "Phillip, is this a good time to talk? Got some updates for you and Brian."

Phillip: "Go for it, good buddy."

Smitty: "Before it slips my mind again, we located that bunker yesterday. Got some other specialized parties planning to recon it. Still have to get a status update about it, though.

"Cap'n Rhodes and our Marines are packing for their trip down to Quantico for a training session on CQB."

Phillip: "Wait one! Are you talking about what I think I heard? That's some pretty serious crap for down on The Mall in D.C., isn't it?"

Smitty: "You're pretty fast on the uptake. They played for keeps out at the rest-area; bullets at my feet told me that much. It's not practical to be training for all possible threats, but we have to be prepared for the most logical one. I was just on the phone to Rocky and told him our self-determined primary area of responsibility will be The Mall east to west, Capitol to the Lincoln Memorial and TWH to the Jefferson Memorial. We are not planning to divide our forces to look into all possible diversions, which I believe are gonna be part of their plan. We may send a Gunny or a Platoon Sergeant and a driver to make our own evaluation, but that's about it."

"I hope you and Brian agree with one other arrangement I told Rocky about. And that is, on the ground Rocky, a Captain, is supposed to be in command of all Marines and two platoons of Army soldiers; that also includes both you and Brian. That's because he has the most organizing to coordinate. However, once it all hits the fan, in the air you and Brian are sort of your own unit of two. Any problems with that?"

Phillip: "A little bit unorthodox, but reasonable under the circumstances. We'll make it work-out okay."

Smitty: "That's good to hear. You'll be down in Quantico at the same time the Pendleton Marines and the Army platoons are there. Your job will be to understand and become confident with the choppers you will be introduced to down there; but because of your part of the mission, you and Brian are not specifically scheduled for CQB training. If you have the spare time, you are welcome to observe it if you're interested. I also suggested to Rocky he should look you up so

Order of Succession

you, he, and the Army officers get to know how you all are supposed to fit together. You all can discuss planning for defending the area after you know what mods are being made to your new rides. You need to be comfortable with what's in the works for them.

"Bring civvies and don't get haircuts for awhile. You don't need to stand-out like sore thumbs when you're down on The Mall. And if you or Brian have any questions, by all means contact me directly ASAP. Sorry, but I gotta go."

Phillip: "You must have a non-stop brain; sounds like one serious plan is developing. I'll contact Rocky and see how he's handling his plate. On the rest, roger and out."

ORDER OF SUCCESSION
36 – Modified Choppers at Quantico

Around 06:30, Tuesday, 31-July: The Motel in Waynesboro, Pennsylvania

TIME: 06:35 EDT

{Smitty, thinking to himself: "This is getting terrible; I'm getting used to this hot breakfast buffet. Not so much craving it, but used to it."}

More mystery-meat patties and eggs, but the coffee was what he really craved this morning. Smitty left his maps in his room. But, he grabbed a courtesy copy of the *USA Today* newspaper and quickly browsed through the sections to get a quick feel of what happened in the U.S. yesterday. While working his way through the food, he started the crossword puzzle just to give his mind something else to work on.

{Smitty's inquisitorial brain: "Okay, big boy, anybody call you about recon on that bunker yet? Now get with it; there's more on your plate besides that patty. Git-on with it."}

{Smitty: "No reports yet, but it's only been about sixteen hours or so. Give'em some time to recon the area; they gotta plan and get the teams selected. Take it easy, okay? Yeah, there's a lot of stuff stacking-up on the plate; maybe I need to get some side-board extenders. Ha-ha! Besides Phillip and Brian are due in tonight. Gotta get ready to meet them tomorrow morning down in Quantico."}

Smitty's contact down at Quantico said the modifications on the two helos were nearing completion. Now would be a good time for the pilots to look them over to make sure they like what we did to them. Smitty assured him that the pilots were on their way tonight. They'd make Quantico their first stop tomorrow to give a 'thumbs up or down'. That reminded him that he also had to high-tail it down to

Order of Succession

Quantico at oh-dark-30 to meet them mid morning down there. He, too, wanted to see what mods were made to the choppers.

He planned to take another trip up to the High Point jump-off just to get some current pictures from up there. In a way, he hoped NOT to run across either Bubba or Ray – or anybody else from the plotters, for that matter. Well, he consoled himself, he won't have to worry about the four agents out in California; they should remain the guests of Hard-Ass over at 29 for a little while longer. He made a note to call Hard-Ass about the status of all six of them. He planned to start cleaning-up some loose ends in Waynesboro and clear-out permanently in about ten days. It was fun while it lasted, but that fun was not unlimited; it was quickly coming to an end.

Smitty advised the front desk that he would be leaving early in the morning, anticipating one or two days away. He hoped to return to his same room by Friday evening or so.

Time: Wednesday, 01-August, 03:35 EDT (Motel in Waynesboro)

{Smitty's groggy brain: "Maybe you think getting-up this early is really a great idea, but I got other ideas about that. Who gave you permission to set the alarm for this early, anyway? Whadya say we grab another 40 winks; make that 80 winks – 40 for each of us. Whadya say?"}

{Smitty's response thoughts: "Well, there's one benefit I guess. No mystery meat patties this morning. But I can still get coffee to-go. So, I've got all I need 'til we get out on the Interstate. Hey, I've got it mapped-out; should work okay. Taking I-81 south into Virginia down to I-66 east. Somewhere around Gainesville, we hop-off onto 234 toward I-95. We'll be slightly north of Quantico. So, what's not to like about that, eh, good buddy."}

In theory, this should have worked okay, and it did for the most part when he was headed south. However, over around Gainesville, the traffic began thickening even this early in the morning. Even after a couple of pit-stops and more coffee and a coupla 'breakfast sandwiches' (filled with more of somebody else's morning mystery meat), Smitty was running pretty close to making decent time. He arrived in the Quantico area around 07:15. But at least he didn't have to drive through the middle of the infamous D.C. commuter-traffic jams on I-270 to I-495 to I-95.

ORDER OF SUCCESSION

Around 08:45, he met Phillip and Brian in, where else, the mess hall. At least, there was known meat here – no mystery meat.

The Major and Captain had already been in contact with the techs over at the 'rotary wing' (helicopter) shop. They had an appointment to stop by around 10:15, which was fast approaching. Each grabbed an extra cup of coffee and left for the helo hangar.

Although the shop was staffed by both civilians and Marines, Marine Captain Nichole Swanson greeted them at the door. She introduced the lead helo mechanic, Sergeant Ruben Wilford, who was in charge of the requested modifications. Both were quite proud of the mods they had engineered and installed on the standard Viper chopper. The visiting pilots were invited to look over their handiwork in a work bay near the hangar door. Both Phillip and Brian were duly impressed by the custom work, which included: armaments, an electronic weapons system, improved avionics, and beefed-up shielding. And a couple of prototype weapons for 'field trials'.

For the Viper, the armaments were the most impressive because of the assortment of missile and gun platforms this chopper could now handle including:

- Pylon-mounted, Hellfire and Sidewinder air-to-air missiles. And, just to fill-out the complement, a couple of Hydra rockets.

- Standard weaponry included a 20-mm 3-barreled Gatling gun with an increased magazine capacity of up to 1,000 rounds. Non-standard weaponry was a 7.62-mm GAU-17A Gatling gun. (Which they just happened to find 'lying around'. No further questions asked about it.)

- Auxiliary lighting included some Nightsun® lamps for up to approximately 200-million CP – and the auxiliary alternators to power them.

- A set of ultra high-intensity auxiliary signaling LEDs – multi-colored, no-less.

- But the package that intrigued everybody the most was beta version of a new technology for scrambling the electronic brains in the aggressor's chopper. Some sort of a focused beam of intense

ORDER OF SUCCESSION

radiated digital power to be aimed at the other chopper up to a quarter mile away. Somebody, somewhere wanted to see if this thing really works in action.

They were also equally proud of the mods they made to the Venom Super Huey. This one looked pretty much standard, except for:

- Beefed-up shielding for the floor and up to the tops of the windshields; the same as had been done to the Viper.
- A remote-control 7.62-mm GAU-17/A Gatling gun mounted in the port doorway.
- A 20-mm Gatling gun slung between the skids with the ammo magazine in the belly.
- The same Nightsun® configuration.
- The same set of high-intensity auxiliary signaling LEDs.
- A weird container mounted below the starboard door threshold – the mechanics called it a 'blister pod'. This was something they had designed in their own 'skunk-works'. It could contain either Kevlar® [24] blanket or a Kevlar® [25] cargo net.
- And a set of rubber bladders to hold liquids – also from their 'skunk-works'.

And both helos were now also equipped with some prototype products on loan by the manufacturers for 'evaluation' purposes. One was a new UHP [26]-Laser. Its manufacturer says it is hot enough to cut metal at up to 200 meters – give or take a meter or two. This system had already been installed on the Major's ride – the Viper.

Another prototype on both is a device to jam digital command signals to/from drones (or other devices) using some sort of broad-spectrum transmitter. This system was already installed on the Cap'n's helo.

The Remainder of the morning and most of the afternoon was spent familiarizing the pilots with their new aircraft. A 45-minute test

---

24 CP = Candle Power
25 Kevlar® is an aramid fabric made by DuPont™. It is very strong for its weight and is cut-resistant. It is also used to provide a protective armor for military and other vehicles.
26 (Info: Ultra High Power Laser)

ORDER OF SUCCESSION

flight concluded the introduction around 15:45. The only comment from both pilots was, "Sweet!"

Brian, however, spoke with the Captain and sergeant to see if they could make an addition to the Super Huey. "Would it be possible to add one more blister-pod under the port door? That way the helo could be equipped with one of each type of Kevlar® blanket or net." Sergeant Wilford said he would see if it is possible this late in their delivery schedule.

The mechanics said the helos would be ready to be turned over to them on the following Monday. "Sweet!"

All three stayed down at Quantico that night. Tomorrow they would all drive up to D.C. to recon that area.

ORDER OF SUCCESSION

37 – Parking Spots for the Helos

Nearing 07:30, Tuesday, 31-July: Quantico mess hall, Virginia

TIME: 07:25 EDT

Smitty: "I thought I was growing to like the motel's 'hot breakfast buffet' way too much. This proves there is another way to serve breakfast. We've got an appointment to meet the Garrison Commander Joint Base Myer/McNair at around 12:45. McNair is where one of the helos will be based for the duration of the *Armed Forces* show. I thought that maybe the Major's bird, the Viper, would be a good choice for McNair because of its closeness to The White House and the flight paths used by other helicopters in the area. We can give the proposed LZ and support areas a good once-over and see if this works for you. The location for the other helo is at Fort Myer, across the Potomac from D.C. proper.

I assumed you have your own car, so whenever you all are ready, we can shove off. We'll be going up I-95 to I-495 so we can get on I-395, where it's almost always follow-the-leader, into the south-side of D.C. I printed out some maps for all of us. And here is a CB radio to help if we get separated.

If we do get separated, let's meet inside McNair, not the Main Gate on 2nd Street SW, but inside the 'P' Street SW gate. There's a parking lot at the very first left turn after entering the fort. Oh, McNair is such a small fort, we park the cars and walk everywhere. Just have your IDs ready."

Time: Thursday, 02-August, 12:12 EDT (Fort McNair, Washington, D.C.)

Smitty: "Sorry, but I was just informed that General Baldwin is busy. We are going to meet with the Deputy Commander, Colonel Laughlin. Both he and the General have been briefed that this is a hush-hush assignment until the end of the *Armed Forces Show*. Oh, by the way,

Order of Succession

they are also the same commanders for Fort Myer, which we are scheduled to see tomorrow at 09:30. Let's walk over to the Officer's Club to meet the Colonel; it's just past the end of the 'Generals Row' residences. I understand that the General had two sites in mind at each fort for the helos. We are planning to house one of the helos at each Fort for survivability just in case word of our countermeasures leaks out.

Phillip, for the Viper; that'll be your choice if you like this fort instead of Fort Myer, which we will see tomorrow. Brian, the remaining site is yours for the Super Huey. I know the both of you will decide where to site the helos for how you want to approach this challenge."

They met Colonel Laughlin at 12:40 in the O-Club as he was just finishing lunch. He offered refreshments if anyone wanted water or soda. Because of the warm weather and humidity, everybody asked for just cold water. 15 minutes later, the meet-and-greet was over, and they started the walking tour, south along 2nd Avenue, very near the Washington Channel (a waterway running parallel to the Potomac River that borders the East Potomac Golf Course on its east side and extends northward into the Tidal Basin in front of the Jefferson Memorial).

Phillip mentioned to the Colonel that there seemed to be a lot of really low-flying helicopter traffic parallel to the fort just on the other side of the trees over by the Channel.

Colonel Laughlin agreed that's what it looked like, but there is a FAA [27] rule that required helicopters to fly extremely low in this area because of how near their route is to Ronald Reagan Washington National Airport just across the Potomac from where they were standing. He said it was his understanding that the helicopters had to stay this low until they got further up-river to somewhere near Memorial Bridge where they could go a bit higher if they were going over-land into D.C. But they couldn't get too high because there was a designated flight path directly above the river for commercial jets into and out of National Airport. But don't hold him to that because he was only told this stuff by a friend-of-a-friend."

And then as an after-thought, Colonel Laughlin added, "There is also supposed to be a little-used helicopter landing area almost next-door to the fort. The way I heard the history, it's down at a water-front site on the Anacostia River, I think that's what my buddy said. Well,

---

27   FAA = Federal Aviation Administration

anyway, he said it used to be used to dispatch local choppers for 9-1-1 flights into Washington. But, he thought the city also shut it down for those emergency flights. Nevertheless, he also thought it might still be used just for emergency or overflow flights, just not permanent dispatches. I think I may have heard somebody refer to it as D.C. Police Department Air Support Unit or something like that. I don't know where D.C.'s choppers are kept now, or even if they are the city's, or if they subcontract-out the service. And that's about all I know about that. Oh, the area is also supposed to be called Buzzard Point by some old-timers. It's just over there across the water, only about 500 or 600 meters away as the crow flies. You see that bridge; the landing zone is supposed to be just this side of that bridge. Ya gotta remember as far as I know, I'm giving you hearsay because I never thought to drive around the outside of this fort to just look at stuff like that."

Phillip added this to the notes he already wrote about the restricted flight areas on the west side of McNair. "Say, Colonel, is it possible to drive over there or is it a restricted area"

Laughlin: "I never had any reason to go over there, so I've never been down that way. However, one of our soldiers says he walks over there to do a little catch-and-release fishing. He says he walks over there right out our back gate. Besides, there are lots of docking facilities for private boats right there on the river. You see that building right over there, right across this little park? (He motioned toward a building right outside the perimeter fence with is right arm.) That's the local Coast Guard facility; the soldier says he walks over to the river just to the south of that building. So, I think you can get pretty darn close to that old LZ if you want to."

Phillip: "Thanks, that sounds great. Smitty, Brian, as long as we're already so close, let's check-out what's over there before we leave."

During their walk down 2nd Avenue and the return via 4th and 5th Avenues, Colonel Laughlin pointed-out the two areas that the General was offering the use of until the end of the *Armed Forces Show*. He broke off the tour upon arriving at the Fort's HQ Building and said he would meet them tomorrow morning at 09:30 over at Fort Myer.

When they left McNair, Smitty followed Phillip, turning right out the 'P' Street Gate, heading toward the stadium for the Washington Nationals, which loomed a great deal taller than the surrounding neighborhood. Phillip turned right down one of the streets heading south toward the Anacostia

Order of Succession

River. From there it was only coupla zigs and a zag before Smitty saw the river a coupla blocks away. He just followed Phillip, and in about 90 seconds, they were sitting in front of a couple of buildings behind a chain-link fence topped with concertina barbed-wire. A windsock could be seen on a pole rising above the larger building, which had a sign saying it was a heliport. But, there were no signs indicating any government function – except maybe the 'No Parking' street signs. Maybe just as well on that point.

Phillip parked his car on the grass strip shoulder beside the street and both got out. Smitty didn't know what the Major was up to, but he parked his car behind Phillip's and joined them. Since Phillip and Brian were both in their uniforms, they decided to see if that would carry some weight during a little recon about the other side of the fenced-in buildings. All three approached the fence looking for a call-box. Instead, they found only a sign with a 'For Delivery, Call' number, which Phillip dialed. Pretty soon Phillip was talking to somebody who said he would be out to the gate in a coupla minutes.

A fellow, wearing a work shirt with 'Douglas' embroidered above its left pocket, appeared and introduced himself, "Call me Doug. What do ya need?" Phillip explained the upcoming *Armed Forces Show* and his and Brian's parts in it. And what they had been told about this heliport. And what they would like to do is look at the heliport itself as a possible emergency LZ. You, know just in case something really serious happened over the city and they needed an escape route really fast. They just wanted to see if their choppers could safely land here, considering their size and possible nearby obstructions. Well, Doug said he didn't think there would be a problem, but he'd have to check with the Officer-In-Charge inside. He said he'd be right back. Maybe the uniforms worked their magic.

Pretty soon, Doug returned along with another fellow in uniform in tow. The second fellow was Bernard (call me Bernie), who wore a D.C. Police uniform. Bernie wanted to know why nobody called him to tell him we were coming. Phillip explained that they were just told they were gonna be in the show, and they were scouting the area for an emergency LZ between The Mall and Andrews Air Force Base. And that all we wanted to do was just to verify that our helos would actually safely fit at this heliport and what the restrictions and obstructions might be. That's all. And if everything looks okay, we will ask our chain of command to get in touch with whoever you say is the right contact to get an official okey-dokey on it.

Order of Succession

Bernie said that sounded reasonable, but we would have to sign the Visitor Log and provide an official ID. "Sorry, but the uniforms will not work just by themselves; this facility requires that official ID card." Phillip said he and Brian would vouch for me since I had only a driver's license with me. "Oh, and no pictures are permitted inside the fence." Done deal!

Doug was our guide. He provided information on the best approaches and about flight restrictions. He thought the nearby bridge (South Capitol Street SE) was probably the only real obstruction – aside from the various buildings outside their gates. Then he added, "That *Armed Forces Show* thing must be really a big thing. You guys are the second bunch of guys in the past three weeks asking about our heliport." All three visitors gave each other passing glances.

Smitty: "Say, Doug, do you remember those other guys? Do you remember how they were dressed? How many of them were there and could you describe them. We don't want to step on their toes or duplicate your efforts; maybe we can work something out with them, too."

Doug: "Well, there were three or four of them. Two were wearing uniforms but not yours. Yours are Marine, right; well theirs weren't. I don't really know whose uniforms they were."

Smitty (poking around on his cell-phone): "Say, Doug, we have a bunch of pilots coming-in for the show. Let me show you a coupla pictures, and you tell me if anybody looks like those guys. Then we can coordinate calls to you and your points-of-contact (POC). How's that sound to ya?"

Doug: "Sure. Whacha got?"

Smitty showed Doug some pictures of Bubba and the U-Team. Doug picked out Bubba right away as the one who said he was the chopper pilot. That wasn't too surprising, but Doug also pointed-out one more photo. Ray, Hal's son. That was very unexpected.

Smitty: "That's a big help, Doug. Say, would it be possible to look at the Visitor Log once again when we sign-out. Maybe we can figure-out who the others are. That would really be a great help. By the way, did one of them have a real-southern accent?"

Doug: "Is that what you call it? I ain't never heard of 'piss-ant' before. Is his 'piss-ant' like our 'F-you'?" And all three immediately knew they had to look at the Visitor Log sign-in sheets before they left.

Order of Succession

Smitty: "Well, Doug, we've been doing several of these shows lately, and it's like a contest between us and them to see who finds the best emergency LZs first. So, if they want to claim we owe them some beers we need to know they were here first. Know what I mean? It's getting late in the afternoon, could we buy you, and Bernie, too, if you want, something to wet your whistle on your way home? Your taking Metro aren't you? Not driving cars, I mean. Right?"

Doug led the tour back into the office, where he left them alone for about four minutes with the Visitor Log while he went to talk to Bernie about our offer. While he talked, we copied the names and IDs from Bubba's visit. Smitty took a close-up picture with his cell-phone. Thank goodness for Phillip's and Brian's uniforms; they worked better than we had ever imagined.

Smitty: "Doug, have you ever been to the O-Club over at McNair? Would you like to join us over there? But we gotta go right now in our cars and only for a coupla pops. We gotta vouch for you, so you know it's on the level. Okay?" Doug and Bernie greatly enjoyed their beers in the O-Club. Before Smitty and Phillip took them back to the heliport, they stopped at the on-base convenience store to pick-up something a little stronger for them to take with them. A very good investment for an above-average return already received.

Phillip dropped them off at the Metro stop closest to their usual gate and then followed Smitty as they headed up to the quest quarters at Fort Myer taking Memorial Bridge across the Potomac River. That was an error in judgment because of the traffic, but there was no easy way around D.C. at this time of day.

But now the names were known – four of them – complete with titles and ID numbers. All hoped they were legitimate, but they still had them. Bubba was the pilot – probably military-trained. And, Ray was also something more than just a driver of a big pick-up truck. And one of the other names (real or fictitious) is good old 'piss-ant'. It had been a good day, indeed.

Time: Friday, 03-August, 08:30 EDT (Fort Myer, VA)
Smitty, Phillip, and Brian met for breakfast in the mess hall, where they waited to meet Colonel Laughlin. All three were in civvies; this was

ORDER OF SUCCESSION

Smitty's plan for later in the day. Yes, it's not a good idea to get too used to 'hot breakfast buffets' in motels.

Smitty: "Last night, I called in the name and ID information we picked-up yesterday. My contacts said it might take 'til maybe noon today to get back to me. So, we got that running for us in the background. I am not planning to tell Colonel Laughlin anything about what we discovered because we need to keep that partitioned-off at this time. When we know who's who, I think then we tell Rocky and his Colonel – what's his name – yeah, Gahagen. At least they deserve to know, and we still don't know who else might be involved. Any problems with that approach?"

Both Phillip and Brian shook their heads. "Understood. It's private SCIF material for now."

Colonel Laughlin appeared about 09:20 and got a cup of coffee. He brought a map of Fort Myer to show us where he thought the best sites would be for our purposes – considering the Generals and Mrs. Generals (as he called the wives) and the duration of almost two weeks.

Breakfast and coffees completed, we all rode in the Colonel's SUV. While not a huge fort by any means, Fort Myer is considerably larger than Fort McNair because you can't park and walk everywhere – conveniently. Fort Myer is also different for another reason: Arlington National Cemetery is just on the other side of a low stone wall. And, the horse-drawn caissons are guided down the middle of the fort's main streets on their way to/from funerals in the Cemetery. Fort Myer must be one of the Army's few forts that still has working horses in everyday service. Maybe the only one.

Phillip and Brian were making notes at each of the possible sites about flight approaches, restrictions, and obstacles. Laughlin showed them two possible sites. We returned to the mess hall and grabbed some coffee cups. The Colonel and Smitty made small talk at another table, while the pilots went through each site with hand-motions like chopper into and out of each of them.

Finished, they motioned for us to join them at their table. They laid-out each of the sites and how they felt about each. They told Col. Laughlin their first choices for McNair and Myer with only a couple of comments. Not surprisingly, they were ones originally suggested by General Baldwin. Colonel Laughlin accepted the choices on behalf of the General, and then he excused himself for another appointment.

Order of Succession

Time: Friday, 03-August, 11:56 EDT (Fort Myer, VA)

That done, they had lunch before a final visit to The Mall area. Smitty led them downtown and found a small garage on the north side of The Mall. He planned to show them what he thought was being planned. They walked around TWH to get a feel for the likely ground-zero of an armed confrontation. Maybe they could put their heads together and figure-out how to scare the aggressors into surrendering. Maybe not; probably not. But it would be nice to know the alternatives.

Smitty had suggested wearing comfortable shoes because he was going to take them to Jefferson Memorial – by foot. They headed across The Mall, crossing near The Washington Monument, and passing the Bureau of Engraving and Printing on 15th Street SW.

Smitty: "Look to the west, over there on Maine. See where it sort of curves. Keep that spot in mind. We'll look at it closer on our return trip."

He led them over to the steps of the Jefferson Memorial. Told them to face TWH. And the light bulbs went on in their heads.

Brian: "You weren't friggin' kidding!"

Smitty: "I'm showing you this so you can sorta figure-out from where the plotters can reach-out and touch their target. And touch it fast and damn hard, too. Remember where that spot is on Maine I told you to remember? It's right under the same flight-path from this position. My plan is to have Rocky control this line-of-fire by whatever means necessary."

On their return walk, they stopped at the Maine Avenue SW site so they could imagine the line-of-fire. That would be much worse because of the shorter flight-time, requiring much faster reaction times. "If an outright chopper assault doesn't happen as we think it will . . . well, this is my worst nightmare. This is why Rocky's assignment is so critical."

They circled TWH once again, but this time with that new variable component inserted into their equations.

On to Waynesboro so they could look over the areas up there – Camp David, High Point Road, and the Bunker.

ORDER OF SUCCESSION
38 – Recon the Bunker and Camp David

Around 06:15, Saturday, 04-August: The Motel in Waynesboro, Pennsylvania

TIME: 06:17 EDT

{Smitty's mocking brain: "So, you're back to where we left-off a few days ago, huh? You're anxious to get back to the 'hot breakfast buffet', ain't cha? Just what is wrong wit-cha, anyway? You like this stuff way too much. Oh, wait, whatcha really like is going over to that produce stand and getting some fresh fruit, huh? Don't forgit you owe Fern a picture of that elusive bird of yours. And, don't forget the hot coffee from Mickey D's, neither. That short visit down to Quantico didn't break you of this place did it? Boy, you are some piecea work, you are!"}

And that's what all three found on the next morning's buffet serving line – more mystery-meat patties and re-heated, pancakes, frozen eggs, and potatoes. The coffee was hot, though. Smitty laid-out his plans for this weekend so Phillip and Brian could return to Quantico on Monday morning.

Smitty: "Guys, I have three places I want to show you between today and Monday – High Point, the jump-off place for gliders. It's sort of right around the corner from Camp David – literally, around the corner, but we won't be able to get into it. And, of course, the bunker, assuming nobody is around the area. Your choice which one's first. I still got my 20-day growth and floppy hats so we might even be able to go down into Thurmont without me being recognized. But those are the highlights. I also think you might want to bring along any air charts of the area so you can make notes.

"Oh, I forgot to mention this yesterday, but I did get a callback about those names we found over at the heliport near Fort McNair. Let's just say that, assuming the ID information is correct, we got us some interesting names alright.

Order of Succession

"The first one is the easiest. The one guy I recognize as Ray, is indeed, Ray. Ray Drixler who lives in the Thurmont area. So, he is probably related to Hal, who calls him his son. Hal is supposed to be married to Daisy, who, in turn, is still out at 29. Looks like the family who plots together stays together – in jail, that is. Or something like that.

"The second one, the one I know as Bubba is using the ID of a Colonel Seth Delong, who is supposed to be in the US Army, working outta, wait 'til you hear this, the friggin' National Security Agency, assigned to some sorta think-tank on counter-terrorism. I don't know how true that is because when I met him, it certainly wasn't in that kind of think-tank environment. I requested a picture from his ID folder to see if it's the same guy I know. Or, maybe if he's just using somebody else's ID.

"The third guy is the one I think is our favorite "piss-ant" Voice on the POTUS phone. The ID number belongs to one Lieutenant General Hamilton Calhoun, currently stationed at the Pentagon, formerly the post commander at Fort Rucker, Alabama, which is also where Colonel Bubba was stationed. Coincidence? I don't know. And you know, by the way, Fort Rucker has a whole hell of a lot of choppers of all sorts down there!

"The fourth guy on the heliport sign-in sheet is an unknown. The name is Spencer Forsythe; however, that ID number belonged to a doctor in California, now deceased. So, this guy is some sort of player, but we can't figure him out yet.

"This is the latest on the players on the aggressor's side; we're still assembling our team. But this helps choosing the right players. I'll meet you in the parking lot in about 15, okay?"

Time: Saturday, 04-August, 07:11 EDT (Motel in Waynesboro, PA)

Ah, a calm Saturday! They had the hot breakfast buffet at 06:30. So much for sleeping-in late, but they did have things to do, places to go, things to see, and some people to avoid seeing. Smitty had jotted-down a possible itinerary of where he wanted to take them and sorta a rough timetable. But they sat around talking until 08:16, which was not the early start he had in his mind. By quarter to nine, they were in their civvies and in the car with their maps, flight charts, and cameras. Smitty drove, of course. He had also thrown his birding books into the trunk as well – just in case. He did his best to make

Order of Succession

today's excursion into a circle as much as possible so they didn't have to re-trace their route. Didn't quite work out that way, though.

Time: Saturday, 04-August, 10:07 EDT (High Rock, glider jump-off area)

The first stop on this tour was High Rock so they could sorta play tourists taking in the sights. Smitty had no hopes of catching Bubba up there today, but he could show Phillip and Brian the place so they could mark their charts. When they arrived, there were only about a half dozen pickups parked around the area; by the time they left, it was a baker's dozen.

They looked over the edge and marveled at the birds playing in the thermals below them – just like they didn't have a care in the world except for the thermal updrafts. They also took note of the posted warning sign about this P-40 area turning into R-4009. Phillip said they would have to look that up when they got back to find-out exactly where the invisible borders were located.

Thank goodness, Bubba and Ray did not show up while they were lookin' around. That would have been terribly awkward.

Time: Saturday, 04-August, 11:16 EDT (High Rock, glider jump-off area)

Next stop was the long-secreted red barn. Along the way, they stopped off at the produce stand so Smitty could chat-up Fern about showing the birding area to his new buddies from the Mid-Atlantic Ornithologists' Society. This was one of the things they had discussed over breakfast – how Phillip and Brian were going to certify Smitty's (oops, make that, Terry's) find of a seldom-seen bird. That's the cover they were going to use for wandering back down the dirt lane. Smitty wanted to reinforce that in Fern's mind – especially if the Maryland State policeman was around the area again. They also bought some fresh fruit and something to drink, too – all to-go.

Out of the parking lot, right on Route 550 and another quick right onto Debold. Smitty parked the car as far off the road as he could, and they walked down the dirt lane, this time not trying to be quiet just in case they were being observed by that same fella who pulled-out of the lane after Smitty first located the bunker. All along the lane, Smitty kept up the birding chatter motioning where he said he saw the bird and took pictures of it. But, even though Phillip and Brian seemed interested in the bird, they knew that the real target down this lane was buried in the hillside across the meadow. Once near the red barn, they stood so that Smitty had his back toward the bunker and kept motioning and pointing where he finally saw that elusive bird. The other two were busy looking at the bunker but agreeing with everything Smitty was saying and even made notes about 'certifying' his sighting. They also took 'certifying' photos, with telephoto lenses, making sure the bunker was in most of them – just in case. They made their way back to the car and decided a break was in order.

Time: Saturday, 04-August, 12:22 EDT (Shoulder of Debold Road, Frederick County, Maryland)

Smitty thought about taking them to The Treadle, but they all sorta nixed that idea simply because they didn't know who might see them and recognize Smitty, even though he now had a short beard, a mustache, and longer hair. Instead, they opted to go north to Emmitsburg to a restaurant, the Ott House, right on the town square for lunch, figuring that the odds of not being seen by any of the plotters favored them up there. During lunch, Phillip asked a wild question about finding some sort of landmark that they could use as an orientation marker if they had to fly up to this area. Preferably, one that could be seen both during the day and especially at night – again, just in case. Smitty had to admit that he didn't have a clue about that, but asked Phillip to let him think about it during lunch.

After lunch, Smitty was going to make a quick pass by Hal's place and The Treadle, so he drove back down US 15.

However, before they even left Emmitsburg, Smitty had an 'aha; moment: "Phillip, does that landmark have to be land itself or could it be just something you can see from the air?"

Phillip: "Preferably something that can be easily picked-up at night. What did you have in mind?"

Smitty: "I think I've got just the ticket for you. We can drive to it on our way. Okay?"

Phillip: "Drive to it? Sure, why not, I guess."

ORDER OF SUCCESSION

Just after getting on US 15 from South Seton Avenue, Smitty took the exit for Mount St. Mary's University. Then they followed campus roads to reach St. Anthony Road, which he followed to Grotto Road and turned onto that, following it up to a small parking lot alongside a glass-walled Catholic church, where he parked the car. They all got out of the car, and still looking at the church, Phillip asked, "Were you thinking about using this church for a landmark? It's going to be awful difficult to see at night, dontcha think?"

Time: Saturday, 04-August, 14:07 EDT (Parking lot at the end of Grotto Road)

Smitty: "Probably so, if you are only thinking about the church building in front of us, but if you expand your horizons, what would you say to something that's over 100 feet tall and lit-up at night? That ought to be pretty easy to pick-out at night, dontcha think?"

Phillip: "Damn straight something like that would be great. Oops, sorry, I shouldn't say that here, should I, considering this church in front of us?"

Smitty: "Give a gander at the tower behind us; see how nice and tall it is? There's a statue of the Blessed Mother, Mary, Jesus' Mother, on top of it. And most nights, it is lit-up with flood lights. Do ya think this 100-foot lit-up tower with a statue on top could act as a landmark for whatever you are thinking about?"

Phillip: "Boy, would it. Brian, definitely mark this tower on our charts."

Smitty: "And Camp David is right over these mountains here roughly in that direction (motioning roughly south-south-west as he was speaking). Roughly, about eight miles, as the helo flies. And our bunker is roughly six miles due west from this spot. The glider jump-off cliff is roughly less than nine further along pretty much the same vector as the bunker, give or take a few degrees. I thought both of you might like this tower as a landmark.

"Plus, if you need an airport for whatever the reason, there's a civilian one almost directly south of here and east of downtown Frederick, and its right down U.S. 15, which we will be on in just a few minutes. It's the one to which the F-16s out of Andrews escort a lot of the wayward pilots after they get lost and fly into the restricted airspace over in D.C. And if

Order of Succession

you need a military air-base, there's an Air National Guard base down in Martinsburg, West Virginia. Follow I-81 south from the Potomac River, and, as they say around here, ya can't miss it off on the east side of I-81. I'm trying to make you comfortable with emergency LZs for your choppers."

Phillip: "And that you have my good man. You sure you aren't a chopper pilot?"

Smitty: "I take that as a compliment, but I'm gonna have to take the 5th on that. I have to keep you in suspense."

Time: Saturday, 04-August, 14:32 EDT (Parking lot at the end of Grotto Road)

Smitty: "The last item on my agenda is a secret place that everybody knows about – Camp David. I can't get us in to it right now. Make that I don't want to get us inside the wire because we don't know who's who – the good-guys or the plotters. We don't want to tip any hands yet. But since it's inside a federal park, we can drive around it on park roads so you can get a lay-of-the-land so-to-speak. On your maps, I'm gonna drive down US 15 to the north end of Thurmont and exit at Route 550. I'll take you past The Treadle and some other interesting points so you can sorta get the feel of the area. But I'm not planning to stop and sight-see for the same reason; I don't know who's out-and-about. Then we are going to leave Thurmont on MD-77 and head for the area around Camp David, roughly west from Thurmont. But first, I'm gonna pull into another fruit market right along 15 just a coupla miles before we get to the 550 turn-off into Thurmont."

So, that's what Smitty did – gave them a short tour of Thurmont. His version, just hitting the highlights took less than 15 minutes, including the stop light at Main and Water streets. He cruised past The Treadle so they could gawk at it for a few seconds.

Smitty: "That's where Daisy or Darlene Zoe worked as a waitress. There's even a small, private Camp David Museum inside." He continued down Frederick Road and turned right to take the underpass under US 15. He even pulled into the Food Lion parking lot in a small shopping center on a hilltop overlooking Thurmont. He hoped to get some sort of site-seeing view because it was above the city streets. But nature got in the way; the trees had grown too high to really see much of anything.

Order of Succession

He exited the parking lot and turned right on Tippin Drive and followed that over to MD-77, where he turned left up toward the parklands. Once they reached the roads their maps showed surrounding Camp David, they turned into tourists and drove slowly, checking the roads against their maps and charts. All matched perfectly.

After they finished meandering around the hills, Smitty continued west on 77 to the intersection of MD-77, Stottlemyer Road, and Foxville Deerfield Road, where he turned right onto Foxville. He followed Foxville until he veered right onto Manahan, which skirted the west side of the Camp David restricted area and, interestingly, some public campgrounds. He followed Manahan down to MD-550, where he asked Brian to drive, so he could sit in the rear seat on the far side. Then Smitty asked Brian to take 550 to the right. And he guided Brian to the turn-off for Hal's welding shop, while he was slouching down in the rear seat. They got to see the welding shop where Hal, the ostensible leader of the plot, worked. This ended the tour. Smitty gave Brian directions to get back to their motel.

After they freshened-up, dinner-time was calling. Smitty took them up to the Hickory Bridge Farm Restaurant in which he first discovered the painting of the red barn. Just because.

ORDER OF SUCCESSION

39 – Recaps

Just past 06:30, Sunday, 05-August: The Motel in Waynesboro, Pennsylvania

TIME: 06:35 EDT

More, mystery-meat patties and eggs, but oh, the coffee! Smitty left his maps in his room. But, he grabbed a copy of *The Washington Post*, which he had found at a newsstand, and quickly browsed the sections to get a quick feel of what's happened in the US and the world the past weekend. While picking his way through the food, he started the crossword puzzle to give his mind something else to occupy itself.

Phillip and Brian showed-up almost an hour later. Both were planning to return to Quantico this morning directly from the breakfast table. Phillip and Brian were planning how they could deal with all sorts of possibilities. Plus, they had come-up with a couple of minor modifications for the helicopters.

In a few days, Smitty was also going down to Quantico to meet the Army platoons that had been committed for this training.

Time: Sunday, 05-August, 09:48 EDT (At the Waynesboro motel)

Smitty had developed an ominous feeling that this quiet morning was just a lull in an approaching storm. It was a good time to resupply some of his toilet articles and get some note-taking supplies. After dressing in his floppy hat and sun-glasses, he found the housekeeping staff and paid them again for not cleaning his room daily. They gave him directions, and he walked out to the street, turning left toward Waynesboro's 'downtown'. They had assured him that there were drugstores maybe a mile or so that way. As usual, they were right.

The weather was comfortable for walking right now, but he was sure it was going to get a lot warmer just past noon. Better get his walk in now. Sure enough, he found a CVS near the Mickey D's

ORDER OF SUCCESSION

he'd been stopping at for his morning coffee ever since he arrived in town. He found everything he needed, paid, and left on his walk back toward the motel. He stopped at Mickey D's for a coffee to-go. The return walk gave him lots of time to think.

{Smitty, sort of mumbling: "Actually, the word 'assault' doesn't seem like the right word. With the munitions in the bunker and the weaponry available to these plotters, the Secret Service would certainly be on the shorter end of the stick immediately after the first missile left its launching tube. But an 'assault' just sorta fits, but it's not exactly right. It certainly won't be a long drawn-out fire-fight. These plotters don't plan to 'assault' da WH in order to capture it. They plan to flat-out raze it down to the ground with their first missiles in the first minute of the fight. The word 'blitz' is more like it. Yeah, like 'blitzkrieg' from WWII – fast, furious, over-whelming. A 'blitz' is what this will be. As long as TWH is razed to the ground, they win. They don't care if the Secret Service, the government, or anybody else wants to claim ownership of the ashes; they can have all they want. The defenders' side can own the burning remains, and the aggressors still win. They win with the imagery of having destroyed the most symbolic seat of all power in the United States – and also for a major part of the rest of world, too. Suppose simultaneously, they fire a missile into Camp David. Two symbols for them, and zero for our side. And, they don't even have to assassinate the President.

"And you know about those supposedly secret and super strong underground bunkers for the rest of the Government – you know, the ones to which Congress can evacuate themselves so they can hunker-down – well, what the hell good would they be anyway? That really secret one back in the '70s and 80s down in West Virginia, what was that one anyway? Oh yeah, that bunker at the Greenbrier Hotel in White Sulphur Springs, West Virginia. Yeah that's the one. Well, once the secret got out that it was there, well, now they even give tours through it to the paying tourists. And the other one up in the Catoctin Mountains near Camp David – that one's so secret that it's in Wikipedia and any number of other web-sites, complete with layouts of the entrances and everything. Just stuff a coupla missiles down each entrance and the exit tunnel and see how many friggin' Congress people and Senators are gonna want to go inside willingly if there's the slightest chance it's gonna be their tomb. How many, ya think? They might even be more willing to take their chances on the outside among their 'fellow Americans'. On second

Order of Succession

thought, maybe they wouldn't want to be stuck among some highly pissed-off 'fellow Americans', either. Maybe it would be safer behind the blast-proof doors with the millions of tons of mountain on top of them. At least then the PO'ed Americans would know exactly where their damn leaders were. All safe and sound inside, while the average 'Joe six-pack' Americans are left outside to face head-on whatever the danger is."}

{Smitty's mocking brain: "And then what, smarty-pants? So, TWH is turned into a smoking hole in the ground. What are you gonna do to stop it? Can it even be stopped? Huh? Huh?"}

{Smitty: "Good questions, Brain. All good questions. Well, we are gonna try our damnedest to stop it. What do ya think we've been planning here, anyway, a Sunday tea-party on the back lawn?

"But your other question is even more important. What happens then? Oh, SHIT! This is what's gonna happen sure as there's white on rice and skunks stink to high heaven after they're run-over. This is what is gonna friggin' happen. The President must replace the Secretaries in his Cabinet, right? We all heard him say that on TV last week that he's gonna ask the Congress to okay all of his appointees on an expedited basis. You know what that means, dontcha? He's asking Congress to not investigate or vet anybody. Don't screw with checking-up on them or anything else. Take his word that he can run the Government by using their skills and personal networks. And then guess what? Com'n, guess."}

{Smitty's brain's response: "I don't know what comes next. Why dontcha tell me, huh? I can see you're itching to. Go ahead and tell me. Surprise me, smarty-pants. Go ahead."}

{Smitty: "Here's what's gonna happen. Get this. All of the new Secretaries, the ones Congress isn't supposed to check-out, will be in place to run the Government under a 'War Powers Act' or some other friggin' Presidential Executive Order. They don't have to worry about anybody saying it's unconstitutional or anything like that. They are gonna be able to do whatever the hell they want, and there's not gonna be anybody able to stop them after TWH is gone. They're gonna change the Federal Government without any elections; without anybody's permission; period, done deal. Fiat accompli without a civil war or anything. Over and done with, and you won't even see it on TV News because those damn lily-livered shows are just looking for ratings and advertising bucks. Give'em a real story and nobody's still around who

ORDER OF SUCCESSION

has the experience and the depth of experience to know what they are even lookin' at. Nobody's gonna know it even happened for at least a year – or maybe even two or three. That's way too long to back out of the new Government without bloodshed, without a real honest-to-goodness civil war. Just a few weeks ago, we saw the opening attacks out at that California rest-area. But this is gonna be the real crowning event. Pure and simple, if they can get away with it. What a plan! Damn!"}

{Brain: "Tell you what; you tell a pretty damn good story. I gotta cogitate on this for a while. Get a hold of me after lunch and after you make some phone calls."}

Time: Sunday, 05-August, 13:10 EDT (At the Waynesboro motel)

After what he thought was enough time to field some recon teams, Smitty placed a call to find-out how things were going about scouting that bunker

Smitty: "Velma, Terry Pedrozo here. I'm calling about the status of a recon request about that ammo bunker I reported yesterday. I hope you have something favorable to report on that."

Velma: "Yeah, well, yeah got some preliminary recon stuff. I'm not one of the analysts you understand, but I think you got it pretty spot-on. I think we fielded three teams. I'm saying 'I think' because one of the original two teams called in a third team, okay?

"Team one was a 'husband and wife real estate sales team' that searched for the owners of land around your coordinates. They were supposedly looking for sellers of property in that area for one of their buyers. By the sound of it, they got a bite from an owner near the meadow and the bunker. They are supposed to go out and talk-up a sale and take pictures of the property to show to their buyer. Supposed to go out later this afternoon.

"Okay, now team two is a couple of Maryland DNR rangers looking for a wounded bear on the other side of your building from the interested real estate seller. So, they would have been a lot closer to the bunker. They were out there this morning. The only information I have to tell you is that they got close-ups of the bunker through the trees. When they got closer to the building, they saw little red flashing lights under the eaves. Their assumption is that the building has lots of sensors on it and inside it. It's the ones that may be inside that

Order of Succession

concerns them most. One mistake breaching the doors and maybe the whole bunker goes sky-high. Preliminary suggestions include waiting for them to open the doors and then sort of rush them; maybe nothing will happen if they can't trigger the detonators. Another possibility might be to create a 'natural emergency' of some sort like a fire or something. Maybe the building alarms will notify the other end that something is wrong up there. Or maybe shut off the commercial power; maybe they'll get notified wherever they are.

"The third team is actually a helicopter and a truck. The chopper is equipped with ground-penetrating radar gear. The plan is for the chopper to have a serious mechanical problem that causes it to land in the meadow. The truck is driven by the 'repair techs' sent out to get the chopper into the air again. It, too, has ground-penetrating radar gear aboard and will try to drive over the underground storage area to get an idea of how big it is and maybe what's down inside it. That scenario is set to go tomorrow, so there's nothing to really tell you about yet. That's all I got so far."

Smitty: "So far, this is great. You have no idea how helpful this has been. I'll call you again tomorrow in the late afternoon. Thanks again."

ORDER OF SUCCESSION

40 – Learning New Skills

Just past 07:00, Sunday, 05-August: The Motel in Waynesboro, Pennsylvania

TIME: 07:10 EDT

The previous night, Smitty decided it was high time to meet his teams down at Quantico, Virginia. He was planning to drive down there this morning to get acquainted – with some California folks again, and with others for the first time.

But first, one last motel breakfast before checking-out. Still more mystery-meat patties and eggs all the same as all the previous mornings. The coffee, while not spectacular, was unusually good for a breakfast buffet offering. Smitty had already packed his belongings and his other tools – maps, cameras, binoculars; they were just waiting to be carried down to the car. "Where's the local paper or *USA Today*? Maybe there's a crossword puzzle that offers a challenge before I leave here – for good."

After eating, he brought a cup of coffee with him back to the room. He visually swept the room to make sure the pile of gear he stacked near the door contained everything he had brought into the room over the past coupla weeks. When he was satisfied that the pile was complete, he ferried all of it down to the parking lot and packed it into the car. He returned to the room for a final check to make sure there was nothing lying under the bed, forgotten in a dresser drawer, and the like. He also found the housekeeping staff and thanked them for taking such good care of him while he was here. He also told them he would remember this motel if he was in the area again; then off he went to pay the bill and depart.

He Drove West To Pick-Up I-81 And Headed South. Because he really didn't have to be there until tomorrow morning, he took what he hoped would be a more relaxing drive than through traffic on I-95 South. He continued on I-81, passing Martinsburg, West Virginia, and Winchester, Virginia.

Order of Succession

Somewhere just past Mt. Jackson, Virginia, he saw a building on a frontage road on the west side of I-81 that looked interesting, Route 11 Potato Chips. He pulled off I-81 at the next exit and with the help of his GPS, worked his way back the side roads to the plant and pulled into the parking lot, parked, and walked into the 'sales room'. He was fortunate this morning; they were 'frying' new batches of chips. A very interesting operation. After a visit to the restroom and buying a few bags of really fresh chips, Smitty headed back to southbound I-81.

He turned eastward on I-66 near Strasburg, Virginia, continuing toward Gainesville, Virginia, where he finally headed south again on Virginia Highway-234, following it to I-95 and Route 1. Then it was just a matter of following the signs to Marine Corps Base Quantico.

Smitty arrived in the area around 13:14 and stopped at the Visitors Center to confirm that his teams were already on-base. He also asked for directions to the FBI's billets, where he already had a room reserved.

Time: Monday, 06-August, 14:10 (FBI Billets, Quantico, VA)

Time to call Rhodes, Jenkins, and Hauser. He made a note to have Rhodes contact the two platoon officers from The Old Guard, Bravo and Delta Companies. Might as well get them all up to speed on what's gonna happen over the next coupla weeks. Time's awastin'.

He unpacked his gear and set-up shop for the next coupla weeks – probably be just a coupla days, though. He checked for messages, and, finding none, he set-up a small conference area at one end of the mess hall, which was supposed to be for their exclusive use – the mess hall nearest the FBI Training Center. That done, Smitty invited his three old partners and their Gunnies and Coms plus the two platoon officers from The Old Guard and their Platoon Sergeants to join him in his new conference area.

Time: Monday, 06-August, 15:05 EDT (FBI Training Center, Quantico, VA)

Smitty: "Glad all of you could make this initial meet-and greet. First, of all, welcome to Quantico. Are all of your platoons here yet?" All Captains answered that they were. "That's a good start for this mission. During this meeting I hope to acquaint you with how the situation is

ORDER OF SUCCESSION

advancing now and why you are down here so your troops won't be leaderless during the first coupla hours tomorrow morning. I left some envelopes with directions for you at the barracks, and it looks like you all got them. Cap'n Rhodes, please ask your Gunnies to come-on inside and join the meeting; platoon officers from The Old Guard, please do the same with your Platoon Sergeants because they are gonna havta implement the final plans that are developed down here over the next two weeks. We'll run through the introductions and get started. Then we need to have a planning session about how to deal with the probable threat we believe is coming in a few weeks. We need good planners knowledgeable about urban conditions, so anybody with specific Close-Quarters-Battle experience in urban conditions is definitely welcome, but let's try to keep the group under 20 or so for this afternoon.

"First-off, introductions are in order. I'll start them and then excuse myself for about ten minutes. I am the first to admit that the Army officers and their sergeants are at a slight disadvantage right now. The Marines here have already been personally involved with this situation since it began out in California in the middle of July, and they are aware of who some of the players are. Wait on that; it is more correct to say the Marines know what the players sound like, but none of us have seen any of the ones we are going to meet together. The Marines, at all levels, are going to bring the Army personnel up to speed ASAP. The two Army Captains joining our effort are: Captain Duane Calhoun, US Army, platoon Commander, Bravo Company, The Old Guard, and Captain Gerald Lambert, US Army, Company XO [28] Delta Company, The Old Guard. Please carry-on around the table; I'll be back shortly. Cap'n Rhodes, please join me ASAP after you introduce yourself and explain the reason why you will be in charge." Smitty delivered the last request like it was an order; Rocky immediately realized something was amiss.

As Rhodes joined Smitty: "Smitty, what's up?"

Smitty: "Get to know Army Captain Duane Calhoun really well and really fast. During the last week, Philip, Brian, and I discovered that there could be a Lieutenant General involved in the plot. Let's just say a Light General who likes to use 'piss-ant' in his speech patterns and who is currently supposed to be assigned to the Pentagon. One who had been at Fort Rucker, Alabama, at the same time as one Colonel Seth Delong was.

---

28 XO = Executive Officer

Order of Succession

This colonel could very well be our Bubba, who I personally observed flying a hang-glider. Guess what, choppers and hang-gliders. I think these two are only some of our bad-guys. But, here is why you need to watch Old Guard Captain Calhoun – both he and the Lieutenant General share the same name – Calhoun, and both were stationed at Fort Rucker at the same time as Colonel Delong was also there. Right now, we do not know if the Captain out there in our meeting is personally involved, or if he just has the same last name from a different branch of the Calhoun family. Even more frightening, if they are father and son. Feel him out and if he looks the least bit screwy, we are going to have to somehow isolate him really fast from some of the aspects of this operation."

Rhodes: "Wow, what a coincidence! Understood. I might get Gunny Cornell involved to buddy-up to the Captain's Platoon Sergeant. Okay with you?"

Smitty: "It's your command. Do what you think is best. By the way, when does your C.O., Colonel Gahagen, show-up if he's coming?"

Rhodes: "Oh, he's definitely coming. But he won't show-up until the middle of next week, though. You know, I certainly hope this doesn't turn-out to be a real-life test for my promotion. There are so many twists in this situation, how could I ever be graded? A simple pass or fail? What a mess that would be; I could be passed over for the rest of my career."

Smitty: "Not if I have anything to do with it. I got plans for you, Rocky; big plans. Let's get back to our meeting."

Smitty (back in the meeting): "Now that we know each other, if there are no questions, let's continue."

One of The Old Guard Captains: "Well, I do have a question or two. First, what is this all about. Our Commander just said be here on time and they'll fill you in, and then I can tell him. Is this some sort of secret operation? And last, why were we picked? What are we supposed to bring to this operation?"

Smitty: "All good questions. I'll answer your questions in reverse order. Last, your soldiers are expected to bring some knowledge about D.C. itself and its local streets to this operation. We expect that they have wandered around the D.C. area and especially around The White House for some time – and certainly a lot more frequently than the Marines

ORDER OF SUCCESSION

from Pendleton have. We expect they may have a certain feel for what looks normal and right on the streets and what looks out of place. In other words, eyes and ears on the ground.

"Next, The Old Guard was picked because they are recognized as 'being' D.C. In other words, the locals know you are supposed to be here; you don't look like tourists because your troops have seen much of what's here and just keep walking instead of stopping to point and gawk. You should understand that we did not pick your companies or you personally. Your Battalion Colonel did that. However, we did ask for officers and non-coms with Top Secret, or higher, clearances. You will be 'read-in' for items that we classify as higher than a simple TS; you will also be advised when that happens.

"Yes, this is considered to be a Top Secret operation at this time – from the second you entered Quantico. You and your soldiers are restricted to NOT TALKING ABOUT THIS UNTIL AFTER IT HAS BEEN COMPLETED AND MAYBE NOT EVEN THEN FOR YEARS AFTER THAT. And, no, you cannot tell your Colonel or Company Commander anything specific about this unless he has the proper security clearances and the specific need-to-know – and then, only after the mission is completed. You may tell him only that it is some sorta 'security detail' for the *Armed Forces Show*. And that is all at this time. You will also be required to NOT TELL ANYONE about those items without a need-to-know. And since Cap'n Rhodes and I control the classification for this project, YOU CANNOT TALK ABOUT THIS WITH ANYONE NOT IN THIS ROOM. Or, I will personally prosecute your case.

"You will be provided all the information you need to fulfill your mission while here. You may consult with Captain Rhodes over there (Smitty motioned with his right arm) because he and his Gunnies were there for the literal opening shots, no pun intended, in an I-8 rest-area in the Mojave Desert in southern California. They have been instructed to bring you up to speed as quickly as they can. For that reason, you Army Captains and Platoon Sergeants are going to have to attend some additional familiarization meetings led by the Marines because they lived through those beginning shots and know exactly what went-on from almost the very beginning. Those meetings will be in the afternoons and evenings after your soldiers and the Marines go through the CQB training courses. I am also expecting you to attend that CQB training,

Order of Succession

too, because you are gonna be on the streets along with your soldiers. The familiarization meetings won't take long – only about an hour a day for the week. And you are expected to ask all the questions you want, and the Marines will answer you if they have the information. Any other questions? None. Good. Please take a break for about 10."

Time: Monday, 06-August, 16:15 EDT (FBI Training Center, Quantico, VA)

Smitty returns and continues addressing the Army members: "Captains and sergeants just in case you have not been informed yet, let me be the one who tells you. With the permission of your chain of command several things have been slightly altered solely for the purposes of this exercise.

"To begin with, and probably the most difficult for those of you in the Army, your new chain of command for this effort is through Marine Captain Rhodes over there. There is nothing against the Army, but Cap'n Rhodes has first-hand experience with some of the bad-guys on the other side of this plot.

"Next, Cap'n Rhodes will fill you all in about what we are facing. I say again, this information will be considered Top Secret, privileged, and on a need-to-know basis. If anyone does not have at least a Top Secret clearance, they will be asked to leave during the briefing. This means that your troops are not to be told unless all hell breaks loose. Exceptions may be made on a case-by-case basis for command NCOs if necessary. We already briefly touched on that earlier. And, we will somehow establish ground-rules for a work-around, as needed.

"That's followed by: many of your troops will be in civilian clothes during the actual field assignment. They will have to be able recognize the Marines because most of them will also be in civvies. I also know that The Old Guard requires white-wall haircuts. Those will be suspended for the duration of this assignment. We need both the Army troops and the Marines to blend-in as much as possible with every-day visitors on and around The Mall. After we all decide what the assignments for the various platoons and companies are, I suggest that the troops and Marines wear civvies to the training sessions so everybody recognizes everybody else as they will be seeing them on the streets of D.C.

ORDER OF SUCCESSION

"Oh, yeah, finally, as of now, you are no longer The Old Guard from Virginia, and the Marines are not from California, either. You are now an Army company from Idaho here for some training purposes. The Marines working this assignment are also not from Pendleton; they are from Texas and Florida. You all will also be issued fictitious ID Cards for this assignment, which must definitely be returned at its conclusion.

"The Quantico Marines have set-up water in the outer room. The Marine mess hall will have meals for both services to accommodate our training schedule. Only our two groups are to be served at the same time in the same mess hall; no other Marine companies, or civilians, for that matter, are to eat with your soldiers and Marines. If there is a stranger, ask him for some ID and ask him to leave – officers included.

"Major Phillip Jenkins and Cap'n Brian Hauser (Smitty motioned in their direction) will be our only air-power. For the duration, their helos will be stationed on-post at both Fort McNair and Fort Myer for security reasons. For those of you who used to practice on the respective Parade Grounds, practices will continue as normal; however, a parking lot at McNair and part of Myer's motor pool have been posted for restricted access for the duration of the *Armed Forces Show*.

"They have already requested that they would like to speak with any and all Army personnel who may have personal experience down around The Mall and both forts. Here's your soldiers' chance for free beers. Anything else, Major, Captain? (Both shook their heads.)

"Oh, I forgot, the FBI has NOT been read into this assignment; they just know they have been asked to provide their facility down here to provide support for Close-Quarter-Battle training provided by instructors who have been flown in solely for this training. They, too, have not been read-in as to the reason. (In a forceful, lowered voice) PLEASE KEEP IT THAT WAY. Chow for Army and Marines is scheduled for 17:30 sharp in this mess hall and is described in your information packs. The mess hall will be ours alone for the duration. They will be set-up for breakfast at 06:00, and the first class tomorrow morning is scheduled for 07:30. Lunch is scheduled for 13:00. After the brief familiarization, both Army and Marines in this group will meet after chow to decide which company is best suited for various tasks. Captain Calhoun and Captain Lambert, your soldiers may go wherever they want while here at Quantico, just advise them not to stand-out; we do not need to have some overzealous,

Order of Succession

by-the-book guard asking questions. If there are no other questions, grab some water, and meet the FBI and CQB trainers outside in 15; they are going to give you a quick overview of their Training Center. See that your troops and Marines are ready to eat at 17:30 or it will be closed to them. I'll see you in the mess hall at 18:45."

Time: Monday, 06-August, 18:45 EDT (Mess Hall, Quantico, VA)

Both the Army and Marine companies ate together – but at their own respective tables. Somehow, the word leaked-out about the Army reporting to the Marines. "That was just plain unheard of." "Are we gonna let them do this to us, The Old Guard?" The air was filled with a 'WTH is going on' attitude. Ketchup, hot sauce, and free pizza and beer would not have improved the taste of what everybody thought tomorrow morning was gonna bring. "No sir, this is just FUBAR'ed already."

Smitty motioned to Rocky, Phillip, Brian, the Gunnies, Captain Calhoun, Captain Lambert, and both Army Platoon Sergeants to take seats at the tables located at the end of the mess hall. This was not so much a show of force, but rather a show of unity. Smitty introduced himself: "Call me Smitty, no rank, just Smitty. I realize you all are wondering just what the WTF is going on. What is so important enough to spoil your weekend in D.C.? Well, if our guesses are right, we are here to be part of history – something that has never happened in The United States in anyone's lifetime. If our intel is right, we will be involved in attempted aggression; our job is to prevent it from being successful on our watch. And then it will be your privilege and honor to mop-up afterwards."

The mess hall was now deathly quiet. Questioning looks were exchanged: "Did you hear what I just heard?" There was no noise from the mess hall kitchen or the dish-wash room. All of the staff was clustered around the serving line; all wearing quizzical looks. Smitty invited them to join the others because they weren't going anywhere else after what they had heard. And this is when Smitty gave all of them the 'this is Top Secret, and you are personally responsible to keep it that way' speech. "If you think you *cannot* do this, then all you need to do is stand-up and leave right now. I'll wait until only those who can do this are the only ones remaining in the room. Same goes for you, too (motioning toward the mess hall staff). Your Captains and Platoon Sergeants have been briefed and will be responsible for you successfully accomplishing

Order of Succession

this mission. They said you are, and their word is good enough for me. Don't make them regret trusting you. You know they won't like that. Not one bit. And you won't like living in Leavenworth for the next few years, either. The offer to leave is still open for another 60 seconds. If you feel you *just cannot keep your mouths shut*, get up and get out right now while the gettin's good. No punishments or extra duty at this point. Afterwards, I cannot guarantee. 30 seconds remaining.

"Sorry, folks from the mess hall, but at this point this mess hall is now also closed to you. Cap'n, Rhodes, please have a Gunny escort them out and secure those doors.

(31 seconds later) "Tomorrow morning you begin short, but intense, training sessions. If you brought civvies, you are encouraged to wear them because most of you will be wearing them on this mission. Get used to them now. Also learn to recognize each other without uniforms and emblems of rank showing. That also includes recognizing the Marines and they you. You will be encouraged to NOT use titles in the field. Military-related nick-names are also not acceptable. Get used to that now and quickly. Your officers and sergeants are aware of this – good only for this mission.

"If any of you are really familiar with downtown D.C., we need to speak with you after the training sessions tomorrow. And we really need to pick your brains if you are really familiar with the areas around The Mall – not a shopping mall, but the grass mall between the Capitol Building and the Lincoln Memorial. And since The Old Guard is frequently involved with ceremonies on the grounds of The White House, we need to definitely talk to you if you have been inside the fence surrounding The White House. You get an extra beer for that little talk.

"One thing to remember is that we are deadly serious here. Why? Because the aggressors are planning to be deadly, too.

"Normally, I would take questions at this point, but I am going to direct you to your chains of command so they can familiarize you with your roles during this mission. Thank-you one and all. See you at 06:00 tomorrow for chow. Good night."

And Smitty turned and walked out. All soldiers and Marines gathered closer to the tables. At this point, they took the message about no uniform and no rank to heart. They asked questions and

Order of Succession

didn't mind if somebody from another company, or even another service for that matter, thought they had answers. They rapidly understood there was no handbook for this assignment, and it was their personal responsibility to understand it and get it done right. The discussions continued for another 90 minutes.

Time: Tuesday, 07-August, 06:00 EDT (Mess Hall, Quantico, VA)

Smitty (at the front of the room): "Your platoon commanders gave me lists of questions. I will sort them while you are chowing-down and then answer the more important ones beginning at 06:30. Enjoy breakfast."

Promptly at 06:30, Smitty called for silence and began answering questions and continued until 07:30, when he announced an end. "You all have good questions; we will see if we can include some specifics in the training. For now, get more fluids and go to the head – sorry, go to the latrine for some of you. They're both behind the same door so you won't get lost. Your instructors from the FBI and CQB will be here in 20 to pick you up. Be ready."

ORDER OF SUCCESSION

41 – Moving to New TDY Quarters

Around 06:20, Sunday, 19-August: Quantico Mess Hall

TIME: 06:25 EDT

Smitty: "May I have your attention please? Today is your last day here. We hope you have begun to understand how an aggressor in a Close-Quarter-Battle environment thinks. By the same token, now that you know what to look for, we believe each of you will also look at other tourists on The Mall in a different light. We fully understand this is a big burden to place upon you. We firmly believe that you will be our excellent eyes and ears on the street for us.

"For the next two weeks, your assignments are to walk and wander around downtown D.C. getting familiar with your company's or platoon's assigned area of responsibility. Your Captains and Sergeants will fill you in about the exact boundaries of that area. The same areas will be patrolled by both Army and Marines in the same foot patrol squad to avoid complaints of favoritism, if you catch my drift. Whether you are Army or Marine, your chain of command is through the sergeant in charge of that squad – regardless if he is Army or Marine. Fully integrated. Got that?

"We also are ordering you not to get together with your buddies back at The Old Guard for obvious reasons. Also, that order includes no calling, texting, e-mailing them, etc. until you are permanently released from this assignment. In order to make it easier for you to do that, we have arranged for hotel rooms for you around the area. And shuttle buses to take you to and from The Mall area.

"Because you will not be living on-post, we understand that you will need to spend money at least to eat. You will each be issued one credit-type of card to cover your usual per-diem expenses. Don't lose it, and don't over-use it. And they all must be returned at the end of the assignment.

Order of Succession

The rooms are taken care of on a different, special account. If anyone asks about the arrangements, you are on a special-study field-trip sponsored by a university in upper New York State to study government in action in real-life. Keep in mind that New York is also the home of West Point, but you are not from The Point. This will be covered when you are issued your cards. Also please keep the receipts of all your purchases.

"If our collective intel is correct, the bad-guys will need to create at least one diversion in an effort to keep people's mind off what will really be going on around them in real time. One type is the probability they could disrupt cell-phone service. So, we are also providing you with special radios that look a great deal like cell-phones; however, these operate on a separate, private, secure network. The bad-guys may also use more than one diversion to keep the civilian population unbalanced. Well, at least, that's a tactic we might consider doing. We have already pre-programmed the radios with the numbers of all of your teams' members, basically, everybody in this room. Plus a few of the buttons that are for emergencies in red. For example: Our air support is shown as 'Helo' and Mall support is 'Monuments'. These will be monitored 24/7 for the duration. Don't mess with them unless you really need or see something that is extremely out of the ordinary or very important. So, you had better know who's who and their names, too. And, of course, these phones – sorry, make that radios – must also be returned.

"The rest of today is a travel day for you up to D.C. to your temporary quarters. Tomorrow, your assignment begins for real. And keep your uniforms in your locked duffle bags; we do not need to have nosey housekeepers poking around and finding anything that doesn't track with your cover story.

"Your officers and sergeants have all of the details. Thank-you for attending these classes. Everything will work-out okay because of your assistance Your assignments are ready for you at those tables over there. And one final order: You all are one team. For the purposes of this assignment, you are neither Army nor Marine; you are one joint, cohesive unit. Consider any officer or sergeant as one of your own. Listen-up to them; they may have insight or orders from your temporary chain of command. You must understand that if anything happens in your assigned territory and you must contact the nearest in your chain. Count on it. Your transportation leaves in 90 minutes. Thank-you again."

Order of Succession

Time: Sunday, 19-August, 08:05 EDT (Mess Hall, Quantico, VA)

Smitty and the officers, Gunnies, and Platoon Sergeants gathered one last time for one last meeting and any last questions. After all were satisfied that everybody knew what was going-on and how to deal with situations, they left for their transportation. Except for Rhodes, Phillip, Brian, Cornell, and the two Platoon Sergeants. Smitty informed these men that they now formed the primary cadre for the duration of the operation. There was still additional ground to cover. And besides, there were two separate vans to transport them to their quarters in the D.C. area – quarters not with their soldiers and Marines.

Smitty: "Platoon Sergeant Emery Colman from B Company and Platoon Sergeant Harlan Crandall from D Company, I've read your service records. This is why I want you in our inner circle. Sing-out if anything I read is incorrect. You both have CQB experience under live fire in either Iraq and/or Afghanistan, and you both have Top Secret clearances, right? (Both confirmed with a nod.) I've seen the records of both of your Captains; neither have your experiences? To the best of your knowledge, is that correct? (Again, both nodded yes.) This is another reason we need your experience. We are going to rely on you to guide your Captains to get the results we may very well need in the next two weeks.

Right now we – that includes all of the rest of this cadre team – are going to read you into the rest of what happened a little over two months ago out at the Buckman Springs Rest Area along I-8 out in the Mojave Desert plus the follow-up discoveries in the last month. This information has neither been distributed to your official chain of command, nor to most in the U.S. government because, quite bluntly, we do not know who's on which side.

"Platoon Sergeant Colman, your Captain, Captain Calhoun, is among those we do not know enough about because of his relationship certain Lieutenant General Hamilton Calhoun, whom we determined in the past few days is his father – about whom we have some doubts. I am not saying he is a good-guy or a bad-guy; we just do not know which side of the fence your Captain is on right now. For that reason, I am asking if you want to remain in this inner team here or if you want to walk out now. It's your choice, but we gotta know right now. What's your decision Platoon Sergeant Emery Colman?"

Order of Succession

Colman: "What a download that is. (He sat silently for ten seconds.) Okay, I'm in it for this here team, now. Let's get on with it."

Smitty: "I thought so. (Turning to the rest of the team.) Bring them up to speed as fast as you can. We have this mess hall for the rest of the morning. I'll get the coffee and snacks."

So, for the next three hours, the newest members of the inner circle were told everything that happened out in the desert. Smitty brought them up to speed on the bunker, the heliport in D.C., and what Forts McNair and Myer were going to be used for.

Before the meeting finally ended, Phillip and Brian asked both if they had any experience with CQB using choppers. Both nodded and said, "A little." Phillip invited them over to the hangar for some brainstorming and a briefing about what they may have to coordinate on the ground.

Smitty: "When you get up to D.C., get settled-in quickly; our walk-arounds begin tomorrow around 09:15. We waited to make sure that you both were willing to work this assignment before telling you that, although Cap'n Rhodes here has been given the overall responsibility, he still has a back-up in command, his Colonel, a Colonel Michael Gahagen, also out of Pendleton. Colonel Gahagen has also been out at the Rest Area, but not in the same capacity as Cap'n Rhodes. Our arrangement is that Colonel Gahagen will be here primarily as an observer – unless all hell-breaks-loose and we need higher brass on the ground immediately. The Captain's Marines have already been advised that any of the Sergeants in this room, whether Army or Marine, also has decision-making ability and will be obeyed. Basically, we did not want to freeze you out. And then the situation with Cap'n Calhoun just popped-up. So, our counter to that was to sort of freeze-out both Army Captains until we get a warm feeling about one or both. Do you understand how this boiled-down, because we, as a multi-service team, need to have your cooperation?"

Both Platoon Sergeants agreed – up to a limit – that they are still responsible to their own Captains, and nothing was really worthwhile getting crosswise with them. Also, both thought the concerns about Captain Calhoun were unfounded.

Smitty: "So noted. Please keep this under your hats until we get this ironed-out. Thanks again."

Order of Succession

42 – Getting' the Skinny in D.C.

Around 07:30, Monday, 20-August: D.C. Hotel Coffee Shop

TIME: MONDAY, 20-AUGUST, 07:32 EDT (D.C., hotel coffee shop)

Smitty (still wearing a beard, his floppy hat, sunglasses, and somewhat-used-looking clothes: "Good morning to y'all. I thought I would be the early one, but I can see nobody sleeps late around here. Emery and Harlan (deliberately not using ranks), I brought these for you to wear to keep the sun out of your eyes. (As he laid some sunglasses and floppy hats on the table). We need to look at a few spots that will fall directly into your area of expertise. Let me get a cup of coffee and we can look at these maps I brought along; they're touristy types as part of our roles."

Bringing his cup back to the table, Smitty continued: "I marked some lines-of-sight on them, particularly this one. It's this one that we are most concerned with. (He traced it with his index finger on the map to show where it was in a satellite perspective, but not in real life.) This is our primary route this morning; this and the other one that falls directly under the longer one. (As a couple of nearby tables filled with guests, the subject changed.) Say, how about the game last night, huh? Don't that homer in the top of the 9th beat all? Well, shall we get movin' here?"

Time: Monday, 20-August, 09:25 EDT (Near the south side of The Mall)

Smitty: "I think we should work our way around the Tidal Basin to look at the objective from the furthest possible/probable launch site first. That way you can visualize what the bad-guys might see if this fits into their plan. This may take a slight change of perspective if you're used to The Mall as a nice place to be on a weekend instead of what it might be in ten days or so."

Order of Succession

They made small talk as they walked past the Bureau of Engraving and Printing on 15th Street SW and skirted the Tidal Basin.

They approached the steps of the Jefferson Memorial and climbed them and played tourist by going inside and reading the inside walls while they circled the statue. On their way out, they paused on the eastern side of the steps of the extremely broad staircase.

Smitty spoke (in a hushed voice): "Check-out the view toward TWH right over there. You can see it clearly. And THAT is the problem. If we can see it, a missile can, too. This is what I believe we need to be concerned about. Roger?"

Emery: "Sonvabitch, now I wish you had not pointed this out. I've been here for almost two years and never saw it with this in mind – even though I was looking straight at it. I roger your concern big time."

Harlan said much the same, but added: "Where's this second problem area you said was right near this one?"

Smitty: "You're lookin' at it right now. What you don't see is that it is much closer to the target. Check the map about half way. Let's walk this route in reverse, but this time, with recon in mind."

So, off they went, down the steps, retracing their path around the Tidal Basin in reverse. This time, the maps beckoned them back to the straight line drawn on them. Smitty guided them to the Maine Avenue spot that was his next biggest concern.

Smitty: "If you stand right here (pointing to an approximate spot), you should be able to see both TWH in front of us and the Jefferson Memorial behind us. As you can see, these lines-of sight overlay each other for one hell of an opportunity for the right kind of aggressors. This is what I, sorry, make that we, would like for you to figure-out how to take both these spots out of their equation. We need some fresh eyes on it and some creative new ideas. Give it a coupla days of playing like cops-and-robbers, and let me know what you think."

They finished back on The Mall looking at another sketch highlighting where the *Armed Forces Show* was going to be laid out on the grass and surrounding streets. "Give this a going-over to see what the risks might be. And last, but maybe even more important, if you were on the other side, how might you take down TWH? What would you use and how would you apply it. Look at it this way, this upcoming show on this here Mall probably brings all of the necessary equipment you might ever need right here to the very site. Within a stone's throw of the intended target."

Harlan: "What do ya say we find a bench in the shade facing TWH?" So, the search was on until they spotted one on the other side of The Mall. "We might be able to solve both of the Jefferson / Maine Avenue problems. It's way too late to plant grown trees to make an instant forest, but how about something like a temporary barrier by the trees, like maybe a giant screen showing the Armed Forces goodwill or something. Otherwise Emery and I will have to keep a rotating platoon wandering that area. You know, keeping road maintenance work postponed and out of the area temporarily and no work at Jefferson that requires trucks on the Tidal Basin side."

Emery: "I think we now understand why the trip down to Quantico was called for. But, I also think that probably the only way to take-out TWH is by air, that is, with an aerial assault. I mean why would somebody do a full frontal ground assault during the show. But wait a sec. That would almost be the ideal time to do it. All of the hardware is already here – the weapon-systems, all of it, except the ammunition, presumably. Nah, wait; I still prefer helicopters. Definitely, not a ground assault"

Smitty: "Okay, assuming that they use choppers, how would you use them? Okay, Harlan, how would you defend against Emery? These are the situations we are probably facing. Let's get together in about three days, shall we? How about this Thursday, same bench at, say 13:30?"

Emery: "Roger. That ought to give us enough time to plot how we would do it and see if they are doable."

Time: Thursday, 23-August, 13:03 EDT (Walking on the south side of The Mall)

Smitty's phone rings just as he opens a water bottle. "Terry, here."

Platoon Sergeant Colman, "Tony? I was calling for . . . I forgot. Yeah, Terry, our hotel is letting us use their breakfast room. Come on over; we have some maps that'll show you what we dreamed-up. Hope you don't mind the change."

ORDER OF SUCCESSION

Smitty: "Not a problem. Mind if I bring a coupla pilots?"

Colman: "Not at all; the more thinkers the better."

Time: Thursday, 23-August, 13:42 EDT (Hotel breakfast room, closed doors)

Colman: "Welcome, Terry, Phillip, and Brian. Glad you're all here. Harlan and I spent a few hours shooting the breeze and scribbling about this task, and we came up with these ideas. Now we need a sanity check, if you know what I mean."

Phillip: "Can't have too many ideas here, we're anxious to see whatcha got. Oh, just FYI, we've been working with some of the local FAA folks who hooked us up with their local TRACON and the tower over at Reagan National. We think we have an arrangement for some special treatment for helicopters during the *Armed Forces Show* so we can demonstrate some helo maneuvers over The Mall. We're hoping that will cover some of our activities and patterns. We also devised an emergency call-sign for Andrews Tower, Reagan National Tower, and the local TRACON – just in case something goes terribly wrong down near The Mall. The call-sign we chose may sound hokey, but we think '*Buckman Jacumba*' is highly unlikely to be confused with anything else. Notify one of us, and we will call it in. In theory, they will shut down all other air traffic so we can have 'cleared airspace'. Here's a list of our regular call-signs and the emergency one. If you hear the later on your radios, you will know there's gonna be some crap-hitting-the-fan damn close to you and/or TWH real soon. Keep those secure. Didn't want to steal your thunder, but thought maybe I could help with some more background info."

Colman: "We don't know just yet; let's see how yours fits with ours. Okay, Harlan, unroll the maps and let's find-out if the pieces fit together – or if we're even in the same ballpark playing the same game.

"Harlan and I both agree that the most logical, at least to us, is to use one or more, choppers. But the way to use them effectively, in this city, evaded us for a while until we walked the same streets and areas and our troops are also walking around. Then, we think the lights came-on. We noticed the methods the police and fire departments respond use to various sites. We decided to start by taking them out of the equation so they wouldn't be available to respond en-masse to our primary target, TWH. We marked TWH with big red dot just so we can find it quickly on the map.

"Then we would create two diversions if we had limited resources. And, three if we had a few more resources; the third diversion is added to the first two. Now, about the first diversion, look at the blue lines over in this area to the north and east of TWH. We wanted this diversion to require both police and fire responses over a wide front, like along a couple blocks of one street. Not to create mass destruction, but enough to pull response personnel into an area and sort of get them stuck there for an hour or more. Here's how we might do this one. Harlan, pass out those news clippings and see what they think. These clippings happened in real life in D.C., so we just copied them along maybe two blocks of this street here. It's a major street for traffic in and out of this area, so if we get it bottled-up . . . well, use your imagination if it is done at the right time of day – like maybe afternoon rush-hour on a Friday. Okay, that's the first one, directing attention and resources over there and bottling them up in place.

"Now for the second one, we resorted to a 'brute force' diversion – these orange lines over here south and west of TWH. We figure this one will put the city into a shut-down for the rest of the day. This diversion, literally takes this area out of the picture for quite a while because there are no alternate routes in or out. (As he drew his finger across the diversion's intended target). The police will be grid-locked for a long time because they won't be able to move their squad-cars either, so those officers are sort of frozen in-place. Without flames, chances are good the fire department won't respond immediately, but if we add some flames and smoke, you know they will try to respond, just to be on the safe side. They will also be grid-locked in-place. Sure it might be destructive, but we think it would be damn effective and real fast to implement, too.

"Along with whichever diversion is first or if there's only one, we would include some cell-phone jammers just to raise the public's anxiety level. We don't, however, think the jammers would be really necessary for two diversions because civilians will jam their own cell networks by trying to make lots of calls themselves. And note, that depending whichever diversion is done first, it sort of drives people toward the other one, and they both become grid-locked by traffic.

Order of Succession

"The third diversion would be over here to the north where we placed some green lines. This area is not as sensitive as the other two, and it can be avoided if you want to drive the back-streets. But if you get enough traffic of drivers wanting to get out, why, you effectively grid-lock this area, too. And with grid-locked police and other emergency response vehicles, the city is literally shut-down – nobody can respond to anything in these areas. Now, we need that sanity check."

Smitty: "Wow! You boys put some thought into this. I like your thinking and the results."

Colman: "Thanks. Harlan and I walked all three areas and dug-up roughly the quantity of vehicles and the times when the most traffic tries to squeeze through these funnels. Our best guess is that the evening rush hour would probably be the worst for tying-up traffic to grid-lock the area around TWH. I know, who would have ever thought that, huh!! We think the blue and orange areas would probably cause the most fear and panic for commuters. There are available side and back roads that could bypass the green area; but they would become clogged after all of the Internet and GPS units begin advising commuters where the closest alternate route is. Everybody makes a bee-line for them, and, bam, they're jammed too – especially, if the orange diversion has been activated in the destructive manner we dreamed-up.

"We also came-up with some thoughts about the aggressors' chopper, too. We think . . . Harlan, why don't you describe this?"

Platoon Sergeant Crandall: "Roger. Here's what we thought might be effective for their chopper. (He laid some pictures on the table.) If their chopper were disguised like a relatively neutral entity or company, such as one of these in the pictures, most people would not recognize it as an immediate threat and wouldn't give it a second look. The pilot could use air-space to look like it's going about its normal business until it's close enough to change roles to aggressor. "If they use the right armament, it could probably destroy TWH almost within five minutes or so."

Phillip: "You guys ever eavesdrop on a conversation about a month and a half ago? Terry, if two independent groups come-up with the same plan, that's 100%, and we probably have a winner with it, dontcha think? Harlan, you guys got anything else about this chopper brainstorm you wanna share?"

Order of Succession

Harlan: "Well, yeah, sorta. We also think the bad-guys would not want to fly a still disguised, chopper around for several days if it was fully-armed. I mean, like what if something happened and it crashed; there'd be an awful lot of questions. So, we think their weapons systems will be pre-installed and then loaded roughly the same day they plan to attack. Look at the map again. We marked some places where a disguised chopper could land or be staged and armed at the last minute; look for red circles. We eliminated the military facilities for the obvious reason of too many eyes not in on the plot. But there are quite a few heliports around this town, including some on roofs like at hospitals. We just marked those within maybe 15 or 20 miles of TWH for a really fast assault run. Running low or high, fast, and lookin' like it belongs there, who's gonna second guess its purpose until, well, until it's too late to defend against it. Just some more food for thought."

This had turned-out better than Terry hoped for. The room turned silent. While the pilots and sergeants gathered into a small cluster and discussed each diversion and circle for why this and not that, Terry left the room to gather some coffee and bottled water. This had gone a lot better than planned.

Time: Friday, 24-August, 07:13 (Hotel breakfast room)

Smitty spent the rest of yesterday with the map the sergeants had drawn-up. He walked the diversion areas, visualizing how commuters would react to these diversions and how the police and fire departments might respond – if they could even get to them, and then could they get out again. Not too easily at all; all of them were stuck in there along with all of the civilians, too. He liked what he saw; Emery and Harlan had done a good job – no, make that a great job.

Smitty: "Thank-you all for coming to this status meeting. I've got some notes and areas to have your troops pay special attention to (as he passed-out some smaller, marked-up maps and notes stapled together.) Because the start of the *Armed Forces Show* is fast approaching, please have them report anything that looks out of the ordinary, and I mean ANYTHING that looks different than the last time they walked the area. Things like street work – like down on Maine Avenue – utility work and barricades, digging-up the streets, stuff like that. Maybe new scaffolding on the outside of a building, or a crane that wasn't there yesterday. ANYTHING and EVERYTHING that looks different."

Order of Succession
43 – Night Maneuvers

Around 21:06, Wednesday, 29-August: Hotel Coffee Shop

TIME: 21:06 EDT

Smitty's cell-phone rang. The caller ID showed the number for Larry the sat-op tech.

Smitty: "Larry, whatcha got?"

Larry: "Well, you know how you, Andy, and I were working on a glider, one of those 'you can't see them types? Well, every once in a while I used to check the site, that jump-off point not too far from Camp David. Never saw any activity until this evening. In theory, that place is supposed to be closed-down near dusk; but this evening looks like the same guys are assembling a glider. I got a hold of Andy, the radar guy for Camp David, and he's ready to go looking if you are."

Smitty: "I tell you what, let me conference you with a coupla guys who might be able to shed some light on the situation if they can get there in time. Is that okay?"

Larry: "I just came-on duty, so go for it. I'll wait for ya."

Smitty: "Will do. Be right back."

Smitty called Phillip on another phone and explained the situation. Fortunately, Phillip and Brian were still trying to get the lay-of-the-land by running some night exercises sorta northwest of D.C., and, luckily, just a bit north of the Frederick airport area. Camp David was a ways away, but they were willing to try to make it in time before the glider disappeared. Conference away.

Smitty: "Larry, here's Phillip. He's enroute to the Camp David area now. Tell him what you got and let's see if he can help us."

Larry and Phillip exchanged coordinates of the sites in question. They headed north, following U.S. 15. Thurmont soon appeared under the chopper, so High Rock and Camp David weren't that much further. Now, all Phillip had to do was locate the landmark he was planning to use to navigate cross-country – the lighted tower up near Mount Saint Mary's University – and turn almost due west to the jump-off point.

Time: Wednesday, 29-August, 21:28 EDT (Hotel Coffee Shop)

Larry: "Ghost-1, Andy, and Terry are on here, too. I think we have you. You're a little late; the glider jumped-off already. Andy's gonna give you some coordinates he's been tracking. We would like to see if you can find it. I mean, well you know, to see if we got its radar profile right."

Ghost-1: "Heading for the new coordinates. We're goin' cross-country and don't have to follow the updrafts. Be there in less than a minute." "Okay, Andy, assuming you can see the glider and us, where is it in relation to us?"

Andy: "You should be almost right on top of him. He's a little to your left, looks like, he's trying to follow the contour of the hillside. Say, you got any access to tunable radar? I'll send you the freqs to set it to, if you can use that.

Ghost-1: "Send away." About 15 seconds later: "Got them. We are dialing the freqs now." About another 15 seconds: "Is his profile supposed to look like, what would you call it, a 'disturbance'?"

Andy: "Bingo! You must be looking at the same thing I am."

Phillip tried to slide in right behind the target without flying into it. As a precaution, Phillip tried using the FLIR unit to see if the glider could be picked-up using that. No luck; the FLIR is out for now. He told Brian to get the camera and the Nightsun® ready. When he was sure that he was as close as he should get above and behind the glider, he told Brian to turn on the light and see what they had. The whole operation was nearing the outer boundary of Camp David.

The glider was instantly visible – all black; the pilot was startled as all get-out, to say the least. The glider's next maneuver was evasive, trying to escape the light. Sorry, no such luck. So, its pilot attempted to find an open area to land it without capture. His final effort was trying to fly it back over some hills toward the Sabillasville School across Highway 550 from Smitty's produce stand.

Order of Succession

Ghost-1: "Larry, Andy, did you get all of that? At least, you now know what that radar profile looks like. If you didn't hear us, the FLIR unit could not detect it. Say, if either of you have contact with Camp David security, call and let them know where to look for their intruder. And make sure they take possession of the glider, too. Thank-you for the entertainment tonight; we really enjoyed it. Out."

Time: Wednesday, 29-August, 22:15 EDT (Hotel Coffee Shop)

Smitty had monitored the entire engagement. When it ended, he placed a coupla calls to contacts he knew he could trust. Basically, he told them that this would be an ideal time for the President to be 'out of town' for about a week or so. If nothing else, try running an 'evacuation drill' for TWH personnel, President included. Schedule it near the very end of the Armed Forces Show on The Mall. Do not take him to Camp David; we know it is vulnerable or already compromised. How about taking him up to Site R instead? Say, would it be possible to take the entire Cabinet with him to Site R for say a long weekend, too?

ORDER OF SUCCESSION
44 – A Helluva Party Boat

Around 20:20, Wednesday, 29-August: Pentagon Lagoon Yacht Basin

TIME: Wednesday, 29-August, 20:21 EDT

The crew of the 30-foot craft, *In The Open*, untied its mooring lines and noisily boarded. They had been busy taking 'party' supplies on-board all day. They told the owners of neighboring boats they were getting ready for a moonlight cruise down the Potomac to around Fort Washington Park, maybe as far as Indian Head. Going all the way down to the Chesapeake Bay would take too much time and burn too much fuel. Just a moonlight 'party-boat' fishing cruise for a group of buddies; that's all.

After navigating out onto the Potomac and turning south, the crew set out fishing poles and cooler chests and then quickly readied the supplies for their real tasks. The cruiser slowed to drifting speed as it began its journey under the 14th Street Bridges (actually, two bridges and a separate train trestle). The *In The Open* began the passage, but the *Under Your Nose* exited from under the bridges. Not only was the name changed, but so were the registration numbers. The hull had been disguised by adding 'slip-on' fake ladders and 'stick-on' porthole cut-outs. Different colored stripes were added to the cabin. As the *Under Your Nose* passed Reagan National Airport, it turned to port and headed for Haines Point, where it turned around again and headed back up the Potomac.

The *Under Your Nose* slowed again and dropped anchor under the railroad trestle. Two SCUBA divers silently slipped into the water and swam to the nearest concrete pier on the starboard side and dived below the surface. Then they swam over to several bridge piers on the port side of the boat.

The *Under Your Nose* moved up-river to the 14th Street Bridge, where the same procedure took place again. Only at this bridge, four divers were in the water. They also worked their way sideways, starboard

Order of Succession

to port (east to west) across the river, as well as staggering the bridge piers they visited. They did this under both spans of the bridge.

After the divers were finished with their work, the *Under Your Nose* drifted back under the bridges and reemerged again as the *In The Open* once again, continuing its journey back up-stream to its home dock.

By the time it returned to its slip in the Yacht Basin, the crew had eaten all the food and consumed all of the beverages on-board. As proof of their hard partying, the crew left stacks of empties, pizza boxes, and other garbage near the dumpsters, being extra careful to leave some litter along the slips.

Part 4 –
The Game Begins; Place Your Bets

Order of Succession
45 – Act I – The Show Begins

Around 05:06, Friday, 31-August: (On The Mall)

TIME: 05:10 EDT

Despite being dog-tired from researching the most likely scenarios, the wear and tear of the pressure continued to build. Smitty's adrenalin level must have been rising because he couldn't sleep as much or as well at night any more. He decided it was a great time to go down to The Mall to see how the show was coming together. All of the displays by all the branches of the Armed Forces were assembled during the last two days to be ready for the scheduled 11:00 opening to the public. Nothing like breakfast among tanks and tents, cannons and cooks, aircraft and anti-aircraft weapons, weapons, and widgets and missiles. He quickly cruised up and down the branches, aisles, roped-off areas just checking if anything was out of the ordinary. As requested, all of the gear that shoots anything was pointing south – away from TWH.

Smitty also noted that, for this show, the Army and Navy were also going to invite the public to share '*Mess Hall Meals*' and '*Galley Chow*' to be served in large tents. They were even anticipating having to take reservations.

Everything looked like it was it should – like everything belonged; which was just another reason for him to worry. Like it belonged there – both a relief and a threat.

Time: Friday, 31-August, 09:25 EDT (Hotel breakfast room)

The show was scheduled to open to the public at 11:00 this morning. This was the last scheduled meeting of Smitty and the other officers and sergeants before the official opening. There was nothing else they could think of or plan for now. Collectively, the next ten days will record how their fellow citizens will talk about them for the rest of their lives. History is truly written by the victors, and it is a cruel master.

ORDER OF SUCCESSION

Smitty told the meeting that they all exceeded his expectations and that their efforts were greatly appreciated. "Now is the time to be especially observant especially around those areas that were identified as possible diversion and traffic-choke sites. If anything looks out of place, call somebody to check it out along with you. I think now would be a good time for the officers and sergeants to be dressed in uniform for the duration of this show. If push comes to shove, the uniform speaks with more authority than civvies – if you catch my drift here.

"Above all, do not become distracted and lose sight of the bigger picture. In advance, I need to thank-you for your upcoming efforts. Pass that on to your troops, too. Keep your ears and eyes open."

Time: Friday, 07-September, 10:09 EDT (Sitting on a bench on The Mall)

Smitty sat, thinking how fortunate the entire team was. Here it is the eighth day, and nothing had happened during the first seven days; like nada and zilch. However, with only three days remaining and the show winding down if the bad-guys don't do something very soon, they are going to lose the advantage of having lots of commuters in town.

{Smitty's inquisitorial brain: "You sure this was a good idea? I mean all the way from talking to the guys on the POTUS phone to getting the military to jump through your hoops? And how about all those EMs working under aliases, and you expecting them to keep quite? Boy, you really must think you're something else – an untouchable – huh? Well, if this works out the way you thought, all you guys are gonna be heroes, huh? And if it doesn't work out that way, well, you're gonna be recorded as one of the biggest hoaxers ever. And those troops you got involved, well, they are really gonna have something to write in their autobiographies – and you know all of them are gonna have to write a book or two about their experiences even if it was only walking up and down the same twenty blocks of Constitution and Independence Avenues for two weeks with nothing to show for it except tired feet. Hell, they'll even be on all the news shows, talk shows, and morning shows, and do you know what's gonna be the topic du jour? You and your outsized sense that you knew all about this, that, and the other about how they were gonna remake the U.S. government from the inside out – only truly from the outside, but nobody else is gonna know that, are they? How'd I ever get hitched-up to you anyway? Hey,

Order of Succession

you still day-dreamin' while your radio's goin' off? Why dontcha pay attention to this mess you built, huh?"}

Time: Friday, 07-September, 10:15 EDT (Sitting on a bench on The Mall) Sure enough Smitty's radio was alerting him. *{Smitty mumbled: "Thanks. I almost zoned-out."}*

Terry: "Terry. Over."

Platoon Sergeant Harlan Crandall: "Terry, I don't know if this qualifies for any of your bad gut alarms, but there are two work trucks setting-up shop at both Maine Ave and Jefferson. Need somebody to check them-out and send them away any way they can. Over."

Terry: "What's your location? Over."

Crandall: "Jeff. Over."

Terry: "On my way. Passing by Maine Ave on the way. Get hold of Lambert and a vehicle. Meet me at Maine. Contact civvies and have them circle around truck at Jeff. Over."

Crandall: "Roger. Out."

Smitty took off at a fast jog, hoping to meet Lambert en-route. He must have been thinking way too loud because Cap'n Lambert pulled-up next to him at the next stop light. Smitty scrambled into the Humvee before it had even stopped rolling. Quickly, they decided to park near the Maine Avenue truck even if it meant blocking traffic. The parked work truck blocked the left lane of Maine Avenue exactly in a spot in line with TWH and Jefferson – not a good sign. The doors wore those magnetic signs identifying some road construction company from Virginia. But magnetic signs are easily made – and removed as needed.

Lambert: "Morning guys. What's going on here?"

One worker pointed to another guy with a clipboard, and as Lambert moved toward Clipboard, Smitty noticed the first guy fell-in lock-step behind Lambert, then followed by a second guy. At this point, Smitty got out of the Humvee and drew his pistol out of its holster – just in case. He also keyed his radio, "Harlan, watch-out at Jeff. Maine may be compromised already."

Order of Succession

Lambert to Clipboard: "Morning sir, I'm just checking on things about that *Armed Forces* show right over there on The Mall. We thought the D.C. Streets Department agreed not do any work in several areas for the duration of our show. This was one of the areas. So, I am just checking things out. You understand, right?"

The Clipboard guy became very agitated and began pointing to his work-orders on the clipboard. Lambert asked if he could look at the orders and maybe he could help straighten things out with D.C. Streets and everybody could get back to work. Clipboard guy wasn't gonna play nice; he wasn't planning to show the friggin' Army anything about his job; not one damn thing. Smitty advanced as silently as he could and said, "Does that mean you won't open the truck and let us look inside?"

Clipboard: "You're damn right about that. Get the hell outta here right friggin' now or I'll call your damn boss and have him tell you to get the hell outta here."

Smitty (making sure Clipboard and the other two saw his pistol out and in his hand): "I am gonna make this suggestion one time. Call your friggin' boss right now if you think it's gonna help. And while we wait for him, you hand the Captain there the keys to your truck very gently. Then all three of you guys sit on this curb right over here right now. And be quick about it. Cap'n, wait for me,"

Then he keyed the radio: "Harlan. Aggressive show over here. Read me the signs on the side of the truck over there. Over."

Sergeant Harlan read the signs. The same magnetic signs for the same company. Not looking too good.

Smitty: "Malibu Beach (Rhodes). Over."

Cap'n Rhodes: "Terry. Over."

Smitty: "If you got wheels, Guard Delta needs authority at Jeff. Right now. We may have a matching team at Maine Ave site. Very aggressive here. Over."

Rhodes: "Roger that. We're gone. Out."

Smitty returned his attention to Clipboard and cohort. "Hey, you with the Clipboard, get up and walk very slowly toward the truck and point-

Order of Succession

out which key opens the doors. Cap'n, remain to the side and make sure you are not in my line-of-fire. Roger?"

Lambert (drawing his own sidearm): "Roger that."

Smitty: "Clipboard, open the side door, and do not make any funny moves because too much lead is not a healthy diet. Got that? Answer me?"

Clipboard: "Yeah, I got that, but you're gonna be the one in a friggin' lot of trouble. Our boss doesn't like to be screwed with." Clipboard opened one of the doors just a bit and left it ajar. Smitty motioned him to open it all the way.

Clipboard: "I'm telling you, you're screwing with the wrong people. They're gonna screw you right back this afternoon. For damn sure, you're gonna wish you didn't screw with me."

Smitty: "Say, Clipboard, any one of your friends think a lot of people are 'piss-ants'? Huh?"

Clipboard swung around, his jaw slack in surprise. "How'd you know ... Oops." Big oops there, Clipboard buddy.

Smitty: "Don't worry about calling him to come over here and fix this screwed-up mess you're in. Ain't gonna do you one lick of good right about now, you 'piss-ant'. Ain't that 'bout what he'd say, piss-ant, right? Am I close? No never-mind now, your asses belong to me now. Cap'n, why dontcha open the door just a little bit wider so you can look inside. Just look, don't touch anything. Careful now; if it doesn't want to open easily, do not force it. Clipboard, go sit with your buddies and breathe the air while it's still free to you."

Lambert gingerly pulled the door open by its edge, not the handle. "Holy shit! Sure as hell, this ain't a road-work truck; there's a full-blown missile system in here. Now what?"

Smitty: "Cap'n make sure you don't touch anything when you close the door to the ajar position; we don't need the public to see this right now. You got your sidearm out; cover these two while I make some calls."

Lambert: "You got that. (Turning his attention to the so-called workers) Sit there with your hands in the open. Do not try anything that you will regret, or I may enjoy shooting you. Do you understand?"

Smitty: "Malibu Beach. Over."

Order of Succession

Rhodes: "Here. Whacha got? Over."

Smitty: "Bad-guys with missiles. More than one. Approach your guys with care and sidearms out. Think we will need EOD and Gahagen for muscle. Get Bravo Cap'n or not; your call. Over."

Rhodes: "Roger for most of that. No Bravo yet."

Smitty: "If any Gunnies or Platoon Sergeants are armed, call 'em and send two my way. Over."

Rhodes: "All armed. Two your way. There in 5. Out."

True to Rocky's word, Gunny Johnson and Platoon Sergeant Colman appeared in 4:34 and parked their HUMVEE on the grassy divider island, with sidearms drawn. Lambert opened the truck door for them and then cautiously closed it again. The Platoon Sergeant called some MPs from MDW and requested enough transportation for the three bad-guys here and four more at Jefferson – all in separate cars with two MPs each as guards. And hand-cuffs and leg-restraints and no sirens or lights. Within two minutes, Sergeant Winthrop (EOD) appeared, looked the truck over, and called-in some missile specialists, who fortunately just happened to be down on The Mall supporting the show.

Smitty told the sergeants that he and Cap'n Lambert were going to Jefferson and that Colonel Gahagen was on his way to both sites. And that Cap'n Calhoun had not been officially informed yet. And off they went to Jefferson with Lambert at the wheel.

(En route) Lambert: "What was that about Duane? Didn't you tell him?"

Smitty: "Sorry, sir, right now, that's on a need-to-know basis. And you may not tell him anything about that yet either. Understood?"

Lambert (with a quizzical look): "Yeah, I guess so, but I don't like that at all."

Smitty: "Understood." He keyed the radio: "Malibu. Status? Over."

Rhodes: "We have workers isolated, but truck not opened yet. Over."

Smitty: "Wait before opening truck. Wait for EOD Sgt to get there. Let him open it and call for specialists. Over."

Rhodes: "Roger. Colonel just showed-up. Where first? Over."

Order of Succession

Smitty: "Platoon Sergeant called for MP transport for ours first; yours second. Colonel go to Maine Ave to see before gone. Over."

Rhodes: "He's on way. Out."

Smitty and Rhodes conferenced-in Phillip and Brian to ensure they were now aware of what happened over around the Jefferson and Maine sites. "Guys, if this was the beginning, the fat lady hasn't sung her aria yet. This opera ain't over yet. It's just getting' started! Phillip, Brian, I think your parts are coming-up before 16:00 because they can't let too many commuters get past their choke-points wherever they are. Are your helos working okay? Yeah, I know, sure they are, but please make sure. We'll include you in the meeting at hotel as soon as we get there. Thank-you for working this TDY assignment. It is really is important. Call you from there."

Basically, this meeting just brought everybody up to speed about this morning's capture of two teams equipped with missiles. It was decided that the walking teams should concentrate on diversion areas blue and orange beginning now. Change into uniforms as quickly as possible. And pray for the best outcome.

ORDER OF SUCCESSION

46 – Act II – Smoke and Poor Doug

Just past 14:20, Friday, 07-September: (Breakfast room at hotel)

TIME: 14:21 EDT

Smitty noticed his hands were trembling slightly and he felt a bit nauseated after this morning's captures. He took a short meal break in the hotel's coffee shop because he hadn't eaten since dinner last night. He sensed that the next twelve hours were going to be even worse.

{*Smitty's mocking brain: "Whadya mean sensed? You know it in your gut. You can feel it gnawing in there already. You know it's gonna be a real bitch of an afternoon. You can admit it; go ahead. You know it is. Besides, I can't tell anybody without you knowing about it. Suck it up. You and your team will come out okay. Trust me, will ya?"*}

Time: Friday, 07-September, 14:32 EDT (Hotel coffee shop)

Nothing in the menu looked like he couldn't live without it. He settled for a BLT sandwich along with a chef's salad, honey-mustard dressing, croutons, and coffee. Maybe that was it: no coffee since 5 o'clock this morning.

{*Smitty's brain in advising mode: "You know, you really do drink a lot of that stuff. Maybe you should cut back to just one pot instead of two. Some people are addicted to lots of things; yours is coffee. You know that dontcha? You need coffee, really need it."*}

{*Smitty, responding: "So what. I like the taste of coffee. Where's the food? Don't they know how important it is that I am up for this afternoon? Come on where's the damn food? Ah, here it is now; finally. It all looks so good; just what I needed."*}

{*Brain, advising again: "You gonna eat all of this? Man, there's a lot there. You sure about this? Go ahead make a pig of yourself."*}

351

Order of Succession

Time: Friday, 07-September, 14:52 EDT (Hotel coffee shop)

The radio came to life. "Terry. Bravo Guard here. Over."

{Smitty, preparing himself: "Oh, please, don't let this mean that I was right about this plot. Couldn't I have made this a mistake? It would be so much simpler if I were wrong. This isn't something a person really wants to be right about."}

Smitty: "Terry here. Over."

Colman: "Problems in Area Blue. Call me on lima-lima. Over."

Smitty: "Roger. Out."

{Smitty's puzzled brain: "Call by lima lima? What could be that important I have ta use a telephone? Oh, shit, I hope it really is that important.}

Smitty: "(Trying to sound relaxed) So, Emery, what's up. Why the telephone?"

Colman: "What's up are man-hole covers; they're flying all over the place. (Smitty immediately tensed-up again.) And there's fire – like real live flames – flowing down the gutters for three blocks so far. Parked cars are in flames. Some of the corner storm drains are also spouting flames. TV news crews just got here a coupla minutes ago. And, by the way, civilians complaining that nobody has any bars. A cell-jammer must be in use already."

Smitty: "Okay, now. Did you or anybody on your team see anything before the flames? Anything, like trucks with leaking tanks or hoses? Anything at all."

Colman: "I know I didn't see anything. I just turned the corner, and it was all in flames already. The police and fire department just showed-up. You can hear their sirens. They want everybody to evacuate the area. I'm being pushed toward a side street that isn't burning. What now?"

Smitty: "Your work up there is done. Notify your squads, and you all see if you can head over toward the orange area. Keep your eyes peeled along the way you go. Be careful; the game has just turned deadly serious. Call me when you get to wherever. Okay? Time to get your platoon into camo's right quick; we don't want to be confused with . . . well, with the bad-guys."

Colman: "Roger. I'm gone."

Order of Succession

Time: Friday, 07-September, 15:14 EDT (On way back to The Mall)

The radio intruded once again.

{Smitty's cynical brain: "That radio is sure busy; sounds like something bad is starting. Doesn't it ever shut off for a while? But how are you gonna finish eating? I know, I know, you're just too important to be eating now. All hell might be breaking loose and you don't want to be caught with food in your mouth; you might sound like you've been drinking or something. A real big shot now, huh? Why dontcha have 'your people' take care of this stuff? Oh, wait these are 'your people, aren't they?"}

Smitty: "Ghost-1, over."

Radio: "Ghost-1. Pick-up Air Lima Lima. Over."

Smitty: "Ghost-1. Roger. Out." And sure enough, as he finished the 't' in out, his secure cell rang.

Smitty (checking the caller's name display): "Phillip, what's up?"

Phillip: "I called on your cell because we don't know who is monitoring what. Be advised: Radio chatter on local police freq about gun-fire at that heliport over at Buzzard Point. Too far to drive under current conditions. Crew is prepping bird for flight. I'm gonna lift-off to check it out. Already advised Brian that this could be the beginning of what we were training for. He and crew are prepping his helo, too, but he's gonna stay on the ground 'til I observe."

Smitty: "Roger. Keep us advised."

Time: Friday, 07-September, 15:17 EDT (At Fort McNair)

Major Jenkins gets the clear-signal from the ground crew; he spools-up his helo and lifts into a hover.

{Brain: "Wish the hell we had more time to practice with these mod'ed weapons. Too late to moan about it now."}

He finessed the controls so that his helo already pointed up-river before he's even above the nearest building. Up and gone. He flips a coupla switches in the cockpit, and the status lights on the armament displays indicate "ARMED"

353

Order of Succession

Time: Friday, 07-September, 15:23 EDT (Above heliport)

There is a column of expanding smoke rising from the direction of the heliport. Jenkins is the first to arrive above the heliport only to realize the smoke is rising from all over the heliport and the nearby South Capitol Street Bridge. There is also more smoke rising further up-river toward the east; a quick check of the navigation charts shows another bridge in that general direction.

{Phillip's analyzing brain: "Looks like the shit is starting to hit the fan. Check the heliport first. Leave the new smoke for later. Gotta find a spot to land this helo. Get with it. NOW. Out."}

Instinct took over. Phillip keyed the radio, "Andrews Tower, Ghost-1."

Tower: "Ghost-1, go ahead."

Ghost-1: "I am on approach to Buzzard Point Heliport, trying to find an LZ. Advise D.C. Response Team that there appears to be a war-zone down there. Also there is smoke rising from the nearby bridge. Smoke up-river, too; my charts say it is near – *wait-one* while I look it up on my charts – I-695 or the Navy Yard. Will advise when on ground. Out."

Tower: "Roger. Will advise D.C. Police. Out."

Ghost-1: "Ghost-1 to Air Lima."

Smitty: "Air Lima here, over."

Ghost-1: "It's begun. Continue monitoring my transmissions. Advise Rocky and Army as needed. Out."

A quick glance at the Capitol Street Bridge told Phillip it had been attacked at least on the down-river side – the outbound lanes.

{Phillip's brain, still analyzing: "Wrong kind of smoke and flames. It was hit with a friggin' missile, wasn't it? Damn right it was. Find your LZ, dammit, right NOW. The prop-wash is spreading all the loose crap fast. Get your helo on the ground; find-out what happened here first. Get your ass on the ground."}

Ghost-1 (aloud): "What the hell hit this place? Where can I put this thing down? It'll fit over there on the other side of the hangar. That'll havta do." He was forced to land closer to the Anacostia River than he preferred; the rear rotor extended just a tad over the river and on a slight down-slope toward the river. Phillip shut the lift rotor down because he didn't want to suck any of the flying debris into his engine. Making sure he was wearing his sidearm with a full magazine, Phillip got out trying to find anybody who could tell him what happened and who did it. He was immediately hit by the stench of explosives – missile warhead explosives. Making his way around the rubble and used-to-be-a-chopper parts, he noticed the main gate from the access road was open and sorta hanging at weird angles – the wrong way for a missile attack from inside the heliport.

Finally, Phillip spotted somebody still walking – Officer Bernie, walking in a daze – and ran over to him.

Major: "Officer Bernie, isn't it? I was listening to the radio and heard something happened up here. What's going on?"

Officer Bernie (his speech quite 'shaky'): "Oh, yeah, you're the Major, aren't you? I recognize you and your uniform. Hell, it's not what's goin' on. It's more like what isn't going on. Man alive, what a mess this is! This chopper radios-in for an emergency landing about 14:45; says he's got engine trouble. So, we bring him in; right over there (motions with his arm just a little nearer than the Major's helo). He sets down, and then somebody in a truck rams his way through the front gate right over there. . . . Ya know, the one you came through a few weeks ago, that one. Well, anyway, they try to drive right over to the chopper with the engine trouble; you know, just like they were waitin' for it to be on the ground. Well, Doug runs-out of the office over there and tries to stop the truck. Well, they up and shoot him, not once, but it sounded like they emptied half a magazine into him. We gotta call in for an ambulance, but I think we'll havta call the coroner instead. Those damn bastards, why did they havta do that? I ask ya, why, huh? Doug was a real nice guy. Why?"

Phillip hadn't expected this, but in his mind it sorta fit with what he saw out at the rest-area. "Bernie, I'm sorry to hear about Doug. Yeah, he seemed like an awful nice guy. I'm sorry, but can we get back to the truck and chopper? Let's see if we can help catch whoever did this to Doug. Did you recognize anybody in either the truck or helicopter? Did you see what they did when the truck got over to the helicopter? Anything will help."

Officer Bernie (still visibly 'disconnected'): "Why did they havta do that? Okay, back on track for a little while, then I'm gonna sit down somewhere and cry. I didn't recognize anybody in the truck, but then again, I didn't see everybody's face; they were wearing masks, yeah, ski-masks. At least three of 'em. When they got over to the chopper, they

Order of Succession

backed-up right to the chopper's belly door, and real close, too. Three of 'em bailed-out of the truck and grabbed a lotta stuff outta the rear and pushed whatever it was into the chopper's belly door. When they finished-up, they slammed the door shut, got in, and drove outta here like the world was on fire. And they tried to pull as much of the damaged gate back into the hole they made. All that did was make it hard to get in or out. Did I tell you, the truck was a full-ton van, ya know like a workman's heavy-duty van. Only it was a full ton, not a half or a three-quarter ton. It had a weird license plate; something like US Government or something like that. But, that can't be right, can it? U.S. Government, and then they do something like this. Why?"

Phillip: "Was it white? And what about the people in the chopper? Did you recognize anyone? What did the chopper look like? What did the stuff look like; the stuff they handed over to the chopper crew?"

Office Bernie: "Yeah, the van was white, and it had this logo or sticker on it. I never saw anything alike it before, so I drew it so's I remember it later during the questioning. Here look at it; take a picture of it if that'll help catch those bastards. But you can't have it; I gotta save it for, you know, when I'm questioned."

Phillip took a picture of Bernie's sketch with his cell-phone. Bernie was right; indeed, it was a strange looking logo or maybe a parking sticker. That'll havta wait for later. "Thanks, Bernie. Anything special or different about the chopper? What about the chopper crew, did you recognize anybody? And the cargo; can you describe anything about it?"

Office Bernie: "Why, I ask you. Why'd they havta go and shoot Doug; he didn't hurt them none. Why? Oh, yeah, the chopper was painted-up up like a news helicopter; but I didn't recognize its station call sign. It wasn't any local station that I heard of; not even from Baltimore; nosiree. Where do ya think WTFU Channel 37 [29] is located? I took a picture of it with my cell-phone. Here, look. I can send it to ya if you want."

Phillip: "You bet I want that. Here's mine; transfer away." And tapping them together – done.

Officer Bernie: "Where was I? Oh yeah. The chopper pilot looked a good deal like one of the guys that came here before you guys did. What

---

29 Both 'WTFU' and 'Channel 37' were unassigned in the Washington, D.C. area at the time this book was written.

was his name now? I'd havta check the visitor log; I can't remember right now. Why did they do that?"

Phillip: "Bernie, here look at these guys on my phone. Is he one of these?"

Officer Bernie (paging through the photos): "Nope. Nope. Nope. Wait a minute, I think this guy coulda been the pilot. He was one of those guys in the register. And this next one; this guy was inside the belly door; I'd bet on that." Bernie picked-out Bubba and Ray.

Phillip: "Anything about the cargo that was handed into the chopper? Can you describe any of that stuff?"

Officer Bernie: "Lots of long, square-looking boxes. Maybe 15 or 20 boxes with snap fasteners on the tops. They sorta looked like large plastic map cases. And some smaller tubes. The larger boxes were about this size on the ends (gesturing with his hands); I didn't get a good look at the lengths. But they were covered by tarps. The small tubes were maybe this big around (again, gesturing with his hands like a small coffee can); but I don't know how long. Then they highballed it outta here like they were on fire. Right through the gate; did ya see what they did to that gate? That's all I remember. Oh, wait, there's more before I forget. When the chopper lifted-off, it faced down-river, then rotated left so he was broadside to up-river. And then fired a missile from the port side belly-door into the bridge. Then that bastard continued his rotation so his port-side was facin' us and fired another missile at us. That bastard; why did they have to shoot Doug?"

Sirens were approaching the area. Lotsa sirens were closing in on the heliport. The Major didn't need to get hung-up with the local police; not right now. Other things were a lot higher on his priority list; that's for damn sure.

Phillip: "Thank-you, Bernie. You have been a great help. You really have. I gotta go now."

Officer Bernie: "I gotta another clue for you. As they were unloading the stuff, one of the boxes fell and hit the pad; and part of an end-piece broke off. Wanna see it?"

Phillip: "You bet; how fast can we look at it?"

Order of Succession

Bernie ran over to the hangar with Phillip hot on his trail. Phillip took a picture of the box-end with what looked like a lot of alphanumeric strings of characters on it. But what really caught his attention was an odor on the inside surface of the end cap. An odor Phillip had smelled before on a container for a missile. Not a good sign. Now, he raced back to his helo and spooled-up the rotor. The sirens were now outside of what remained of the front gate as Phillip worked the controls and lifted-off with the nose already tilted down, heading up-river toward the smoking bridge before the first police car skidded to a halt right where his chopper had just been.

The nearest bridge had a huge hole where its outbound lanes used to be, taking the bridge completely out of service. Monday morning was going to be a commuters' nightmare. Following the river, Phillip was led right to the second bridge, I-695, which also took a missile strike to its outbound lanes.

{Phillip's stunned brain: "So far, two bridges out of service. It really has begun, hasn't it? And the afternoon is still young. Make your reports and get refueled; it might be a long evening.}

Phillip keyed his radio and advised Andrews Tower. This was quickly followed by a cell-phone call to "Air Lima" to advise about the scene over at Buzzard Point.

Air Lima: "What did-cha find."

Phillip: "Bad news. I believe they are now armed with missiles. The heliport was hit with a rocket as were two nearby bridges. None of these are in any of our color-coded diversion zones. The chopper is disguised as a news helicopter from an unknown TV station. I'm sending the picture. And worst news, they killed Doug over here. Guess who Officer Bernie thinks may be in the news chopper? Would you believe your buddies, Bubba and Ray. Brian and I are goin' big-game-hunting ASAP, live and hot."

Air Lima: "Be careful, but light 'em up if you havta. What can I do from here on The Mall?"

Phillip: "Get a hold of Rocky and the others. Advise them not to raise any weapons toward our helos because we will assume they are hostiles. Clear all the civilians off The Mall if you can; there may be a whole lotta crap fallin' from the skies real soon. He's got about

ORDER OF SUCCESSION

a 15 minutes lead on us, so we gotta figure out why he hasn't done anything else yet or where he could be waiting or hiding."

The Major, advised Brian, who was still waiting on the ground at Fort Myer, to spool-up and get his hunting license in order and that all his 'tagging' equipment was ready and hot. He also told Andrews Tower, Reagan National Tower, and the local TRACON to activate 'Buckman Jacumba' immediately. And to advise others on their emergency lists: "Clear-out all airspace above the Potomac, The Mall, and especially around TWH. Prepare yourselves; whatever you heard about lots of stuff happening on The Mall may about to become true." Phillip also sent the news-chopper's picture to all parties involved.

ORDER OF SUCCESSION

47 – Act III, Scene I – Forget Coming-In On Monday!

Not quite 16:00, Friday, 07-September: (Hunting on The Potomac)

TIME: 15:51 EDT

Major Jenkins thought the day was still too young and too little damage had been done at outlying targets – except for poor Doug. And TWH had not been touched yet. He presumed that skirmish at the heliport was just the opening shots. He headed back over to Fort McNair to top of his tanks before the real action and night arrived.

Time: Friday, 07-September, 16:01 EDT (On The Mall)

Smitty, sitting on a Mall bench, was just checking his watch when he heard an enormous, steadily-increasing growl approaching from the south side of The Mall – from the direction of the orange diversion area. Not only did he hear it, he also *felt* the earth beneath his feet *shudder* and keep *quivering* for several seconds. Instinctively, Smitty looked toward the orange area. South of The Mall, a rising wide plume of smoke and dust, like a volcanic cloud, rapidly grew taller, billowing outward and expanding, filling the evening sky above Washington's waterfront and the Potomac.

    Air Lima (on his radio): "Ghost-1. Over."

    Phillip: "Ghost-1. Over."

    Air Lima: "What was that explosion? Look over at the orange diversion area. What just happened over there?"

    Phillip: "Just departed McNair after top off. Best guess, I'd say their orange diversion was just activated. Remember the 14th Street bridges? Several spans of road-decking between piers are gone; there's nothing but air where the road used to be. Some of the piers are gone, too. Advise Rocky and everybody that we are really going hunting for bad-guys now. Out."

Order of Succession

Ghost-1's next radio call was to the Andrews Towers and the TRACON to verify *Backman Jacumba* had been activated to cease all outbound flights and divert all inbound and air-traffic away from Reagan National ASAP. All air traffic to and from Reagan should be grounded. As far as we are concerned, there should be only three helicopters in the air in the area – two Marines and one bad-guy. The Marines' transponders are already set to the pre-arranged signals. The Marines need to know where the third guy is or we will find it and bring it down one way or another. Out.

Time: Friday, 07-September, 16:02 EDT (On The Mall)

While he was talking to Phillip, Smitty's phone indicated a second call – from California, yet.

{Smitty's pre-occupied brain: "WTH is calling me right now. With all of the crap hitting the fan right now, who the hell thinks it's so damned important to talk right now. Your choice, ignore or answer. Whatcha gonna do? Com'n get with the program: ignore or answer; it can't be that hard; make a damn decision will ya?"}

Smitty (answer, it is): "Yo."

Caller: "Hard-Ass here. Is this Smitty?"

Smitty: "What's your rank and location?"

Hard-Ass: "Rank is Major at 29 Palms, Psych interrogation. Need to talk about the last four FBI agents. Smitty, zat you?"

Smitty: "Terry here. Sorry, Major, I didn't recognize your number, and we've been pretty busy back here in the last hour. Watch the news; it's started. What can I do for you?"

Hard-Ass: "Fire in the streets and some bridges blown-up, right?"

Smitty: "How the hell did you know? Is that crap on the news out there already? What else do ya know about?"

Hard-Ass: "Well about 15 minutes ago two of the fake agents became really antsy. They talked about being left out of all the action back there. And something about doing most of the recon, and then some other bastards are gonna get all the glory for bringin' the Newnited States into existence. They seem to be quite motivated right about now, sayin' by

Order of Succession

17:45 it'll all be over. So, what the hell's goin' on back there? And no I haven't seen or heard any reports about anything back there. Fill me in; I need some ammo when I talk to these guys again."

Smitty took all of 15 seconds to give the Major the highlights. "Sir, how'd you know about the street fires and bridges? We need all the info you can provide. Right now, Phillip and Brian are, how did he describe it, 'out huntin' big game'. They're out looking for a chopper disguised as a TV news chopper that's loaded with enough missiles to bring down not only TWH but probably just about everything for blocks around it. You got anything that can help us? Please say you do."

Hard-Ass: "Well, I might. Agent Phelps said 'RFK' one time. That doesn't mean anything to me right now; haven't had time to research it yet. What's her name, Daisy, gave me a real surprised look for about half a second when I mentioned RFK to her. And then she caught herself and went back to her usual blank stare. That's about all I got for you. I'll keep my ears and eyes peeled for both broadcast news and chatter among our guests. Give a call when you can."

Time: Friday, 07-September, 16:03 EDT (At the former 14th Street Bridge[s])

And, indeed, this area will really be a gigantic, lengthy diversion for an extended lengthy period of time – probably in the order of at least a year or two for a completely permanent replacement. All three bridges are completely out of service after losing at least six road-deck spans each between various piers. Plus, some of their supporting concrete columns, as well. The pattern of explosions was staggered across the three bridge roadways and dropped highway decking into the Potomac, extended completely across the river – just not in one continuous line of rubble. Basically, enough rubble for another entire bridge was dumped into the river – all of it underwater, especially the support columns. And all of the debris would have to be removed before new construction can begin. With three separate bridges down, moving the cranes and barges around will be a logistical nightmare – especially, for rebuilding the middle bridge.

The demolition's implementation dumped some cars into the Potomac River, unfortunately drowning some drivers and passengers. Other cars were left, high and dry – but stranded, on still-standing columns and spans with no way to get off except to jump into the river or wait for rescuers in

ORDER OF SUCCESSION

either boats or helicopters. This evening's rush hour immediately turned into a rush weekend; nothing moved, in southwest D.C., absolutely nothing. Monday morning would be a really big problem, too, because there were insufficient bridges to carry all the displaced traffic. Commuters would have to leave their homes hours much earlier than usual – like maybe leave at maybe 3-o'clock in the morning – without a specific bridge to drive to.

Time: Friday, 07-September, 16:05 EDT (Back at The Mall)

Smitty on his phone: "Sergeant Colman, you've been around D.C. for some time now, right? Can't waste time right now; I need to pick your brain real fast. Does 'RFK' mean anything to ya? Com'n, real fast."

Colman (after almost five seconds, which seemed like an eternity to Smitty): "The only thing I can think of off-hand is the old RFK Stadium. It's been sitting unused for years ever since the Washington Redskins built their own stadium years ago in the mid-90s up in Maryland between D.C. and Baltimore. Sorry, but that's the only thing that comes to mind on short notice. Hope it helps."

Smitty: "Of course, it is. I completely forgot all about that. Yes. You have been a tremendous help. Gotta go."

Time: Friday, 07-September, 16:07 EDT (Back at The Mall)

Air Lima (radioing Phillip): "Ghost-1, how much of a problem is it to get over to RFK?"

Ghost-1: "RFK? What's an RFK? Right now we are searching the obvious places hunting for a helo that shouldn't be there – like hovering under the bridges, rooftops, and places where it might not be that out of place for news chopper to set down in a park or something. I'm lookin' on the east side; Brian's doin' the same on the west side. Now what's this RFK? And why are you askin' about it?"

Air Lima: "Major 29 called sayin' that Agent Phelps slipped-up one time and mentioned 'RFK' one time and then clammed-up. Also got a very brief reaction from Daisy before she also went 'blank' again. Sergeant Colman said the only thing he could think of was old RFK Stadium. The Washington Redskins used to play there up until the mid-90s. Could a stadium hide a chopper like the one you're hunting?"

Order of Succession

Ghost-1: "Hot damn. Out in the open with only the tall walls to hide them. Where is that RFK Stadium? Do you know?"

Air Lima: "Funny you should ask. Been asking Google while we were talking. Basically, find the Capitol Building and fly directly due east. Almost as far east as the Lincoln Memorial is west. It's a big round stadium-lookin' structure sittin' right near the river."

Ghost-1: "Roger; got the coordinates. Will advise Ghost-2 to move closer to this side of the Potomac. Out." Ghost-1 also requested Potomac Consolidated TRACON to look at radar records for the last hour concentrating on the Buzzard Point heliport for a single chopper lifting-off and heading up-river. What was its direction and speed? And did it go toward RFK Stadium?

Time: Friday, 07-September, 16:08 EDT (Toward RFK Stadium)

{Ghost-1's brain, advising again: "Okay, get your rear in gear, good buddy. Use the lady on top of the Capitol Building right over there as a guide and put this sucker into hyperdrive right now. Did you hear me? What are you lookin' at? We're supposed to be goin' thata way, over to the east, didn't you say? So, what's the hold-up, huh?"}

{While heading toward RFK, Ghost-1 mouthed the words and wondered aloud: "This airspace is supposed to be closed. What's that medevac helo doin' flying over there? Maybe he thinks that medevac marking lets him go wherever he wants whenever he wants. We'll see about that."}

Keying his radio: "Andrews Tower, what's that helo to my south doin' out here now?"

Andrews Tower: "Ghost-1, we do not have any request for a medevac chopper. Only you, Ghost-2, and the bad-guy TV Traffic chopper are supposed to be out there. Over."

Ghost-1: "Andrews, you wouldn't have a spare AWACS E-3 looking for something to do would-cha? Need to keep track of where these civilian pilots are flying. Local TRACON does not seem to be in control yet. Over."

Andrews: "No E-3s on tarmac. Going to alternate freq, *wait-one*." Less than 30 seconds later: "Ghost-1, found one airborne on training

Order of Succession

flight over southern Virginia – a big one, a 767. Still want him? I'll re-vector him to this area. Says he's been watching you guys anyway. Be in full range in about 5 minutes."

Ghost-1: "Give him our locations and transponder data. The third one I'm lookin' at doesn't belong here – especially flyin' in our cleared air now. Get local TRACON to search for his origination and his transponder info. This guy's gonna screw us all up. On way to RFK. Out."

Andrews: "RFK. Roger. Out."

Smitty dialed the number for SAT-Recon on his secure phone; it rang through to the sat operators. "Larry, Terry here. Say, you wouldn't have a satellite handy that's got a view of The Mall in D.C., would ya? Need to have view of overall activity right fast. Ya got one overhead now? Great. You should see only three active choppers. Two will be Ghost-1 and -2. We believe the third one is the bad-guys' bird. Andrews found an AWACS bird; one of those will show-up, too. My call-sign is 'Air Lima'. You got my number. Thanks again, Larry."

Ghost-1: "Air Lima, over."

Air Lima: "Ghost-1, go ahead."

Ghost-1: "Air, this is getting real serious. Clear The Mall ASAP. Get the civilians outta there right now. Close it down early. Old Guard to control road access into area ASAP. Rocky needs command authority because bigger than all hell, all this shit is comin' his way really BIG TIME. Do you roger that? Over."

Air Lima: "Roger. Clearing already began when orange area went up. Safe hunting. Got a call in for an AWACS when it's in position. And a high flyin' sat-recon bird that'll be on-line in 15-minutes. Out."

{Ghost-1's mind: "Okay, now, got that taken care of; gotta get to target site. Let's move it."}

Ghost-1 approached RFK at full speed and then pulled a 360 around the parking lots. No sight of any chopper anywhere.

{Ghost-1's mind: "Okay, now let's give a look inside the stadium; just be careful about it, okay?"}

Order of Succession

Ghost-1 armed his weapon systems and took his helo up high above the edge of the stadium in a nose down attitude. No chopper in there either. Just a big pile of colored sheet-plastic looking stuff blowing in the breeze. That in itself looked familiar, but also highly suspicious. Ghost-1 pulled his phone out and thumbed through Officer Bernie's pictures. (Out loud) "There it is. The picture of the TV news chopper. Same colors. Oh, shit, now what?" He swooped down almost to grass level and let his prop-wash move the debris around. "That's it. The WTFU Channel 37 decals. They changed the news chopper into a medevac helo. Dastardly bastards." His helo erupted upward out of the stadium, nose tilted, heading due west, radio already keyed.

Ghost-1: "Andrews, where did that medevac go? That's the bad-guy now. They pulled off the TV news decals. Now flyin' as a medevac going to help at the mess they created. Where is it now?"

Andrews: "Echo-3 says it vectored toward up-river on the Potomac. Ghost-2 advised. Over."

Ghost-1: "Andrews, out. Ghost-2, you're closer. Didya find him along Potomac yet? You got hunting authority; smoke 'em if you havta. Comin' over-land; I'll be on your 3 in less than 60. Out."

Time: Friday, 07-September, 16:18 EDT (Approaching Potomac at Memorial Bridge)

Ghost-2: "Ghost-1, are you on my 3 yet?"

Ghost-1: "Negative. Approaching your 6. You wanna flush him out? Over."

Ghost-2: "Roger. Havta approach careful. If he's under the bridge, there's not much headroom. Let's do it on 5. Out."

Ghost-1 and 2 slipped-sideways west to east down opposite sides of Memorial Bridge. The rabbit didn't flush out of hiding; he simply wasn't there. There wasn't enough room overhead to safely hover under there anyway.

"Ghost-1 and 2, this is Echo-3. Over"

Ghost-2: "Echo-3, go ahead."

ORDER OF SUCCESSION

Echo-3: "Ghost-2, bogey disappeared around northwest side of Memorial Bridge. No acquisition since. Over."

Ghost-2: "Echo-3, not here; need a better guess. Andrews, where are the helipads in this area? Some place a medevac chopper could set down and not draw a crowd. Need a place where he can set down fast and hide in plain sight without attracting notice. Echo-3, can you check any hospitals for choppers on their pads and the transponder code you tracked? Gonna check out the island in the river next. Out."

Air Lima: "Echo-3, this is Air Lima. There'll be a recon-sat overhead within 7."

Echo-3: "Roger. Hope his cameras are on to capture upcoming action. Out."

Ghost-1 and 2 flew over to Theodore Roosevelt Island, slipping-sideways past both sides simultaneously. The rabbit must really be hiding in his hole, and he knows exactly where it is. They hovered at the north end of the island to re-evaluate.

{Ghost-1's now calmer brain: "Hey dummy, slow down and think this over. You think you know what his target is, right? And it's right over there, right? The 'eye-in-the-sky' says he went this way, right? So, why does it look like you are chasing him toward his target? Well, at least it does look that way to me; but what do I know. Think about this: Is there any clock-time that the rabbit hasta pop out of his hole? Could be, but I don't think so. So, why are you chasin' him. So, you're gonna say, 'To keep him away from TWH.' Okay, dummy, but he's leadin' you to his target, isn't he? How's that gonna keep him away from the target? How's this working-out for you? You need a new plan and right quick, dummy.}

The radio brought the reflections to a screechin' halt.

Radio: "Ghost-1, Andrews. Two hospitals near your location. Georgetown University to your north, northwest on the other side of Key Bridge. That's the next up-river bridge from your location. Look for the tall buildings on the bluff above the river. Second hospital. George Washington almost due east from your location. Near big traffic circle. Near corner of K Street and New Hampshire. Maybe six blocks from the Kennedy Center right there on the river. That's all I got in your area. There's a third hospital about seven klicks up-river on east bank of river; it's named Sibley. Landmarks: Reservoirs

ORDER OF SUCCESSION

beside river just past Georgetown; continue. Second reservoir is Dalecarlia; do not pass this one. About half a klick before this one. That's all of 'em. Good huntin'. Advise. Out."

Time: Friday, 07-September, 16:43 EDT (Hovering near Roosevelt Island)

Radio: "Echo-3, here. Doesn't look alike any choppers on either of the first pads. Can't see the third right now; river bluffs in the way from this position. Movin' into position above Potomac north of D.C. Gonna' be doin' 'lazy 8s' to the north. Andrews, advise TRACON of new station. Out. Spoke too soon. Something popped-up in the area of hospital three. Headin' for the river now. Heading down-river toward your location. Low and fast in your direction. There's a bridge up-river from your location. He's gotta a choice to make. River channel too narrow to flare-out on south side. He can go low and wide over Georgetown on the north side. Your choice. Approaching the last reservoirs up-river from your location. He slowed forward, but climbing and turning south. He's gonna come-in behind ya' with a straight shot into D.C. from Arlington Cemetery. He's gonna . . . "

Ghost-1: "Echo-3, not on our watch. We're outta here. Advise of changes. Out." "Air Lima, comin' your way. Don't know where it's headed. Get everybody outta the way." "Andrews, we're goin' to TWH cross-country. Raise contacts on your console and advise two Marine helos are friends. Medevac is not friendly at this time. We do not want to get shot at, and they don't want us to engage them either. You copy all that? Over."

Andrews: "Roger all that. All consoles on Lima Limas advising contacts and TRACON." "Echo-3, you got three and only three airborne over D.C. now? Over."

Echo-3: "Roger, only three at this time." "Ghost team: Target hovering over Arlington end of bridge. Turning 180; now facing Cemetery. What the hell is he doin' down there? Nose down, nose up, twice, and a 180 facing D.C. What the hell was that about."

Ghost-1: "It is a salute called 'Ave, Imperator, morituri te salutant.' It means 'Those who are about to die, salute you.' The pilot is either military or trained by the military. He was paying his respects to those who have gone before him, and he expects to join them. The last 180

Order of Succession

faces him toward his goal, and he knows we are in his way. They are gonna make this a fight to the death; there is no way out for him now. He is ready to visit all of his power and weapons upon all who stand in his way. When he moves toward us, the waiting is over; he is not afraid of dying in pursuit of winning or killing us in the process."

ORDER OF SUCCESSION

48 – Act III, Scene II – Missiles Away

Not Quite 17:15, Friday, 07-September: (West end of Memorial Bridge)

TIME: 17:15 EDT

Echo-3: "Bogie moving slowly east toward Lincoln Memorial. *Wait-one.* He's turning south down-stream before getting to Memorial Bridge. Following Potomac south at about 30 klicks. Hovering at 14th Street Bridge. Turning east and slowly crossing the Potomac. It looks like he's surveying the damage. Like he's just looking at his handiwork. Ghost-1, this is weird; never seen it before."

Ghost-1: "Echo-3. Roger on his location. Ghosts waiting. Systems armed and hot."

Echo-3: "Roger, Ghost. Still only three airborne. Turning up-river toward Lincoln Memorial, much slower than down-river. Approaching Lincoln and turning east. *Wait-one.* Changing flight direction again. Crossing behind Lincoln on river side. Now turning east again. Slowly following tree-line along – map says Constitution Avenue. Along north end of Lincoln, proceeding east. Passing Vietnam Wall. Stopping and hovering about halfway to your location. He's rising above treetops. What the hell . . . Missile away north. We see three missiles away to North. Chopper instant turn south across The Mall. Instant contact for all three. Whatever it was, there ain't much left standing any more. Holy sshhh . . . Can anyone confirm what used to be there? Over"

Air Lima: "Echo-3, Air Lima here. Not far from my position. Does it look like maybe four blocks west on Constitution from the Ellipse, like maybe 20th or 21st Streets? Over."

Echo-3: "Roger. "What used to be there? Over."

ORDER OF SUCCESSION

Air Lima: "The Federal Reserve Bank. Whoever's flying that chopper must really be PO'ed big time at the banks. Come Monday morning, money's gonna be really tight. Maybe that's part of the plan. Out."

Larry: "Air Lima, Sat-Op here. Cameras on. Did I just see what I think I saw? Three missiles at the Federal Reserve Bank? Are you kidding me? The Federal Reserve? Just what the hell are you mixed-up in?"

Air Lima: "Sat-Op, your visuals correct; keep recording video. More serious stuff coming next. Out."

Ghost-1: "Air Lima, advise Rocky and Army to get ready to take charge of all wreckage – whoever it is. Follow the action; can't control where it's goin' next. Out."

{Ghost-1's suddenly-concerned brain: "I got a stupid question for all you deep thinkers. You ever take a good look around The Mall from this height, huh? Well, have ya? Didn't think so. This is, what do ya call it, oh yeah, a 'target-rich environment'. But these are all the wrong types of targets; they're all, how do you guys say, they are all collateral damage. Between these three choppers and all of the munitions, you all are equipped to blow the living shit outta everything you can lay your eyes on here. Give a look at all of the buildings with people in them. And how about all the stone-work, the monuments. Say, did you know that the Washington Monument just over there is just lay-up construction to get that high; quite a feat, dontcha think? You boys with these toys better not fly into that thing; it might fall apart and bury one of youse under the falling stones. Can you imagine how much all that stuff weighs, huh. It'd take weeks to dig down just to get to youse' chopper, wouldn't it? You sure you want to take that chance? Hey, dummy, did you think this plan through? Really, you can tell me the truth, did ya jus' happen ta think about this? Well?"}

Ghost-1 (mouthing the words): "Tried to, but it's too late now to think any more about it; we're in it now." And with that, Phillip rotated his helo to face Arlington Cemetery and then also nodded its nose down and up. "Ave, Imperator, morituri te salutant."

Meanwhile Over At Reagan National Tower:

Traffic Controller: "Hey, Boss-man, where are you? You gotta see this! TRACON's radar feed shows some big-assed plane doing lazy-8s

Order of Succession

above us. WTF is goin' on over there. Boss-man, you're missin' a great show; wish I knew what we're watchin'. Hey, where you at?

"Hey, boss-man, I thought this was just supposed to be a training exercise. You been listening to these transmissions? Is this for real or what?" Just then, the radio said ". . . three missiles away . . .". And something on the other side of the Lincoln Memorial lit-up the sky, and the controller felt his tower shudder and sway ever so slightly. "Three missiles! This looks and feels like it's for real. Is this connected with the 14th Street Bridge being blown up? I'll bet it is. Too bad all the trees on the other side of the river are in the way; we'd have a ring-side seat. Well, maybe a balcony seat. Hey, boss-man, what's TRACON sayin'?"

Boss-man: "Keep watchin'. We're seein' history in the makin'. Know what I mean? Some place above us, there's even an AWACS playing spotter for the good-guys. You don't really want to know what TRACON's talkin' about. Keep watchin'; they're gonna come ask us what shit hit what fan and when. Mark my words; we're gonna be talkin' to all sorts of folks who wouldn't want to talk to us any other time. Mark my words."

Echo-3: "Ghost-1, he's movin' further across The Mall fast. Passing FDR and MLK Memorials. Skirting the Tidal Basin. He's really moving; making a wide turn to port and sliding into a hover behind the Jefferson Memorial. Hey, can anyone monitor radio transmissions from that chopper? Be nice to know what's next. Still hovering."

Air Lima: "Ghost-1, hope you gotta a plan for an airborne launch of a missile from Jeff."

Ghost-1: "Me too." "Ghost-2, wide spectrum jammers on? UHP-Lasers armed?"

Ghost-2: "Roger. Both armed and seeking."

Larry: "Air Lima, you talkin' like this is a hot missile attack. The biggest target across from Jefferson is . . . is The White House. Oh, my God, The White House! Are you shittin' me? Camera recorders on for sure with immediate backup redundancy. The effing White House! I don't believe it!"

Order of Succession

Echo-3: "What's he doin' now? He's slipping-sideways to the east side of Jeff."

Ghost-1: "Ghost-2, you ready?"

Ghost-2 (keyed his radio, but Echo-3 took control of air): "North-bound missile away. Sonovabitch, it's headed straight for . . ." Echo-3 didn't finish.

In anticipation, Ghost-1 had flipped his jammers on before the launch and had the missile in his sights when he pressed the 'Fire' button of his laser. The record tapes showed Ghost-2 was only milliseconds slower. The tapes also showed the missile bursting into a cloud of flame, scattering debris over the north center of The Mall – just west of the Washington Monument – but way too damn close to the Ellipse and da WH.

{Ghost-1's brain in overdrive: "But, hell, we were able to stop his first attempt. How many more does he have? That could be a big problem – a real big problem – if any follow-up missiles have faster flight times. And now the bad-guys know we have some counter-measures. That means he can make educated guesses what they might be. It will be a VERY BIG problem if he moves closer and hovers over the Maine Avenue site and fires . . . God, have mercy on all of us."}

Echo-3: "Two more small somethings airborne near medevac chopper. They just appeared. Flight paths out both sides of Jefferson; they're heading toward TWH, too. Maybe small drones or something like that. Over."

Ghost-2: "Ghost-1, take the chopper. Ghost-2 is searching for new bogies now."

Echo-3: "Ghost-2, bogies still headed for TWH; about a half-a-mile apart. Coming over Tidal Basin probably going over the Vietnam Wall. Gaining altitude to clear trees. Still heading north. Approaching open air over The Mall."

Ghost-2: "Got 'em in sights. UHP-Laser and missiles locked-on both. UHP acquiring target on automatic." With the sounding of the 'acquisition' lock-on tone in his headset, Ghost-2 pressed 'Fire'. The closest drone's explosive charge went-off like most firework shows' grand finale – except it shot all the fireworks simultaneously. For a brief instant, The Mall was flooded with brilliant light and a sound like 100s of 'Flash-Bang' grenades all detonating all at once. The concussion wave even rocked Ghost-2's

Order of Succession

helo. Anybody left around the displays on The Mall was probably more than a bit disoriented, to say the least, if they were still on their feet.

Ghost-2: "Second one's gonna be a lot closer. UHP locked on. Pucker-up." The flight path of the second drone was more easterly. The drone flew just past the mall-side of the Washington Monument and then over some civilian buildings. It looked like the intended path would be an attack from the south-east – maybe over the Commerce Department Building or one of the hotels. Wait for it or stalk it, that's the question. Ghost-2 decided to split the difference. He flew eastward toward Commerce, waiting for his weapons to signal a lock-on. He witnessed the previous drone explode and felt its concussion. His plan was to press 'Fire' and get the hell out of Dodge as fast as he could. Lock-on tone in his headset solved the intercept-it game at a comfortable distance from TWH.

{Ghost-2's adrenalized and dreading brain: "There's gonna be one helacious blast and lots of broken glass all over everything in sight. Hope there aren't people down there in Freedom Plaza. And no guests are looking out of that hotel's windows. What are ya waiting for? Times awastin'; press the damn button, will ya?}

Ghost-2: "Weapons engaged. Fired." The UHP-Laser's beam burned through the drone's fuselage and reached something that definitely didn't like the sudden, terrible heat. Drone-2 also detonated its explosive charge all at one time. A lot of glass windows needed to be replaced around Freedom Plaza starting tomorrow morning. At least three major hotels and the D.C. Government Building, not to mention other office buildings, would keep a window company going for months. Oh, and the cranes and workers, too! DC Metro Police is gonna need lots of overtime to protect the property behind all those now-empty window frames. (What Ghost-2 didn't realize is that the fictitious aunt who was gonna stay in the top-floor room hotel opposite the Treasury Building, the one that Greg, the bell-hop showed to one of the recon teams, would have had a really first class vantage point – if the window had survived.)

Ghost-2: "Both drones down. Ghost-1, chopper is yours. Keep advised."

Air Lima: "Andrews Tower, you got room for Echo-3 on tarmac at your location?" "Echo-3, be prepared for a long weekend at Andrews. Confirm? Over."

Echo-3: "I guess. If they got space, we're gonna have the time."

ORDER OF SUCCESSION

Air Lima: "Echo-3, keep your data intact. And do not talk to anyone about what you just got tangled-up in. That's an order. Confirm, Echo-3? Over."

Echo-3: "Roger on that." "Andrews, park us close to a mess hall and beds. Close to 12 hours in air. Not provisioned for a real mission. Will also need refueling and resupply. Over."

Andrews: "Roger. Working on that for you. Everybody, keep Andrews advised. Out."

Time: Friday, 07-September, 17:19 EDT (Above the Ellipse)

Ghost-1: "Ghost-2, surprised by The Fed. I guess TWH is now his primary target. I hope my helo's got the weapons for this. You know where to find me. Try to stay high outta my guns. Confirm. Over."

Ghost-2: "Roger. Out."

Ghost-1: "Air Lima, clear anybody remaining from Ellipse and The Mall. He's on the other side trying to make sure the missiles have enough distance to arm in flight." "Andrews, keep D.C. emergency personnel out of area. Do not want friendly-fire casualties."

Echo-3: "Bogie's moving toward center of Mall. We got negative visual on you. It's all yours. Out.

Ghost-1: "Roger."

Time: Friday, 07-September, 17:22 EDT (Above the Ellipse)

Echo-3: "Ghost-1, aggressor is moving slowly toward your position on the river side of Washington Monument."

Ghost-1: "Echo-3, when he fired last missile, what was his orientation? Facing us or a side-door launch? Which door?"

Echo-3: "*Wait-one* – good call, port door launch. *Wait-one*. Looked-up first launches. Same launch door."

Ghost-1: "Roger."

Instead of having an all-out air assault and defense above The Mall, Phillip tried hailing the other pilot to try to talk him out of it. He

375

ORDER OF SUCCESSION

didn't think the pilot would cooperate because of the attack on The Federal Reserve. But it was worth trying. "Pilot of medevac chopper, please respond. Over."

Pilot: "You don't want to defend against me; you'll die in the effort. Just slide aside and let us finish our job. I promise I won't down you. Over."

Ghost-1: "I think you are wrong to follow this plan of yours. You know I can't just slide away and let you shoot at TWH. You know it is my job to protect it, dontcha, Colonel Delong."

Delong: "How'd you know my . . . Never mind; it doesn't matter now. It's set then; see you on the battlefield."

Ghost-1: "It was the 'Ave, Imperator' maneuver. That's how."

Time: Friday, 07-September, 17:24 EDT (Above the Ellipse)

Echo-3:" Ghost-1, he's advancing toward your position on the river side of the Washington Monument. This is going to be too close-quartered; he's yours. Out."

Delong advanced toward TWH, crossing over the Maine Avenue site where the first 'missile-in-a-van' bad-guys were arrested. Then he feinted a turn to his port-side – toward the river. He didn't show the port-side door of his chopper. Ghost-1 was in his way. He re-vectored back to straight-ahead toward TWH. Delong now turned to his starboard, exposing his port-side door; it was closed. Suddenly, his crew slid it open. Ghost-1 was now looking straight down the barrels of several missile launch tubes.

Instinctively, Phillip thumbed the trigger on his 20-mm cannon (actually, an enhanced, lightweight mini-gun), whose barrels unleashed 50 projectiles at the medevac helo. Delong anticipated the response and jerked his helo out of the path just in time. The bullets, having missed their target, continued across the rest of The Mall and struck the Department of Agriculture Building over on Independence Avenue.

{Ghost-1's mocking brain: "Good shooting buddy. Ya missed the entire target; not a scratch, one. But ya did hit that building behind it. Yeah, it wasn't movin' so ya had a better chance of hittin' it. It couldn't get outta your way. Boy, there's gonna be some paperwork on that one. Next time, ya wanna try for a building that can jump outta your way; less paperwork. Didn't check your background, did ya? Boy, what a dummy."}

Order of Succession

{Ghost-1's inquiring mind: "Okay, now what's next?"}

Delong nudged his phony medevac chopper out past the river-side of the Washington Monument. The port door was now wide open, but he quickly brought it back to his port. Was that an 'oops' on his part? Delong decided he needed an advantage of some sort – any sort. But he had to survive long enough to get close enough to TWH to complete his mission. He flew his helo toward the Capitol-side boundary of the Ellipse. Ghost-1 slid eastward to block and maybe cause a bit of a retreat. Delong did not retreat; blocking was the only alternative left.

Once again, Delong turned to expose the open port door. This time, Ghost-1 anticipated this move and immediately fired another 50 rounds of 20-mm. This time, however, several rounds penetrated the medevac chopper directly behind the belly door, but he could not see any obvious damage. Furthermore, Delong didn't jerk his ride out of the bullets' paths as if something went suddenly wrong. At least, this was proof that Ghost-1 had figured-out how to hit the medevac helo. The bad part was that there was still more paperwork in his future. The rest of the rounds stitched down the western side of the Washington Monument, leaving pock marks down the middle 150 feet of the Monument. Small clouds of stone dust were instantly visible.

{Ghost-1's mocking brain: "Wasn't it just re-opened a few years ago after repairs from an earthquake? Probably have to close it again for more inspections. Damn the paperwork is gonna be serious on this one. You need a new nickname. How about 'Gunner? No, wait, it's gonna be 'Vandal'; yep, 'Vandal' fits you to a 'T'. What a mess this is turning into. Good shootin', Vandal. At this rate, if you live, you'll never get outta town. You'll havta extend your tour of duty just to fill-out all of the paperwork. Say, does D.C. have any laws against dischargin' a firearm inside D.C.? More paperwork. That pilot, Delong, probably won't have any paperwork to fill-out. He hasn't discharged any firearms in D.C. – just some missiles is all. Betcha there's no law against dischargin' a missile in D.C. Boy, are you gonna be in for it. What a sucker! Get with the program here and hit something that needs hittin', would ya?"}

{Ghost-1 (talking to himself): "I'm gonna hit him; he ain't gonna get away with just some bruising. Ya got that straight. Okay, now, let's get down to business."}

Order of Succession

Delong pushed his helo north at roof-top height above 14th Street NW past the Commerce Building. Ghost-1 followed him high over 15th Street. Suddenly, Delong turned his helo and shot upward, turning to his starboard, exposing the open port door toward TWH at a slight angle. Ghost-1 placed some more rounds into the tail section of the helo. The helo lurched a bit further to starboard; these rounds must have hit something or someone. The next missile in the launch tube did fire, but missed TWH completely. When The Fed is gone, who needs a Treasury Building anyway? And so, there was a new, smoking skeleton near The Mall. This one was way too close to TWH; there are no more sacrificial buildings next to da WH on this side. Way too close.

Ghost-1: "Colonel, set your chopper down and shut it down. You know you can't win this thing. Please just set it down and shut it down."

Delong: "Whoever you are, you know I can't do that. I have not completed my mission yet. Can't do that until then. Can't surrender while I still have some missiles. Would you?"

And with that, Delong swung his chopper around so the port door, once again, faced in the general direction of TWH. Ghost-1 saw the medevac chopper behaved jerkily; control was not good enough for fast maneuvers. Nonetheless, Delong nursed it to stay in the air. But that open door still posed a serious threat. The chopper jerked as two missiles launched. Both missiles struck buildings, just not their intended target, TWH. One missile struck the Eisenhower Executive Office Building on the west side of the TWH. The other missile went wider still; the Corcoran Museum now had a smoking, open-air display of its collections of fine art. Gonna be lots of damned paperwork for both of those hits.

Ghost-1: "If that's the way it's gotta be, you're gonna get your way starting now." And with that, Ghost-1 fired another volley of 20-mm at the wounded medevac. More paperwork as some of the rounds hit a few buildings and hotels along 14th and 15th Streets. Ghost-1 was positive that most of the rounds passed right through the medevac helo; it wasn't heavy enough to stop or contain them within itself. Plus, it didn't look like there was any armored shielding on Delong's helo. He probably wasn't expecting to have any opposition, especially from a custom-modified, tricked-out, armed to the teeth Marine chopper, either. Good luck for the buildings and monuments around the The Mall.

Order of Succession

{Ghost-1's still-mocking brain: "You really are gonna be old enough to retire after filling-out all of the paperwork, aren't-cha? Is that really what you're aiming for? Sorry, couldn't help but make a pun out of your handiwork. He's got the holes in his bird, and you can't shoot worth shit. Boy, some hero, you're turning out to be. Get with the friggin' program, here. Straighten-up and fly right, okay? Couldn't help that one, either. Did-cha get the message here? Then do it."}

Delong's chopper was wounded, but still flying, albeit with a slight yaw angle toward its port side. Delong attempted to gain height; his helo did, indeed, rise, but much slower than before his last encounter with Ghost-1. He continued to gain height, gaining enough to rise above the nearby tree-tops. He maneuvered around to the north side of Lafayette Park, immediately across blocked-off Pennsylvania Avenue directly in front of TWH. With the Hay Adams Hotel to his starboard, Delong labored trying to keep his helo steady so the port door still faced TWH. With TWH behind him, Ghost-1 faced Delong's helo across Lafayette Park.

Ghost-1: "Ghost-2, put your Nightsuns® on his cockpit – into it if you can. Cripple his sense of level. If that doesn't work, one of my missiles is aimed for that door. Roger?"

Before Ghost-1 finished, Ghost-2's Nightsuns® lit-up the nose of the medevac chopper. Ghost-2 even threw-in the red/blue pulsating lasers to further confuse its pilot. (Ghost-2 immediately took on the appearance of an airborne police cruiser pulling over a high-flying offender – only Ghost-2's lights were many times brighter and backed-up with more firepower than any police car could safely carry.) "Roger. Done."

Ghost-1: "When he lands, drop your blanket over him. Roger?"

Ghost-2: "Roger. Ready."

Ghost-1: "Medevac pilot, your helo appears to be dying. Please land and shut it down. Do you roger that?"

Delong: "What makes you think there's anything wrong with this chopper? It's still up in the air isn't it?"

Ghost-1: "You are broadside to me. There's a laser guided missile armed and aimed, just waiting for me to press the launch button. I will

Order of Succession

not launch if you set it down and shut it down. Set it down and shut it down now. Do you roger?"

Delong: "Roger. But before that, I'll kill your bird, too." He tried to turn his wounded helo to face Ghost-1. It was sluggish to say the least.

Ghost-1: "Don't do this. You don't need to do this. I will keep my word. Set it down and shut it down now, or I will shoot you out of the air. Do not do this. You don't need to do this. Do not do this. Out."

Ghost-1: "Ghost-2, blanket ready? Over."

Ghost-2: "Roger."

Ghost-1's chopper also had three mounted Nightsuns® – one on each of the outboard pylons and the third directly beneath the front of the cockpit – he estimated for a total of, oh, maybe 205 million cp. Ought to be hot enough to melt the paint off the medevac chopper. One by one, Phillip turned all three on; he felt the electrical amperage load all three of them placed on his alternators – sort of a deep moan like pulling-out large nails from thick wood using a crow-bar – causing the engine to adjust for the additional load.

Delong kept trying to turn. Phillip turned on his targeting laser and aimed it at the center of Delong's helo. "Colonel, we don't have to do this. Please set it down on the grass and shut it down. We do not have to do this. Just set it down and shut it down."

Phillip turned on his jammers, and simultaneously aimed the UHP-Laser. Maybe he could convince Delong into surrendering by just cutting the medevac chopper apart. The laser started to slice through the fuselage near the front edge of the side door opening, just behind the cockpit, so Delong would notice what was happening to his helo. Next target for the laser was the engine area. Smoke and the smell from burning metal are difficult to ignore. Phillip shut off the jammers so he could talk to the medevac pilot. "Colonel, set it down and shut it down. I don't want to slice-up your helo and cause injury if I don't have to. Set it down and shut it down now."

Delong: "No way, my mission is not finished. Ain't gonna happen. Nosiree. No way."

Jammers back on, and the cutting laser continued cutting its way toward the engine. Increased smoke and a little flame. "Ghost-2, going all the way. Ready? Out." The hot UHP-Laser cut something flammable; the

Order of Succession

flames became intense. One of the conspirators jumped out of the starboard door; he must have become very desperate because the helo was still over 75 feet up. Another one jumped as the helo descended to about 50 feet. Probably only Delong was still on board. The laser kept cutting. The helo began to rotate in place; the laser must have cut a control cable or something. "Ghost-2, got that weight at the ready? Force him down with it."

Ghost-2: "Roger." And Ghost-2 rose about 50 feet above the medevac chopper and began lowering two linked, water-filled bladders – about 300 pounds of water – to force the chopper down without too much collateral damage to the surroundings. Expecting the bladders to break when they contacted the whirling rotor blades, Ghost-2 released it at 30 feet above the rotor and darted to what he thought would be a safe distance – up, up, and over nearby tree-tops. Indeed, one blade on the fake medevac chopper's rotor broke and unbalanced the rotor causing the chopper to tumble toward the ground. Ghost-2 edged back from the trees, but remained above the tumbling destruction.

Ghost-1: "Malibu and Myer, your area for containment is in Lafayette Park on the north side of TWH. Need medics and ambulances for at least three. Need EOD and coms at the site. Out."

The medevac chopper was now lying on its starboard side. The open port door was facing up, leaving the launchers exposed. Ghost-2 activated a switch for the equipment added on the starboard side of his helo. Out rolled the cargo-net-looking device. Only this net was made out of Kevlar®. It was intended to contain any of the missiles if they tried to launch or cooked-off. Ghost-2 flew it over the disabled medevac and stretched the net out like spreading a blanket on a fire, and hit the 'Release' button. Next, Ghost-2 repeated the process for the equipment in the port-side pod of his helo, and laid a solid Kevlar® blanket across the top of the net, hoping to smother the flames.

Ghost-1 landed his helo on the paved area of Pennsylvania Avenue in front of TWH, tail rotor toward TWH. He left the engine running but shut down the large, overhead lift rotor. He did not, however, immediately disarm his weapon systems. He surveyed the debris and two bodies littering the once pristine park in front of the Executive Mansion and slowly shook his head, silently mouthing, "Whatever caused them to take this path must have been ever so powerful. A power unto itself."

Order of Succession

Ghost-1 confirmed he was still wearing his customized Colt 1911 sidearm and that it had a full magazine of .45-caliber rounds plus two spare magazines. If he was gonna be out of his gunship, he was gonna carry something with a bit more oomph than the standard, military-issue 9-mm. Just before leaving the cockpit, Phillip finally disarmed his weapons systems. Grabbing a portable radio and the nearest fire extinguisher, Ghost-1 climbed out of his almost best friend and began walking cautiously across Lafayette Park. He felt the adrenaline draining away, but remained wary nonetheless; we still don't know who's who and what side they are on. Whoever these folks are, he realized he had just put their plan, and maybe themselves, into a new world of hurt and fear. "They ain't gonna be friendly. Not in the least."

Ghost-1: "Ghost-2, watch for more bad-guys. I'm gonna check on the pilot and the two crew who jumped. Out."

Ghost-2: "Roger. Doin' tight 8s above. Watch out. Out"

{Ghost-1's wary brain: "Hey you brave boy, circle a little farther out of the debris field. You don't know anything about them, and you're just gonna waltz right through their chili? Oh, ain't you the brave idiot. Circle out a little farther, will ya? We don't wanna get bumped-off here on the ground in their territory. Hey, dummy, you listening there? Move farther out, or wait for Rocky. By the way, where the hell is he anyway?"}

Not such a bad idea for a runaway brain; Ghost-1 moved away from the center of the debris field and toward its periphery.

Ghost-1 made his way to the wreckage of the fallen medevac chopper and located the front end under the Kevlar® tarps. He found what he hoped was the cockpit and lifted the blankets with his left hand, while holding his cocked .45 in his right – just in case.

{Ghost-1's still wary brain: "Showing a little caution; I like that a lot better. That's better. Don't need to be caught flat-footed now, okay?"}

The odor of smoke, burned metal, and spilled AV fuel assaulted his nostrils, starting to nauseate him. He thought he saw a body in there and pulled the blankets a little higher. The fresh air must have hit a smoldering ember or something because now he saw flames sprouting from where the belly of the helo had been.

Order of Succession

{Ghost-1's mocking brain: "Great, that's just what you need – a fire starting where the remaining missiles are. Aren't you proud to start this because you wanted to pull that pilot out. Now what, huh? Oh, wait, you brought a fire extinguisher; think this might be a reason to use it? Well, what are ya waitin' for, an engraved invitation? Pull the pin and activate it, dummy. Do I havta do all the thinking?"}

Ghost-1 holstered his Colt .45, pulled the extinguisher's pin, aimed at the fire and 'foamed' away. Fortunately, the fire died 'down and out'. The extinguisher felt like it was almost empty, so Ghost-1 tossed it aside – away from most of the debris. Filling his right hand with his .45 again, Ghost-1 reached in with his left hand again, grabbed the pilot's clothing, and pulled as hard as possible. He was able to move the pilot's upper torso far enough to move Delong's head into fresher air. Ghost-1 pulled harder and finally freed the pilot so he could be pulled completely out from under the tarps. Ghost-1 found some reasonably flat debris on which to prop-up the pilot's upper body. But a quick scan of Delong confirmed there were some very serious wounds – jagged metal protruded from the right side of his flight suit, some other wounds that looked like shrapnel, but the worst were his legs and feet – twisted at impossible angles. The lower half of his flight suit was completely blood-soaked. The pilot would be in a real world of hurt if the medics didn't get to him real soon. And the body felt broken – broken and wet, blood wet – all over. Ghost-1 propped-up the pilot so he was sort of lying at about 45-degrees above the ground.

Ghost-1: "Are you Colonel Delong? I've got water; need some? Here, drink it anyway. Colonel, listen-up. I can't pull you away any further. I don't want to do any more damage to ya than maybe I did already. Just hang in there; the medics are on their way. Look, while we wait, tell me something. Who dreamed-up this plan? Who's the leader of the pack, here? Who's the head honcho? We gotta see what we can do to fix this as soon as we can."

Delong: "I'm pretty banged-up inside; I know I don't have that much time left. It's a long story, and I don't have that much time. You want to know who started this whole plot, dontcha. Well, I don't know who it was. The only thing I can say is that I think it started over there. (Delong motioned with his wounded left hand, pointing the thumb back

Order of Succession

at da WH.) For all I know, it might even be 'The Man' himself over there. Wouldn't that be a kick in the ass, huh? 'The Man' himself plottin' his own transition. Who'd ever believe that for a story?"

A loud, caustic voice from behind Ghost-1: "Colonel, you're a damn traitor to the cause. You cain't even pilot a friggin' chopper right to git the job done; what a damn screw-up you are! And now you up and want to friggin' rat-out our team. Hey, you, flyboy, okay you whipped us. Now, get outta da way so's I can see my so-called 'team-leader'."

Without turning to face the new voice, Ghost-1 flexed his fingers around his .45 like a batter in the on-deck circle does to his bat preparing for his turn at bat.

{Ghost-1's mocking brain: "You're plannin' to be some sort of hero, ain't-cha? You're trying to figure-out if you should try to spin around and face the voice, ain't-cha? Well suppose you're already in his gun-sights. All so fired-up to get to the pilot, you walked right past armed crew members. Smart move, DUMMY. Now what? Huh?"}

Ghost-1: "Hey voice, I don't know who you are, but I'm gonna move to my left real slow so you can speak directly to the Colonel here. Okay, I'm gonna duck-walk to my left beginning now." And with that, Ghost-1 moved cautiously to his left.

Voice: "That's good; don't go too far, Major. It is much better talking to Bubba's face than your back. Say, Bubba, you look like you're hurtin' some. Think you can hold-out 'til the medics get here? I don't think ya can. Do you?"

Delong: "That you Hal? Voice sounds like you. Yeah, I'm banged-up real good. How you doin'? You and Ray; how are both of you doin'?"

Hal: "Ah-huh. Yeah, it's me alright. I think one of my legs is broken from the fall outta your damn chopper. Ray; I think Ray's dead; he took a round from this here flyboy's bigger gun. Ray's dead because you screwed up. You said nobody would ever think of looking for missiles in a medevac chopper, didn't-cha? Well, if nobody would ever think of it, why the hell were they here just waitin' for us? Huh? Can you answer me that, you screw-up? We believed ya, and now I'm a cripple; ya know they can't fix me-up so I'll ever walk right again. I'm a cripple, and Ray's dead. Some friggin' team leader you are. You friggin' has-been, you screwed-up big-time. Well, maybe Daisy did better than we did; she

Order of Succession

wasn't on your team. Maybe she's still alive. Don't know where the hell she is, but maybe she's still alive. God rest her soul. But I keep comin' back to you. You hurtin' real bad, huh? Well, the medics ain't here yet, are they? And you're in a world of hurt, ain't-cha. Although I hate you and wish you all the pain in the world, I tell ya what I'm gonna do for ya. I'm gonna put you outta your friggin' misery, just like the friggin' dog you are. And to think I believed in you; you and the leaders of this here friggin' plot, to help the average American get out from under the thumb of this here God-awful friggin' gubamint we got controllin' us. Here's what I'm gonna do for you. Eat friggin' lead, you friggin' bastard."

And as the words sank into Ghost-1's mind, Hal fired most of the rounds in his 9-mm pistol's magazine at the dying Colonel, whose body shook from each impact. Ghost-1 rolled on the ground into a position to return fire. He triple-tapped the .45. The bigger dog barked a lot louder and reached-out far harder, silencing the smaller one – for good. Hal joined his son Ray. Just that much more blood and brain matter spattering on the grass in the once peaceful park. And just that much more paperwork.

Lafayette Park, directly across Pennsylvania Avenue from TWH, used to be known as a protestors' park, sort of like Hyde Park in London. This day, it played host to one of the most visible and over-reported protests America had ever seen. Now, if only the citizens could be told what it was really all about, that's the biggest issue. If only. . . . Probably never gonna happen.

ORDER OF SUCCESSION

49– Act IV, Scene I – Securing Sites

Around 17:45, Friday, 07-September: (Lafayette Park, across from The White House)

TIME: 17:43 EDT

Ghost-1: "Echo-3, Ghost-1. Who else do you see in the area? Over."

Echo-3: "Ghost-1, everything looks clear. Nothing registering except two Ghosts. Over."

Ghost-1: "Roger. You got fuel for another 2-1/2 to3 hours? Over."

Echo-3: "Can do about 2. 3 hours really pushing tanks. Over."

Ghost "Andrews, Ghost-1. Can you make room for Echo-3 in 2? Needs fuel and hot-standby position on tarmac. Needs priority take-off position for the next 72 hours. Copy? Over."

Andrews: "Copy. Echo-3, priority approach and take-off positions all set. Call when ready. Out."

Echo-3: "Andrews, Roger. Ghost-1, appreciate the real-live training exercise. Call again anytime. Still doing lazy 8s over D.C. Andrews, look for us in about 2. Need a vector from your northwest someplace around Theodore Roosevelt Island, where we became active. Copy? Out"

Andrews: "Air Lima, if Echo-3 doesn't have bogeys in 2, can we return air-space in D.C. area back to TRACON and Reagan Tower? Over."

Air Lima: "Negative on that. Keep airspace clear for flights to/from Pentagon in approx 90 minutes. Out."

Ghost-1: "Ghost-2, this area is getting tight for space. Can you find a secured LZ and set it down? Over."

Order of Succession

Ghost-2: "Got one picked-out already. The Marine name on the helo really helps around here. See you in about 10. Out."

Meanwhile Over At Reagan National Tower:

"Hey, boss-man, where you been? You missed a great show. Better than any training exercise I was ever in. Was that a real, honest-to-goodness helicopter gun-fight over downtown D.C.? Looked real to us. Sure wish we had some pictures from the top-side. That would have been real sweet. Think they'll let us get that in our next budget' after all, we are the closest to the Capitol, aren't we? That would be really sweet, wouldn't it? Sounds like Lafayette Park will be off-limits for quite a while, maybe a week. They probably wouldn't let us look at it up-close, would they? I mean we are almost cousins to Andrews; I'll bet they can get to see the park, what do ya think?"

Boss-man: "TRACON says Andrews Tower advised if the AWACS doesn't see anything else in the area, we may get our air traffic back in about four to six hours. Maybe. Better get your breaks and meals in now 'cause it is gonna get hectic when the airlines get to re-route to us again. No breaks 'til maybe 23:00 hours."

Air Traffic Controller: "You did just say there was an AWACS up there, right? Oh, man, that would have been a real sweet place to be for the last hour, dontcha think? Hey, can we put our radar on him? Can we try to track him?"

Boss-man: "Not only no, but hell no. You do not even want to think about tracking him. Are you outta yur ever-lovin' friggin' mind? You think after whatever that live-fire was over there above D.C. that your tracking radar is gonna look friendly to that bird. Hell's bells, man we don't know what other assets they were controllin' do ya? Just even look like some other unfriendly, and it'd be just as easy for them to vector those hot choppers or God-knows-what else they got up their sleeves to this tower and bring that live-fire exercise right on our asses, too. You'll be so old when you get out, they will have forgotten your Social Security Number. No radar on that bird. Got it? They look at that signal and back-trace it to us and then to you. And that's the end of that."

ORDER OF SUCCESSION

Time: Friday, 07-September, 17:48 EDT (Lafayette Park, D.C.)

Finally, a whole convoy of Army and Marine vehicles showed-up at the crash site in Lafayette Park. Three Captains (Rhodes, Calhoun, and Lambert) and one Colonel (Gahagen), all parked their vehicles on the pavement on both sides of Ghost-1's helo. Although Colonel Gahagen had the rank in the group, his agreement was to let Captain Rhodes run the show until real muscle was needed; to his credit, Gahagen abided by that agreement – albeit, with a certain 'itch'.. And Rhodes knew it really hurt the Colonel to stay out of this event, so he invited the Colonel into the 'clean-up' conferences – as an observer. Besides, Smitty and Rhodes had plans to use Gahagen for a special project on Sunday – or maybe even tonight depending on timing.

Rhodes: "As we saw during the past hour, there are several sites that need to be secured. I scribbled a list of sites as the fire-fight progressed. Here are copies of my list for each of you. Colonel, sir, here's a copy for you. Note that these sites include the diversion sites, especially, the 14th Street Bridges and the railroad bridge that used to be beside it. Some planning will be necessary for traffic control on Monday morning' but all areas will be off-limits for civilians until we are straight about what D.C. departments are capable of so they can provide their own clean-up and security details. Oh, yeah, don't forget the heliport where this all started this afternoon is also one of the sites, too.

"I also have a call into Bethesda Naval Hospital to send medics, a forensics team, and a team of Navy medical examiners to clear the human remains out of this park before we can get to work on the ground over there (broadly pointing toward all of Lafayette Park).

"I already have Marine EOD personnel looking at the remains of the medevac chopper to find out what kind of armament is still on-board. They will handle deactivation and/or destruction of anything that is unstable or unsafe.

"Our Marine coms sergeant is setting-up a coms center to be used by all of us.

"Back to the list of sites to be secured. Which Old Guard company is the better equipped to handle these? Which areas, and what will you need? How do you want to split them-up? And I have two platoons of Marines at your disposal; use them wherever you need a presence. You choose who goes where and how many. The Marines you see here will remain here and form the core of our primary support group. We have slots for some liaison personnel from The Old Guard if you have any spare troops to fill them.

"One of you captains from The Old Guard, call-up your Colonel and advise that you will probably be extended to support this incident for at least of the rest of this week and into next week. Colonel Gahagen, would you mind discussing that with The Old Guard Battalion Commander? Thank-you, sir."

"If there are no questions, let's make this happen by 08:00 tomorrow morning."

Brian (Loudly, From Outside The Group Area):

"Hey, this chopper is parked illegally; does anybody know where the pilot is? He's gonna havta move it or pay for a ticket, impoundment, and tow charges."

Phillip: "Brian, you just can't let a good joke go to waste, can you? Where did you park your helo."

Brian: "Well, you did say a secured LZ, didn't ya? It's sittin' in a nice patch of grass that doesn't have any debris scattered all over it like you have over here. And it has a fence and a security detail 24/7/365. It's right on the other side of that white building right there. And you know what else? They don't have any problems that my helo is loaded-hot, either. And they even let me keep my loaded sidearm, too. Right friendly, they are. Told ya, having '*US Marines*' on the side of that helo carries weight around here right now. But damn, no valet service; I had to park my own. Can you beat that?

"Aside from all of that BS, are you okay? Any wounds, cuts, anything?"

Phillip: "Nope. Nothing. Good to-go. You?"

Brian: "Nothing here, either. And a lot better than our three bad-guys over there. A damn-sight better."

Phillip: "Say, anybody seen Smitty? Rhodes, you seen Smitty yet?"

Time: Friday, 07-September, 18:32 EDT (Lafayette Park, D.C.)

Smitty (to Rhodes): "Cap'n, can I borrow one of the other Captains and

Order of Succession

the Colonel for a short time. Gonna send them over to the Secret Service Guards to find-out and confirm where the President and his Cabinet Secretaries are right now. Also want to request the Secret Service conduct a room-by-room search of TWH to ensure that nothing's been planted in it. They can use their own dogs. Okay?"

Rhodes: "Roger. Colonel Gahagen, sir, would you and Captain Calhoun meet Smitty over there? He'll fill you in about a short assignment. Thank-you, sirs."

The three met near the tail rotor of Ghost-1's helo. Smitty explained that the Secret Service responds faster to more 'brass', but Captain Calhoun can explain the reasoning better because he is more familiar with the area around here in D.C. "You might request that the Secret Service evacuate TWH during this search and to route all personnel through scanners as they exit just as a precaution. Is that okay with both of you? Captain Calhoun, if you need to get Cap'n Lambert to take over some of your troops, now would be the time to do that. Thank-you." Captain Calhoun saluted and turned smartly and trotted over to Cap'n Lambert.

Smitty (to Gahagen): "Colonel, we have a situation that you can really help us with. Several days ago, we discovered a potential conflict-of-interest situation involving Cap'n Calhoun over there. Please stay with me about this. After you and the Cap'n get the Secret Service moving, we want both of you to become involved in a trip over to The Pentagon. Part of that trip will be to use some 'brass muscle' on any JAG officer we can scare-up at this hour to join us on that trip and to witness that everything was by-the-book. Okay so far, sir?"

Gahagen: "So far, yes. But why is this trip so important that we need a JAG officer?"

Smitty: "This is where the conflict-of-interest sorta comes into play. We are intending to go to The Pentagon and take a Lieutenant General Hamilton Calhoun into custody as being a co-conspirator in this matter. It is also our understanding that the Cap'n is the General's son. We would like you to sorta feel him out about any sympathies he may have in this case. We would like you to keep him busy until he accompanies the Secret Service in TWH for their search. At that time, we should be ready for our little trip and one of the sergeants will replace him in TWH. Will you do this with us, sir?"

Order of Succession

Gahagen: "Can-do; will-do. Quite frankly, I had not anticipated anything involving a general."

Smitty: "If you understand what I told you so far and agree, please nod in the affirmative or I have to end at this point." Gahagen weighed the offer for a few seconds, then nodded. "Thank-you, sir. Consider yourself being 'read-in' at the highest security clearance in existence for the following information." Smitty continued as they moved to a more deserted area of the park. "The medevac pilot provided sorta a 'deathbed' piece of information about this plot, a much deeper conspirator or even the controller of the plot; we're trying to check it out now. Right now, Cap'n Rhodes, both Ghost pilots and I know what's goin' on; you make the fourth person. We are working this as a group; in other words, we dispensed with rank as a perk. Please consider this as a full-dress rehearsal for more to come later. And please keep this on the very-highest need-to-know basis. By the way, be prepared for visiting other offices and ensuring that the JAG officer is aware of what we are going to be doing."

Time: Friday, 07-September, 18:58 EDT (Lafayette Park, D.C.)

Smitty: "Cap'n Rhodes, I found a Navy JAG officer over at Fort Myer who, unfortunately for her, had not left her office yet. Lieutenant Commander (LCDR) Sheila Weekes will be accompanying us to The Pentagon this evening. She will, however, need transportation from over at J.B. Fort Myer to The Pentagon. Due to the traffic roadblocks, how about sending Cap'n Hauser to pick her up and bring her over to The Pentagon. If nothing else, a ride in Ghost-2 ought to be impressive as all get-out after everything that went down on The Mall. And have Brian refuel while he's at it. By the way, is Gunny Cornell available for an easy assignment?"

Rhodes: "Roger to all three. How did you ever guess this was goin' be this exciting two months ago? When you throw a party, do all of your guests always havta do all the work?"

Smitty: "If I can get them to come over and play in my sandbox, they usually have to do some of the shoveling, too. By the way, my contacts say that the Lieutenant General is still in his office. When we assemble over in the hall outside his office, Sergeant Coms can dial him from the POTUS Phone and you can speak to General 'piss-ant' Calhoun. How does that sound?"

Order of Succession

Rhodes: "That oughta be a shocker, alright. Hey, I just thought about transportation. With all of the bridges down and out, how are we gonna get there?"

Smitty: "I used your Colonel's name – he doesn't know it yet – when I called the Marine Helicopter Squadron One (HMX-1), over at Joint Base Andrews Naval Air Facility. They are gonna have six helos from their fleet of Marine-1s out on the Ellipse in 10-minutes after notification we are ready for troop transport to the Pentagon. Ghost-1 is gonna fly this here baby over as an escort. Andrews Tower will notify TRACON and Reagan Tower that this is a priority flight. No other air traffic will be permitted until further notification. Pentagon guards are cordoning-off an area in the parking lot for up to ten helos. Ghost-1 is also gonna refuel prior to goin' to the Pentagon. Keep this area clear so he can re-land again.

"Hey, I've been playing with a wild-ass idea; what do ya think of this? You remember that old movie, oh what the hell was it, *Blue Thunder*, I think. When the pilot puts his helo into 'silent mode' and hovers outside the window. Remember that scene? Well, how about hovering outside the general's office window as the POTUS Phone calls him. Wouldn't that be the greatest 'piss-ant' moment?"

Time: Friday, 07-September, 19:33 EDT (Lafayette Park, D.C.)

Dusk begins falling in downtown D.C. And, of course, the only newsworthy story on all stations around the country is the 'helicopter fire-fight around TWH' and the damage to 'our national monuments and buildings' but 'thank goodness that TWH was spared any damage'. "But we are continually being refused access into an insanely large restricted area of Washington, D.C." There are even allegations of 'the government is taking away our first amendment rights to report the news to you, our viewers, who are entitled to know everything'. Not to mention that, 'there are no government spokespeople to tell us anything'. Well, that part is absolutely true because NOBODY KNOWS ANYTHING SO FAR. THEY REALLY DON'T because they are trapped in the same traffic jams where everybody else is, and they have no idea what the hell happened anyway.

Major Jenkins, mumbling to himself, "Well, what do you want? Some of your own damn spokespeople are the damn plotters to replace your damn first amendment! What do ya think of that? Come fly with

Order of Succession

us when there's some bastard intent on blowing your ass outta the sky because you are in his friggin' way to his friggin' target. Come suit-up with us and I'll personally appoint you the nose gunner and missile target. Let's see if you lose sphincter control and your underwear still comes back sparkling white. What the hell do you want anyway? Well, I can't give you any of that while it's still happening. You idiots with perfectly white teeth and sprayed-stiff hair, get the hell outta here and actually do something useful for once. Damn it, anyway." He lifted to a hover then did a 180 up-an-over TWH on his way back to Fort McNair to refuel and re-arm. He returned to the park in 20 minutes, already primed for the next flight.

Ever since the events began to unfold several hours ago, the press and media reporters had been forced outside all restricted areas – as had everyone else. Those found trespassing had been transported to a 'holding area' on the other side of The Mall 'for personnel safety reasons'. As a result, they complained loudly and threatened even more loudly. One of the Platoon Sergeants charged with securing that area got back in their faces and assigned them '. . . to sit on that step over there so it doesn't move until I tell you it's safe to stand-up again'. They complained loudly that they demanded '. . . to go to where the action was' or they were going to sue for having their first amendment rights being taken away. He said he understood their problem, so he took them on a personal 'tour' of the area, pointing-out very-recent bullet pock-marks on the various buildings in this area. And then, the entire group was also personally guided behind the restricted area over at the Washington Monument to look at the pock-marks on its side. He ensured they got close-up pictures and interviews with anyone standing around in those areas who wanted 'to speak to the press'. Several armed soldiers and Marines walked beside and behind this 'group of tourists'. They were released from his 'tour' after about three hours, after his parting speech about the reason for these temporarily restricted areas.

ORDER OF SUCCESSION

50– Act IV, Scene II – Raiding The Pentagon

Around 19:55, Friday, 07-September: (Lafayette Park, across from The White House)

TIME: 19: 57 EDT

Smitty found Gunny Cornell over near the coms table. Gunny just located a portable generator and just cranked it up. He was gonna have lights and power for this area of the park any way he could. His Marines had established a secured area around the park, including blocks on both sides of, and adjacent to, the park; he extended the security perimeter up to, and including, the Hay Adams Hotel entrance.

Then he scouted-up an officer from the White House Secret Service detail and sorta convinced him to join him on 'short walk' over to the Hays to have a short 'discussion' with the management, whose actual participation was restricted to listening and doing what was 'suggested' to them. They requested to speak to the on-duty manager ASAP. "We have a small security problem we hope you can help us with. You no doubt are aware of the activity over there at the White House earlier tonight, right? We would greatly appreciate it if you will close down your roof for a few days. At the present time we consider it a security violation to have ANYBODY –ANYBODY AT ALL – up on the rooftop for any reason. The Secret Service, here, will advise when you can reopen the roof. Can you help us with that or should we have an armed Marine or soldier posted in plain view verifying that the roof area remained completely unoccupied until further notice?" The manager reluctantly acquiesced. "Thank-you, sir, we really appreciate your cooperation in this matter." Having delivered the message, they returned to the White House grounds.

Smitty: "How'd you like a cushy job right now? Got one with your name written all over it, right over there inside TWH. Whadya say?"

Order of Succession

Cornell: "That's right generous of you. Yessiree, it sure is. But I'll betcha you got something much more interesting up your sleeve. We've already been piddling around here doin' nothin' for too long. I'll bet you guys are planning something else to go along with this. Maybe not the aerial fire-fight again, but somethin' real different. If that's not an order from the Cap'n, I'd like to wait for the next shoe to drop. Maybe one of the other Gunnies or even PFC Berkeley or PFC Thompson would get a kick outta being inside TWH. What do ya got planned, anyway?"

Smitty: "You're on to me; you know me too well. But, as an alternative, I also thought you might also like to go for an airborne trip tonight. You up for that, Gunny."

Cornell: "Are you kiddin'; where do I sign-up. It's already done; you want to assign a Gunny or PFC inside TWH? You just tell me how many, when, and where; I'll round 'em up right now."

Smitty: "A Marine EOD Tech can do the work of an Army Cap'n, right? Whoever you choose is gonna relieve Army Cap'n Calhoun and personally escort the Cap'n over to me and then return to TWH to assist the Secret Service's search of TWH for anything that even looks like it doesn't belong in there. That's why the EOD is part of this – maybe even two of them. Your choice and then tell Cap'n Rhodes we agreed to this because you wanted to take a joy-ride in a helo at night to see the city's lights at night. Okay."

Cornell: "Done. Many thanks."

Time: Friday, 07-September, 20:15 EDT (Lafayette Park, D.C.)

Coms still had the POTUS Phone, all carefully packed and charged.

Smitty: "Okay, Coms, you ready? Corporal Knight still taking over? Pack-up that POTUS Phone and get ready. Meet over by Ghost-1's helo."

Coms: "Roger to both. On my way."

Smitty: "Gunny Cornell, we need five squads of Army troops and Marines ready for a night ride – one squad per chopper. Meet-up over by Ghost-1's helo."

Smitty: "Brian, you know who you're meeting' over at Fort Myer and where, right? Leave early to refuel. And make sure she can deal

Order of Succession

with helos. Besides, we may need your spot on the lawn. Meet cha at our 'reserved' helo pad at The Pentagon. Their regular one should be secured by the time you arrive."

Smitty: "Say, Colonel Gahagen, did the Secret Service confirm where the President and his Cabinet are? This is important for our next phase."

Gahagen: "Well, they tried to be rather cagey about the official whereabouts at first. You know, the usual 'at an undisclosed secure location B.S.'. You were right; they became more cooperative after I got all irate-like and poking-fingers-in-their-chests while indicating my Marines put their lives on the line to protect their damn little guard shack. And it is still possible that we can obliterate it on our way out within the next hour. But, the short answer is the President is participating in some sort of evacuation exercise in Site R, just as you suggested. The Cabinet, however, is still here in D.C., with no specific locations. How's that for security – no specific locations? Probably at restaurants or at home."

Smitty: "We're forming up over near Ghost-1's helo for this next phase. This is the Phase I told you about. Helo transport is laid-on for a quick trip across the river. Ghost-2 already left to get the JAG officer and will meet us over there."

Smitty: "Captain Lambert, Gunny Cornell selected a total of five squads to proceed to the LZ on the Ellipse. Verify each squad has a senior sergeant. Everybody to be armed. But no inserted magazines during the flight."

Smitty: "Captain Calhoun and Colonel Gahagen, please join me over near the coms table. We have an item that must be ironed-out immediately.

(Arriving at the coms table) "Captain Calhoun, our information indicates you are the son of Lieutenant General Hamilton Calhoun. Is this correct?"

Captain Calhoun: "Well, yes, that's correct. But what's that got to do with me and this attempted assault on TWH?"

Smitty: "This next phase is to take one of the conspirators into custody, your father. I, make that we, think it is best if you are not directly involved with this phase. Any comments?" Even in the fading light, Smitty noticed the Captain's face go pale; then it turned red.

Order of Succession

Captain Calhoun: "You've gotta be wrong. My father would never be involved with something like this. Never. I certainly don't want to stay here; I want to go and face him. You gotta be ever so wrong. I want to go. I need to go with you, sir."

Smitty: "I fully understand. Colonel, what's your opinion? The helos are waitin'."

Colonel Gahagen: "I trust him. I'll take him in my chopper and keep him on a short leash. Captain, you do understand that you are not to interfere regardless where this leads. And no phones or arms on my chopper. You will be there strictly as an observer. Do you agree, Captain."

Captain Calhoun: "Yes, sir, I understand and agree. Here's my phone, radio, and sidearm. Where are those helos?"

Colonel Gahagen stared at Smitty for a few seconds, not fully comprehending what Smitty was up to. But he had been correct on quite a few things, in fact, almost all of them so far. Gahagen also realized that he now had an extra responsibility he hadn't expected. "Captain, follow me over to the helos; I've got some things to pick-up over near Ghost-1 on the way."

Air Lima (on radio to Andrews): "Andrews Tower, is Echo-3 in position? Echo-3 will be looking for 6 new helos plus Ghost-1 from our position. Ghost-2 will be coming from J.B. Myer. No one else allowed in this cleared airspace at this time. Out."

Andrews Tower: "Air Lima, roger that. National Tower and TRACON advised. Echo-3 tracking now. Out."

Time: Friday, 07-September, 20:33 EDT (Lafayette Park, D.C.)

Air Lima: "Everybody mount-up with your own squad. Colonel and Captain Calhoun, your chopper is that one over there; it will be the last to arrive at our destination. I'll meet you at our new LZ." "Andrews Tower, we have lift-off as soon as Ghost-1 hovers above the Ellipse. Good, Ghost-1 is up now. We are on our way."

As Smitty climbed aboard, his pilot was already lifting-off. No time was wasted. In all, seven choppers formed-up, and, as Ghost-1 headed westward down The Mall, the other six followed. The reporters and cameras were held well behind barriers on The Mall. They were

Order of Succession

forced to track them with binoculars and those huge telephoto lenses – those big, white lenses with which they can read labels on your clothes from four miles away. Fortunately, the gaggle of news-people couldn't physically follow the helos on the ground; the roads were still gridlocked going on five hours after the 14th Street Bridge was destroyed.

Using radar, Andrews followed them over to The Pentagon. Not to be forgotten, Reagan Tower did the same visually – at least as far as the trees and buildings would permit. Their cordoned-off LZ area was located near the South Parking Entrance, two sides away from General Calhoun's office above the North Mall Terrace side. As the helos' skids touched the asphalt, the occupants bailed out both sides and ran to their assigned assembly areas.

Rhodes: "Captain Lambert, we need one squad to secure the 'official' heliport located just around that corner. If the choppers aren't ours from this primary mission, they do not land, and they do not lift off. Period. That heliport is now shut down until further notice. Period. Your troops can fire live rounds to secure that heliport if they have to. Is that understood? Ghost-2 is on its way with the JAG officer from J.B. Myer; his approach is from over there. (Pointing toward Fort Myer.) He is supposed to land in our designated area, not in the usual area. He will fly around this perimeter to reach our LZ. DO NOT FIRE ON HIM. He will return fire back with so many live rounds and missiles you won't be able to count all of them until the end of next month. If you're still living, that is." The soldiers and Marines quickly snapped and locked full magazines into their weapons and formed a perimeter-guard around the now quarantined LZ.

Ghost-2 appeared on schedule and landed near the other helos. LCDR Sheila Weekes managed to exit the helo as gracefully as possible; the first step from the belly was an unexpectedly long one. She hustled over to the mass of soldiers at the entrance doors. "Is there a Smitty here? I need to talk with him ASAP."

Smitty: "Major, I'm glad you could make this late meeting. You're probably wondering just what the hell is going on around here. First clue is that this is part of the destruction of the 14th Street Bridge and the attempted aerial assault on TWH this afternoon, etc. We need you to ensure we do nothing illegal when take a conspirator into custody."

Weekes: "You mean here at The Pentagon. You're kidding me, right? You better be kidding me. You're not serious about that, are you?"

Order of Succession

Smitty: "Ma'am, we are as serious as cancer. And I, make that, we, expect you to be the JAG officer on all of our custody apprehensions stretching into or past this weekend. Isn't that right Colonel Gahagen?"

Gahagen: "Ma'am, your participation has been authorized by your chain of command up to and including SECNAV, who, by the way bailed-out of their offices due to a horrendous traffic jam. Yes, ma'am, we are not kidding in the slightest about our expectations for your functions."

(Well, a slight fib. Because this plan was developed so late, SECNAV could not be informed yet, and besides he had also left early because of the traffic. But there was also a small element of some truth. A message was left on his known phone numbers. Regardless, LCDR Weekes would be too busy to check all of that out right now anyway.)

One squad remained around the transport helos, which were spooling down. The rest of the detachment advanced to the entrance doors, where the guards initially refused admittance because all the soldiers and Marines were in battle-dress, and, even worse, they were fully armed. Colonel Gahagen used his finesse and just simply ordered the guards to step aside or his Marines were going to make their post most uninhabitable by the time they got finished with it – if it was still there. He even commandeered one of the guards to act as a guide to reach their objective by the fastest route – and the quietest one, too. Three Marines were left to secure this entrance and to ensure that no alarms were sounded to alert the conspirator.

Once they reached the corridor nearest the General's office, all remained concealed around the corner from the corridor running past that office.

Air Lima (quietly): "Ghost-1, what's FLIR tell you about the office? Over."

Ghost-1: "Occupied by two people. Over."

Air Lima: "Continue FLIR. POTUS call going out . . . now." (Pointing his left index finger at Coms, who pressed the magic buttons, heard the ringing, and handed the phone to Cap'n Rhodes.)

Air Lima: "Ghost-1, status?"

Ghost-1: "Two startled people. One is going over to the phone. Hesitating. Reaching for it. I think you're on. Over."

Order of Succession

Cap'n Rhodes began speaking: "Say, is this the same contact we spoke to when the President was supposedly kidnapped at that rest-area out in the California desert? Glad to hear you're still alive and kicking. (And Rhodes gave the high sign to Smitty, who motioned the soldiers and Marines down both sides of the corridor [finger to his lips].) Say, I hear that there was a lot of activity this evening back there in D.C.; you know around da WH. What happened? Oh, really, some piss-ant terrorists had an aerial fire-fight near da WH. Really, some terrorists, huh?"

Air Lima: "Ghost-1, Nightsun® and pulsing lasers any time. Go." And with that, the inside of the general's office turned brighter than day. "Status? Over."

Ghost-1: "Startled is too polite. I think they're coming your way. Fast."

Smitty motioned to the soldiers and Marines to watch the office door. They didn't have to wait long. The Lieutenant General and a Colonel ran into the corridor and faced about 20 rifles. The General stammered something about he'll court-martial all of these piss-ant soldiers. Rhodes was still holding the POTUS Phone.

Rhodes: "So, we figured-out who the right piss-ant conspirator is, huh?" as he waved the phone at the General. "I bet the chopper pilot that he couldn't get you all to willingly come out of your office on your own. I guess I lost; I owe him a beer. General, please come with us peacefully and nobody gets hurt. LCDR, is this legal so far? Would you please read the General his rights?"

Weekes: "Oh, my God; you weren't kidding!" And she read the General his rights.

Smitty: "Hey, piss-ant General, my wife, Rita, you remember using her name, right? Well, Rita did not appreciate the way you used her name during one of your calls on this phone. But she still sends you her very best – me and my best buddies here. See you around, piss-ant."

Rhodes (now addressing the colonel who also exited the office): "Colonel, I do not know who you are right now, but would you please also accompany the General. For the time being, you are not under arrest, but you will be in our custody because we don't want to lose track of you until you are fully vetted and identified. Do you understand everything I have told you."

Order of Succession

Unidentified Colonel: "Just one effing second here, I just stopped in to see General Calhoun before leaving for home. I'm a colonel; you're only a Captain. I'm on my way home right now. Get outta my way, Captain." Wrong attitude; wrong words; oh, ever so wrong under the circumstances.

Gahagen's voice (echoing in the recently emptied corridor from behind the uniformed Marines behind and to the right of the JAG officer) was quickly followed by the Colonel himself as he tapped shoulders of Marines and soldiers – who quickly gave him room to pass: "Please excuse me for butting-in, Captain Rhodes. I may be able to help here. (Assuming a battlefield command posture, he turned sharply toward the unidentified colonel, his voice changing from quasi-mild-mannered into full command mode.) I am a Colonel, a Marine Colonel. I'm this Captain's commanding officer. You, sir, have just screwed-up big time. The Captain here was only going to detain you until you are properly identified. I, on the other hand, now feel detention is much too lenient for you under the current situation brought about by your friend, the general here. My eagle just sank his talons into your eagle, and both my eagle and I do not care one Flying Eff about your DOR, either. You, sir, are now under arrest beginning with drinking alcohol in a government building, but primarily for being an arrogant, self-appointed, pompous jackass during war-time. We'll fill in other charges as we fill-out the arrest paperwork. (Turning slightly to speak to a nearby sergeant) After the JAG officer reads him his rights, Gunny, put the bracelets on him and lead him out of here. (Turning to face the colonel again) And, sir, let me tell you personally, you don't screw with a Marine Captain when he tells you to do something; you do it without giving him any lip. You are going to have more than enough time to reflect on these personal imperfections of yours during the next few months. LCDR Weekes, read him his rights."

This was not something LCDR Weekes had ever seen before. She read the unidentified colonel his rights as his handcuffs were tightened just a bit. And his face which had been such a striking shade of red, quickly paled as Gahagen's words really sank-in. Weekes quickly stepped aside.

Order of Succession

{The colonel's now over loaded brain: "Say what? Hey, buddy, I kept telling you to learn when to shut-up, but, no, you always gotta be Colonel Ratchet Jaw. See where it gotcha. I'll bet this Marine colonel is really arresting you under war-time conditions. He didn't look like he cared much about your full-bird insignia. And just where the hell is he sending you that it's gonna be for months to adjust your attitude? Looks like it's for real to me. Feel those 'cuffs?}

Gahagen: "Gunny, load him up in a different helo than the General's; he's going for a ride tonight. Captain, your prisoners are ready for transport."

Both of the Calhouns faced each other for a few brief seconds. The General hung his head; the Captain turned his back toward his father and pounded the nearest wall three times with his right fist. "Why did you? Why?"

The Pentagon guard/guide led them back down to the entrance doors without saying a word. He was witnessing history – history involving two of the worst a-holes in the whole damn Pentagon and didn't want to spoil it. Gonna have lots to tell his buddies in about seven minutes. Yessiree, lots to talk about tonight at their Guard Desk. Yessiree! They might even invite some of their guard buddies over from the other guard stations just to fill them in and regale them with his eye-witness arrests in the Generals Ring. Yessiree, gonna be a hot time tonight!

Time: Friday, 07-September, 21:43 EDT (Pentagon Parking Lot)

The soldiers and Marines securing the Guard Station and the LZ were recalled and boarded on their helos. The prisoners were loaded on-board separate choppers along with their guards, who made sure they were properly belted-in.

As Weekes belted-in into Ghost-2, her mind quickly wandered off to what might take place next or to whom she was gonna havta read them their rights. It strayed up the chain of command – all the way up to . . . She caught her wild imagination and mouthed, "Nah, it can't be that high! Can't be . . . can it?" With Brian at the controls, Ghost-2 lifted-off and found its place in the formation, now headed to Andrews for a secured LZ near the AWACS plane's priority position on the tarmac. Echo-3 landed 26 minutes later.

ORDER OF SUCCESSION

Armed APs greeted the helos as they landed. Both prisoners were escorted to separate cells in separate buildings.

Rhodes to Gahagen: "Colonel, sir, I know that a lot of people are gonna want to interrogate the Light General, so I planned to keep him confined locally. However, what if the Marines were to take charge of that other colonel and hold him in a secured Marine facility? Your thoughts, sir?"

Gahagen: "My thoughts exactly. How about a secured facility within 29 Palms? There's a fellow out there who goes by the nick-name of Hard-Ass. I think he'd just love to talk to our colonel. What doya think? (with a slightly malicious wink)"

Rhodes: "Yes, sir, that would certainly meet our security requirements. There's an Air Force cargo flight out to Edwards with an ETD in about 45-minutes. Two Marine choppers from 29 will be flying past Edwards returning from Yuma within about 15-minutes of the plane's ETA at Edwards. They'll wait if the plane's late. Sir?"

Gahagen: "Sounds too good to be true doesn't it. Make it so. This is a lot more exciting than sittin' in a motel room waitin' for something to happen. What else ya got slated for tonight?"

Rhodes: "Gotta advise Air Traffic Control that the transport plane is okayed to make its flight on time and then close the airspace again. And advise the JAG officer that one of the prisoners is being moved to a more secure location. An introduction with the General is in order; gotta get Smitty, JAG, you, of course, Coms, and a coupla others for that. Then we gotta have a group conference about what we're gonna havta do about the replacement Cabinet Secretaries and, of course, POTUS. We gotta get the LCDR to decide if/when we involve the Chief Justice from SCOTUS and/or whoever is in charge of the Justice Department right now.

"Let me get a hold of the LCDR and get her on track about the colonel's transfer. I'll bring her along to the interrogation session. Sir, could you get me some coffee or water; I'm awfully dry right now? See you in 15 at the holding cell. Thanks."

Cap'n Rhodes found the LCDR sitting on a mechanics rolling stool just slowly shaking her head as if in some sort of a stupor. Rhodes intruded into her daze and invited her to accompany him to the General's interrogation. Her reaction was not exactly enthusiastic – more like being roused from a deep, deep sleep. On the way over to the cell, Rhodes brought her up to speed about what was planned for the weekend. Everybody was going to be very busy, including JAG Officer LCDR Weekes.

Weekes resigned herself to the fact that her paperwork better be the best CYA-type she ever produced. At the rate things were escalating, there very well could be some very, very powerful and well-connected people standing in front of her as she read them their rights. They were probably going to be people who run the Federal Government, and she was expected to read them their rights.

{Weekes' stunned brain: "Maybe if you changed your perspective maybe that would help. How about if you are only there to make sure the 'I's were dotted' and the 'T's crossed' during the process. After all, you are not really the person arresting anybody, are you. No, you're just making sure the correct words are said. Yeah, that's better already. Okay, changing the point of view works pretty well."}

Now Weekes suddenly realized that she, like most Americans, couldn't even name the Chief Justice of the Supreme Court to save their own lives. She had heard his name in news reports, of course, but now that she may have to talk directly about some politically-sensitive pending arrests . . . well, now she thought she better do some very fast research. What the hell is his name. And how about the Attorney General over at the Justice Department. She knew he just resigned in the last month or so, but she didn't know if a new one was appointed yet or if he/she was confirmed yet? Just who was running the damned Justice Department today at quitting time; she flat-out didn't know. Maybe no one knew.

And who's running TWH and the rest of the Federal Government now that the President is nowhere to be found? That's another good question. Nobody at her pay-grade would be expected to know this stuff. Would they? And who would expect them to know it? More good questions. Does anybody have any accurate answers tonight? Not likely.

When they arrived, Rhodes gave Gahagen a silent signal that he didn't think Weekes was really up to the task right now.

ORDER OF SUCCESSION

During the initial interrogation, the General admitted to knowing about the POTUS Phone. It would be impossible to deny that he called it from his office phone. Too many damned telephone call-records stored away would fill a life-time. And his use of 'piss-ant' so often? Well, that also is a slam-dunk for anybody investigating him. So, after his name, rank, and serial number and those admissions, Lieutenant General Hamilton Calhoun requested his lawyer; LCDR Weekes was there to ensure that happened. End of interrogation.

Even if they could ask him about visiting the Buzzard Point Heliport, signing-in in the visitor's logbook, and using 'piss-ant' while there, he had just shut-down that probe for now. The same had to be said about 'Clipboard' down at the Maine Avenue site, the one with the missile-launching road-work truck. That one would not be answered here, either. At least, not tonight.

Time: 22:46 EDT (Andrews Air Force Base)

The unidentified colonel's plane for Edwards left on time with the colonel hand-cuffed to a canvas jump seat. Four armed guards were posted in rotating 2-man shifts. The Marine choppers also had four armed guards waiting for their prisoner. The Marines up at 29 would be waiting for him; Hard-Ass was also prepared. The colonel's life is going to change so much for just being a smart-ass with an ego-mouth. Poor egotistical sucker.

ORDER OF SUCCESSION
51– Perp Walks, Not Quite

Around 22:45, Friday, 07-September: (Joint Base Andrews', Pilots' Ready Room)

TIME: 22:46 EDT

The conferees occupied a Pilots' Ready Room just off the tarmac near the AWACS plane. News of the conference spread like wild-fire. All ranks – officer and enlisted – and some civilians – all wanted a seat, any seat just to listen to history before the news media got hold of it and twisted it out of shape. Sorry, guys, you were all out of luck; the room was closed to all spectators. In other words, GO AWAY.

They laid-out the basics of the strategy for dealing with the Cabinet and the President. The JAG LCDR was given the responsibility for contacting the Chief Justice of SCOTUS and for figuring-out who was running the Justice Department, and for getting both of them to tomorrow's 09:30 conference in this same room.

Additionally, she was also assigned to find-out who the ranking officials of both the Senate and the House of Representatives are, as well as those for both major political parties. Subsequently, she was supposed to invite them to tomorrow's meeting as well. If anyone could not be contacted, she was supposed to invite their chief of staff in their stead.

And find some more JAG officers for Sunday and Monday.

Smitty suggested that PFCs Berkeley and Thompson would be good choices for a computer search of some Cabinet Department for their chains of command and for background on the respective Secretaries, as well. Rhodes agreed. A radio conversation indicated they were spot-on. A chopper would pick-up Berkeley and Thompson Saturday morning on the Ellipse at 06:30 sharp. Berkeley was going to get to use some new PCs and high-speed Internet connections over at The Pentagon; who wouldn't jump at that. However, he had to produce the search results by COB Saturday. But COB didn't have to

ORDER OF SUCCESSION

be at 17:00, so he figured he had some built-in slack. Chuck Berkeley slept well all Friday night – up until their scheduled lift-off.

The conference broke-up around 00:43 and agreed to reconvene at 09:15 later in the morning.

Time: Saturday, 08-September, 09:05 EDT (Andrews' Pilots' Ready Room)

The Andrews' mess halls furnished coffee, water bottles, fruit, pastries, and sandwiches in amounts adequate for an invasion – an invasions of politicians, all expecting their richly-deserved dues.

Smitty: "Is the AWACS crew represented here? If, yes, we can get you outta here early."

Echo-3 Commander: "Here. How can Echo-3 help out?"

Smitty: "Here is a condensed version of what we came-up with last night. Can you support this?" He slid a single sheet across the table.

Echo-3 Commander: "I believe we know what you all are looking for. Yes, we can support this with the addition of one other step. We need to have a no-fly zone covering the areas you intend to operate in. Otherwise, there will be so many media helos out there, they may cause their own accidents. We can spot them, but we cannot control them; it would be far better, from our perspective, if they all didn't look like 'hostiles', if you know what I mean."

Smitty: "Thank-you and noted." "Andrews Tower, you here? Good. Can you work on that with TRACON and Reagan Tower? I see you nodding yes, so Echo-3 you're free to make sure your bird will be fully operational when we start this. Oh, by the way, it looks like we may be using up to six to eight helos in addition to the Ghosts, so your points are well taken. Thank-you and good flying."

Time: Saturday, 08-September, 09:25 EDT (Andrews' Pilots' Ready Room)

The official briefing meeting began with introductions all around. This was followed by 90 minutes of how the events developed; steps taken to counter these events; and how the assault on TWH was stopped.

Order of Succession

During these 90 minutes (and one break at the mid-point), all of the guests nodded their heads as if in understanding of the actions, reactions, and conclusions.

Time: Saturday, 08-September, 11:33 EDT (Andrews' Pilots' Ready Room)

Some participants thanked the active military for their service in stopping so much of the possible damage to downtown D.C. as well as for bringing all of this to their attention before reading about it in *The Washington Post* and other major dailies – and seeing it on all the TV news shows.

However, during the follow-up Q&A session, all that agreeable head-nodding deteriorated into dissent.

The politicians split along party lines. Those in the same party as President Jacobson pronounced the President as incapable of being a party to such plotting. And the other party denounced the President as not only capable of plotting something like this, but also declared him to be completely capable of leading such a plot, as well.

Both parties agreed on at least one point: If we pursue arresting the President and the Cabinet, they will hold hearings and pursue charges against all of the people involved in this 'grandiose usurpation of constitutional powers by the military'.

The new Attorney General said that the Department of Justice (DOJ) would probably pursue trials for all concerned if they went forward with plans for bringing the President and Cabinet Secretaries to face their concept of 'military' justice.

The Chief Justice of SCOTUS said that, while he could not bring charges against anyone so far, he was more concerned by the 'overwhelming lack of evidence' against anyone but General Calhoun and the fake FBI agents out in California.

All adjourned to the buffet tables to chow-down on free food before they scurried off to catch-up to their regular weekend activities.

Time: Saturday, 08-September, 13:17 EDT (Andrews' Pilots' Ready Room)

The atmosphere in the Ready Room turned heavy and oppressive.

ORDER OF SUCCESSION

Following the departure of the shakers and movers in the U.S. Government, the remainder of the participants (those who had actually saved the butts of those same politicians), gathered to discuss their next move – or even if there was one left to pursue.

Smitty: "Thank-you one and all for all of your efforts so far. There were obviously at least two visions of reality in this room this morning. Just as obvious, the threats to pursue charges against any or all of us puts a damper on most future actions on our part primarily for the reasons that the Chief Justice mentioned. That is, unfortunately, we, make that I, do not have any iron-clad, rock solid proof. For that reason, I guess the best course now is to fold my tent and abandon any further overt steps. Any other comments are more than welcome. The floor is yours. Anybody?"

No one accepted the invitation with the exception of a few, who congratulated Smitty and a few others as having followed the patriotic path, but the politicians . . . well, you know those friggin' politicians were only looking-out to save their own jobs, positions of power, and retirements. Deserting the country during this apparent coup just did not warrant any place on their lists of top priorities.

Smitty: "So, I guess the thing to do now is for everybody to fold-up shop and go home. And thank all of you for trying to do the right thing."

Each respective command changed plans as required. The AWACS commander changed the destination of the plane. Andrews Tower notified TRACON and Reagan Tower they could return to normal operations in three hours. The Old Guard companies reclaimed command of their own officers and Platoon Sergeants and formulated plans to return to their barracks at Fort Myer while still maintaining a crowd-control stance around the buildings damaged during the aerial fire-fight in D.C. All was returning to normal again.

LCDR Sheila Weekes was overjoyed.

Time: Saturday, 08-September, 14:24 EDT (Andrews' Pilots' Ready Room)

Smitty motioned to Phillip, Brian, and Rocky to join him at a vacant table in the nearly empty room. "I just want to thank-you personally for believing in me. I know we had it straight, but it just didn't fall

Order of Succession

into place the right way. I'm so sorry that I got you all involved – you and your units. I hoped we could do the right thing for the country, but it was not to be. We missed the 14th Street Bridge, but at least I believe we saved quite a few lives in D.C., what with the missiles and all. Anybody up for a farewell flight?"

Phillip: "Where to and what did you have in mind?"

Smitty: "Site R to return Jacobson to . . . I don't know whether to Camp David or TWH. Haven't quite decided yet."

Rocky: "Well, as personal guards for Jacobson, sure, why not." There was just a hint of scorn in his answer.

Smitty: "Let me make a few calls before we leave. Gotta let some folks know to put a hold on some departures. And if you got one of these, bring it along." He waved a small electronic device at them and then slid it back into his pocket. Every one raised theirs, smiled slyly, and slowly nodded their heads in agreement.

Both Phillip and Brian immediately rose and made for the helos, borrowed from the Marine-1 fleet, to get them fueled and ready for flight.

Time: Saturday, 08-September, 14:56 EDT (Andrews' Flight Line)

Both helos lifted-off and headed almost due north from Andrews – actually, maybe eight degrees, or so, west of north.

Andrews Tower: "Ghost-1 and 2, two more helos joining your flight. Fly safely."

Ghost-1: "Andrews, who is third helo? Over."

Before Andrews could respond: "Ghost-1, this is western Ghost-3. Needed at least three to make a proper escort. You got four now. Out."

Brain turned to look at Rocky, who sort of gave fist-pump. Rocky: "If I didn't know better, I think he sounds an awful lot like Colonel Gahagen. Ask him if he's Malibu Slumlord." Brian keyed the mic and asked Ghost-3.

Ghost-3: "Roger that. Got some buddies in the bird. Out"

Rocky: "YES!! There's a squad of Gunnies joining us for this little trip. Let me get a hold of Air Lima. This'll tickle him."

ORDER OF SUCCESSION

Rocky: "Just as I suspected. There's gonna be a slight change in passenger loading. Here's what Air is suggesting." Rocky read his notes to Ghost-2.

Time: Saturday, 08-September, 15:45 EDT (Site R)

The helos landed at Site R – between the 'A' and 'B' doorways.

When the presidential party appeared, Plan C was put into action – and that is to separate the President from his Secret Service detail. The President was guided over to Ghost-1, which already had Smitty and, now, Gahagen in it as well as Phillip as pilot. Two Marine Gunnies were posted outside the door – dressed not in the usual Marine Full-Dress, blue uniforms, but in Marine Battle uniforms, complete with M-4 rifles, loaded magazines locked in-place. After Jacobson was on-board, the Secret Service agents started to come on board, but the Gunnies pointed them to next helo over their objections. Smitty appeared in the door-way and pointed to the next helo and told them their charge was in safe hands. The agents recognized Smitty and, looking at each other, shrugged their shoulders and hustled on over to Ghost-3, only to discover they were getting the last seats because of all the Marines, who forced them to sit not together, but each between two fully armed Marines, who made sure the agents were belted-in really tightly and requested their radios and firearms, which, of course raised red flags. But, whacha gonna do . . . Ghost-4 had room for the balance of the agents and more Marines – same scenario. Ghost-2, with Brian and Rocky on board, now also had the balance of Marines and soldiers who left Andrews in the additional helos

Plan C opened as planned: The President had been separated from his protection detail. The next part of Plan C began to unfold after lift-off. Ghost-3 and Ghost-4 now led the formation, heading south on a course toward Andrews. Ghost-1 and Ghost-2 followed the formation and peeled-off the formation at the tower at Mount St. Mary's University and flew cross-country back toward Camp David. Echo-3, which had monitored the air-space along the entire route, now flew lazy-8s above, and 'Satellite' Larry monitored an even wider area.

Time: Saturday, 08-September, 16:23 EDT (Camp David)

Ghost-1 landed on the regular helipad, while Ghost-2 set-down on the employee parking lot, which wasn't crowded because it was the weekend and President Jacobson was not expected. The occupants of Ghost-1 hustled into a nearby building, where they found a decent-sized room to have a conversation. One of the Marines found a buddy on-post and scrounged up some coffee and sandwiches.

As expected, Jacobson had been highly suspicious when he first got on-board without his regular security detail back at Site R. His uneasiness was somewhat relieved when he saw Smitty, whom he recognized from one of his earlier security details. But now, landing just after lift-off mere miles away, he again became quite apprehensive. Everybody reached into their pockets and thumbed their digital recorders on.

Smitty: "President Jacobson, I know what you must be thinking right about now. We are not kidnapping you or holding you as a hostage. We just want to have a conversation with you about what's goin' on and that you approved all of it because it looks very suspicious to us – frankly, quite suspicious. Some of us put our lives on-the-line doing what we knew had to be done. All of our careers are still on-the-line. Your Secret Service detail is safe; they are being detained over at Andrews until we finish this conversation."

Smitty, introduced the primary people in the room as those who were personally involved in yesterday's fire-fight in D.C. He also told Jacobson that he and this group of American Heroes would appreciate a little private conversation with Jacobson before he returned to The White House.

Each narrated their story of participation in the events leading up to yesterday in D.C. It was obvious that Jacobson was not listening intently or was just plain bored – as if he was pre-occupied with more important matters Lots of 'I see's' and other non-committal comments'.

However, Phillip's narrative was, obviously, more action-packed than the others; he concluded his tale with Bubba's death-bed quasi-accusation about all the planning and control emanating from TWH. Jacobson's demeanor changed to attentive. "Who was that pilot, again?"

Phillip: "Former Air Force Colonel Seth Delong; he was also nick-named 'Bubba'. Used to be assigned to Fort Rucker, Alabama; the same place Lieutenant General Hamilton Calhoun was assigned at the same time."

Jacobson: "I do not know any Colonel Seth Delong. I do know General Calhoun, though. And you said this Delong said I had something

Order of Succession

to do with yesterday's attack on TWH? I don't know him. Period. Why would I attack TWH; I live there for cryin'-out-loud! He must be wrong about this. When I get back, I'll call him into the Oval Office and get this straightened out right then."

Phillip: "You can't do that, sir; he died in my arms yesterday evening. Delong pointed toward TWH and said he believed control came from over there and that he would not be surprised if it went all the way up to 'The Man', which I assumed meant you. And then he was shot to death by a fellow conspirator on the medevac helo, the one firing the missiles."

Jacobson: "Missiles? What missiles? I was told late last night that that somebody fired some shots at TWH. Nobody said anything about a missile attack. You're kidding me right? Missiles, you gotta be be jokin', right? Who was this other guy on the chopper? Missiles! Oh, my God! You're not joking are you?"

Phillip: "His name is, or was, Hal Drixler before I shot and killed him. He had a welding shop in Thurmont, just a little ways over the hill from us right now. And, yes, missiles were used on a number of buildings. The Federal Reserve and the Treasury Buildings are smoldering holes in the ground. And both the Eisenhower Executive Office and the Corcoran Gallery of Art now have huge gaping holes in their sides. Yes, indeed, missiles were used. And the 14th Street Bridge was also destroyed. Did you know about that, sir?"

Smitty immediately recognized the slight change in Phillip's tone of voice toward Jacobson. The 'sir' gave it away.

Jacobson: "What do you mean the 14th Street Bridge was destroyed? That's an essential commuter artery, isn't it?"

Smitty: "It *was* essential until Friday's evening rush hour, when it was blown-up. It and the nearby rail bridge are now lying in the Potomac. And a couple of other bridges across the Anacostia River are still standing, but useless. You have been saying that somebody was telling you what happened yesterday, right? Yet you don't have any of the facts correct. Who has been giving you these news flashes?"

Jacobson: "Why should I trust you? For all I know right now, you may have kidnapped me and are holding me for ransom of some sort. You should know, of all people, that we don't ransom hostages."

Order of Succession

Smitty: "We understand your concern about us. Okay, you must know somebody up here that you do trust. Call him and ask him or turn-on that TV and change channels until you find a news report. With all of the destruction yesterday, it will still be the only major news event on TV for the next week or so. Or I'll call Larry to zap me some video from yesterday's satellite feeds. Or how about backup from the AWACS plane circling above us right now. Call your man up here and ask him. Here's your POTUS Phone you had out in California when you were really kidnapped. Use it if you like."

Jacobson: "You really are serious, aren't you? Okay, let me call somebody who I believe will be straight with me." He dialed and spoke to three people – as if triple-checking the information. Jacobson face turned ashen after the first call; after the third one, it was really drained – really pasty. "All three agree with your description. You're asking me to name an old friend. That's going to be very difficult for me to do."

Gahagen (who had been silent up until now): "Sir, can we play a little game, okay? Does this old friend have access to military armaments, either directly or indirectly? Did your old friend help you with selecting some or all of the new members of your Cabinet? Did he vouch for how good each of these people is? Do you really know any of the new Cabinet Secretaries or anything about them? I mean really know them? Do you like their work in your administration? How did he explain all the murder and destruction out at that rest-area out in the California desert? Does this old friend have unrestricted access inside TWH?"

Jacobson (now appearing to speculate he had been played for a sucker): "Oh, my God. Every answer points toward the same person. How could he do this to me? How could he betray me like this?" Jacobson's face turned from pasty to livid in record time. "The one that fits the bill, in all categories, is my party's majority leader in the Senate, Senator Marion O'Donoghue. You've got to be wrong about this. Give me my phone; I'll call that guy right now and settle it. And, no, I don't know that much about all those Cabinet Secretaries; Marion said they were all good people who could manage their Agencies as we directed. I went along with him on that. I've been conned for sure!"

Smitty: "Mr. President, how did this Senator O'Donoghue explain the events at the rest-area?

ORDER OF SUCCESSION

Jacobson: "He said it was a training exercise. I was never given any follow-up on it. Why, what really happened?"

Smitty: "Aside from somebody shooting at me with a hunting rifle, killing all of the remaining agents on your security detail, blowing-up an overpass on I-8, some local sheriff's deputies being killed, a helicopter attack on our Marines in the rest area, remote-controlled weapons, and some other nasty business – not much else."

Jacobson: "That's not what I was told by the Senator – and not by the Secret Service, either, I might add."

Smitty (addressing Jacobson): "Sir, please get a cup of coffee or something over there while we discuss this turn of events. Have a sandwich while you're at it. Trust me, we won't take long."

Smitty: (turning to the others after Jacobson was out of earshot): "Is he truthin' us, playin' us, or just a really good liar? Rocky, can you get a hold of PFC Berkeley or Thompson and see if he can figure out how to run a background check on the Senator, and fast, too?"

Time: Saturday, 08-September, 18:06 EDT (Camp David)

The group decided Colonel Gahagen should present their findings to Jacobson. They also decided that this would be a test to see if it would be worthwhile to proceed further depending on how Jacobson responds.

Gahagen (addressing Jacobson): "Sir, we had a background check done on the Senator; we double- and triple-checked it, pulling it from several different databases. One thing that popped-up was that he has business ties with at least 11 of the new Cabinet Secretaries, primarily through ownership and cross-ownership interests of various companies that do lots of business with the Federal Government. And these other parties were confirmed as your new Cabinet Secretaries controlling the government departments charged with regulating the areas of the economy in which their former companies operate. There seems to be several conflicts-of-interest.

"Our quick check also disclosed that the Senator also belongs to at least two somewhat secret groups, which covertly advocate dynamic changes to the U.S. Government by any means necessary. Prior to this morning's meeting, I ordered two Marines to begin locating background information about the newly-confirmed Secretaries. They are still at it trying to follow intertwined leads across all 15 appointees. Of the eleven he has finished, he reports that approximately 85 percent of those have four or more similar possible conflicts with other government departments. Some of these began through common employers and some were at financial institutions with ties to those companies and others in the same field. Furthermore, they also belong to social organizations pressing for changes to rules and regulations that are under the direct control of these new Secretaries. These are either the same organizations the Senator belongs to or are quite similar to them."

"Basically, their brief analysis is that the U.S. Government is now controlled by an extremely small group of people, all tightly intertwined and uniquely positioned, and who are pushing for specialized private gains while simultaneously enacting and enforcing serious changes inside the Government without any legislative actions. And, publicly they are telling the citizens how well this administration is 'working for the American people'. Here is a list of the organizations they have found so far and who is associated with them. Would you like to look at the list on my phone or shall I send it to yours?"

Jacobson: "Mine, please. Tap mine and I should have it."

Gahagen: "Yes, sir. (He tapped his to Jacobson's.) You should have it now."

Jacobson thumbed through the document and began mumbling to himself. "I would never associate with this guy. I know, about this company and these four, too; they're as crooked as corkscrews. Why would I do business with these lying SOBs? This Secretary controls this department and still has financial ties to the companies it is supposed control? That shouldn't be allowed. And I trusted my old friend for advice. What a fool I am! Okay, guys, how do we fix this and fast? By Monday morning, if possible? How can we do it that fast?"

Smitty handed this off to Gahagen motioning with an up-turned palm. In other words, whatever the Colonel decides to do, everybody gains glory or hangs together.

Gahagen: "Sir, we had some teams composed of Marines and Old Guard soldiers already assigned to this task. However, following this morning's meeting over at Andrews, we staged a stand-down of these

Order of Succession

plans and were preparing to return to our normal duty assignments at our usual posts. That also included taking you into custody based on the suspicions of Colonel Delong, the pilot of the aggressor chopper. This conversation has turned me around to the point of believing that you were, indeed duped. That, or you were just plain stuuu . . . (Gahagen didn't finish his quickly deteriorating attempt at sort of humor.). As I was saying, sir, all of our teams are still in place waiting for our decision – your decision. For example: The AWACS, Echo 3, plane is circling overhead as we speak. If you decide to implement those plans, Echo-3 will guide our choppers and advise where other planes and choppers are in relation to our target LZs. If your decision is a no-go, the AWACS heads back to its home base as soon as it gets the word. We also have one company of Marines at the ready, and two platoons from The Old Guard standing-by over at Fort Myer, not to mention Andrews Tower, the Reagan National Tower, and the local TRACON waiting for a go/no-go. We do not have anybody at The Pentagon advised of this situation because we are still not positive about who is on which side – with the exception of General Calhoun, that is. If this is a go, we will have by-passed all officers above all our levels, which is a serious situation for all of us, as you can well imagine."

Jacobson: "Will you help me regain control of the Government? How about orders directly from the CINC? I think I am still the CINC, aren't I? They haven't usurped that power yet have they?"

Gahagen, looking around the room for consensus, using hand signals, it was decided. "Sir, put the orders in writing, and we launch our original Plan A."

Jacobson: "I'll hand-write orders from me to you on this piece of paper. It doesn't have the Oval Office logo and watermark, but it does have Camp David printed on it." And so, Plan A began with hand-written orders on a Camp David paper napkin.

ORDER OF SUCCESSION

52– Pack Your Overnight Bags

Around 19:00, Saturday, 08-September: (Camp David)

TIME: 19:02 EDT

Gahagen: "We now have what I consider our marching orders direct from our CINC. Let's make this happen."

Cap'n Rhodes queried PFC Berkeley about progress with the background check on the Senator. Berkeley had uncovered even more ties to an increasing number of leaders of big business – domestic and foreign – through multiple off-shore accounts. Rhodes instructed him to make sure the paper trails are as easy to follow as possible. Then print-out what they already have and make about 40 copies, and then hand-carry them in a box or pouch to Rhodes' location. "Cap'n Brian Hauser will provide transport from your location. And do not let the pouch outta your hands."

Rhodes raised Gunny Cornell on the radio and instructed him to have APs from Andrews take over custody of the Secret Service agents (who were not presently under arrest). The APs are to just keep them 'contained' and not to permit any contact with their offices. And then Gunny Cornell had to load as many armed soldiers and Marines as possible into the choppers deploying to the Ellipse. Their mission is to restrain the new passengers just as they did the agents. And, oh yeah, prepare for about a week stay at our location.

Cornell: "Yes, sir. You really mean this is really goin' down, dontcha? Consider it done."

Rhodes: "Yeah, it's gonna happen. Orders straight from CINC. Standby for the go-signal."

Order of Succession

Major Jenkins raised Andrews Tower with orders to make as many choppers as possible from Marine Helicopter Squadron One (HMX-1) available, fueled, and ready for transportation duty from the Ellipse to/from Camp David. Each helo needed room for at least three passengers and three armed Marines or Army soldiers on-board – or four plus four, if possible. Andrews was to await our signal for the flight over to The Ellipse. While Andrews waited, they again had to order the air-space over D.C. and the Maryland and Virginia suburbs to be closed to all air traffic by 20:15 hours for at least two days. This was to include the flight paths all the way to Camp David plus a 10-mile restricted buffer zone on each side of that path. That 'P-40' Zone just increased dramatically in size.

The Air Force fighter squadrons at Andrews were advised of the 'newly-expanded' restricted zone, R-4009. The pilots were given authority to keep all intruding aircraft out of the zone or force them to land using whatever force the pilots decide to use. The pilots all asked for their orders to be repeated. 'Air combat here in America? Put that in writing with a signature'.

Rhodes: "Echo-3. Over."

Echo-3: "Go ahead Malibu."

Malibu Beach: "You all may need to refuel for an extended mission beginning around 21:30 hours. And once it actually begins, the news media are gonna be comin' out of the woodwork trying to follow our vehicles. We just need to know who's where. Ghost-1 will provide low-altitude defense if necessary. Andrews Tower will advise how large the new 'P-40' restricted area is and where its new boundaries will now be. All airspace inside that will then be reclassified to 'prohibited'. There will be lots of choppers to and from Tango Whiskey Hotel and Charley Delta. We need to know if anybody else flies within that area. Do you roger?"

Echo-3: "Roger that. Returning to refuel for extended mission. Out."

Cap'n Brian Hauser contacted our JAG officer, LCDR Weekes, with instructions to scare-up more JAG officers – up to four more if she can find that many. And, yes, from multiple services, if necessary. He was to provide transportation between the earlier LZ in the Pentagon parking lot and Charley Delta.

ORDER OF SUCCESSION

Gahagen's job was to deal with the higher profile government employees who had been at the meeting earlier in the morning. Specifically, the Chief Justice and the Attorney General, who were peeved about being disturbed twice in one day regarding a problem they thought they had already resolved. Gahagen, in military fashion, advised each to pack an overnight bag for about a two or three days' stay.

Then Gahagen contacted The Old Guard Battalion Commander to have the two platoons to fuel-up their Humvees, each of which was to have an armed, senior NCO in charge of picking-up high-ranking passengers and transporting them to The Ellipse. The assigned assembly area was Lafayette Park on the north side of TWH, while the assigned LZ was the Ellipse on the south side.

What Colonel Gahagen didn't tell The Old Guard's colonel, was that, after consulting with Smitty and Rhodes, it was decided to create some transparency with the news media. To that end, Gahagen also included the names of up to five media reporters to the list of passengers. Each was with one of the four major TV networks and was usually its designated 'White House correspondent'. The fifth was a reporter from *The Washington Post*. These five were supposed to document the impending proceedings and distribute their documents to the rest of the United States and the world. These reporters were to be under similar communications restrictions as the other passengers were while in the air – however, retaining some privileges the others were not going to have while on the ground at Camp David. They would either fly in any vacant seats on the choppers or have to ride in Humvees. First choice goes to the earliest arrivals.

Jacobson raised the OIC, a Navy Commander, for Camp David and instructed him to prepare for about 40 to 50 guests and to organize parking facilities for Humvees, helos, and buses. And more beverages and food are also needed where they already were. CINC also authorized 'local purchases' for anything the OIC needed. Done. Let's 'invite' the guests.

Time: Saturday, 08-September, 21:34 EDT (Lafayette Park and the Ellipse)

Cap'n Duane Calhoun, The Old Guard, Bravo Company, handed-out addresses and maps for picking-up Cabinet Secretaries in sequential order. They were to pick-up the first one and transport him/her to the

Order of Succession

Ellipse, then go pick-up the next on the list. With eight Humvees it shouldn't take too long.

Platoon Sergeants Emery Colman and Harlan Crandall and other Platoon Sergeants were each armed with a loaded side-arm and were provided with a script of what to tell their assigned pick-ups. Basically:

"Because of the incidents yesterday afternoon, the President requests that you join him for further discussions. Although we are military, we are only providing transportation to his location. We must depart immediately. Please grab a coat and an overnight bag. We'll help you carry it to the Humvee that's waiting for you."

Followed by transportation to the Ellipse to board the helicopters.

The same procedure also applied to Senate Majority Leader, Senator Marion O'Donoghue. He was to be picked-up first and boarded immediately into a dedicated helo with him as the only passenger – not counting one Marine Gunny and one Army Sergeant – both armed.

The Chief Justice and Attorney General would be picked-up first and flown immediately to Charley Delta in their own helo, piloted by Ghost-2 and the normal flight crew onboard.

Cap'n Calhoun also handed the list of media reporters to two Humvee drivers, also with an armed Sergeant (strictly for show). The invitation he extended to the reporters was more like an invitation than an order: (The implications were obvious and absolute, however.)

"Because of the incidents yesterday afternoon, the President is offering five media reporters an invitation to join him and to observe and report about further discussions. Your name is on my list. If you are interested, please grab a coat and an overnight bag for maybe three days. Although we are military, we are only providing transportation to his location. We must depart immediately. We'll help you carry it to the Humvee that's waiting for you. If you are not interested, there are other names further down on this list."

(That last part was a slight fib; these five were the only ones because of time-constraints.)

Not a single one reporter turned-down this invitation. Not one.

Order of Succession

Time: Saturday, 08-September, 22:07 EDT (Lafayette Park and the Ellipse)

Cap'n Rhodes gave the 'go-ahead', and the Humvees departed the park to pick-up their respective Secretaries. During the lull between departures and returns of the Humvees, Cap'n Calhoun walked over to a Secret Service guard shack and used the restroom and got another cup of coffee. Of course, the agents wanted to know what was going on and what the mission was tonight. "Sorry. I can't tell ya. Keep checking TV and *The Post* over the next few days, though; there should be one helluva story."

Cap'n Gerald Lambert, The Old Guard, Delta Company, was assigned to direct Humvee traffic on the Ellipse and boarding the bewildered, new passengers onto the waiting helos, making sure that cell-phones, radios, and other devices were bagged and stored in secured boxes. He also ensured that either soldiers or Marines sat between each of the civilians and who made sure their belts were appropriately tight.

As the first batch of returning Humvees pulled-up into the Ellipse, Cap'n Lambert directed them to the their assigned helo and instructed them 'don't tear-up the grass out there'. "Drop 'em-off and go get the next one." He also noticed the Secretaries' faces – some concerned, some not; some biting their lips, others reluctant to surrender their electronic leashes. But most checked and rechecked their watches again and again and again.

Three media reporters were lucky enough to get flying seats. They reluctantly surrendered their phones and other electronic gear; however, they were assured all of it would be returned at the destination – unlike the Secretaries'. Their fears were much different than those of the secretaries. They may have to write their stories by hand – using old-fashioned pen and paper. The two remaining reporters hustled to get seats in any Humvee headed in the right direction – even though they had no idea what that direction was.

Time: Sunday, 09-September, 00:22 EDT (Lafayette Park and the Ellipse)

Fortunately, Ghost-2 departed first. He arrived first and off-loaded his passengers, including PFCs Berkeley and Thompson and four additional

ORDER OF SUCCESSION

JAG officers, including two from the Army, one each from the Air Force and the Navy – all in various states of disbelief and confusion. If LCDR Weekes was supposed to lead this mixed staff of unknowns into the uncharted frontier of JAG-dom, she certainly had her work cut-out for her – and, as previously, was rather fearful of it.

Ghost-2 returned to the Ellipse to pick-up the Chief Justice and the AG.

After the Senator and all of the Secretaries were safely on their ways to Camp David all remaining soldiers and Marines, not assigned to the helos, loaded into the Humvees. Cap'n Calhoun formed the Humvees into a convoy and headed north toward Camp David.

D.C. Metropolitan Police provided an escort bypassing all blocked-off streets north on Wisconsin Avenue all the way to I-495 (a.k.a. 'The Beltway') north of Bethesda. Maryland State Police (MSP) directed the motorcade onto the closed lanes of the I-495 (a.k.a. 'The Outer Loop') and then onto I-270, which had also been closed all the way to Frederick, Maryland, where the motorcade was routed onto north US-15. Similarly, US-15 was also closed all the way to Thurmont, where MD-77 was also closed, in both directions, all the way into the Catoctin Mountains.

None of the police officers had any information about all of the closures, but about 100% were positive it had everything to do with last Friday's fire-fight down in D.C. Maybe 110%.

Following the departure of the last helo, Cap'n Lambert returned control of the Ellipse back to the Secret Service and claimed his usual seat in his Humvee, the shotgun seat. A reporter reluctantly moved into a rear seat, fearing the complete loss of the trip. Yes, this was going to be a big piece of history not to be missed. Cap'n Lambert felt for the grip of his sidearm and made sure there was a magazine in it and the spare one at his waist. He tapped his driver's right shoulder and made the signal for 'move out now'. His driver drove the Humvee through the D.C. streets north on Wisconsin quite a bit above the speed limit until he was the last vehicle in the motorcade before the motorcade passed through Bethesda. He drove like his 'low-flying license' was about to expire.

The fifth reporter was a little late getting to the helos, so he or she should be in one of the Humvees in the motorcade. If he/she missed the seat, some editor is really going to be PO'ed with that reporter.

Order of Succession

Time: Sunday, 09-September, 01:17 EDT (Camp David)

The helos approached Camp David by following Highway US-15 north out of Frederick, passing over Thurmont, and turning to port near the lighted tower at Mount St. Mary's University. The first helos landed on the usual LZ. The later ones were forced to unload their passengers and fly over to the newly-requisitioned, overflow LZ located over the hill at the Sabillasville School. The Old Guard dispatched soldiers and Marines to set-up the perimeter guard for the helos. Regardless of the traffic jam, all passengers were delivered safely.

Ghost-1 knew the helos and Humvees would be thirsty before their last trip if this meeting went as he thought it probably could. He contacted Andrews Tower with a request for a couple of fuel tankers to be standing-by on this side of the D.C. traffic jams – still in grid-lock in some areas. Andrews said they would look into that – one for helos and one for the Humvees, right? It was the part about where to get them that was the big problem right now. An hour later, Andrews raised Ghost-1.

Andrews: "Ghost-1. Over."

Ghost-1: "Roger."

Andrews: "Fuel trucks laid-on from Martinsburg Reserve. Meet helos and Humvees at Hagerstown Airport. They need about 2-1/2 hours to load-up and get there. Airport's ready to receive trucks and your flights at the far east end of their runway – where the perimeter road goes under the runway. Call ahead for lights. Will that work for you?"

Ghost-1: "That's a big Roger on that. Works fine for us. Don't know when fireworks will be over at this station. We'll ferry passengers to airport and form-up there before final flights. Thanks for scouting them up. Stand-by for updates."

Chuck Berkeley took personal pleasure knowing that only the two lowly PFCs knew exactly what this was all about, and those 'official' bozos didn't know that both PFCs had developed the critical evidence enclosed in his pouch (actually, his personal camo back-pack) and one copy-paper box. PFC Berkeley doubled-timed over to the meeting building and found Cap'n Rhodes. Thompson followed with his own 'pouch' – the box. They moved their meeting into the kitchen area, where Berkeley unpacked his pouch and handed the contents over to Rhodes. He also handed Cap'n Rhodes two thumb drives with all of the

Order of Succession

documents stored on them. He policed-up the pouch, saluted, turned smartly, and left the showboating to others. Both he and Thompson remained in the building – in the kitchen. Who would after being this close to history? He found the latrine, got a cup of coffee and some snack-chow, and sat on an out-of-the-way chair in the kitchen, anxiously waiting for the real show to begin.

Cap'n Rhodes sorted through the contents of the pouch, making distribution piles. Thoughtfully, PFC Berkeley included additional copies of his findings – not including the ten copies he made for himself and stored them in a separate compartment of his bag along with three additional thumb drives with everything he dug-up about the Senator and Cabinet Secretaries stored on them, protected by 16-character alpha-numeric passwords. In a few years, this stuff might be valuable. Well, one never knows if these could turn into a retirement account or just a nuisance to move from place to place. Ya just never knew.

Colonel Gahagen addressed the new guests with the basics of this meeting: grab refreshments (over there), the latrines are over that way, and your seats are over here. Please get comfortable. And please note that both video and audio recording will be activated during the rest of the proceedings.

Physically, the chairs were arranged similar to SAT and college testing halls – with large spaces between the chairs to allow proctors to watch for copying and passing of notes.

The first three reporters – the lucky ones who flew in on a helo – were pulled off to the side by Colonel Gahagen and told they were the first ones to arrive and guided them to the impromptu 'press pool' – those chairs and tables over there by that wall.

President Jacobson was standing in the kitchen area where he had been studying the PFCs' reports. He was plainly visible to the Senator and Cabinet Secretaries through the kitchen's serving window. Jacobson looked around the kitchen, spotted the PFCs still seated in what they thought was an out-of-the-way 'safe zone', and motioned them to join him at the counter. Berkeley gave him a startled look and returned a questioning look – like 'Who? Me?' And got a presidential look – no, make that a CINC look – for 'Yes, you and right now, dammit!' They both hustled over to the counter like they were on roller skates. This

Order of Succession

mini conference with only the President and two (lowly) PFCs sent more than a ripple through the assembled high-powered guests: "Why should a PFC be talking to 'The Man'?" "What the hell could they be talking about for 15 minutes?" If they could only have been a fly on the wall in the kitchen, they would have heard how the evidence against them was laid-out. But worst of all, how damning it all is.

The Humvees with the two remaining reporters finally pulled into the parking area, scattering gravel and dust as they slid to a stop as near to the building as possible. Both reporters literally threw their bags and stuff out and hit the ground running. The last reporter slipped on some loose gravel, fell flat – almost doing a face-plant in the parking lot – ripping the right knee of his pants, skinning both hands and his left shin. But he collected himself and his gear and hustled to catch up to the others as if his life (and reputation) depended on getting into that room where all the action was supposed to take place as quickly as possible.

{Breathless brain: "That Army guy who rousted me out of a comfortable evening with the family better not have been pulling my leg. If half of what he said is true, I bet this will be a real scoop. Better be true, dammit, or I'm gonna expose the Army's incompetence and its audacity for keeping us from the news site around The White House. Who do they think they are anyway?"}

Both burst into the room, where a Marine guard slowed them to a crawl by requesting ID cards to match against his list of pre-approved attendees. Colonel Gahagen personally identified them and sent them, packing their stuff, 'over to the press pool by that wall over there'. Looking at their colleagues already there, "What the hell is going on here?" Hey, has it started yet?" "Did we miss anything?"

{Breathless brain: "Looks like the Army guys were right. Looks like something big might be brewing. Guess you better thank those boys in uniform."}

Gahagen also had the reporters' electronic devices returned to them along with an order masquerading as a request, "As a courtesy to President Jacobson, please do not use these devices in this room so you will not disturb the proceedings – no calls, no beeps, no nuthin' with the exception of your digital recorders. As long as the proceedings are underway, please use just your recorders. If any of you has a digital video camera, you may set that up as well. However, because of the space limitations in this room, that one video must be shared with all of your colleagues as the pool video feed. We, the Government, would also greatly appreciate three courtesy copies of that entire video as well. However, during any breaks in the events, all of you are more than welcome to use all your other gear, such as phones, laptops, tablets, and the like in here or if you go outside this building. Do you have any questions? None. Then thank-you for observing these few simple courtesies." Of course, no one had any.

{Confused brains: "Questions about what? Hell we don't even know what the hell is goin' on here yet! How can we have any questions? Is this guy friggin' serious?" "Okay now, let's slow your attitude down a bit 'til we see what's gonna happen, okay?"}

After Gahagen got the go-ahead signal from the kitchen area, in his best command voice, he approached the center of the table facing the Senator and Secretaries and finally announced to the rest of the room, "Ladies and Gentlemen, The President of The United States of America" and promptly withdrew to the kitchen to join the others watching history in the making.

The reporters were all eyes and ears, with pens and paper at the ready for taking notes; their recorders all turned-on to catch, not only the words, but also the tone, nuances, and inflections as well. All had at least two recorders; one had three, another one had four.

President Jacobson walked quickly and purposely to the center of the room, facing his Cabinet Secretaries and the Senator. Jacobson, usually relatively quiet and reserved, a man who didn't mind meeting people at least half-way, began to demonstrate his firm, authoritative, and in-charge CINC-mode – a style rarely, if ever, seen before. Before he began to speak to his so-called Cabinet of 'experts', he held a sheaf of papers in each of his hands, slowly shaking his head from side to side. Finally, he turned to face his Secretaries and shook the papers in both hands at his Secretaries, slowly shaking both hands up and down in short movements. He slowly cast his penetrating gaze across the room from his left to his right, stopping his movement to shake his fistsful of papers at each Secretary all the while looking each directly and squarely in their eyes, the papers still flapping in the calm air. After he finished facing the final Secretary, Jacobson finally threw those in

Order of Succession

his right hand forcefully down on the table in front of him, with a snap of his wrist, displaying a face and attitude of disappointment, disgust, and utter contempt. He cast his stare across the Secretaries ending back at the Senator without saying a word, letting his demeanor and ire speak for themselves.

He motioned to Cap'n Rhodes (still in his battle uniform) to pass-out the individual reports about each of the respective guests, each receiving their own. As Rhodes distributed the respective reports face-down to each of the guests, President Jacobson told the Cabinet Secretaries, "Just to clear the air about the presence of the armed services here today, they are here because of me. In my capacity as CINC(Commander in Chief), I commanded them to provide these services and duties, such as transportation and the like, because . . . well, because I trust them to be relatively neutral in this particular situation. Unlike you all, they are not involved in the coup attempt that climaxed with Friday's destruction down there in D.C. They put their lives, reputations, and possibly their personal freedoms on the line to preserve these United States. That attempted coup that I mentioned is what we are here to resolve, and I am going to behead it at this meeting." Rhodes continued distributing the reports while Jacobson spoke, laying complete stacks of all the same reports on the table at which the JAG officers were seated. He handed separate complete stacks to each Attorney General Pamela McAllister and the Chief Justice Gary Paulings from SCOTUS. Continuing in the direction of the kitchen, Cap'n Rhodes distributed five complete sets of copies of the reports to the 'press pool' After Jacobson backed away from the podium, Rhodes leaned over the podium, and gave some brief instructions to the Cabinet Secretaries and the Senator about how they could (or should) refute their respective reports. Rhodes kept thinking that if anything goes wrong with this whole gambit, our collective fat is in the fire now for damn sure; those media reporters will skin each of us alive for damn sure. Rhodes exited into the kitchen and joined the PFCs and the Colonel to follow along as Jacobson unfolded the show. Smitty joined them moments later.

The reporters didn't wait for permission to open their copies; what could happen to them now, anyway. As they thumbed through the Secretaries' and the Senator's reports, there were muted and hushed, "Oh my God, have you seen this one yet?" "What were they effing thinking?" "How could they think this would go unnoticed?"

428

ORDER OF SUCCESSION

"Holy s—t!" They highlighted almost everything, everywhere. The JAG officers noticed all of the reporters' activity and figured-out most of what they were mouthing to each other – and why. The JAGs wasted no time coming up to speed reading through their copies of the reports. None more so than LCDR Weekes. Her worst nightmares were starting to come true.

{Formerly 'shrinking violet' brain: "Sheila, baby, what did you get yourself into? Why did you hang around Friday night, huh? You were even on the right side of the Potomac; there weren't any traffic jams on the Fort Myer's side.

"So now you arrested one General and some stupid Colonel who didn't know enough to shut-up and play nice with fully-armed Marines. What the hell is his name anyway? Still don't know. And now you're leading all these JAGs. To do what?

"POTUS is gonna have them effing arrested, isn't he? Oh, don't tell me we gotta read all of these Secretaries and the Senator their rights! I'll bet we're gonna arrest most of the leaders of the Executive Branch of the government. What did you get yourself into? Why me? Conference with the JAGs now and get a plan together if it comes to that. Start looking through those reports right now, Sheila baby. Then plan going on leave Tuesday."}

Jacobson began: "After I heard what actually happened on this past Friday down in Washington, and I must tell you I personally even double-checked, no make that quadruple-checked, everything I was told. I was greatly saddened to learn that someone would attempt to assassinate me in The White House. That someone I thought I knew as a friend. I counted my blessings because I was in an evacuation exercise near here at Site R. At least I was safe, or so I thought. But those dastardly bastards were willing to blow-up The White House with its staff still working inside it and the Secret Service guards outside, too. (Now, turning to face O'Donoghue:) Weren't they, Senator? I'll get to that in a few minutes. Maybe.

"Interestingly, when I was supposed to return to The White House yesterday from Site R, my transportation was provided by some folks who had been at that rest-area in the Mojave Desert out in California about two months ago, where I was informed that I was just acting a part

Order of Succession

for a training exercise for the Secret Service. (Now facing the Senator straight-on as he spoke to the entire room:) Isn't that what you told me, Senator? And all of those Secret Services agents who were killed. What kind of training is that? And all along, you had very different plans for my signature to fast-track the appointments of these here friggin' Secretaries, didn't you?"

(Now looking around the group of Secretaries): "As I read through these reports, my mood changed from one of disbelief to one of extreme disappointment then to one of anger. I realized that all of you are probably working together in concert to achieve a much different goal than I and my former Cabinet members were. They are all gone now, but you all know that already don't you? And you, you friggin' bastards, are all still effing here, working to change my administration into something even I won't recognize at the end of my term. You are working to achieve a purpose that does not seem to benefit the average citizens of this country. Not one iota, does it? The benefits of this new, covert, underhanded plan, however, will be shared by a very small, select group, won't they? Y'all used to work for them. You might even still be paid by them under-the-table as far as I know. And you would probably go back to work for them so you can collect your rewards for effing the rest of the citizens of this country. Well, before this here meeting, that may have been your plans. But, shit happens and plans get derailed. You're now looking at the new chief derailer-in-chief.

"As I interpret the intent of your actions, y'all are planning to permanently codify 'privatizing the benefits and socializing the costs or losses' through new laws and regulations dreamed-up on the fly. Basically, you are planning to legalize mandatory laws to permanently screw the average American until long after you all have retired and moved-on, taking all the ill-gotten gains with you while the average American won't be able to afford any retirement. Well, here's an effing news flash for you: That ain't gonna happen on my watch. Period. Got that? It just ain't going to effing happen. And after we settle your hash here, your corporate buddies are my new administration's next targets. My next order to the AG is to make that happen as the very first priority. Sorry, you won't be able to warn them because you're going to be very busy on your own cases. Take my word for that."

ORDER OF SUCCESSION

Turning to face the AG, "Attorney General McAllister, do you understand your new marching orders?"

AG McAllister: "Yes sir. Consider them underway the very second these proceedings conclude."

Jacobson, now in a more moderate voice toward the Senator and Secretaries: "All of you now, please go ahead and read these reports I had prepared about your own respective backgrounds. I think I am not stretching too far if I say you are probably also aware of many similar ties and conflicts-of-interest shown in each others' reports. If something, anything at all, is out of place and incorrect about yours, speak-up now so we can discuss it openly and correct the inaccuracies if necessary, here and now, and in the open. Tell me where and how these reports are wrong. How and where I am wrong. I'll wait for thirty minutes by the clock on that wall over there. Time begins now." Jacobson pointed at the clock with his right index finger and then snapped his fingers, indicating the start of timing.

Jacobson turned smartly and headed toward the rest-room; however, when Senator O'Donoghue tried to follow, one Gunny and one Platoon Sergeant posted themselves at the latrine door, barring his way. The Senator resignedly returned to his seat. Jacobson's next stop was the kitchen for a break. When he entered, softly he asked no one in-particular, "How am I doin' so far? Just wait for the second act if no one challenges me."

At this first official break in the proceedings, all five of the reporters grabbed their cell-phones and tablets and tried to get hold of their respective bosses and/or editors – even if it was nearing 2:30 AM. The biggest story in American politics was about to break, and each had to get space allocated for it on their networks and in newsprint. Unfortunately, none of them took advantage of the break to go to the head before the story continued.

Jacobson filled another cup with coffee and checked his watch. "Time's up out there." He walked through the door back into the main room again promptly at the 30-minute mark.

Jacobson began Act Two: "Okay now. Let's discuss this openly. Who among you is going to tell me his or her respective report is incorrect? And where the errors are? Who wants to lead off?" No one challenged his/her respective report. Not a one.

Jacobson: "So, if no one attempts to challenge his or her own, I have to assume that you all agree with the reports in your hands." Verbally, Jacobson went around the room asking each person individually if his/her report was accurate. Each answered, yes; none of them challenged their reports. Private Berkeley started breathing again, realizing they had hit all homers, with no strikes. The JAG officers were busy scribbling notes on the respective reports they had divided-up amongst themselves.

The press pool was also ultra-busy, as one might expect, flipping pages, marking more points and pages, all shaking their heads in disbelief. But one good result was that they were muttering amongst themselves as a team; no one, single reporter was going to get his/her own personal 'stop-the-presses' scoop story. This was going to be a 'group report' to the nation – one the media wrote themselves, free of the usual political pressures. A real story full of meat and no fluff – 'just the facts, ma'am'.

Jacobson: "The disclosures in these reports run counter to my former administration's goals for this term. They run counter to good and open government. They have all the aspects of collusion and a full-blown conspiracy. They have all the earmarks of coordinated corruption. But, most of all I am disappointed in myself for agreeing to nominate, and subsequently, appoint all you thieving bastards to your offices on the word of someone I thought was an old friend. To me, these are evidence that the sole reason for your appointments was to aggregate and consolidate the authority and power of the Federal Government, the Executive Branch, that is, to provide personal gain by taking the same from all our fellow citizens. That intent is not good for the country; it is not good for its citizens.

"To me, these are treasonous, and I will treat them as such. Shortly, before you leave Camp David, all of you will immediately be relieved of all authority in your respective Departments and Agencies. You will immediately be replaced by the most senior, qualified, existing government employee by Monday morning – employees who have actually run these same Departments that you, total strangers, were supposed to actually lead for the benefit of the entire country. Those calls are already being made." (That part was a posturing bluff, but it

ORDER OF SUCCESSION

could be made real in just a few minutes. Gahagen motioned to Berkeley and Thompson. They conferred briefly and quickly, and both nodded that they understood their next assignment – finding-out exactly who those government employees are.)

Jacobson (now facing the Chief Justice and Attorney General): "Does POTUS have the authority that we previously discussed before midnight? Do I have that power and authority right now?"

Attorney General Pamela McAllister: "Yes, I think you do, Mr. President. Your orders, Sir?"

Chief Justice Gary Paulings: "Well, this is sort of precedent-setting, isn't it? I think that as CINC, President Jacobson could probably proceed and then wait for it to be argued in the Courts. For now, yeah, sure I agree with the AG. Proceed as we discussed."

Jacobson (now facing all of the accused in the room): "Thank-you all for verifying the information contained in these respective reports as being accurate and true. Do not worry about resigning; I just fired your asses right effing now. You are all laid-off with no severance or other benefits except for 'three hots and a cot' at government expense. Colonel Gahagen, proceed as we previously discussed. And, all of you thieving bastards, please remember that the military present here tonight are acting on my orders because civilian personnel could not be located quickly enough because of all the destruction down in D.C." With that, Jacobson left the room and returned to the kitchen. He breathed as if a giant weight had been lifted off his shoulders.

Ten minutes later, while Gahagen addressed the Senator and the Secretaries in the larger room, Jacobson approached Smitty, Berkeley, Thompson, Rhodes, Jenkins, and Hauser. He thanked each one for being brave enough to risk their careers (and maybe their lives) and shook each of their hands. And then he sat down on a kitchen stool and breathed deeply several times. He sat in the 'quiet area' with a cup of cold coffee in his slightly quivering hands, right alongside Berkeley, who didn't say much other than to ask where they could find some PCs with access to the Internet. Jacobson, now much calmer, invited Berkeley and Thompson up to the Main House, Aspen, where he was sure they could find something. Once there, Jacobson told them to look around the place while he cleaned-up in his own bedroom.

ORDER OF SUCCESSION

Time: Sunday, 09-September, 03:48 EDT (Camp David)

Meanwhile out in the main room, Colonel Gahagen was already busy addressing all of the guests – (former) Secretaries and the Senator: "Under authority granted to me by my Commander in Chief, I am arresting each of you for bribery, corruption, conspiracy to commit theft from The United States of America, conspiracy to commit sedition, sedition, conspiracy to commit treason, and for treason against The United States of America. You may also be charged with, and prosecuted for, violation of the Espionage Act, Section 793(d) in particular.

"The JAG officers over at that table (as he pointed directly at it) will call each of you up by name and read your rights to you in order to ensure all the wording is correct. Attorney General Pamela McAllister will assign Department of Justice Attorneys to prosecute you and all others who may be discovered to be co-conspirators in this plot, both within the Government now and/or in civilian life. The United States of America will not provide defense attorneys to any of the accused and/or those arrested. Chief Justice Gary Paulings will verify the proceedings taken here today, Sunday, 09-September at approximately 03:48 hours, were performed in accordance with laws of the United States in effect at that time. Your passports are hereby revoked. You will be held in temporary custody in the brig at the United States Marine Corps facility at Quantico, Virginia. Some of your fellow conspirators will also be held in a different Marine brig. None of you should expect bail or bond because that privilege will not be made available to you at this time."

Gahagen (turning to the JAG officers and motioning to Cap'n Rhodes): "Gentlemen and Ma'ams, please proceed with reading the prisoners their rights. Gunnies and Platoon Sergeants, please handcuff the prisoners after they have been read their rights. Cap'n, load the prisoners in their helicopters and secure them for transport to Quantico. Major Jenkins, notify Echo-3 and Andrews Tower of these events so they can monitor air transport and confirm that D.C. airspace is still closed to all others. Also close all airspace down to Quantico during transportation of these prisoners. Also provide transportation for the President's Secret Security detail from Andrews to this location. And advise Major Rollins to arrest his guests, as well, with the exception of the two California locals and that 'unidentified' colonel. Cap'n Hauser,

Order of Succession

provide transportation for the JAG officers following their work at this location. Make this happen. Thank-you all."

The new prisoners were in a daze; like "WTF just happened here?" "That Senator said a lot of planning went into this; nothing could possibly go wrong." "Are they really effing serious?" "What's this effing Espionage Act, Section whatever he said?" "What'd I do that it adds up to treason?" "Hey, can I buy my way out of this bogus charge; I already have things to do scheduled for next week?" "Am I gonna havta spend time in jail?" "In the movies, don't they always say you get sent to Leavenworth; what the hell is Leavenworth and where is it?" "Anybody know any good defense attorneys who have experience with treason cases?" A million new questions, and only a handful of answers. None good.

Jenkins (back in his helo): "Andrews and Echo 3."

Andrews: "Andrews here."

Echo 3: "Echo 3 same."

Ghost-1: "We're loading-up for a flight to Andrews with rest going to Quantico. All stopping at Hagerstown Airport to top off birds. Humvees will follow. We are moving in 10 with intervals about 5 apart. All in Hagerstown in 60. Out."

Andrews and Echo 3: "Roger." "Roger."

Time: Sunday, 09-September, 08:18 EDT (Camp David)

In the presence of the Chief Justice and the AG, Jacobson placed a conference call to four more interested parties – the majority and minority leaders of both The House of Representatives and The Senate – or the next in their hierarchy if they were not available. He added each to the conference bridge as they answered. Jointly, he advised them of what had transpired in the last few hours. Major Jenkins and Captain Hauser provided immediate transportation from The White House to Camp David for strategy meetings.

Time: Sunday, 09-September, 12:03 EDT (Camp David)

Berkeley, Thompson, and Colonel Gahagen met with POTUS Jacobson and the majority and minority leaders of both The House and The Senate. Berkeley handed-over the list that he and Thompson

Order of Succession

created of existing senior government employees who could possibly actually run the various Departments and Agencies that are now leaderless. Thompson also provided as much background information about each as he was able to find – just so there would not be another 'conflict of interest' instance. The politicians agreed with these choices of 'care-takers' with little negotiation.

In order to keep the new-found transparency window still open, Jacobson invited the 'press pool' to watch and listen what was happening to keep 'our government running' on Monday morning. He also gave them the final list of names they had decided could do the job with the understanding that his (Jacobson's) personal assistant down in D.C. was currently calling these people so Jacobson could personal talk with each, ask them questions, and ask them if they would accept their new responsibilities. Then, and only then, would each be 'sworn-in'. Until that time, this list identifies the best-qualified we have been able to find in just the past few hours. Jacobson also asked that the media show some restraint about reporting about these people because they are not aware of what is going to happen in their lives by our hands. The reporters thanked POTUS and scribbled notes on all the pages.

Time: Sunday, 09-September, 12:36 EDT (Camp David)

POTUS Jacobson, AG McAllister, and Chief Justice Paulings spent the afternoon coordinating the upcoming cases that promised to take years to resolve.

The reporters never broke-up their quickly-formed collaboration starting from the 'firing of the Secretaries' and their arrests to the present. They were piecing together a combined story of all that had happened live in front of them. Each of them got the 'by-line' in alphabetical order.

Time: Monday, 10-September, 09:10 EDT (Camp David)

Smitty still had a tab running at his recent hotel in D.C.; he hitched a ride down to D.C. in one of The Old Guard's Humvees.

He and the Captains and the Platoon Sergeants walked the streets around The Mall just decompressing over how close the plot had come to being successful. Well, the 14th Street Bridge was going to be out of service for months, or maybe even a couple of years, regardless of how

Order of Succession

much money the Federal Government throws at it. You just cannot wish it to be rebuilt; that takes engineering drawings, engineered material, specialized equipment, and skilled workers. The Fed and the Treasury buildings: Well, the shared opinion was "I hope they backed-up all of their computers off-site, or money fluidity is gonna be a real hell for a coupla weeks." "Today, it is already a real serious bitch; there's no liquidity anywhere" "I hope they didn't keep any real-money reserves in there; that'd take a long time to re-construct the ashes into anything that looked like an honest-to-goodness greenback."

Smitty: "Has the thought ever crossed your minds, if Jacobson was truthin' us or just playin' us? Was he part of the plot or not? We probably will never know for sure, will we?"

But PFC Berkeley could probably tell them a thing or two. While he had access to all that gear at the Pentagon, he pulled a background check on Jacobson, too, and saved the newly-found information on his three thumb drives – all password protected. Just something for the good old retirement account – just maybe.

At the end of the night, Smitty wondered where he parked his car on Friday. Maybe it was towed already. Oh, well, it's a rental anyway.

Order of Succession

ORDER OF SUCCESSION

Appendix 1 – The Order of Succession

The Constitution Of The United States provides just the specific, basic guidelines for presidential succession – that is, president to vice-president. Only the basics.

In 1947, Congress passed a new law, the Presidential Succession Act of 1947, in order to expand the depth of government officials (elected and unelected) who can assume Presidential powers in times of death, impeachment, and/or emergencies. Today, following this law, the Order of Succession now includes the following government officials:

The Order of Presidential Succession (following the Succession Act of 1947)
- President
- Vice President
- Speaker of the House of Representatives
- President Pro Tempore of the Senate
- Secretary of State
- Secretary of the Treasury
- Secretary of Defense
- Attorney General
- Secretary of the Interior
- Secretary of Agriculture
- Secretary of Commerce
- Secretary of Labor
- Secretary of Health and Human Services
- Secretary of Housing and Urban Development
- Secretary of Transportation

ORDER OF SUCCESSION

- Secretary of Energy
- Secretary of Education
- Secretary of Veterans Affairs
- Secretary of Homeland Security

ORDER OF SUCCESSION

Appendix 2 – Additional Quotes From Thomas Jefferson

Thomas Jefferson, one of the founding fathers of the United States of America, is credited with pertinent observations about government based on first-hand, on the front experience – perhaps like no other American's, and certainly, not since the Revolutionary War.

There are a great many quotes attributed to Thomas Jefferson. The following quotes were selected to reflect the thoughts, beliefs, and political positions of Hal, one of the main characters of this book, and, possibly, how he came to embrace those. And of how he felt he was protecting "The Union" in his own defiant way. Note that there are numerous other quotes attributed to Jefferson on a wide variety of subjects. While those are also insightful, they are not pertinent to Hal's beliefs. Read-up on them, especially, the ones on God and religion.

"Laws that forbid the carrying of arms...disarm only those who are neither inclined nor determined to commit crimes. Such laws make things worse for the assaulted and better for the assailants; they serve rather to encourage than to prevent homicides, for an unarmed man may be attacked with greater confidence than an armed man." (Quote attributed to Cesare Beccaria, an Italian politician and philosopher.)

A free people [claim] their rights as derived from the laws of nature, and not as the gift of their chief magistrate.

A wise and frugal government, which shall restrain men from injuring one another, which shall leave them otherwise free to regulate their own pursuits of industry and improvement, and

Order of Succession

shall not take from the mouth of labor and bread it has earned. This is the sum of good government.

American government is to leave their citizens free, neither restraining nor aiding them in their pursuits.

An elective despotism was not the government we fought for.

God forbid we should ever be twenty years without such a rebellion. The people cannot be all, and always, well informed. The part which is wrong will be discontented, in proportion to the importance of the facts they misconceive. If they remain quiet under such misconceptions, it is lethargy, the forerunner of death to the public liberty. And what country can preserve its liberties, if its rulers are not warned from time to time, that this people preserve the spirit of resistance? Let them take arms. The remedy is to set them right as to the facts, pardon, and pacify them. What signify a few lives lost in a century or two? The tree of liberty must be refreshed from time to time, with the blood of patriots and tyrants. It is its natural manure.

History, in general, only informs us what bad government is.

I am not a friend to a very energetic government. It is always oppressive.

I predict future happiness for Americans if they can prevent the government from wasting the labors of the people under the pretense of taking care of them.

I think myself that we have more machinery of government than is necessary, too many parasites living on the labor of the industrious. (And this was back in the late 1700's!)

I would rather be exposed to the inconveniences attending too

ORDER OF SUCCESSION

much liberty than to those attending too small a degree of it.

In a government bottomed on the will of all, the liberty of every individual citizen becomes interesting to all.

In matters of style, swim with the current;

In matters of principle, stand like a rock.

Liberty is the great parent of science and of virtue; and a nation will be great in both in proportion as it is free.

Most bad government has grown out of too much government.

No man has a natural right to commit aggression on the equal rights of another, and this is all from which the laws ought to restrain him.

Of liberty I would say that, in the whole plenitude of its extent, it is unobstructed action according to our will. But rightful liberty is unobstructed action according to our will within limits drawn around us by the equal rights of others. I do not add "within the limits of the law," because law is often but the tyrant's will, and always so when it violates the right of an individual.

Sometimes it is said that man cannot be trusted with the government of himself. Can he, then, be trusted with the government of others?

The beauty of the Second Amendment is that it will not be needed until they try to take it.

The democracy will cease to exist when you take away from

ORDER OF SUCCESSION

those who are willing to work and give to those who would not.

The man who reads nothing at all is better than educated than the man who reads nothing but newspapers.

The natural progress of things is for liberty to yield and government to gain ground.

The price of freedom is eternal vigilance.

The right of self-government does not comprehend the government of others.

The spirit of resistance to government is so valuable on certain occasions that I wish it to be always kept alive. It will often be exercised when wrong, but better so than not to be exercised at all.

The strongest reason for the people to retain the right to keep and bear arms is, as a last resort, to protect themselves against tyranny in government.

The two enemies of the people are criminals and government, so let us tie the second down with the chains of the Constitution so the second will not become the legalized version of the first.

Timid men prefer the calm of despotism to the tempestuous sea of liberty.

To compel a man to furnish funds for the propagation of ideas he disbelieves and abhors is sinful and tyrannical.

To take from one because it is thought that his own industry and that of his father's has acquired too much, in order to spare to others, who, or whose fathers, have not exercised equal

ORDER OF SUCCESSION

industry and skill, is to violate arbitrarily the first principle of association—the guarantee to every one of a free exercise of his industry and the fruits acquired by it.

Were we directed from Washington when to sow and when to reap, we should soon want bread.

What country can preserve its liberties if its rulers are not warned from time to time that their people preserve the spirit of resistance?

When the people fear their government, there is tyranny; when the government fears the people, there is liberty.

When wrongs are pressed because it is believed they will be borne, resistance becomes morality.

ORDER OF SUCCESSION

Appendix 3 – Abbreviations and Acronyms

Abbreviation / Acronym	Meaning
4WD	Four Wheel Drive
a.k.a.	Also Known As
AAA	American Automobile Association
AC	Air Conditioning
AFB	Air Force Base
AFL-CIO	American Federation of Labor-Congress of Industrial Organizations
AG	Attorney General
AP	Air Police (The military police of the United States Air Force.)
ASAP	As Soon As Possible
AWACS	Airborne Warning And Control System (E-3A aircraft)
AYCE	All You Can Eat
BAL	Blind Ass Luck
BDU	Battle Dress Uniform
BLT	Bacon, Lettuce, and Tomato (sandwich)
BMG	Browning Machine Gun
BS	Bull Shit
C&C	Command and Control
CB	Citizen Band (Radio)
CC	Central Command

Order of Succession

Abbreviation / Acronym	Meaning
CD	Camp David
CG	Commanding General
CHP	California Highway Patrol
CI	Counterintelligence
CIA	Central Intelligence Agency
CINC	Commander in Chief
CO	Commanding Officer
COB	Close Of Business
Coms and coms	Communications (NOTE: Coms [with a capital "C"] can also refer to the person – e.g., the Communications Sergeant, in this case.)
cp	Candle Power
CQB	Close-Quarters-Battle
CSI ™	Crime Scene Investigation
CVS	Drugstore chain. At one time in the past, the initials 'CVS' supposedly stood for 'Consumer Value Store', but now they reportedly stand for 'Convenience, Value and Service' according to the parent corporation, CVS.
CYA	Cover Your Ass
D.C.	District of Columbia
DNR	Department of Natural Resources (basically, Maryland Game Wardens)
DOJ	Department Of Justice
DOR	Date Of Rank
DSLR	Digital Single Lens Reflex (Camera)
DU	Depleted Uranium
EDT	Eastern Daylight Time
EEOB	Eisenhower Executive Office Building

447

Order of Succession

EM	Enlisted Men (In the military, soldiers as opposed to officers)
EOD	Explosive Ordnance Disposal
ETA	Estimated Time of Arrival
ETD	Estimated Time of Departure
FAA	Federal Aviation Administration
FBI	Federal Bureau of investigation
FDR	(President) Franklin Delano Roosevelt
FEMA	Federal Emergency Management Agency
FLIR	Forward Looking Infrared Radiometer (Thermal Imaging Heat Sensors)
FN Herstal	Manufactured by FN Manufacturing (Fabrique Nationale of Herstal Group, Belgium)
FUBAR	Fouled-Up Beyond All Repair (or words to that effect)
Full Scope/Lifestyle, Poly	Polygraph (a.k.a. Lie Detector)
FYI	For Your Information
GPR	Ground-Penetrating Radar
GPS	Global Positioning System
Gunny	Gunnery Sergeant (United States Marine Corps)
HQ	Headquarter(s)
HUMVEE and HMMWV	High Mobility Multipurpose Wheeled Vehicle (the new Jeep)
HVAC	Heating, Ventilating, and Air-Conditioning
ICBM	Inter-Continental Ballistic Missile
IED	Improvised Explosive Devices

Order of Succession

IEDD	Improvised Explosive Device Disposal
JAG	Judge Advocate General
J.B.	Joint Base
JSF	Joint Strike Fighter
KKK	Ku Klux Klan
LASER or laser	Light Amplification by Stimulated Emission of Radiation
LCDR	Lieutenant Commander
LED	Light Emitting Diode
LL	Lima Lima = Land Line = Call by Telephone
LZ	Landing Zone
MDW	Military District of Washington (that is, the District of Columbia area)
MLK	Martin Luther King
MOS	Military Occupational Specialty
MP	Military Police
MSP	Maryland State Police
NCOIC	Non-Commissioned Officer In Charge
NEOB	New Executive Office Building
NRA	National Rifle Association
NRO	National Reconnaissance Office
NSA	National Security Agency
OEOB	Old Executive Office Building
OIC	Officer In Charge
PDQ	Pretty Damn Quick

Order of Succession

PDT	Pacific Daylight Time
PFC	Private First Class
PO'ed	Pissed Off
POC	Point Of Contact
POE	Port Of Entry (a border crossing)
Poly	Polygraph
POTUS	President Of The United States
POW	Prisoner Of War
PR	Public Relations
Pushes	Radio Frequencies
Q&A	Question and Answer
QT	Quiet (as in "on the QT)
RFK	Robert F. Kennedy (An old Football Stadium in D.C.)
RSVP	From the French phrase, 'Répondez s'il vous plaît', meaning 'please reply'
S.O.B.	Son Of a Bitch
SAP	Special Access Programs
SAT	Satellite (as in Sat-Phone)
SCI	Sensitive Compartmented Information
SCIF	Secure Compartmentalized Information Facility
SCOTUS	Supreme Court of the United States
SCUBA	Self-Contained Underwater Breathing Apparatus
SECNAV	Secretary of the Navy
Sgt	Sergeant
SNAFU	Situation Normal All Fouled Up
SOP	Standard Operating Procedures
SOS	Same Old Shit; Same Old Stuff; Shit on a Shingle

Order of Succession

SWA	Southwest Asia (i.e., Iraq and Afghanistan)	
SWAG	Scientific Wild-Ass Guess	
TDY	Temporary Duty Assignment	
TDY	Temporary Duty	
TRACON	Terminal Radar Approach Control (Air Traffic Control)	
TSA	Transportation Security Administration	
TWH	The White House	
da WH	The White House	
UHP	Ultra High Power (Laser)	
USMC	United States Marine Corps	
U-Team	Team Of Unknowns (e.g., We don't know anything about them.)	
WTF	What The Fuck or Who The Fuck	
WTFU	Wake The Fuck Up (Slang)	
WTH	What The Hell or Who The Hell or What The Heck	
WWII	The Second World War; World War 2	
XO	Executive Officer (2nd in command of an Army Company)	

Made in the USA
Middletown, DE
26 August 2019